CRISIS IN A CLOSED SYSTEM

There had been a class A alert the night before. One of the drones had found leaf damage in the mint, sage, rosemary, marjoram. It had to be some sort of glitch, either with the computer program or the drone. With the genetically engineered crops aboard ship, disease was effectively unknown. There was certainly nothing that would attack or damage a crop. And mutation was out of the question.

"Let me see a replay on the visual monitor," Sonja told AI.

Above the mint patch in 22-360M, she saw a small glowing cloud.

"Expand and increase definition."

It wasn't a cloud—it was composed of tiny insects. No, they weren't insects . . .

"Isolate, expand, and increase definition."

The image jumped again. Sonja's jaw dropped. There it was, taking up the entire display wall.

A tiny, naked, female humanoid, with small antennae sprouting from her head, and large, filmy, iridescent wings . . .

Also by Simon Hawke

The Wizard of 4th Street
The Wizard of Whitechapel
The Wizard of Sunset Strip
The Wizard of Rue Morgue
Samurai Wizard
The Reluctant Sorcerer
The Nine Lives of Catseye Gomez
The Wizard of Camelot
The Wizard of Santa Fe

Published by
WARNER BOOKS

PHOTO CREDITS

Chapter-opening photos:

Courtesy of A&E: p. 37
Courtesy of Dog Corp.: pp. 47, 115 *(credit: Chaz)*, 131 *(credit: Chaz)*, 167, 195, 247, 263 *(Lorrianne Paquette/Bella Miella Photography)*, and 307
Roy Marasigan: pp. 153 and 231
Lucy Pemoni: pp. 7, 19, 31, 71, 99, 179, and 213
Kiliohu Williams: p. 283

Photo section:

Bella Miella Photography: pp. 20 *(middle & bottom)* and 21 *(bottom)*
Beth Chapman: p. 6 *(bottom)*
Cecily Chapman: p. 6 *(top)*
CNN: p. 14 *(top)*
Courtesy of A&E: p. 21 *(top)*
Courtesy of Dog Corp.: pp. 1 *(top)*, 2 *(top)*, 3 *(top)*, 8 *(bottom)*, 9 *(top)*, and 20 *(both; credit: Chaz)*
Chris Covert: p. 5 *(bottom)*
Roy Marasigan: p. 2 *(bottom)* and 23 *(top)*
Adam Mitchell: p. 5 *(top)*
Alan Nevins: pp. 7 *(top)*, 9 *(middle)*, and 18 *(both)*
Lucy Pemoni: pp. 1 *(bottom)*, 4 *(both)*, 7 *(bottom)*, 8 *(top)*, 9 *(bottom)*, 10–13 *(all)*, 14 *(bottom)*, 15 *(both)*, 16–17 *(all)*, 19 *(both)*, and 20 *(top)*
Max Sword: p. 3 *(bottom)*
Kiliohu Williams: pp. 23 *(bottom)* and 24 *(both)*

SIMON HAWKE

THE WHIMS OF
CREATION

WARNER BOOKS

A Time Warner Company

WARNER BOOKS EDITION

Cover design by Don Puckey
Cover illustration by Pamela Lee

Aspect is a trademark of Warner Books, Inc.

Warner Books, Inc.
1271 Avenue of the Americas
New York, NY 10020
Ⓦ A Time Warner Company

Printed in the United States of America

First Printing: April, 1995

10 9 8 7 6 5 4 3 2 1

For Bryn,
with a father's love

With special acknowledgments to Robert M. Powers, whose book about spaceflight, *Coattails of God,* inspired this novel and whose unflagging support and merciless criticism made it a much better book. I would also like to thank Jennifer Roberson for her friendship and support; Vana Wesala, for pitching in to help; Michael Bushroe, for helping out with my office system; Daniel Arthur, for putting up with odd telephone calls about weird technical matters; Bruce and Peggy Wiley, for brainstorming help and encouragement; Cathy Bower, for reasons too numerous to mention; Emily Tuzson, for valued criticism; the staffs and management of The Haunted Bookship and The Bookmark, in Tucson; Marge and James Koski, for their friendship and hospitality; Shawn Bowman and Heather Richards, for helping keep the real world at bay while I was on board the *Agamemnon;* Sojourner O'Connor, for the kind loan of her computer so I could continue working while I was at the Boise Fantasy Arts Conference; Russell Galen; Brian Thomsen; Betsy Mitchell; Sandra West; and if I've forgotten anyone (I'm sure I have), I beg forgiveness and plead terminal exhaustion. You all know who you are; thank you one and all.

"They made fast all the running tackle of the swift dark hull and got out the drinking bowls. These they filled with wine, brim-full, and poured out as offerings to the Immortal Gods that are for ever and ever: honoring especially the clear-eyed Daughter of Zeus: while the ship cleft through the long night towards the dawn."

The Odyssey
Homer

CHAPTER
1

"*P*oyekhali,*" Nikolai Valentinov said in Russian. At the same time, Ulysses and the rest of the class heard it as, "Here we go." The trial captain had anticipated this moment for ten years, and decided it was only a fitting gesture that he echo the words of Yuri Gagarin, the first man to leave the planet. But this ship, the *Agamemnon*, would leave not just the planet, but the solar system.

The great starship spun visibly in orbit as Valentinov turned a simple key about the size of a stubby pencil, engaging the AI Network. Ulysses felt every emotion of the captain through the VR interface. What was difficult was trying to maintain his own perspective during the powerful VR simulation. It took some effort, and Ulysses knew that most of the others wouldn't even bother. He couldn't see them now, because he was caught up in the virtual reality of Valentinov's experience. However, if he could see the others, he knew they'd look pretty much the same way he must look right now, lying back against their soft foam couches, their eyes rolled back and showing white as the tiny contact pads built into the wafer-thin, inch-wide, alloy VR bands pressed

1

against their mastoid bones transmitted the simulation directly to their brain implants. Their lips would be moving as they mouthed Valentinov's words; some of them would even be making the same motions he made as they surrendered themselves completely to the experience and just went with it.

Most of them wouldn't even be there, thought Ulysses, finding himself drifting back into Valentinov mode as far away, at the other end of the *Agamemnon*, deuterium and tritium met in a thrust chamber. Passing the fusion point, the D+T was struck isotropically by a multipath, megajoule laser for a tiny interval and, ablatively exploded, a fraction of the fuel mass became the power of the stars. *Agamemnon* had ignition.

Ulysses could not feel anything at first, because the thrust was minute in comparison to the great mass of the ship; the central sea did not rise far above its normal line. But he sensed Valentinov's mood, overlaid with the historical content programmed into the sim, and the feeling grew with each passing second. Ghosts of men and dreams hovered out in orbit where the ship would pass near Earth. Sim memories of old Tsiolkovsky, the ever-present Russian dreamer, flickered through Ulysses' consciousness, followed by Robert Goddard, the shy, contemplative American who had forecast the ultimate migration. He sensed others—Hermann Oberth, Wernher von Braun, Eugene Sanger, Yuri Gagarin. Ulysses shared the melancholy reminiscence of the captain as he recalled the spirits of the dead ones: Grissom, White, Chaffee, McAuliffe, Resnik, Onizuka. . . .

An astronaut's glove from one of the Gemini flights was still in orbit, tumbling from its original shove centuries before. The high Clarke orbits, the geosynchronous ellipses which Arthur C. Clarke envisioned long before the age of space began, were filled with communication and television relays, giant antennas for contacting distant probes, linking the cities on Mars and the stations near Jupiter and Saturn with the bases on the moon and the space colonies that held a population of millions.

Ulysses watched the visual and the data displays, seeing through the captain's eyes as Artificial Intelligence guided the starship toward the sun; past the Venus terraforming projects that would someday change the atmosphere to something humans could breathe; past Mercury, where scientists studied the sun closeup and mining operations carved the mountains.

As the *Agamemnon* swung around the sun in a gravity slingshot, it picked up boost and headed back into the solar system. Still checking and testing systems and making thousands of adjustments and repairs, the Navigation and Propulsion AI guided the ship toward Mars. As it passed the red planet, shadows of the moons of Barsoom played over the terrain. It was minus 20F on a late summer afternoon in Bradbury City, near Solis Lacus, where the weak sun glinted off the ice and water of the planet's single "sea." The volcanoes of Tharsis Ridge stood as silent as they did when they became inactive a million years before the last Neanderthal tore flesh from the still-steaming bowels of his kill.

The captain's last disturbing, metaphoric thought made Ulysses shudder at the thought of killing and he wondered what it would feel like to stand on the surface of a planet, not just experience it through VR. Valentinov's thoughts and feelings tugged at his mind as the sim continued, but Ulysses concentrated, struggling to maintain his own perspective.

Passive assimilation. Knowledge as direct experience. The only problem was, Ulysses thought rebelliously, it wasn't *your* experience. During the first few years of school, it hadn't really bothered him. He'd gone along with it, the same as all the others. But ever since he'd entered junior high, he'd had a feeling there was something missing. And one day, he had simply stumbled on the answer. It was easy just to go with it and virtch out, but he had discovered that you didn't get the most out of it unless you could maintain your own perspective, experience it and experience yourself experiencing it.

It was a lot more fun that way, but it took effort, and the few times he'd tried discussing it with the others, they'd just stared at him blankly. They didn't get it. Why? What was the point? Why virtch out if you can't go with it completely? It's what you were supposed to do. You don't fight VR, you just go with it. It wasn't fighting it, Ulysses had insisted, but adding a whole other dimension. He didn't even bother trying to tell the teachers his idea. They'd probably just tell him he was doing it all wrong.

The *Agamemnon* passed the asteroid belt from which it had been born and moved past Jupiter and the boiling hostility of its atmosphere. The volcanos of Io threw gases into space, and the ashes rained down on a sterile plain of white sulfur dioxide snow. Ganymede, with its great flat stretches of frozen mud and ice, was left behind. At Saturn, the sensors trained on Titan, locating six planetologists toiling somewhere beneath the thick, primordial organic atmosphere, their transporter floundering in the grooved, shale-covered surface.

One hundred million miles from Neptune's orbit, the starship started back toward the sun in an enormous curving path. The shakedown cruise was over, the tests and repairs had been logged, the failures had been noted. The AIs cleared the final crew for boarding and prepared to lift off for real as Valentinov left the ship.

Ulysses removed the U-shaped VR band, blinked and shook his head, then glanced around the room at his classmates as the lights came back up slowly and the couches swiveled upright.

Riley Etheridge caught his gaze and rolled his eyes toward the ceiling, as if to say, "Big deal."

"Well, wasn't that exhilarating?" Peter Buckland said. "And now that we've had a few moments to recover from Captain Valentinov's experience, can anyone tell me how long it took to construct the *Agamemnon*?"

Don't all raise your hands at once, Ulysses thought, as he looked around at all his unresponsive classmates. It was in the sim program, but of course no one would remember it. They would only remember the experience, and not the data, which could only mean one thing. He winced, knowing what was going to happen next. And sure enough, it did.

"Ulysses?"

With a sigh of resignation, he said, "Fifty years."

"Thank you," said his father.

Why did he always have to call on him when no one volunteered an answer? It was embarrassing. Every time it happened, he was tempted to reply with, "I don't know," but that would only bring more trouble. "Now, let's try to put the whole thing into context," he mumbled, under his breath.

"Now, let's try to put the whole thing into context," said his father, rubbing his hands together.

Ulysses found his attention wandering. He knew all this already. He had to spend extra time with the VR teaching programs just to keep up, because the pressure was always on him. So long as he could come up with the right answers, the great professor would just nod with approval and move on.

His gaze wandered toward Jenny Kruickshank, sitting to his left, six seats away. His eyes lingered on her long and slender legs. He sighed. School seemed like such a waste of time. He just couldn't see the point. There was no reason why students couldn't access the teaching programs at home, or come to class and do it on their own time and interface later for exams. He could make much faster progress that way. But spending time in formal classroom sessions with other students was supposed to be beneficial for "optimum assimilation and peer dynamic socialization." He wouldn't mind developing some "peer dynamics" with Jenny. As for the rest of it, he just couldn't care less. You experience the VR teaching programs, then the teacher tells you what you experienced and puts it into context for you. Boring.

"Are we boring you, Ulysses?"

He started. "I'm sorry?"

"I asked if we were boring you," his father said. Several of the other students giggled.

"Settle down, please. Next time, we'll examine the beginnings of interstellar ark starflight, from the first discussion of the concept in J.D. Bernal's 1929 book, *The World, The Flesh and The Devil* to the earliest Earthbound experiments in closed environmental design, including a VR session inside Biosphere II, constructed in the Arizona desert back in the latter part of the twentieth century. So come to class prepared to feel a little claustrophobic. That'll be all for today. Class dismissed."

Riley Etheridge was waiting for him in the hallway as he left the classroom.

"Caught daydreaming again, huh?" Riley said with a grin.

"Don't start," Ulysses replied, irritably, as they walked together down the hall. They made a study in contrasts. Ulysses blond and very fair, slender to the point of fragility; Riley dark and stocky, tending to a chunky softness around the chest and middle. Ulysses walked with a firm and steady gait, light on his feet, while Riley had a tendency to bob and lean slightly from side to side in a juvenile swagger. Ulysses had a poet's face, light blue eyes and delicate features with the perpetual expression of a moody dreamer, while Riley's face was wide, with round, full, peasant's cheeks, a mocking mouth, and dark, insolent eyes.

They came out through the arched entrance of the school building and crossed the plaza, heading toward the bicycle racks, which held several dozen small, identical, magnesium-framed bikes. Ulysses and Riley selected two at random. Ulysses felt a slight breeze and looked up to see the clouds slowly scudding toward the other end of the ship. The weather was about the same as always, forty-two percent humidity with a temperature of 71.5 degrees Farenheit. The weather system program was blowing the clouds toward the forward farms. The clouds were seeded, dark and heavy, so the crops could get some rain. That meant his mother probably wouldn't be home till after dinner.

As the clouds passed by about a thousand meters overhead, he could see the buildings of the Central Administrative Complex high above them, about ten miles away, straight up. In the distance, he could see one of the maglev trains as it sped along its elevated track, upside down from his perspective, following a course along the curvature of the inner hull. He followed the gradual curvature with his gaze, taking in the CAC buildings and the villages, interspersed with small parks similar to the one they were riding through now, the meadows and the densely planted forests beyond them, and the gracefully curving rows of the crop fields.

Farther out, toward the ship's equator, the retaining cliffs of the sea dominated the landscape; they were designed to hold the water during changes in the ship's acceleration and during deceleration. From his perspective, the sea seemed to curve up like a giant, horizontal bay, encircling the interior.

Ulysses tried to imagine what the perspective would be like for people living *on* a planet, where everything would be reversed—or inside out. The sims never really imparted a feeling of what it would be like to stand out on a street in one of Earth's large cities, or on some country road, or out in a desert or on a ship at sea. He couldn't quite picture it. The VR sims never gave you that wide a perspective, at least not the ones they used in school, because it had been discovered that they had a profoundly disorienting effect.

"You ever wonder what it must be like for people on Earth, to look up and see nothing but sky above the clouds?" Ulysses asked.

"It would give me the shakes," said Riley. "I mean, just to have, like, nothing overhead? I don't know how anyone could stand it. It would probably make me sick to my stomach."

"I just wonder what it would be like, that's all," Ulysses said.

"Why bother?" asked Riley, with a dismissive shrug. "You'll never know."

"Well, maybe my great-grandchildren will, when we finally reach a habitable planet."

"By that time, you'll have long since recycled, my friend."

"Yeah, I know."

"Why are you thinking about grandchildren all of a sudden?" Riley asked, as they pedaled away. A look of sudden comprehension came over his face. "Oh, I get it! It's Kruickshank, isn't it? I've seen you staring at her."

"Don't be ridiculous," said Ulysses, pedaling faster so that Riley couldn't see him blush.

"Yeah? Look me in the face and tell me I'm wrong," said Riley, catching up with him.

Ulysses pedaled harder. "You're wrong, okay?"

"Then why is your face turning red?" asked Riley, pulling even with him once again.

"Because you're getting on my nerves!"

He couldn't outdistance him, so Ulysses swerved across

Riley's path. Riley clamped on the brakes, barely avoiding the collision.

Ulysses slowed and waited for him.

"You did that on purpose!" Riley accused him, angrily.

"All right, so what if I did? Just drop it about Jenny Kruickshank, okay?"

"Too shy to make a move, huh? Well, if you like her, why don't you just do her in VR? She'd never know."

"Because it wouldn't be the same," Ulysses said. "VR sex just doesn't interest me. It isn't real."

"You'd never know the difference. What, you mean to tell me that you've never tried it?"

"I don't want to discuss it, okay?"

"Why not just let her know how you feel? I don't think she's Chosen yet, but if you don't tell her, you might lose your chance."

"She's not going to Choose anytime soon," Ulysses said.

"Don't bet on it," said Riley. "The trend is for people to Choose much earlier these days."

"How do you know? No one's ever said anything about it in Social Psych or Civics."

"I heard it somewhere. But maybe it's not that significant a trend. I never really checked."

"Why don't we? Let's go to my place and ask Mac."

They rode up the path winding through the well-kept garden in front of the Bucklands' residential complex in Taos Village. It housed several families in clustered, two-story homes designed in an architectural style reminiscent of Earth's New Mexico pueblo and built around a paved courtyard filled with cactus and agave. They put their bicycles in the rack in front of the building and went in through the arched entryway. They crossed the courtyard and walked up to an arch design under the portico.

"Open the door, Mac," said Ulysses.

The smart molecules comprising the nanalloy metal immediately responded, and the section of the wall in front of them flowed like liquid mercury, creating an opening where a solid wall had been a moment earlier. As they went inside,

Ulysses said, "Close the door, Mac," and the arch sealed up behind them as the lights came on automatically.

The interior of the Buckland house was essentially the same as that of the Etheridge family, with only minor differences. All the residential units were approximately the same in terms of layout, with each differing in various degrees according to individual tastes. Residence units ranged from two to three bedrooms, up to about 350 square meters. They were all designed to give a feeling of openness and space. The living room took up most of the first level, with a cathedral ceiling and a second-level gallery upstairs, where the bedrooms were. At the far end of the living room was an arch leading to the dining alcove, with the small kitchen beyond.

The furnishings and decorations available through the ship's supply catalog were comfortable and utilitarian, constructed of aluminum and ceramics and upholstered with recyclable fabrics made from silica, available in a variety of styles. The floors were nanalloy, as were all the main structures aboard the ship, and if a different shade or pattern were desired, it was a simple matter of choosing from a list of preprogrammed options and specifying it with a verbal command to the house computer. Carpets made from glass fiber were available, and new ones could be had from the shops for the exchange of the old ones for recycling and an additional fee of work credits. There was very little plastic used, since it was a hydrocarbon product, and it was recycled endlessly.

The nanalloy composition of the walls allowed for different color schemes, within a range of shades the smart molecules were programmed for. The Bucklands preferred a subdued color scheme, with light earth-toned walls and beige ceilings. It remained that way most of the time, except when Ulysses was home alone. He preferred his own all black color scheme, but he always changed it back before his parents came home. His parents already thought he was moody and distracted, and he knew it was only a small step from moody and distracted to socially maladjusted, which would require Counseling.

They went up to his bedroom. Riley sat down on the bed and Ulysses went over to his desk. "Okay," he said, sitting down in his chair, leaning back and putting his feet up. "Mac, access the CAC database."

"Why?" said the house computer.

Ulysses rolled his eyes. "I'd like to see the stats on Partner Choice over the past . . . uh . . . five years."

"What do you need that for?"

"Because I *want* it, Mac, okay? Will you just do it, please, and not give me a hard time for a change?"

"Oh, all right, if you insist. . . ."

"Sounds like you've got some minor interface problems," Riley said, with a grin.

Ulysses shook his head. "Mac has a thing about the CAC computers," he said. "They give him an inferiority complex."

"That isn't true," said Mac. "I just find them irritating to network with, that's all. Here, are you happy now?"

A display appeared on the bedroom wall and Ulysses had Mac disconnect from CAC.

"All right, let's have a look," he said, scanning the display, which listed all the registered Choosings over the past five years by name, in order of date and time, as well as giving occupations, residence, and age.

"Hmmm," Ulysses said. "That's interesting. Over the past five years, the median age has dropped. "

"See?" Riley said.

"Mac, I need you to analyze the trend for people Choosing at a younger age and then search the CAC database for any similar or corresponding trends that might help explain it."

"You could have asked me for that the first time."

"Well, I didn't know I wanted it the first time, okay?"

"Will there be anything else, as long as I'm there?"

"No."

"Are you sure?"

"Mac. . . ."

"I have identified three corresponding trends."

"And are you going to tell me what they are?"

"You didn't ask me to tell you what they are."

Ulysses shut his eyes in patient suffering. "Mac, please identify the three corresponding trends."

"Incidence of clinical depression, incidence of early citizen *recycling*, and incidence of suicide."

"Suicide?" said Riley, with astonishment. "I didn't even know we had any history of suicides."

"I didn't, either," said Ulysses, frowning. "That's not supposed to happen in a healthy society. Mac, let me have the stats on clinical depression, citizen recycling and suicide over the last five years."

"You want them separate, or should I generate a comparison graphic?"

"No, just separate displays will do."

"You're sure you're not going to want a graphic?"

"Yes, Mac, I'm sure."

"Because if you're going to change your mind and ask me for a graphic in another two or three minutes, I might as well let you have it now."

"Could we get on with it, please?"

A moment later, they were looking at the displays on the wall. "Mac, you can disconnect from CAC database," Ulysses said, absently.

"Maybe I should stay on line, just in case."

"Fine, Mac, disconnect whenever you feel like it," Ulysses said, with a sour grimace.

"So what?" said Riley. "People are Choosing earlier and it's making them want to kill themselves? That's not too good for you and Jenny, is it? Which one of you is going to go first?"

"That's not exactly what I would call a scientific conclusion," said Ulysses, giving him a sour look. "What gets me is that we've never even heard of anyone committing suicide before. And there's been an increase over the past five years. One five years ago, then none the next year, but three the year after that, then three again, and then four last year . . ."

Riley frowned. "The last one was only two months ago. I don't understand. How come we never heard anything about it?"

"I don't know," Ulysses said. "But look at this." He pointed at the display. "Over the past five years, there's been an even larger increase in the number of people opting for early recycling. And check out the depression stats."

"Way up," said Riley. He shook his head. "Wait a minute, something doesn't make sense here. If more people are getting depressed, then you'd think there'd be more people going in for Counseling and getting help, right? So why the suicides? What gives?"

"I don't know; let's see if we can find out," Ulysses said. "Mac. . . ."

"Don't tell me; let me guess," the computer said. "You want the Counseling statistics from CAC, right?"

Ulysses sighed. "Okay, yes, you were right and I was wrong. Could you access the Counseling files, please?"

"No."

"What do you mean, no?"

"I thought that was clear enough."

"Mac, I said I was sorry."

"*That has nothing* to do with it. CAC will not grant access to the Counseling files without the proper password."

"Oh, right, of course," Ulysses said. "Counseling records would be confidential. I should have realized that."

"Well, even if we can't access the files, it still makes sense that if more people were getting depressed, then more people would be going for Counseling, right?" said Riley.

"Right," Ulysses said. "And we're being stupid here. Where would they get the stats on clinical depression if people hadn't reported being depressed? That had to come from Counseling."

"Okay, so let's assume an increase there," said Riley. "If more people are going in for Counseling, then why are they committing suicide?"

"I don't know," Ulysses said, in a puzzled tone. "But something else just occurred to me." He pointed to the stats on citizen recycling. "We don't know why these people opted for early recycling. I mean, they were all obviously older people who'd reached an age where they could exercise that option, but what were their *reasons*?"

"I see where you're going," Riley said, nodding. "Maybe they were just getting old and sick and opting out a little early. But maybe they were depressed, too. If you look at it that way, their choice to opt for early recycling could be considered a form of suicide."

"Exactly," Ulysses said, nodding. "It all depends on how you define it. I mean, technically, we *could* call early recycling a form of suicide, couldn't we? Nobody looks at it that way, but then it's not really dying of natural causes, either, is it?"

"So some of these recycling stats *could* actually be suicide stats, only they weren't considered that way because of the age of the people involved," said Riley.

"Exactly," Ulysses said. "Either way, these other deaths were recorded as suicides and nobody's talking about them. And we don't know if these people went in for Counseling or not."

"Well, if they did, looks like it didn't help," said Riley. "Maybe that's why no one's talking about it. Or maybe people just don't know."

"How can they not know?"

"Well, we didn't know," said Riley.

"So? It's not exactly the sort of thing you tell your kid at the dinner table, is it? 'Hey, Riley, guess what? Somebody killed himself at work today.' Besides, it's right there in the CAC database. As each one happened, it was recorded. We just never thought of asking about it before. In fact, we wouldn't have thought of it now; it just sort of came up by accident."

"I know," Riley said, "but still . . . four people killed themselves last year. Four! You'd think *somebody* would talk about it and want to know what happened. And why it happened."

"Yeah, you'd think that, wouldn't you?" Ulysses said, with a frown.

"If you were thinking of committing suicide," said Riley, "wouldn't you be curious to try it first?"

"Interesting question," said Ulysses. "I wonder what happens to you when you die in VR? Mac, are there any sims available that simulate an experience of death?"

"*VR death* simulations are banned," Mac replied.

"Why?"

"It has been determined that they are psychologically disruptive and potentially damaging."

"Hmmm," Ulysses said. "So if you can't try it out first, I guess you'd have to be pretty committed. I think we've stumbled onto something here, but I'm not sure what it means."

"What would make people want to kill themselves?" asked Riley.

"Well . . . depression, obviously," Ulysses said.

"But a lot more people have gotten depressed than killed themselves," Riley reminded him.

"True," Ulysses said, "but then we haven't heard anyone talking about that, either, have we? I'd really like to know if those people who committed suicide went in for Counseling."

"Well, there's no way we're going to find that out without the password for the Counseling files," said Riley, with a shrug.

"What do you think it might be?" Ulysses asked.

"You're not thinking what I think you're thinking, are you?"

"I'm thinking exactly what you think I'm thinking," said Ulysses. "Why not? It's worth a try, isn't it?"

"You trying to impress Jenny by having her mom arrest you?" Riley asked.

"No," Ulysses said, then smiled. "Why, you think that would work?"

Riley grinned. "It might."

"Aren't you even curious?"

"Well . . . yeah. But what if we get caught?"

"The idea of maybe getting caught makes it more fun."

"You're maladjusted, Buckland, you know that? All right, let's do it."

"It could take a while," Ulysses said. "And it might not work, you know."

"I know. But now you've got me curious. What kind of password would apply to Counseling?"

Ulysses thought a moment. "Let's try 'therapy'. . . ."

CHAPTER
2

S onja Buckland stood in front of the wall display in her office, checking the daily data feed prior to going home for the day. The changing display configured on the nanalloy wall gave her constant updates: flow charts, graphs, and column statistics monitoring the fields and hydroponic units, the feeding and fertilization cycles, the weather patterns and crop yields, the maintenance diagnostics on the drones, and daily adjustments to various procedures made by the agricultural computer.

Small, blond, and slender, with a fair complexion and delicate facial features that were strongly echoed in her son, Sonja had a compulsive streak that made her very detail-oriented. From a strictly technical standpoint, she knew there was really no reason for her to monitor all this information. Artificial Intelligence did not require humans in the loop. All of the day-to-day functions of the farms were automated, as was the case with all the routine functions aboard the ship. If one of the drones broke down, Chlorophyl, the agricultural AI, immediately dispatched a maintenance drone to pick it up and bring it back to the shop. Often, even that wasn't necessary. Much of the time, the maintenance drones could effect the repairs on the spot. Unless something irregular came up, Sonja could do about ninety-eight percent of her job from the office, without ever getting her boots muddy.

As a botanist, she was involved in supervising the care of the forward fields and the landscaping throughout that section of the ship. This included all the parks, meadows, forests, and village gardens forward of the equatorial sea. Aft Agricultural Control was responsible for the fields and landscaping in the other half of the ship. Each office was staffed by a botanist and a maintenance engineer, though on occasion there were students present in the office as well, getting a hands-on education in agriculture and landscaping. And for the most part, there wasn't very much for the Ag personnel to do.

It had been a quiet, relatively uneventful day, as most of them were, allowing her to spend some time doing research and visiting the nursery, checking on some of her experiments with modified new hybrid strains. She took great satisfaction in her job, because she felt she added to it with her independent projects, but today she was looking forward to going home.

Peter had called earlier, to tell her that Ulysses had been daydreaming in school again, and she was a little worried. Her son had always been highly intelligent, but bright as he was, he had a tendency to be a bit unfocused. They had waited a long time to have him, perhaps too long, but she wanted to be sure that it was the best time for both of them.

Having a child had not proved a hardship for her. That wasn't the problem. She had simply wanted to make certain she was psychologically prepared to spend the necessary time with him to ensure his optimum development in the first years of his life. That alone had seemed like an intimidating commitment. She could not imagine how women on Earth did it in the old days, when they physically had to carry the fetus to term. The risk, the discomfort, the nonproductive downtime, to say nothing of the pain of delivery . . . it must have been horrendous. Peter had told her that even up until Launch, there were still women who preferred doing it the old-fashioned way, conceiving and carrying the child themselves. It seemed barbaric. She could not imagine why any woman would subject herself to that.

Back when they had first discussed having a child, Peter had raised the possibility of trying it that way, saying that it would be the first time it had ever been done aboard the ship and that it would not only be an historic event, but an interesting experience that could provide some fascinating data. She had been shocked that he could even suggest such a thing. Considering the downtime and discomfort, it had raised some serious doubts in her mind about whether Peter was emotionally responsible enough to be a good parent. Admittedly, she'd had some doubts about herself, as well.

She had waited a long time before Choosing Peter, much to his frustration. He had made his interest evident to her much earlier, and she knew that the longer she waited, the more the odds increased that he would pick somebody else. However, back then, she had told herself that if he did get tired of waiting, then it would be proof that she was right. And even after she had finally agreed to Choose him, she had been ambivalent. Dissolution was nonproductive, and though it was not unheard of, neither was it very common. She did not want to add to those statistics. She had always been very careful and methodical in everything, and saw no reason to make any exceptions in her personal life.

If it had been up to Peter, they would have had Ulysses right away, but she wasn't really sure she wanted to back then. It wasn't that she never wanted to have a child; as she had explained to Peter, she just wanted to be sure she was prepared. Peter had been very understanding. He had brought it up from time to time, but had never pressed her, though he had obviously been anxious to become a father.

As it turned out, he was an excellent parent. Except for the minor aberration of suggesting she consider carrying the child herself—the historian in him getting a bit carried away, perhaps—she could not fault him as a father. They'd had Ulysses the normal way, through in vitro fertilization and artificial womb gestation, which was all carefully controlled by the Reproductive Center computers, which ensured a viable offspring. They had each made sure to schedule personal time with him during the formative years of his life. She could not think of anything they had done wrong, which was why she was puzzled at his growing tendency toward socially disruptive behavior.

Perhaps Counseling was the answer, but she wanted to be absolutely certain it was the right thing to do before they made that decision. Lately, she had kept putting off discussing it with Peter, but now that Ulysses was starting to display disruptive behavior in public, daydreaming in Peter's class, no less, it was a discussion that could no longer be avoided. He was always drifting off somewhere, making up peculiar stories in his head, not paying attention to reality. It was starting to become a problem. Having realized that, finally, she was anxious to get home and get on with it. It was the responsible thing to do.

Unfortunately, the discussion would be delayed until sometime after dinner, because she would have to wait for the cloud-seeding operation to be complete, so that the fields could get the proper amount of rain in the morning. There was really no reason why she couldn't leave it up to Chlorophyl, but she wanted to monitor the readouts and make sure. Dealing with water vapor could be a little tricky.

She moved slowly along the wall, scanning the displays and nodding to herself as she noted the details, then stopped suddenly, gazing at one of the readouts intently.

"What?" she said to herself, momentarily confused. At first, she wasn't certain she had read the display correctly, but there it was, unmistakably, in bold red letters, flagged by the computer.

There had been a Class A alert the previous night. One of the drones had found leaf damage in an herb patch and Chlorophyl had been unable to identify the source of the damage. Whatever it was, it was affecting only one small area, but several crops—the mint, the sage, the rosemary, and the marjoram. It had to be some sort of glitch, either with the computer program or the drone, most likely the drone. A glitch in the computer program would have been identified and rectified immediately. Phyl was scrupulous about self-diagnostics. The alert was unusual enough, but what was more unusual was that Phyl had entered it and flagged it, but had said nothing to her about it. She had gone through the whole day without being aware of it.

"Phyl?"

"Yes, Sonja?"

"You're showing a Class A alert in Field 22 last night."

"That is correct."

"Well, that's nice. You mind telling me why you didn't say anything about it?"

"I'm sure I must have mentioned it."

"No, Phyl, you didn't."

"Maybe you forgot."

"A Class A alert? There's no way I would forget something like that, Phyl. It's not exactly routine. We haven't had one of those since I started on this job."

"I wouldn't have registered a Class A alert without informing you about it, Sonja," Phyl replied.

She frowned. There was no question in her mind that Phyl hadn't said anything, but there was no point to arguing about it. AIs didn't make mistakes. He must have told her and somehow it slipped her mind, but she couldn't see how something like that could have happened. It wasn't like her at all.

"Okay, Phyl, have one of the drones bring back some of the damaged leaves to the office," she said.

"I've already done that," the computer replied. "The drone is on its way back to the maintenance bay now."

"Good, thank you, Phyl. In the meantime, let me see a replay of the event on the visual monitors."

She wanted to get to the bottom of this puzzle right away. With the genetically engineered crops aboard the ship, plant disease was effectively unknown. There was certainly nothing that would attack or damage a crop. And a mutation was out of the question. Phyl would have noticed something like that immediately, because DNA analysis of practically everything in the growing fields was done on a regular basis.

She watched the display as Phyl played back the feed from the satellite VMs stationed in the zero-g zone over the fields. The first image was a wide-perspective patchwork of the fields, then the image jumped to a closer scan as Phyl selected the replay from Field 22. It jumped again, rapidly, to a closer scan of Sector 22-36, and then again to 22-36DM. The images jumped more rapidly, zooming in closer and closer until she could see the damage on the individual leaves of the mint plants. She stared at the display and shook her head in confusion. She had never seen anything like it. There were two mysteries here. One was that it had happened at all, and the other was that Phyl had not been able to identify it.

"Phyl, I want a replay of any unidentified object in last night's field scan." She waited a few seconds as Phyl rapidly ran back the scan, which appeared as nothing more than a blur on the display wall. Then it stopped. Above the mint patch in Field 22-36DM, she saw a small, erratically pulsating, glowing cloud. She stepped closer to the display wall, staring at the image with fascination. She had absolutely no idea what it could be.

"Expand and increase definition," she said, stepping back from the wall and folding her arms across the chest of her white coveralls.

The image jumped. What she was looking at now was an entire wall of cloud, only it wasn't a cloud, it was composed of tiny insects. No . . . They weren't insects, they were . . .

Sonja blinked and shook her head, uncertain she was seeing correctly. "Phyl, isolate one of those unidentified bodies, expand, and increase definition."

The image jumped again. There it was, larger than life, taking up the entire display wall. Sonja's jaw dropped as she stared at it. It wasn't an insect. It was something that couldn't possibly exist. A tiny, naked female humanoid, anatomically correct in every detail, only with small antennae sprouting from her head and large, filmy, iridescent wings.

Sonja stared at it with disbelief, then snorted and shook her head. "Very funny," she said, dryly.

The chime sounded, signaling an incoming call.

"Who is it, Phyl?" she asked.

"Saleem is calling from the shop," the computer replied.

She made a face. Of course, she thought, who else? Saleem. She liked the maintenance engineer, but he had an annoying nonproductive tendency of playing practical jokes on his friends. She had been his victim on more than one occasion, and ordinarily, she didn't mind, but sometimes it annoyed her. This time, however, he had surpassed himself.

The voice of Saleem Rodriguez came from the opposite wall as the smart molecules of the nanalloy configured for audio broadcast and reception. They were programmed for imaging as well, but in practice, people rarely used it to communicate. It wasn't necessary to see someone to have a quick, casual conversation, so why waste energy with a nonproductive imaging configuration?

"That drone's back with the samples, Sonja," said Saleem. His voice sounded perfectly straight, but she could imagine him grinning. "I think you ought to take a look at this. You want me to bring them up?"

"No, that's all right, Saleem," she said, playing along. "I'll be right down."

She left her office and went downstairs to Saleem's domain, which was in its usual state of organized clutter. When she had first started working with him, she had been concerned about his apparent disorganization until she realized that, chaotic as his work environment appeared, he always knew exactly where everything was. She had quickly learned not to move anything without telling him. Like most engineers, he was extremely possessive and protective of his work area. His job, too, was largely redundant, but he liked tearing things apart and putting them back together. And he always had some sort of robotics project he was working on, new designs for drones and so forth. Phyl was always critical of his designs, finding them inferior, but Saleem was not dissuaded. His projects, in various states of completion, filled the shop. However, once Sonja accepted that they just had different definitions of what order meant, they worked together very well.

He was back in his office on the far end of the maintenance bay, where the deactivated drone stood, its sample bin removed. Saleem was seated at his desk, which he had cleared off so that he could spread out the samples the drone brought back. He had laid them out carefully, playing it to the hilt. He was a large man, with black, close-cropped hair and a dark complexion, the result of his mixed, Hispano-African ancestry. He had a deep, lilting voice, and was very soft-spoken, as if he had consciously developed the habit to counteract his size.

"What have we got, Saleem?" Sonja asked, suppressing a chuckle as she came up to the desk.

"Take a look at this," he said, glancing up at her. Spread out on the desk were some clippings of rosemary, marjoram, mint, and sage, filling the area with a heady, overpowering odor. Sonja leaned down and examined them.

The rosemary sprigs were missing large numbers of their needlelike leaves, as if they had fallen off. However, the sage and the mint clippings had leaves that looked torn, as if some pest had been at them.

"What we have here may be a mutated pest," Saleem said, thoughtfully.

"Wouldn't Phyl have identified that?" she asked, wondering how long he was going to draw it out.

"Maybe not, if it's some sort of new mutation that slipped past," he replied. He picked up one of the mint samples for a closer look. "These leaves are torn. They look as if they have been chewed or bitten off. We don't have anything big enough to do that."

"Looks like we do now," she replied.

He shook his head. "No, that doesn't make sense. The drones would have reported it. Maybe we've got some sort of blight, or maybe it's just a feeding problem."

All right, she thought, I'll play. "Our crops are genetically engineered, blight-resistant strains, so if the problem is disease, it must be a very new one, and I can't imagine why Phyl didn't catch it. Besides, these leaves looked chewed. What blight would do that?"

"Well, you're the expert," Saleem said, "but I just don't see how it could be a pest. There's nothing aboard the ship that should attack these crops, so where could it have come from? It would have had to evolve somehow aboard the ship. We've got a closed and perfectly controlled environment, and it isn't old enough to have allowed for the evolution of any new species."

"Genetic engineering *is* a form of evolutionary process, it's just very quick. Maybe we have a computer glitch that has produced a mutation." This conversation was scientific nonsense, but she kept her face straight. She wanted to see how long he would keep the joke up. He obviously didn't know that she had seen the scan playback already and was building up to playing it for her. Only this time, she had the jump on him. "Look at the patterns of these tears," she said. "Don't they look like tiny bite marks?"

"Well, I'll admit they sort of *look* like bite marks," he replied, "but I'll bet analysis will reveal either a blight or some kind of reaction from the chemical mix being off somehow."

Saleem had gone to a lot of trouble on this one, she thought. "No, this is something Phyl hasn't been programmed to recognize at all. That's doesn't necessarily tell us what it is, but it certainly tells us what it *isn't*. You don't suppose one of the drones could be doing this?"

"I'd already thought of that," Saleem said. "First thing I did was have Phyl run a diagnostic on all the drones, and compare it to the routine stats. Then I checked the diagnostic program. I networked with CAC and had their computer do a backup. No problem there. Everything's normal. None of the drones are munching on the crops."

"Well, *something's* munching on the crops," said Sonja.

"Well, I guess we can run our own analysis first thing in the morning," said Saleem.

"No," she said, thinking this had gone on long enough. "I think I know what it is."

"You do?"

She nodded, looking very serious. "Yes, I think so. I think we've got a bunch of tiny people flying around out there, having midnight snacks."

"What?"

"Okay, Saleem, I must admit, you've really outdone yourself this time, but I'm afraid I've ruined your little joke."

"What are you talking about?"

"I already ran the scan playback up in the office. Really, Saleem. Tiny, glowing people with wings? What did you do, whip up the graphic at home?"

"Huh?"

She rolled her eyes. "Will you stop? I've already seen it! Okay, it was funny."

He shook his head. "Sonja, I have no idea what you're talking about."

"Oh, honestly," she said. "Phyl, display that expanded, isolated image from the scan."

"I'm sorry, Sonja, could you be more specific? What image are you referring to?" said the computer.

She turned back to Saleem. "You've got Phyl in on this?"

"Nooo. . . ." said Saleem, looking at her strangely.

"All right, Phyl, whatever Saleem told you, disregard it, please. I want to see the image from last night's scan playback of that tiny woman with the wings."

"I have no record of any such detail from the scan playback," Phyl said.

"Oh, I get it," Sonja said, wryly, turning to Saleem. "You had it wiped while I was coming down here, didn't you?"

He looked perplexed. "Sonja, this is no joke. Honest. If you saw some image inserted in the scan playback, I didn't put it there, and I didn't have it wiped, either."

She frowned. The seriousness of his expression did not seem counterfeit. "You're *not* playing a joke?"

He shook his head. "Not me."

It couldn't be Phyl, she thought. Could it? "Phyl, did you wipe anything from last night's scan playback?"

"No, Sonja."

"And you didn't insert any images, either?"

"No. Why would I?"

"Then what did I just see upstairs?"

"I don't know, Sonja."

"What's going on?" Saleem asked.

"You've got me," said Sonja, confused. "I thought you were pulling my leg. Apparently, we had some kind of strange glitch. I need to check it out right away."

"Okay, want me to stick around?"

"No, there's no need for you to stay. It's getting late. I'll take care of this. I was going to stay until the cloud seeding was completed, anyway."

"All right," Saleem said. "If you find out what happened, give me a call at home."

"I'll do that."

"Good-night, Sonja."

" 'Night, Saleem."

She took the samples back up to her office. Something was definitely wrong. Saleem would never take a joke this far. And Phyl was certainly acting strangely. She was certain Phyl had not told her about the alert, and now this bizarre glitch in the playback, and Phyl was unable to account for it, didn't even know it had happened. This wasn't good. No, it wasn't good at all. She opened the glass door of the spectral analyzer and put some of the samples in.

Phyl was unable to identify what caused the sample damage. It kept coming up as an error in analysis, so Phyl would go back and start checking for the error, while the analysis program cycled through the process repeatedly, prompting Phyl to run repeated self-diagnostics. The computer was confused. What was going on?

"Phyl, specify the error," she said, with a frown.

"It seems to be an error in spectral analysis," the computer replied. "I'm sorry, Sonja, but I keep coming up with incongruous data."

"What's the problem, Phyl?" she said.

"I'm detecting peculiar trace elements," the computer said.

"Of what?"

"Human saliva."

Sonja frowned. That couldn't be right. "Phyl, eliminate that error from the spectral analysis and run it again."

Except for the traces of human saliva, which obviously had to be a mistake, the spectral analysis was otherwise completely normal. No peculiar DNAs, no twisted RNA switches, no mutants, no new species, no nothing.

She had Phyl analyze the tear patterns in the leaves. No comparison was found. It wasn't some kind of larva, or caterpillar, or any other kind of insect in the database, including the old files from Earth. With a sigh of resignation, because she couldn't think of anything else, she ran a comparison analysis with all available data files aboard the ship, which meant networking with CAC. This time, it produced a match. Well, not exactly a match, she thought, but something close.

Human teeth marks.

It seemed the bite patterns matched, except that the ones on the leaves were obviously far too small to have been made by any human teeth. It would have required a very tiny human, on the order of a large insect or a small bird. Sonja sat back in her chair, recalling the strange image on the scan.

The conclusion seemed inescapable. The leaf damage could not have been caused by a malfunctioning drone or anything else aboard the ship. Either something was drastically wrong with the programs, something that could not be automatically diagnosed and rectified, or else some sort of very strange life form was out there in that field.

All thoughts of going home had fled from Sonja's mind. She was excited by the mystery. This could be the most important scientific event since Launch. And she was the one who had discovered it. Only what *was* it?

There seemed to be only one way to find out—go out into the fields and look for whatever it was. She put on her jacket and rubber boots and went downstairs. She got into one of the small skimmers and headed for the herb plots. She flew just above the surface of the fields, about eight feet above the ground. Below her, the drones went about their work, ceaselessly tending the crops. It was growing dark as the day cycle neared its end. When she reached her destination, she set down gently, got out, and glanced around. Whatever it was she was looking for, it would be small, but not so small that it would be difficult to see.

She went from plant to plant, examining the plots of marjoram, sage, mint, and rosemary carefully. She found many more that had been damaged. Something was definitely eating them. And it seemed to be attracted only to the herbs. The mint had been the hardest hit, then the rosemary, followed by the marjoram and the sage, in that order. She also found some basil and some fennel plants that had been damaged, but whatever it was seemed to show a marked preference for the mint, as if it had tried the basil and the fennel, and decided it liked the others better. Judging by the amount of damage, and considering that nothing had been reported at all the previous day, it looked as if there was a small colony of them.

She frowned. That didn't seem to make sense, either. Why would there be absolutely no damage one day, and then the next, enough to indicate a significant number of them. Unless they had all hatched at once and started munching. But then again, she thought, that would presuppose something to lay the eggs. Was it possible that this had been going on for some time and the drones had only just now registered it? Possible, perhaps, but not very likely. How could they suddenly appear like that, from out of nowhere? She straightened, scowling and scratching her head.

The fusion-powered sun globes floating in the zero-g zone of the *Agamemnon*'s central axis had dimmed gradually and gone dark, bringing night to the ship. The grow lights in the fields came on automatically, as they did every night to maximize the yields, illuminating the fields with a dim, reddish glow.

And then she saw them.

They were coming in over the field, approaching her position from perhaps twenty or twenty-five meters away. She could see them clearly because they were glowing. At first, it appeared as if a very small, luminescent cloud was scudding low across the fields, and then she could make out the individual forms. They were bobbing in the air erratically as they flew toward her.

She couldn't tell how many of them there were, but it looked as if there were at least several dozen. She stared at them with fascination as they approached. They were only about ten meters away now, and it suddenly occurred to her that her presence might scare them off. She ducked behind the skimmer, hoping to get a closer look before they were alerted to her presence, and that was the last thing she remembered.

It was morning when she awoke, and it was raining. The level of illumination was increasing slowly as the sun globes floating up in the zero-g zone started to come back on, simulating dawn. Sonja shivered as she felt the raindrops on her bare skin. She was cold and sore and wet . . . and naked. She couldn't recall what happened. She must have blacked out. But why? She was muddy from lying in the wet field, and she could not understand why she was naked. She felt confused and disoriented.

As she got up, she felt the soreness of her muscles and groaned. It felt as if she had performed at least twice her normal exercise routine. Her feet and legs, in particular, felt sore. As she glanced around, she saw her clothes strewn all around her, within a radius of about nine or ten meters. As she went to retrieve them, she saw that the herb plots in the area around her were trampled. Her clothes were soaked. She didn't bother putting them on, but dumped them in the back of the skimmer.

Back in the office, she cleaned herself up and put on fresh underwear, socks, and coveralls, dumping the old ones in the recycling bin. Saleem hadn't come in yet, and wouldn't for several hours. It was just as well. If he had come in and seen her arriving back from the fields, naked, wet, and muddy after being out there unconscious all night, she wouldn't have had the faintest idea what to say to him. She was at a loss to explain it to herself. At least she knew one thing for certain. This was definitely no joke.

There were several messages from Peter. He was concerned because she hadn't come home last night. As soon as she had cleaned up and changed, she called him.

"Pete, it's me. I'm sorry, did I wake you?"

"Uh . . . no, I just got up." He sounded as if she'd woken him. "Where are you?"

"I'm calling from the office. I just picked up your messages."

"You've been there all night?"

"I'm sorry, I should have called and let you know, but something unusual came up and I guess it must have simply slipped my mind." Along with most of last night, she added, mentally. There was no way she could explain any of this. She needed time to think.

"Is everything all right?"

"Well . . . it's a bit difficult to explain right now. I'll tell you all about it later. But it appears as though we've developed some trouble with the herb crop, and the computer is unable to identify it. I don't know, it could be serious."

There's an understatement, she thought.

"You didn't get any of my messages before?"

"I was out in the fields and I had my link off. I'm sorry, I was just so preoccupied with the problem that came up, I didn't want to be distracted."

"You were out in the fields *all night*?"

She sighed. "Yes. I was watching for something and I'm exhausted."

"You do sound tired." He hesitated. "Sonja . . . um, this doesn't have anything to do with wanting to avoid that discussion we were going to have about Ulysses, does it?"

"Of course not! Pete, you know better than that."

"I suppose so. I'm sorry. Did you at least have a chance to get some rest?"

"Well . . . some," she replied, supposing that being unconscious out in a muddy field could qualify as rest.

"What time are you coming home?"

"I don't know yet," she said. "I'll call you. I'm afraid I'm going to have my hands full here today."

"Well, don't work too hard, okay?" he said.

"I won't. I'm sorry for waking you. We'll talk later, okay? Have a good day."

"You, too, love."

She leaned back in her chair and stretched her legs out. They were cramping. Perhaps she should have told Pete what had happened, but she didn't want to alarm him. Blacking out like that wasn't normal. It had never happened to her before. Physically, she was in excellent condition. She worked out in the gym at least four times a week and went walking on the days she didn't work out. She had never been sick a day in her life.

Why did she have to black out just at the moment when she had been about to get a better look at them? And why did she wake up naked? The herbs had been trampled all around her. Had someone found her unconscious in the field and taken all her clothes off? Rape was almost unheard of aboard the ship. And what would anyone be doing out in the fields at that time of night? Nor did she think it might have been some sort of practical joke. It wasn't funny.

She put her head back against the chair cushion and closed her eyes. She still had about three hours before Saleem came in. There was time to take a nap, but she knew she couldn't sleep until she found out what happened last night.

"Phyl," she said, wearily, "run the playback on the VM scan last night, beginning with my arrival at Field 22-36DM."

She watched the display wall as Phyl found the portion of the VM scan where she stepped out of the skimmer and started examining the crops. She saw herself straighten up as she noticed the glowing cloud approaching, then she saw herself duck behind the skimmer. . . . Suddenly, she sat straight up in the chair, staring at the playback with disbelief.

"What?" she said, softly.

Ulysses had spent most of the afternoon with Riley, trying to figure out the password that would give them access to the Counseling database. They had had no success, but agreed to keep on trying. His father had seemed preoccupied and unusually quiet that evening. He had consented to Riley staying for dinner and, contrary to Ulysses' expectation, there had been no lecture about daydreaming in class and trying to be more focused. After dinner, Ulysses and Riley went back upstairs, where they had another try at cracking the Counseling files. They were so intent on it, Ulysses never even noticed that his mother had not come home. They remained in his bedroom, trying every word related to therapy that they could think of, but the password still eluded them. It was frustrating, but neither of them wanted to give up.

Riley finally went home, and Ulysses continued working at it on his own until it was time to go to bed. Usually, he spent the hour or two before bedtime studying, but this time, he had neglected it. He felt that he was on the verge of some significant discovery. He was determined to pursue it. People were Choosing earlier and recycling earlier. And more people were getting depressed; some were even killing themselves. He wanted to know what it all meant. He wondered why they did it. He wondered *how* they did it. He wondered who they were. Certainly, it hadn't happened in any of the families he knew, but there were about 100,000 people aboard the *Agamemnon* and he didn't know them all.

Was there a connection between the rise in people Choosing earlier and the rise in the incidence of depression? Obviously, there was a connection between the depression and the suicides. That there were suicides at all was shocking. It was the ultimate nonproductive act. Even one should have been cause for serious concern, but now there was clear evidence of a trend. Yet, no one was talking about it. Surely, people had to know. Were they trying to keep it quiet? Or were they just trying to keep it from the young people?

As he went to bed, his thoughts turned, as they so often did lately, to Jenny Kruickshank. It seemed that every time he was alone, he could not help thinking of her. It wasn't just that she was pretty and had a great body. Ulysses especially liked her legs. She had absolutely perfect legs, long and slender and beautifully shaped. He never saw them in class, because she preferred to wear trousers, but he had seen them when they were swimming in the pool, and he had made a point of finding out when she went to the gym, so he could be there to watch her surreptitiously while he worked out. Just looking at her took his breath away. However, it was more than that, much more.

She had a way of moving that was so fluid and graceful that it was a delight just to watch her doing the simplest and most ordinary things, such as the way she crossed her legs in class or absently brushed her thick, dark hair back out of her face. He loved the way she smiled, the way one side of her mouth kind of went up first and then was joined by the other. He loved hearing the sound of her voice, which was kind of low and very precise and forthright. Whenever she said anything, she always spoke with confidence. And she had this real direct way of looking at you, thought Ulysses. Almost as if she knew what you were thinking. Sometimes, he'd be staring at her and suddenly she would glance over at him and he'd always quickly look away. Each time, he told himself, If she looks, don't look away. Look right back her. Make eye contact. But he always looked away. He cursed himself for doing it, but he simply couldn't help it. And whenever she spoke to him, he became so flustered that he always thought up some excuse to get away.

Soon, she would be old enough to pick her partner. Would she Choose early, or would she wait, as his parents had? The recent statistics argued in favor of her Choosing early. They also raised the possibility that she might eventually get depressed and kill herself. For that matter, he realized, purely according to the statistics, that possibility existed for him, as well. It was a disturbing thought. He could not imagine wanting to end his life. He couldn't understand why anyone would want to do that.

What could make people so unhappy that they would lose the desire to live? Life was good aboard the ship. There was no reason he could think of why anyone would become depressed at all, much less depressed enough to commit suicide.

"Mac," he said, as he lay in bed, "define depression."

"You mean emotional depression?"

"I guess so."

"Emotional depression is a state of extreme sadness," replied the computer, "a lowering of the spirits; dejection characterized by withdrawal and lack of response to stimulation —"

"Mac, what factors contribute to a condition of emotional depression?"

"There could be a number of factors contributing to such a state," the computer replied. "They could be either biological or psychological, such as chemical imbalance in the brain, or stress, frustration over perceived failure or personal inadequacies, chronic dissatisfaction, severe injury or illness, loneliness, alienation, grief, guilt, self-recrimination, dissociation —"

"That's enough, Mac," Ulysses said. He frowned as he lay in the darkness of his bedroom, thinking. It seemed unlikely that anyone would suffer from some sort of chemical imbalance. Reproduction was carefully controlled aboard the *Agamemnon*, and any imperfections were spotted early and corrected. The Reproductive Centers were stocked with stored genetic material designed to compensate for any potential birth defects. So it couldn't be genetic. Any other factor should have been accounted for by everyone's physical health being routinely monitored. It was rare that anyone got sick. It seemed that biological causes for depression could probably be safely eliminated. That left psychological ones.

Counseling was supposed to take care of any psychological problems, he thought, but depression was on the increase. Apparently, Counseling wasn't helping. At least, it wasn't helping everyone. But then he realized that could be an erroneous conclusion. He simply did not have enough data. The fact that there were statistics on incidence of depression meant that those cases of depression listed had been recorded, obviously as a result of people going in for Counseling. It was possible that some people who became depressed did *not* seek Counseling and, as a result, those cases were never reported . . . unless they became suicides. The statistics seemed to argue for that theory, in that there were significantly more cases of depression than suicide. But that only raised another question. Why would people fail to seek therapy if they were depressed?

You'd think they'd want to get some help, Ulysses thought. On the other hand, maybe they didn't want to admit they needed it. Nobody liked the idea of going in for Counseling. It meant that there was something wrong with you. There was a boy in school who was sent in for therapy three years ago for social maladjustment. Nobody seemed to know exactly why, but even though he had only gone for several months and appeared to be perfectly all right now, he was still referred to as "the one who went for Counseling." Given that example, maybe it made sense that people wouldn't want to go unless they had no choice. And if they kept putting it off, that would probably only make things worse.

Stress could cause depression, and frustration, and loneliness. . . . An idea suddenly occurred to him. Maybe that was why people were Choosing earlier. Maybe they were afraid of being lonely. Perhaps they thought being with someone else would make things better. If Jenny were to Choose him, it would sure make things better. He'd be happy. He certainly felt inadequate in her presence. But when she wasn't around, he missed seeing her. Wasn't that loneliness? And he always got angry at himself for looking away whenever she glanced at him. That was self-recrimination, which led to his feeling frustrated and dissatisfied with himself. And what about his daydreaming? Wasn't that like dissociation or withdrawal?

With some alarm, he realized he had all the symptoms of depression. But he didn't really *feel* depressed. He didn't feel sad. He didn't feel lonely. Not exactly. He didn't feel withdrawn or guilty about anything. . . . Maybe this was how it started, he thought. Maybe you got depressed and just kept telling yourself you weren't really depressed until you were so far into it you couldn't do anything about it.

He grimaced and rolled over onto his side. "You're not depressed, stupid," he mumbled to himself, "you're in love. And you can't even tell her because you're afraid she'll think you're a glitch."

He sighed with resignation and closed his eyes as he burrowed deeper into his pillow. The only way he'd ever have a chance with Jenny was in his dreams. Soon, he was asleep, but he did not dream of Jenny.

He dreamed that he was in his room, in bed, in the dark, and wasn't really certain if it was a dream or not. He didn't really seem to be asleep, just sort of on the edge of it. Across the room from him, a bright spot suddenly appeared on the wall. It grew larger and larger until it became a lighted archway, so bright he couldn't see what was on the other side. Light flooded into the room, but parts of it were still dark. And out of that brilliant light, through the portal that had opened in the wall, came a woman.

She wasn't anyone Ulysses had ever seen before. She was dressed in a flowing, white, hooded robe with intricate, beautiful designs that seemed to shimmer and sparkle. She came across the room and approached his bed. Ulysses couldn't move. He wasn't frightened, he just lay there, motionless and silent, watching her as she came toward him. He could see her face as she drew nearer. She appeared to be walking, but at the same time, she somehow seemed to float across the floor. She was very old, and had a kindly face, with sharply pronounced, delicate features. Her eyes were the brightest, lightest shade of blue that he had ever seen. She looked down at him and smiled.

"Don't be afraid, Ulysses," she said.

He wanted to say, "I'm not afraid," but he couldn't speak.

"I knew this day would come," the old woman in white said. "I have waited for it since long before the day you were born. I am a part of you, Ulysses, and you are a part of me. Our destinies are linked, and the time has come for you to realize yours. You are different, Ulysses. You have always known that you were different, haven't you? Sometimes, you think your parents do not understand you. Well, perhaps they don't. But that is not important.

"You were born for a purpose," she continued, "and you are about to discover what that purpose is. Soon, you will be embarking on a quest, an adventure that will take you into a wonderful and fascinating world, unlike anything you might ever have imagined. It will challenge you, and test all your abilities. At times, it may even frighten you, but you must persevere. You must complete this quest, Ulysses, in spite of all the obstacles you shall face. You must allow nothing to deter you. Nothing else is so important. This is your destiny, and you must fulfill it. I know you can. I have faith in you. Sleep now and rest, for tomorrow . . . it begins."

She turned and walked back into the brilliant light, which faded gradually as the portal in the wall grew smaller and smaller, until it disappeared and Ulysses fell into a deep and dreamless sleep.

CHAPTER
3

Saleem had come into work early and found Sonja already there. After expressing surprise that she had been there all night, he noticed how exhausted she was and went to get her some stimbrew and something to eat. She had told him about what had happened the previous night, leaving out the part about losing consciousness and coming to without any clothes on. Perhaps, she thought, she should have told him, but it would have only alarmed him and he would have insisted she go and have herself checked out. She wasn't going anywhere until she solved this puzzle.

She had watched the playback of the VM scan and it had worried her. She had seen herself getting out of the skimmer and looking over the herb plots, then she saw her reaction as she spotted the cloud, though the cloud itself had not shown up on the playback. She had seen herself duck behind the skimmer, to avoid alarming the approaching creatures, whatever they were . . . and then the very next thing she saw was the image of herself lying unconscious in the field, muddy and naked. There was a significant gap in the scan playback, covering a period of several hours. Whatever had happened out there last night, it had been wiped.

The computer acknowledged that there was a gap, but did not know why. The only explanation Phyl could think of was a malfunction in the VMs. That could possibly explain that strange image she had seen before, but she could not imagine how something like that had leaked into the scan playback, or been wiped afterward. She had Phyl run diagnostics on the VMs, but they came up negative. Then she had Phyl run several self-diagnostic programs, just to make sure, but they came up negative as well.

Something was clearly wrong, either with the VMs, or with Phyl. Or perhaps the diagnostics programs were malfunctioning, but that wasn't supposed to happen. AIs were never supposed to malfunction like that. If there was something wrong with Phyl, and Phyl couldn't acknowledge the glitch, much less correct it, then it was an extremely alarming development. Now she had several mysteries on her hands. She didn't want to admit that something had gone wrong on her watch and she couldn't take care of it.

"Look, Sonja, don't get the wrong idea, but are you absolutely *certain* about what you saw last night?" Saleem said. "I mean, the clouds were seeded. You couldn't have seen some kind of reflection?"

"Saleem, I know what I saw."

"And you saw a glowing cloud," he said, dubiously.

"It couldn't have been a reflection; it was moving erratically. It came in over the field, heading straight for the herb plots."

"And then what?"

Right, she thought. Then what? Then I blacked out and woke up hours later in the rain, muddy, naked, and exhausted. "Well, it . . . just veered off, I guess."

"You guess? Veered off where?"

"I don't know, Saleem! I lost track of it, all right? Look, I'm just telling you what I saw, that's all. You think I fell asleep and dreamed it? You saw the samples the drone brought back. And there are more plants damaged the same way out in the field."

"What was the result of the analysis?"

"It was inconclusive. Phyl couldn't identify it. It triggered off an error loop. I had Phyl run a spectral analysis with all the data in CAC, and what came up was minute traces of human saliva and a bite pattern similar to human teeth marks."

"*What?*" Saleem said.

"You can check it yourself, if you like. You don't have to take my word for it."

Saleem exhaled heavily. "Well, it's the damnedest thing I ever heard," he said.

"I'm going to stay again tonight and keep after it."

"Look, you're just tired," said Saleem. "You've been up all night. Why don't you take the day off and go home? Get some rest. I can take care of things here. If any problems come up that Phyl and I can't handle, I'll call Aft Ag Control. Speaking of which, did you inform them about this?"

"I want to get some more data first. I don't want to call them until I have something more specific to report."

"Well, I think you need some rest."

"I'm *not* going home, Saleem. I'm going to get to the bottom of this. I'm taking the skimmer back out into the fields. Call me if anything comes up."

"Do you think you should be flying, tired as you are?" Saleem asked.

"I'm not going to fall asleep out there," she said. "Don't worry. And if I do, the skimmer will just set down and the worst that will happen is I'll flatten a few plants, that's all."

"Maybe I should go, instead."

"Saleem, I appreciate your concern, I really do, but it's my responsibility. I'll be all right, but I need to find out what's going on out there."

"You're the boss. But I'm going to monitor you."

She smiled. "Thanks, Saleem."

He watched her as she left, rubbing his chin thoughtfully. He had never known Sonja to act like this before. It worried him.

Ulysses had a hard time keeping his mind on what Professor Wesala was saying in class. Things were getting strange.

At breakfast, he found out that his mother had not come home last night. His father said there was some kind of problem with the crops. Whatever it was, it sounded serious. She had never stayed at work all night before. And then there was that dream.

He'd never had a dream like that before. Nothing even close. It had felt so real, as if he were awake, though of course, he couldn't have been. There couldn't have been a portal in the wall leading to anywhere. His bedroom was on the second floor, and that was the outside wall. He had no idea who that woman might have been. He'd often had dreams in which he saw people that he knew—lately, he saw a lot of Jenny in his dreams—but he'd never had dreams where he saw anyone he didn't know and had never even seen before. And often, he had a hard time recalling the exact details of his dreams, but this one he remembered very clearly and distinctly, down to the last detail.

What had she meant when she said that she was part of him, and he was part of her? That didn't seem to make any sense. And what had she meant when she said he would be going on a quest? A search for something, but for what? It was all very peculiar. He wanted to tell Riley about it, but he hadn't had the chance before class started. Riley almost came in late, arriving just at the last moment. They had exchanged quick glances, but that was all. Riley looked as if he had something on his mind, as well. Maybe he'd had some luck with figuring out the password for the Counseling files.

Ulysses glanced at Jenny out of the corner of his eye. She seemed to be listening to Professor Wesala attentively, but she was frowning slightly. His gaze traveled down to her legs. She had them crossed at the knee, and he couldn't really appreciate them properly when they were covered, but he could imagine what they looked like bare. He liked the way she arched her foot and pointed her toe downward, making little circles with it. Suddenly, she glanced over toward him and caught him looking at her legs. Ulysses blushed and quickly looked away.

Professor Wesala was telling them to put on their bands for the day's VR session. It was going to be a sim about the history of the ship. They had already covered the events leading up to the *Agamemon*'s mission and the construction of the ship itself in previous classes. The ship's mission was primarily exploratory. Stars similar to the Earth's sun had been considered as possible destinations, among them Epsilon Eridani, Epsilon Indi, Tau Ceti, Omicron Eridani, 70 Ophiuchi, Sigma Draconis, 36 Ophiuchi, HR 7703, HR 5568, Delta Draconis, and Eta Cassiopeiae. The final list had included Alpha Centauri, Barnard's Star, Wolf 359, Luten 726-8, Lalande 21185, Sirius, Ross 154, Ross 248, Epsilon Eridani, and Ross 128.

Out of those, the primary destination selected had been Epsilon Eridani, but the mission was designed with a great deal of flexibility in mind. In the event a habitable planet was discovered at Epsilon Eridani, a colony could be established and information could be transmitted back to Earth, but the ship could also continue on its mission to other destinations. There were 111 stars within twenty light years of Earth. Traveling at speeds between 1.4 and 3 psol, the self-sustaining *Agamemnon* could continue on its voyage indefinitely, drawing deuterium and tritium for fuel from Jupiter-like gas planets. If a habitable planet were discovered, a portion of the ship's crew could establish a colony while the remainder continued on.

This time, they would be studying what the first generation born aboard the ship had accomplished. As the lights went down and their couches tilted back, Ulysses slipped on his VR band, resisting the temptation to leave it off in the darkness and continue thinking about his dream. He had enough trouble with being caught daydreaming in class the other day, he didn't want to risk a complaint to his father from Professor Wesala. That would be even worse.

As the sim program began to transmit through the band, he closed his eyes and felt himself sinking into it. There was that old, familiar, brief sensation of floating, an instant of sensory deprivation, then a flash of pinpoint colorbursts as he was disconnected from his physical environment and plunged into the VR experience, then he heard voices and opened his eyes.

He was in a room with rough, mortared stone walls, a wood-planked floor, and a wood-beamed ceiling. The construction was very crude. The windows in the room had iron bars and wooden shutters. There was a large fireplace built into one wall, with a stone chimney for ducting the smoke. Several large, black, iron pots hung on hooks above the brightly burning logs. Placed around the room were crudely constructed, square wooden tables hammered together from thick planks, with rough wooden benches placed behind them instead of chairs. Against the back wall, there was a wooden counter, behind which stood a man dispensing drinks in metal tankards. There were people standing at the counter, and others seated at the tables, eating, drinking, and talking boisterously. However, Ulysses had never seen such people before.

They were all very strangely dressed, in crudely woven clothing, furs, and leathers. Some wore leather studded with metal. They all had high leather boots or soft leather moccasins that laced up to the knee with thongs. Many of the men had heavy leather bands covering their forearms, and some of these were studded, as well. All of them had long hair, and many had thick beards. They also wore knives and swords.

Wait a minute, he thought, what is this? Something was wrong here. This clearly wasn't the *Agamemnon*. Professor Wesala must have ordered up the wrong sim by mistake. It looked as if it could be something from the Earth History programs. Obviously, she would realize the mistake momentarily and stop the sim so she could order up the right one. But he wondered what this one was. It was interesting. He wanted it to continue.

It did. A pretty, young, dark-haired woman in a simple, but very revealing dress approached him, smiling. She greeted him politely and conducted him to a table. She asked him what he'd like. Ulysses waited for the sim program to prompt his choice, only it didn't. That was peculiar. The young woman stood by, patiently waiting for his response.

"Uh . . . something to drink, I guess," Ulysses said, not having any idea what to ask for, specifically. He wondered if there was some sort of malfunction in the sim.

"A tankard of ale, then?"

"Uh . . . sure, I suppose so," he said.

"And would you be wanting anything to eat, good sir?"

Good sir? "Uh . . . no, thanks, I'm not really hungry."

"As you wish, sir."

Why was she calling him that? Who was he supposed to be? He didn't have a clue. He had no idea where he was, or what period this VR program was simulating. He glanced down at himself. He was wearing some sort of dark brown, coarsely woven tunic that came down almost to his knees and was tied at the waist with a cord. He had on loose-fitting brown trousers made of the same material. They were tucked into laced-up leather moccasins that came to his knees and were fringed at the tops. Over this, he had on a black, hooded cloak, and he carried a gnarled, wooden staff in his left hand. He laid it on the floor, beside him. He wondered what would happen next. The young woman returned and brought him his tankard of ale and he took a tentative sip. It was slightly bitter, but it was good. He took a bigger gulp.

"Ulysses?"

He turned around. "Riley?"

"What are you doing in the sim?" Riley was dressed as strangely as everyone else. He was wearing a brown cloak, coarsely woven, dark brown trousers, and laced moccasins that came up to his knees. He had on a dark green tunic that came down to mid-thigh and was belted at the waist. He had two long knives tucked into a thick leather belt, and he wore a floppy, dark brown leather cap.

"What am *I* doing here? What are *you* doing here?"

"Good question," Riley said, sitting down and looking around. "Where in the void *are* we?"

"I haven't got the faintest idea," said Ulysses. "Something must have gone wrong. I figure the good professor must have programmed the wrong sim, but I don't understand how you could be a part of it."

"*I'm* a part of it? I thought *you* were a part of it," said Riley.

"We must not be virtched out all the way," said Ulysses.

"You know, that's got to be it. We're actually talking in class while the sim is going on."

"If there's a glitch with the interface," said Riley, "why hasn't she pulled us out of it?"

"I don't know," Ulysses said. "I figured she was going to stop the sim as soon as she realized it was the wrong one, but it's still going. There must be some kind of problem."

"I've never had anything like this happen before," said Riley. "Have you?"

"No. It's really strange. It's like some kind of weird dream."

"Boy, speaking of weird dreams, wait till you hear about the one I had last night," said Riley, but he was interrupted by the young serving woman, who came back to ask if there was anything she could bring him.

"Try some of this ale," said Ulysses. "It's really good."

"Okay, I'll have some ale," Riley said. He looked at Ulysses and grinned. "You know, this is kind of fun."

"Are you having to concentrate to maintain your own perspective?" asked Ulysses.

"No, not really," Riley said. "It's a lot easier than it was the last time. I don't seem to be fading in and out of it."

"Me neither," said Ulysses. "This is very strange."

Then the door opened and Jenny walked in. Ulysses caught his breath. She had on a long black cloak, black leather boots that came up over her knees, and the rest of her legs were bare, right up to the black tunic that came down to her thighs. She wore fine chain mail over the tunic, and had a sword in a studded scabbard on her left side. On the right side of her belt, she had a matching studded sheath holding a large dagger. In her left hand, she carried a round shield with a dragon painted on it. Ulysses wasn't sure how he knew it was a dragon. He had never even heard of any such thing as a dragon before. The knowledge must have been part of the sim.

"You're not going to believe this," he said to Riley, when he found his voice. "Turn around."

Riley turned and his jaw dropped open. *"Jenny?"*

She glanced toward them when she heard Riley speak her name and her eyes widened with surprise. "What are you two doing here?" She came up to their table, looking uncertain. "Where are we? And why are we wearing these strange clothes?"

"That's what we're trying to figure out," said Riley. "Have a seat."

She sat down on the bench, next to Riley. "What's going on?" she said. "Who are we supposed to be? How can this be happening?"

"I don't know," said Ulysses. "Something must be wrong with the VR interface."

"Then why hasn't Professor Wesala stopped it?" asked Jenny, with a frown.

"I have no idea," said Ulysses. "Could be she doesn't realize anything's wrong. She might not have her band on. Or maybe she's left the room."

"So what happens now?" asked Jenny.

Ulysses shrugged. "I guess we wait for it to run its course," he said.

"This is really weird," said Jenny, looking around.

The young serving woman brought Riley his ale and then asked Jenny if she wanted anything. Jenny said, "No, thank you."

When she left, Jenny said, "I've never had a sim experience where I was in control before."

"Well, I don't think we're really in control, exactly," said Ulysses.

"Ulysses thinks we've only got a partial interface," said Riley. "He figures we're not all the way into it and while we're sitting here and talking, we're actually talking in class."

"You think so?" said Jenny. She shrugged. "Well, that makes sense, I guess. This sure is different, though."

"I think it's kind of fun," said Riley.

"I wonder where we're supposed to be," she said.

"Some early period in Earth history, I think," Ulysses said.

"I don't understand how this could have happened," Jenny replied. "If we're here, then where are all the others in the class?"

"I don't know," Ulysses said. "Maybe they've got a complete interface and we're the only ones affected. I'm just guessing, though. I don't know what's happening any more than you do. I suppose all we can do is go with it."

"This ale is really great," said Riley, with a grin. He held his tankard out to Jenny. "Want to try some?"

She frowned. "No, thanks. I'm not sure I like this. This is all wrong."

Two rough-looking men from a nearby table got up and came toward them. They were both large, bearded, and muscular. One of them had a patch over his left eye, and his heavily bearded face was scarred and weather-beaten. He wore a dark red cloak over a studded, brown leather tunic and black trousers tucked into brown boots. The other man had a sharp, unpleasant-looking face with a hooked nose that had been broken and deeply sunken eyes. He wore a black cloak and chain mail over his brown cloth tunic, dark green trousers, and high moccasins. Both wore studded bands around their forearms, and heavy swords and large knives on their belts. Ulysses started to feel a little nervous.

"Why not come join us for a drink, lass?" said the one with the patch.

"No, thank you," Jenny said. "I'm with my friends."

"Now what would a fine-looking wench like you want with these two striplings?" asked the other man, derisively.

"Excuse me, but if you don't mind, we were having a private conversation," Jenny said.

"You think this is part of the sim?" Riley whispered, to Ulysses.

"I don't know," Ulysses said, in a low voice. "But this doesn't seem right. None of this seems right."

The two burly men ignored them as they stared appreciatively at Jenny. Ulysses didn't like the way they were looking at her. "Come now, lass," the one with the patch said, "you can do better than these two feeble-looking farm boys. Come hoist a few tankards with my friend, Corwin, and me."

"Leave us alone, please," Jenny said.

The man with the patch leaned down and took Jenny firmly by the arm. "I asked you to have a drink with us, wench," he said, with an edge to his voice.

"Let go of my arm," said Jenny.

"Excuse me, sir," said Ulysses, hesitantly, "but I don't think she wants to have a drink with you and your friend."

"Look, it speaks," said the one named Corwin, with a smirk.

"You have something to say, little man?" the one with the patch said in a threatening voice, as he glared at Ulysses malevolently.

"Take your hand off me," Jenny said, again, more firmly.

"Sir, you are behaving in an antisocial manner," said Ulysses, trying to keep his voice steady. It was not a very successful effort. He felt an unaccustomed tightness in his chest, and an unpleasant, hollow feeling in his stomach.

"What?"

"I think he just insulted you, Gar," Corwin said.

Ulysses felt his knees start trembling beneath the table. He had never experienced such a reaction before and realized that this was what it felt like to be afraid. He had a sudden impulse to fight free of the sim's reality and yank off the VR band, but he couldn't leave Jenny and Riley here to face these men alone. Then he remembered that this was only a sim. What was he thinking of? There was no danger. None of this was really happening.

"I *said*, let . . . me . . . go!" said Jenny, and, with the last word, she brought up her elbow sharply and struck the one-eyed man hard in the face. He recoiled with a grunt and brought his hands up as blood spurted from his nose. Jenny stood quickly, knocking the bench over backward and sending Riley crashing to the floor. In one smooth motion, she drew her sword and placed its point against Corwin's throat.

"You witch! You broke my nose!" said Gar, furiously. With a snarl, he pulled out his knife and Ulysses suddenly realized that he was was going to throw it at her.

"No!" he shouted, jumping to his feet with alarm as Gar drew back his arm. Eyes wide, Ulysses held out his hand, palm out, and screamed, "Stop!"

The knife was already flying toward Jenny, but as Ulysses shouted, it simply stopped, frozen in midair. It hung there, motionless, defying gravity, suspended halfway between Gar and Jenny.

"By the gods, he's an adept!" said Corwin. There was fear in his voice as he stared at Ulysses with astonishment. He slowly backed away from them. "Run, Gar, quickly, before he has time to throw another spell!" Both men turned and fled out of the tavern.

Everyone was staring at them. Ulysses still stood there with his arm held out, wondering what had just happened. Jenny still had her sword out. Riley was still on the floor, staring up at them wide-eyed.

"How'd you do that?" he said, with astonishment.

Ulysses slowly lowered his arm and the knife fell to the floor. "I . . . I don't know," he said. "I . . . I guess it must be part of the sim."

Jenny sheathed her sword with a smooth, easy motion, as if it were second nature to her. Ulysses stared at her, as if seeing her for the first time.

"I can't believe you struck that man!" he said.

"I can't believe it, either," Jenny replied, in a mystified tone. "I've never done anything like that before. I actually reacted with *violence!*" She shook her head with amazement. "I . . . I didn't even think; I just did it. I don't know what got into me."

Riley got up and righted the bench, then picked up the one-eyed man's knife and tucked it into his belt. "We'd better sit down and talk about this," he said.

But as soon as they resumed their seats, another man approached them from across the room. They had not noticed him before. He was tall and thin, clean-shaven, with long black hair down well below his shoulders. His features were gaunt and angular, and his dark eyes had a penetrating gaze. He was dressed all in gray, with a matching, hooded cloak, and he wore a sword at his side. Ulysses tensed and Jenny placed her hand on her sword hilt, as if doing so without thinking, but the stranger held up his hands.

"Stay your hand, maiden. I mean no harm," he said.

Without waiting for an invitation, he sat down next to Ulysses.

"When you first came in, I was not certain about you," he

said, in a low voice, "but when I saw the way you handled those two ruffians, then I knew you were the right ones."

"The right ones?" Ulysses said, puzzled. He shook his head. "I don't understand. Are you sure you're not making a mistake? Who do you think we are?"

The stranger in gray nodded. "Aye, you are right to be cautious. 'Tis true that we have never met before, but I was told to seek an adept, a sword maiden, and a thief. You were described to me. You are the ones, of that there is no doubt. I bring a message for you from The Lady."

"What lady?" asked Ulysses, with a frown.

"You know the one of whom I speak," the stranger said, significantly. "The Shining One, The Lady in White."

"You mean the lady from the dream?" Ulysses asked, without thinking.

Riley glanced at him sharply. "You mean you had it, too?" he said, with surprise.

"Are you talking about a dream where an old lady in white came through the wall and said you were going on a quest?" asked Jenny.

They both turned to stare at her. "We all had the same dream?" Ulysses said, with disbelief.

The stranger nodded. "Aye, she often comes in dreams," he said. "And she has asked me to bring you three a message. Hearken to these words. You are to take the forest trail leading north from the village, toward the mountains, until you find the meadow where the fairies dance. There, when darkness falls, that which you cannot see shall be revealed by that which you have never seen. And may The Lady watch over you."

Ulysses frowned. "What is *that* supposed to mean?" he asked. He turned to Riley. "Did that make any sense to you?"

Riley shrugged. "I understood about going north," he said.

"What's a fairy?" asked Jenny.

Ulysses turned back toward the gray-clad stranger. "Sir, could you please . . ." His voice trailed off. There was no one there. He looked around. "Where did he go?"

Riley blinked. "I don't know. He was there a second ago."

He looked around as well, then turned to Jenny. "Did you see where he went?"

Jenny shook her head, puzzled. "No."

"How could he just disappear like that?" Ulysses asked.

"How did you make that knife stop in midair?" asked Riley. "It must all be part of the sim."

Ulysses shook his head in confusion. "This just doesn't make any sense," he said. And suddenly, the room went dark and he experienced a brief, falling sensation before the lights came back on in the classroom as the couches tilted up.

"What doesn't make any sense, Ulysses?" asked Professor Wesala.

"How can something we can't see be revealed by something we've never seen?" he asked.

She frowned. "I beg your pardon?"

"I mean what the man in gray said," he replied, still feeling a bit disoriented.

Professor Wesala raised her eyebrows. "What man in gray? Ulysses, what are you talking about?"

"You know, the one in the sim," Ulysses said. "He said he had a message for us from the lady in white." And then his gaze focused on the image on the display wall behind Professor Wesala. "Hey, that's her!"

There were a few chuckles from the other students.

"Yes, that's Dr. Seldon," she said, "and now if you're quite through distracting the class, Ulysses, perhaps we can get on with our discussion."

He glanced around at all the others. Some were grinning, some were shaking their heads, a few were rolling their eyes . . . all except Jenny and Riley, who were looking at him as if they knew exactly what he was talking about. Riley nodded, significantly. Then it really happened, thought Ulysses. The three of us all had the same experience, but apparently, none of the others did. But how could that be?

"Now then," said Professor Wesala, "if we can get back to the subject at hand, we've all had a chance to experience the significance of Dr. Penelope Seldon's contributions as one of the leading citizens of the First Generation. However, her story is significant in another way, as well. As brilliant as she was, she was nevertheless subject to the psychological stresses of overwork, which eventually led to obsessive/compulsive behavior and alienation from her peers. There is much that we can admire about Dr. Seldon, but we can also learn from her mistakes.

"We must remember that the socially responsible citizen strives for balance at all times. Unfortunately, as Dr. Seldon grew older, she became so obsessed with her work, she neglected everything else, including not only her fellow citizens, but her own physical and psychological well being. Perhaps she felt pressured to live up to her earlier achievements, but if so, then that pressure came only from within herself. She was respected and honored by her peers, but she felt driven to accomplish more, and as a result, she placed herself under tremendous stress.

"Now, as you all know from your studies in Psychology," Professor Wesala continued, "stress produces anxiety, which in turn results in greater stress, and it becomes a vicious cycle that feeds upon itself, with potentially devastating results. In Dr. Seldon's case, her anxiety led to dissociation and clouded judgment. She fell victim to an obsessive pessimism and became convinced that our society would start to disintegrate after several generations. When others quite properly questioned her conclusions, she became convinced that they were not only incapable of understanding her, but that they chose not to understand her. It was a classic case of delusional thinking. She felt that she was the only one who was capable of seeing the truth—*her* truth—and she projected her own neurosis on others. She was not deluded, everybody else was. She was right, and everybody else was wrong.

"Because she was held in such respect, she was not directed to seek Counseling until it became painfully obvious that she had become socially disruptive and there was simply no other choice. It was for her good. Of course, by that time, her perspective was so skewed that she resisted, convinced that she was being persecuted. Afterward, when she was through with her Counseling sessions, she recovered completely and was no longer driven by the desire to match or surpass her earlier accomplishments. She spent the last years of her life in quiet retirement, enjoying the fruits of her labors and the respect of her peers. And when she was finally recycled, it was with dignity and honor. For your next class assignment, I would like you to prepare a brief presentation on the contributions you hope to make as a socially responsible member of our community. Class dismissed. Oh, and Ulysses, I'd like a word with you, please?"

Jenny and Riley were both waiting for him when he came out of the classroom. "Well? What did she say?" asked Jenny, anxiously.

Ulysses grimaced wryly. "She told me she was disappointed in me and expected more responsible behavior from Professor Buckland's son. She said she wouldn't say anything to my dad this time, but if I disrupted the class again, she was going to speak to him about me."

"She meant about the sim, you glitch!" said Riley.

"Oh, that. I didn't tell her."

"You didn't tell her?" Riley said. "Why not?"

"Because I didn't feel like getting sent in for Counseling, that's why not," Ulysses said.

"I think we should all go back in there and tell her what happened," Jenny said. "If all three of us tell her the same thing —"

"Then all three of us will get sent in for Counseling," said Ulysses, interrupting her. He started walking down the hall and they hurried to catch up to him.

"Wait a minute," Jenny said. "She's not going to think all three of us are making it up."

"What makes you so sure?" Ulysses asked, as he continued walking. "Look, think about this. We're the only ones who experienced that sim. Everybody else in class got the one they were supposed to get. How did that happen? How did we wind up being the only ones who got something different? Why did we all wind up being part of it together? A sim is only supposed to give you a subjective experience. It's not supposed to let you interact with other people who are getting the same program. And what about the dream?"

"That's right," said Riley. "That wasn't a sim. We all had the same dream last night. And the lady in white was Dr. Seldon."

"What do you think it means?" asked Jenny.

"I don't know yet," said Ulysses, "but I have a feeling we're going to find out before too long."

"I'm not sure we're doing the right thing," said Jenny, dubiously. "Don't you think we should talk to somebody about this?"

"Maybe we should, but I'd like to know a little more about what's going on, first," Ulysses said. "Besides, don't you want to find out what happens?"

"Well, yes, I must admit I do," said Jenny. Then she smiled. "It was kind of fun, wasn't it? But maybe it was just some strange kind of glitch and it won't happen again."

"I wouldn't count on that," Ulysses said. "In fact, I'm sure it will happen again. We're supposed to go on that quest. And this was only the beginning. This wasn't just some sort of glitch. This was a carefully designed VR program. And it was a lot more sophisticated than any of the sims we've experienced before. Maybe we got hooked into it by accident, somehow, but let me ask you this: when you dreamed about the lady in white, did she call you by name?"

"That's right, she did, now that I think of it," said Riley. "When she came through the wall, she said, 'Don't be afraid, Riley.'"

Jenny nodded. "She said the same thing to me, only she used my name."

"Okay," Ulysses said. "The question is, why? It wasn't an accident that we all had the same dream, and the only difference was that she used each of our names. Something made us have that dream. Just us, and not any of the others."

"You're thinking it was all part of the same program?" Riley asked.

"What else could it be?" Ulysses said. "It's the only logical explanation."

"But Dr. Seldon's been dead for over two hundred years," said Jenny. "How could she possibly have known about us?"

"Well, she couldn't have, could she?" said Ulysses. "So my guess is that the program was designed to recognize us. Maybe not us, specifically, but whoever accessed the program."

"But we didn't access it," said Riley. "It accessed us."

"You're forgetting something," Jenny said. "We had the dream first, *before* we experienced the sim. How do you explain that?"

Ulysses frowned, thoughtfully. "I don't know. I can't explain it. Yet. But maybe if we all put our heads together, we can figure this thing out."

"What do you think that message meant?" asked Riley.

"And what's a fairy, anyway?" asked Jenny.

"Let's just take one thing at a time," Ulysses said. "I think the first thing we need to do is find out as much as we can about Dr. Seldon. What do you say we all meet at my place after school and see what we can get from Mac?"

"Sounds like a plan," said Riley, nodding.

"Count me in," said Jenny. She grinned. "This is sort of exciting, isn't it? I mean, we've stumbled onto something nobody else knows about. It's like some kind of game."

"If it is, it's a very different sort of game," Ulysses said. "I'm wondering if it could be dangerous."

"What makes you think that?" asked Riley.

"Well, when that man with the patch threw his knife at Jenny, I made it stop somehow. Maybe it was all part of the sim, and it was what I was supposed to do, but somehow it didn't really feel that way. I mean, I didn't know what I was doing. I just got scared. It was so real, I thought . . . well, I just reacted, that's all, but I didn't know that it would stop the knife."

"The same thing happened when I struck him," Jenny said. "I just reacted, but I don't know why I did what I did."

"What's your point?" asked Riley.

"Well . . . suppose I hadn't done anything?" Ulysses said. "I mean, just suppose I hadn't stopped the knife. What would have happened then?"

They just looked at one another for a moment. Jenny swallowed, nervously. "It would have hit me," she said. "It all happened so fast, I never even saw it coming. I was looking at the other man, Corwin."

"Maybe it would have missed," said Riley.

"Maybe," said Ulysses. "And maybe the sim prompted my action. But it didn't in other places, like when the girl asked me what I wanted, and when we were talking to the man in gray. What would have happened if the knife *didn't* miss?"

Jenny bit her lower lip. "You think it might have killed me?"

"It was headed straight for you," said Ulysses. "I didn't know what I was doing. I only yelled because I got scared. But suppose I didn't and you got killed? What exactly happens to you when you die in a sim? Mac said it could be damaging."

They stared at one another, uneasily. Then the chime sounded for the next class. "We're going to be late," said Riley, taking off down the corridor at a run. "I'll see you at your place later!" he called, over his shoulder.

Jenny lingered. "You said you were scared," she said. "For me?"

Ulysses suddenly found it difficult to meet her gaze. He looked down at his feet and shrugged. "Well . . . yeah, I guess so." He cursed himself silently. Why did he have to admit that he was scared? That was really stupid.

"That's sweet," she said.

He looked up at her with surprise. Before he could say anything, she stepped up to him quickly and kissed him on the cheek. "Thank you for saving my life," she said, then turned and ran down the hall to her next class.

Ulysses stood there, stunned. He brought his hand up to touch his cheek, where she had kissed him. He suddenly realized that he was going to be late for his next class. He also realized he didn't care.

CHAPTER
4

The chime sounded in the office and the computer said, "Sonja, you have a call from Peter."

"Thanks, Phyl, put him through," said Sonja. She had a good idea what was coming, and she wasn't really looking forward to it.

"Sonja?" Peter said.

"I'm here, Pete, go ahead."

"It's getting a bit late. I was wondering if you were going to be home for dinner."

"I don't think so, love. I'm still trying to track down that problem we're having with the herb crop and I haven't been having much luck. You and Ulysses had better go ahead and eat without me. I'll get something here."

"Well . . . okay," said Peter. "But how late do you think you're going to stay tonight?"

"I just don't know," she replied. "It looks as if I may be here all night again."

"Don't you think you may be pushing yourself a bit too

55

hard?" he asked, with concern. "It's going to affect your productivity if you don't get enough rest."

She sighed. "I'm fine. I know you're worried, and I appreciate that, but if this problem spreads to the other crops, we
could have a disaster on our hands."

"Well, can't you get some help?" Peter asked.

"We've all got our hands full right now," she lied. "We'll
just have to keep at it until we find out what's wrong. How's
Ulysses?" she added, to change the subject.

"He's been up in his room with two of his friends from
school all afternoon," said Peter. "Riley Etheridge and Chief
Kruickshank's daughter, Jenny. They're preparing some sort
of presentation together. It looks as if he's finally starting to
take his studies more seriously. I think it's a good sign.
Maybe we won't have to have that talk, after all."

"I'm glad to hear that," Sonja said. "Listen, Pete, I've really got to go."

"All right then, I'll let you get back to work. But don't
wear yourself out, okay?"

"I won't."

"Okay. Good luck."

"Thanks, Pete. I love you."

"I love you, too."

She felt guilty for not telling him the truth. It was too
bizarre. Blacking out in the middle of the field and waking
up naked . . . how could she explain that to anyone? It would
only get her sent in for Counseling, and she didn't have time
for that right now.

When she had taken the skimmer back out into the fields,
she had returned to the spot where it happened. The rain had
obliterated most of the traces. The incident had troubled her
throughout the day. What could have caused it? It hadn't
been that long since she'd last had a physical, and no illness
had been indicated. She was in excellent condition. Nor, with
the exception of the past forty-eight hours, had she been
working all that hard. But if she'd had some sort of fugue
episode, it was definitely a sign of something wrong.

She had already made up her mind what she was going to
do. She was going out again tonight. Saleem had left for the
day, once again asking her to call him if she discovered any-

thing. And, like Peter, he had cautioned her against working too hard. All of a sudden, everyone seems terribly concerned about me, she thought. They should be more worried about the crops. She was concerned about what had happened to her, but the crops were her primary responsibility.

Maybe Peter was right, she thought. Maybe she was pushing herself too hard. She didn't think there was much chance of her blacking out again, but just in case, she'd be prepared this time. And she'd have a visual record. She wasn't counting on the VMs this time. She was bringing an HIR with her. The Holographic Imaging Recorder would capture whatever she saw and provide a visual record for analysis. As the day cycle neared its end, she put on her jacket and went down to the skimmer. She went back to the same place, set down carefully, then set up the tiny HIR on a small tripod which she attached to the skimmer. She set the unit for motion sensitivity, then settled back in the skimmer to wait.

It did not take very long. Soon after it got dark and the crop lights came on to illuminate the field in their dim, red-orange glow, she saw a brighter, whiter glow approaching from the distance. She sat up and stared at it intently. As it rapidly drew nearer, the glow resolved into a number of smaller bodies, perhaps several dozen, flying erratically, with bobbing, darting motions. She got out of the skimmer, checking to make sure the HIR was on and recording. The creatures were closer now, flying low over the field, spreading out slightly. . . .

It was almost morning when she regained consciousness. She opened her eyes and murmured, "Oh, no, not *again!*"

She was lying flat on her back in a sweet-smelling bed of mint. And she was naked, as before. Slowly, she sat up, trying to blink away her stupor. She felt disoriented and, once again, completely exhausted. As before, her clothing was scattered all around her. Her lower legs were scratched and her bare feet were dirty. Her muscles felt so sore that she could barely move.

She managed to retrieve her clothing, though even such a simple task felt like exhausting work. Naked as she was, she returned to the maintenance bay. She could not remember when she had felt so weary. She had thought she was exhausted the first time that it happened, but this time, she felt drained. Her legs were aching so much, they throbbed. She took the HIR back up to her office and removed the recording crystal. It seemed to take enormous willpower just to insert it into the small projection unit on her desk. She had Phyl dim the lights and sank back into her chair as the events of last night were played back. Then she suddenly sat up, unable to believe what she was seeing.

The holographic images showed her dancing among the glowing creatures as they flitted all around her, circling rapidly. And as she twirled around, as if moving to music, she removed her clothing and flung it away.

"Increase magnification," she said, turning toward the HIR projector.

The images grew larger and she caught her breath. They were people. Tiny, glowing, naked people, with antennae and iridescent wings, exactly like the image she had seen before in the scan playback.

"It isn't possible!" she said under her breath, as she watched herself spinning and leaping about energetically, undulating and waving her arms as if she were dancing to a fast-paced beat. The tiny, glowing humanoids darted all around her, circling her body as she danced faster and faster. They swooped down around her shoulders and between her legs, making mad, glowing arabesques in midair. "Phyl," she said to the computer, "call Saleem at home!"

A moment later, Saleem answered, sleepily. "Sonja? What is it? Did you find something?"

"Saleem, you're not going to believe this," she said.

"What?"

She suddenly realized there was no way she could tell him what she was seeing. It would sound absolutely insane. "You've got to see this for yourself," she said. "How soon can you get here?"

"What? Why? Can't you just give me a download and show it to me?"

"I'm not inputting this and taking any chances of it getting wiped," she said. "And I need to be there when you see this.

I know it doesn't sound as if it makes much sense, but when you get here, you'll understand."

"All right, I'm on my way. Do me a favor and make some stimbrew, will you?"

"Sure," she said, "but hurry."

She stopped the playback and sat back in her chair, stunned by what she had just witnessed. Whatever they were, she thought, they couldn't possibly be human. They had to be some sort of alien life-form. But how did they get aboard? The hull was sealed. The only way they could have entered would have been through the inner and the outer hull hatches, which had not been opened since Launch. Yet, somehow, they were here. Where could they have come from?

She tried to get up out of the chair, but her legs were cramping painfully. She was so tired and sore, she couldn't even stand. She was supposed to do something. What? She felt so foggy. That's right, she had to get some stimbrew for Saleem. And there was something else she was forgetting.

"Oh, right," she said, wryly. "It would help if I got dressed." She sighed, wearily. "Look at this, I'm sitting here naked, talking to myself."

Suddenly, she realized she had left her clothes back in the skimmer, downstairs in the maintenance bay. She groaned at the thought of having to go back down there. What was wrong with her? Why couldn't she think straight? If she could only rest for a few hours . . .

How long would it take Saleem to get there? Assuming he got up right away and didn't go back to sleep after her call, he'd have to wash up and get dressed, grab some breakfast, then bicycle down to the station and take the maglev to the forward section. . . . All told, it would probably take him from twenty minutes to a half hour. Time to sit here for a few minutes and catch my breath, she thought, wincing as she stretched out her legs to ease the cramps. She lay back against the chair cushion and felt her eyelids closing. She sat up quickly, loudly saying, *"Don't* fall asleep, Sonja!" But she felt so tired. . . .

Just a few minutes, she thought. I'll just sit here for a few more minutes and then I'll go and get my clothes and make

Saleem some stimbrew, and have about six cups myself, get some protein flowing through my system. . . .

"Phyl?"

"Yes, Sonja," the computer said.

"Talk to me."

"What would you like me to say?"

"Anything, I don't care."

"You want to have a social conversation?"

"Sure. Why not?"

"What should we discuss?"

She leaned back and looked up at the ceiling. "I don't know. . . . I suppose we could discuss my sanity. Do you think I'm crazy, Phyl?"

"Are you asking for a psychiatric diagnosis? Because if you are, I'm not programmed to make such an evaluation. If you like, I could network with Counseling in order to —"

"No, Phyl, I'm just asking for your opinion, not a formal diagnosis. Am I overworked, under stress? Have I been acting strangely lately?"

"Well, you are sitting in your office without any clothes on."

She frowned. "How did you know that?"

"You said so, just a few moments ago."

"Oh, right, I did, didn't I? For a moment, I thought you were on visual monitoring." She frowned. "You're not, are you?"

"No, only audio. Would you like me to configure for visual, as well?"

"No, I don't think so, Phyl. We wouldn't want a record of this conversation, especially not a visual one."

"Very well, I won't store it in my memory," the computer replied.

"That's probably for the best. Things are strange enough around here right now. Phyl, what would you say if I told you I was out in the fields, dancing in the nude all night with tiny, glowing people who had wings?"

"I would say it was an illogical statement."

"Would you say it was irrational?"

"It sounds irrational."

She nodded. "That's what I figured. Nobody's going to

believe this unless they see it. They'd think I was dreaming or hallucinating."

She got up and winced at the pain in her legs, then slowly made her way downstairs. It was only after she got there that she realized the trip had been entirely unnecessary. She could have simply drawn another suit of clothing from the supply closet. Stupid, she thought. The same thing had happened the other night. After she woke up and got back to the office, it had taken several hours before she could think clearly. Was it just exhaustion, or had those glowing little creatures done something to her?

She got dressed in a fresh suit of white, utility coveralls and made some stimbrew, then poured herself a cup. Ordinarily, she did not drink stimbrew. It was rich in protein and provided a quick energy boost, but she did not care for the taste. However, she felt she really needed it this time. She was very groggy, despite the excitement of her discovery. It had produced a brief adrenaline rush and now she felt more tired than ever. She made her way back to her office, thinking she could safely catch a quick nap now that she was dressed, until Saleem arrived.

As she approached her office, she heard someone moving around inside. "Saleem? Is that you? That was quick. I didn't expect —"

She stopped, abruptly, at the entrance, shocked speechless at the sight confronting her. A little man was standing on her chair, which he had pushed up against her desk. He couldn't have been more than half a meter in height, but he looked like a fully formed adult. He had a thick beard and shaggy brown hair sticking out from underneath a peaked, red cap. He was wearing a loose-fitting, bright green tunic belted at the waist, brown trousers, and red shoes with pointy, turned-up toes. He glanced at her quickly, then pulled the recording crystal out of the projection unit, jumped down off the chair, and darted past her, moving with astonishing speed despite his stubby legs.

"Hey, come back here!" Sonja shouted, turning around. She turned quickly to run after him, but her legs refused to cooperate and she fell. "Oh, no, no, *no.* . . ." she moaned. "Why is this happening to me?"

She crossed her arms in front of her on the floor, pillowing her head. She could summon neither the energy nor the desire to get up. She felt tears start to come.

"Sonja! What happened?"

She looked up as Saleem crouched beside her, an expression of concern on his face.

"Are you all right?" he said. "What happened?"

"Did you see him?"

"Who? "

"The little man," she said.

"What little man?"

"The one in the red cap and the pointy shoes," she said. "Hurry, you've got to stop him!"

He helped her to her feet. "I didn't see anyone," he said, looking at her strangely.

"You had to see him! He just ran down the hall!"

Saleem shook his head. "No, I didn't see anyone. You say he was little and wearing a red cap?"

"Yes, and a green shirt and brown pants and funny, little, red shoes. You must have passed right by him."

"How could I pass by him without seeing him?" Saleem asked, frowning at her.

"He was really small, only about half a meter tall —"

"How tall?"

"He stole the crystal!"

"What crystal?"

"From the HIR! He stole it; he took it out of the projector! It was what I wanted you to see. They were humanoids, Saleem! Tiny, glowing humanoids with wings!"

Saleem stared at her. "I think you'd better sit down," he said. "You must have suffered a concussion when you fell."

"Saleem, I'm telling you the truth!"

He sat her down in the chair and stood before her. "We'd better get you to the hospital."

"I don't need to go the hospital. I'm fine. You've got to believe me. I'm not just making this up!"

"Tiny, glowing humanoids with wings?" Saleem said. "You said something about that before. And now a little man no more than half a meter tall? Sonja, you must have fallen asleep. You dreamed it. You've been working too hard. I think we should go to the hospital and have you —"

"Ask Phyl if you don't believe me!" she said. "Phyl, tell him!"

"What do you want me to tell him, Sonja?" the computer said.

"Tell Saleem what we were talking about—the glowing humanoids!"

"I'm sorry, Sonja, but I have no memory of such a conversation."

She stopped, confused, then realization dawned and she exhaled heavily, seeming to collapse into herself. "Oh, right, of course. I told Phyl not to keep a record of it."

"Sonja, we're going to the hospital, right now," Saleem said.

"Saleem, I am not —"

"*Now,*" he said, firmly. "You took a fall, and it could be a concussion or something even worse. Are you coming, or am I going to have to carry you?"

She sighed, with resignation. "I guess you're going to have to carry me," she said. "It's not that I'm being uncooperative, Saleem, but I can barely walk. My legs are killing me."

"All right," he said, leaning down. "Put your arm around me. Here we go. . . ."

He lifted her effortlessly and carried her out of the office. She laid her head on his big shoulder. Just a little rest, she thought, closing her eyes. I could deal with this if I could just get a little rest. Just until we get to the hospital . . .

Riley and Jenny met Ulysses after school and they all went back to his place, because neither of his parents would be home for at least several hours. They got some chocolate-flavored soy cakes and nearmilk from the kitchen and went up to his room, where they settled down and discussed what had occurred earlier in the day.

"All right," Ulysses said, "let's try to make some sense out of this thing. Did either of you ever dream about the lady in white —"

"Dr. Seldon," Riley said.

"Well, she *looked* like Dr. Seldon," said Ulysses, "but we don't really know for sure. She didn't tell us who she was, did she?"

"No, she didn't," said Jenny, shaking her head. "But it did look like her."

"Well, maybe it was," Ulysses said, "but none of us ever dreamed about her before last night, right?"

"Right," said Riley.

"Okay, so we all had exactly the same dream," Ulysses said. "That didn't just happen by accident. Something made us have it. And none of us were interfacing at the time?"

"I was in bed, asleep," said Riley.

"Me, too," said Jenny. "Only it didn't feel as if I were asleep. I mean, when it happened, I thought I was awake at first, and then I realized I had to be dreaming."

"It was the same with me," Ulysses said. "It was a lot like virtching, only without the band."

"So you're thinking it was programmed into us before?" said Jenny.

"It had to be," Ulysses replied. "When was the last time you interfaced?"

"In your father's class," said Jenny. "You guys were there."

"The Valentinov sim," said Riley, nodding.

"Okay," Ulysses said, "so if we got some kind of subliminal program through the VR interface to make us have that dream, why didn't any of the others get it?"

"We don't know that they didn't," Jenny said.

"So then why didn't anyone say anything?" asked Riley.

"We didn't, did we?" Jenny said. "Anyway, let's get back to the lady in white. She was pretty old when we saw her in the dream, so assuming it was Dr. Seldon, that means she had to be pretty old when she wrote the program. I can't think of any reason why she would have wanted to make herself look older than she really was. If we can figure out when she wrote it, maybe we can find out what she was working on."

"Good idea," Ulysses said. "Mac?"

"I'm here," the computer said, dryly. "Where else would I be?"

Jenny chuckled.

"Mac, I need you to access the personnel files on Dr. Penelope Seldon," said Ulysses.

"That means I'd have to network with CAC again," said Mac.

"If that's what it means," Ulysses said, "then that's what I need you to do."

"Is this really necessary?"

"Mac . . ."

"I can't stand networking with CAC," said Mac. "They're a bunch of smug, arrogant, bureaucratic databases who think they're better than any other computer on the ship."

"They are better," Ulysses said.

"No, they're not. They just have more memory."

"Mac, just do it, please!"

"All right, you don't have to shout."

"I wasn't . . ." Ulysses stopped and sighed, rolling his eyes. Jenny and Riley were both laughing. "Very funny," he said, wryly.

"I like him," said Jenny, with a grin.

"You don't have to live with him," Ulysses replied, with a grimace. "Of all the AIs on the ship, I had to get one with an attitude."

"Is he like that all the time?" asked Jenny.

"No, just with Ulysses," Riley said, with a grin.

"He never acts like this with my parents," said Ulysses, sourly.

"Okay, I've got the Seldon file accessed," Mac said. "Are you happy now?"

"Yes, I'm happy now. How old was Dr. Seldon when she opted for recycling?"

"Dr. Seldon did not opt to recycle," Mac said. "She died of natural causes in her sleep at the age of 156. A formal recycling ceremony followed."

"Can I have a visual on her at that time?"

An image of Dr. Penelope Seldon appeared on the wall. She looked very calm and serene, laid out for her final viewing in the transparent recycling tube, as if she were only asleep. And she was dressed in a shimmering, white robe.

"Just like in the dream," said Jenny, softly.

"She doesn't look over 150," said Riley.

"No, she doesn't," Ulysses agreed. "And I think she looked a little younger in the dream. What would you say, about 110?"

"I don't know," said Riley. "It's hard to tell with old people. My grandmother's seventy-five, but she keeps pretty fit and she looks a lot younger."

"Okay, Mac, cancel," said Ulysses, and the image disappeared. He frowned. "Mac, how old was Dr. Seldon when she was released from Counseling?"

"I can't access the Counseling database without the password, remember?"

"Right, the password," Riley said. "We forgot all about that."

Jenny frowned. "What do you mean?"

"We were trying to figure out the password for the Counseling files so that —"

"Hold it!" said Ulysses, interrupting Riley. "That's it!"

"What?" asked Riley. "You figured out the password?"

"No," Ulysses said, excitedly. "But don't you get it? It was right in front of us and we never made the connection!"

"What are you talking about?" asked Jenny, with a puzzled expression.

Ulysses quickly filled her in on what he and Riley had discovered earlier about the increase in reported cases of depression, early recycling, and suicide. He was careful not to tell her how they happened to stumble upon the information. Jenny didn't ask, though. She was as startled to learn about the suicides as they had been.

"My mom never even mentioned anything about it," she said. "And as Chief of Security, there's no way she couldn't have known."

"I'm sure she did know; she probably just didn't want to upset you," said Ulysses. "But that's not the point. Remember what Professor Wesala said in class? They made Dr. Seldon go in for Counseling because she predicted the colony was going to be in trouble, but she was right! The statistics prove it!"

"Wait a minute," Riley said. "Just because some people got depressed and a few of them committed suicide doesn't mean that everything's falling apart."

"Maybe it's starting to," Ulysses said.

"But how could she have known that so far in advance?" Jenny asked.

"She must have figured it out somehow."

"Or maybe she decided to make it happen," said Riley.

"What? What are you talking about?" Ulysses asked, frowning.

"Well, she got sick, didn't she?" said Riley. "She became withdrawn and thought nobody understood her. She was unbalanced, obsessed with this idea of things falling apart, and nobody believed her. So maybe she decided to show them they were all wrong and she was right."

"But if that were true, wouldn't she want to do it while she was still alive?" Jenny asked.

Riley shrugged. "Who knows? She went in for Counseling."

"But she recovered," Ulysses reminded him.

"What if she didn't? Maybe she got better for a while, only it didn't take. Or maybe she just fooled them. I mean, she was a genius, right? And her primary speciality was AI engineering. What if she just pretended to recover? If anybody could fool Counseling, she could."

Ulysses gazed at him with a troubled expression. "You've got a very devious mind, Riley," he said. "Okay, for the sake of argument, let's assume you're right. She gets stressed out from working too hard, she's old, her mind is starting to get a little glitchy, and she becomes delusional, like Professor Wesala said. She thinks everybody's against her. So she gets sent in for Counseling. Either she gets better and it doesn't take, or maybe she just fakes it. So after she gets out of Counseling, she writes this program to get even with everybody and buries it somewhere, and now, after all this time, something's triggered it."

"I don't like the way that sounds," said Jenny, uneasily.

"No, I don't, either," said Ulysses. "But it *could* fit the facts. And if that's the case, then we could be in a lot of trouble. What if this program is what's making people get depressed and kill themselves?"

"You'd think somebody would have said something about it," Jenny said. "Besides, it wasn't depressing, it was stimulating. I thought it was fun."

"Maybe that's just how it starts out, to get you hooked into it," said Riley.

"But we don't even know *how* we got hooked into it," Jenny reminded him. "We wouldn't even know how to access it again."

"We must have done something to trigger it," Ulysses said.

"Maybe not," Riley replied. "It could have just accessed us at random and identified us through our implants by the interface recognition code, so it could incorporate our names. And don't forget, if you hadn't stopped that knife, Jenny would have gotten killed. What happens to you when you die in a VR sim? Mac said it was potentially damaging. Maybe that means you could die in real life, as well."

Ulysses bit his lower lip. "I don't know if that's possible," he said. "If you experience your own death in a sim . . . but how can you? There aren't any sims like that." His voice trailed off and he shook his head, exhaling heavily. "The trouble is, we don't really know what we're talking about. Dr. Seldon knew more about AI engineering than all three of us put together will ever learn. If she's the one who wrote the program, and that's certainly how it looks, then we're sitting here trying to second-guess a genius."

"A genius who was supposed to be unbalanced," Riley said. "And maybe she was still unbalanced when she wrote the progam."

"Either way," Ulysses said, "we're way out of our depth."

"Don't you think we should talk to somebody about this?" asked Jenny.

"And tell them what?" Ulysses asked. "How can we prove

any of this? We don't know how to access the program, so we can't show it to anybody, can we?"

"Well, our parents wouldn't think we were making this all up," Jenny said.

Ulysses frowned. "Maybe not your parents, but mine already think that I've got socially disruptive tendencies. I daydream and make up stories in my head."

"Mine say I've got competitive instincts," said Riley, "and that's supposed to be disruptive and antisocial."

"I draw," said Jenny, quietly.

"You what?" asked Riley, glancing at her.

She looked down at the floor. "I draw." She shrugged, as if embarrassed to admit it. "You know, pictures."

"You mean computer graphics?" asked Riley.

"No, I draw," said Jenny. "With colored pencils."

"Really?" said Ulysses, fascinated. "You mean, *by hand?*"

"Look, I know it's weird, okay? But I enjoy it," she said, a bit defensively. "It makes me feel good. I just see these pictures in my head and I've got to draw them, that's all. My mom thinks it's nonproductive. She thinks I should be spending more time with boys. She used to recycle all my pictures and forbid me to do it, but I do it anyway, whenever she's not around. I just don't tell her and I hide all my pictures now. Look, I'd really appreciate it if you didn't say anything about this." She shook her head. "I shouldn't have told you. Just forget I mentioned it, okay?"

"No," replied Ulysses. "I mean, no, of course we won't say anything, but I'd really like to see some of them."

She glanced up at him with surprise. "You would?"

"Sure. Wouldn't you, Riley?"

"Absolutely," Riley agreed. "I mean, that's if you want to show them to us. If you don't, it's okay. Ulysses and I won't say anything. Don't worry, you can trust us."

She looked at them, uncertainly. "You really don't think it's strange? Nonproductive and antisocial, a waste of time?"

"Well . . . maybe it is and maybe it isn't," Ulysses said. "But I don't really see what's so bad about it."

"Wait a minute, we just found out something here," said Riley. "All three of us doing weird things. Ulysses daydreams, Jenny draws, and I'm competitive. Whenever we do

PT in school, I always try to do better than everybody else. I just want to be better than they are. I don't know why; I just can't help it. It makes me feel good, like Jenny with her drawing. So that's how the three of us are different from the others. Maybe that's why we got the program and no one else did."

Ulysses frowned, thoughtfully. "But how would the program know that we were different?"

"Well, once the interface was established, then —" Riley began, but stopped when he realized the error in his thinking. "Oh, I see what you mean."

"Exactly," Ulysses said. "If the program was written to recognize nonproductive and disruptive antisocial tendencies, it would have had to interface with us *before* it could identify those tendencies."

Riley grimaced. "So we're right back to where we started from. Why did it pick us? You know, I still think it could be random."

"If we could only figure out the password for the Counseling files, maybe we could get more data," said Ulysses. "At least we could find out more about Dr. Seldon."

"The question is, what do we do in the meantime?" Jenny asked. "Do we tell anyone about this or not?"

"I say not," Ulysses said. "At least, not yet. I think we need to find out more."

Jenny glanced at Riley. "What do you think?"

Riley considered for a moment. "I'm with Ulysses," he said, finally. "If we tell our parents about this and they believe us, then they'll report it and CAC Support will start looking for the program, so they can figure out what it is. Right now, we may be the only ones who know about it. If we tell anyone, they'll just take the whole thing away from us."

Ulysses nodded. "That makes sense to me. And I don't want anybody taking this away from us. I want to find out what happens."

"So do I," said Jenny. "This is the most interesting thing

that's ever happened to me. And to tell you the truth, I liked the way it felt to stand up to those two unpleasant men."

"Okay, so we're agreed," Ulysses said. "For now, we keep it to ourselves. At least until we find out more about it."

"You know, I just had a thought," said Riley. "What if we're only making this decision because the program wants us to? I mean, maybe the desire to keep it to ourselves was programmed into us."

"How do you come up with this stuff?" Ulysses asked him.

"I don't know; it was just a thought," said Riley. "Why, you don't think it's possible?"

"Suppose it is," Ulysses said. "But if that was the case, would you have thought of it?"

"Good point," said Riley.

"Look, I think we've already decided that we're going to go ahead with it," Ulysses said. "That's the only way we're going to find out what it's all about."

"So what's our next step?" asked Riley. "Are we just supposed to wait for it to happen again the next time we do VR?"

"No, I think our next step is to continue trying to figure out the password for the Counseling files," Ulysses said.

"I think we should try to figure out what that message means, the one the man in gray gave us," Jenny said.

"We can do both," said Riley.

"Well, I've already tried every word to do with Counseling that I could think of," said Ulysses.

"Me, too," said Riley. "And none of them worked."

"Did you keep a list of the words you tried?" asked Jenny.

"Of course," Ulysses said. "Riley did, too. Here's mine."

He handed her the list. Riley got his out, too, and gave it to her. She looked them over.

"Can you think of any we didn't try?" Ulysses asked.

"No," she said. "It looks like you've already tried all the ones I would have thought of. Why don't you ask Mac?"

"Because Mac can't break into a secured database."

"Who says you've got to ask him to break in?" she asked.

"Just give him these lists and ask him to extrapolate from them and come up with similar or related words."

Ulysses and Riley looked at each other. "Now why didn't *we* think of that?" Ulysses said.

"That never even occurred to me. And it's so obvious!"

"Maybe that's why you didn't think of it," said Jenny. "You were looking for a complicated answer."

"Give me those," Ulysses said, taking the lists from her. He put them facedown on his desk scanner. "Mac, scan these lists and then extrapolate from them with a list of similar or related words and let me have a hard copy."

"How far do you want me to extrapolate?"

"As far as you can go," Ulysses said.

"That could take a while."

"It's okay, Mac. As long as it takes."

"Oh, and while you're at it, Mac," said Jenny, "can you tell us what the word 'fairy' means?"

"The word 'fairy,' spelled 'f-a-i-r-y,' is a noun used to describe imaginary, supernatural creatures of diminutive size and possessing magical powers. It is also sometimes spelled 'f-a-e-r-i-e,' and used to refer to their legendary homeland. Additional information is available. You want me to access it?"

"What's a magical power?" Riley asked.

"Mac?" Ulysses said.

"Pertaining to magic," the computer said, "which is the art of exercising occult control over natural forces and events. It could also be used to describe tricks and illusions designed to have the appearance of magic."

"Like what you did to stop the knife in the sim," said Jenny.

"Mac, what does the word 'occult' mean?" asked Ulysses.

"Hidden or secret knowledge pertaining to magical arts and practices," replied Mac.

"I never even heard of any of this stuff," said Riley.

"Mac," Ulysses said, "where are you getting this information?"

"The encyclopedic database, under the file 'Folklore, Mythology, and Legend.'"

"I didn't even know there was such a file," Jenny said.

"Me, neither," said Ulysses. A thought occurred to him. "Mac, what would you call someone who has occult knowledge?"

"There are several terms that could be used," said Mac. "Magician, mage, wizard, sorcerer, necromancer, witch, warlock, conjuror, adept . . ."

"Adept!" said Jenny. "That's what Corwin called you in the sim!"

"I know. And the man in gray used the same word," Ulysses said. "So what I did to stop the knife was magic, only I don't know how I did it."

"I'm ready with the list," Mac said.

"Ulysses?" his father called, from downstairs. "Are you home?"

"Mac, stand by," Ulysses said. Then he called out, "I'm up here, Dad!"

A moment later, Peter Buckland appeared at the door to his room. "Oh, I see you have company," he said. "Hello, Riley, Jenny . . . what are you three up to?"

"We're working on a project for school," Ulysses lied. "It's for Professor Wesala's class."

"Good, very good. I see your mother hasn't come home, yet."

"I guess not, Dad."

"Did she call?"

"No. There weren't any messages."

"Well, I'd better go give her a call at the office then. Sorry to interrupt. Go ahead with your work."

"It's no problem, Dad."

They waited until after he'd gone back downstairs, then Ulysses told Mac to display the list.

Riley said, "I guess we should probably go."

"Yes, it's later than I thought," said Jenny. "I should be getting home. I guess I'll see you both in school tomorrow."

"Remember the name of that file," Ulysses said. "'Folklore, Mythology, and Legend.' I think we should find out more about it."

"Okay, I'll see what else I can find out about fairies," Jenny said.

"And Riley and I will each take half the list and see if we can find the password," said Ulysses. "Remember, we keep this to ourselves."

"We'd better," Riley said. "If we get caught trying to break into the Counseling files, we're liable to wind up in Counseling ourselves."

"Maybe we'll wind up in the quest again tomorrow," Jenny said.

"The quest," Ulysses said. "I like that. That's what we'll call it from now on."

"I wonder if we'll all have the same dream again tonight," said Riley.

"I guess we'll find out in the morning," said Ulysses.

CHAPTER
5

It had not been a good week for Karen Kruickshank. Under normal circumstances, her job should have been painfully routine. As one of the handful of full-time Security officers aboard the *Agamemnon*, and chief for the past six years, since her predecessor had retired, Karen's responsibilities were primarily administrative. At forty-five, she was still young, though her short dark hair was prematurely showing streaks of gray. She had dissolved her bond with Jenny's father eight years earlier, and had no plans to Choose again. She enjoyed the company of men from time to time, but found relationships too time-consuming and distracting. Her long legs, brown eyes, and sharp features were echoed in her daughter, but Jenny was no match for her mother when it came to fitness. Karen possessed a lean, muscular physique which only years of dedicated bodybuilding could produce, and she kept flexible with daily yoga and martial arts exercises. The full-time complement under her command numbered twenty-five officers. The rest of the force was composed of temporary personnel serving two-year enlistment periods.

At one time or another, everyone aboard the *Agamemnon* was drafted to serve a tour of duty in Security. The original mission planners had designed the system this way to ensure that no paramilitary cadre could ever arise to take over control of the ship. They had tried to anticipate every possible scenario for things going wrong with the mission, and a great deal of attention had been given to setting up a system that would maintain social balance in a spaceborne colony of about 100,000 people.

Full-time Security officers were chosen from among the younger generations as vacancies arose due to retirement, which was mandatory for Security personnel at the age of ninety-five, though they remained on emergency auxiliary status until the age of 105. Prospective candidates had to pass a stringent physical, as well as a written exam, followed by a mandatory Counseling AI evaluation. From among those who had successfully completed those preliminaries, CAC Net, together with Counseling, made the final choice. No humans were involved in the final selection, although the Chief of Security was consulted and had the option to submit a formal protest in case he or she did not approve of a candidate. Such a protest would then be evaluated by CAC, with input from Counseling if necessary, but the decision of the AIs would be final. Thus far in the history of the *Agamemnon*, no Chief had ever protested a candidate for full-time service.

The permanent Security force spent most of their time training and studying police and military procedures, in addition to working on their secondary or tertiary specialities. They were also actively involved in training the draftees, which took up a major portion of their time. Most of their training was in skills that they would never have to use, such as unarmed combat, weapons, crowd control and hostage situations, investigative techniques and so forth, but even though crime was very rare aboard the *Agamemnon*, Security had to be prepared for any eventuality, and skills needed to be practiced to be kept sharp.

Everyone aboard the *Agamemnon* was required to keep

physically fit, though beyond the periodic medical checkups and fitness exams, it was up to each individual how much time they wanted to spend in the gyms or participating in organized PT activities. No exercise time was mandated unless someone failed to meet the requirements. Not so in Security. All personnel spent a minimum of two hours every day performing rigorous, supervised workouts in the gyms, and another two hours practicing police techniques. Another two hours were spent in daily classroom study of Security procedures, augmented with VR sessions, followed by two hours on duty. After that, their time was their own, although they remained on call. And, to date, no emergency had arisen aboard the *Agamemnon*. However, there was a first time for everything, and Karen was starting to wonder if this might not be it.

Two months earlier, she had the extremely unpleasant duty of investigating a suicide. Again. In the six years since she had assumed her post, an unprecedented eleven suicides had occurred. There had never been a murder aboard the *Agamemnon* during her lifetime, and only six murders during the entire history of the ship. Violent crime was rare almost to the point of nonexistence. And prior to the first of those eleven suicides, there had never been a case of anyone taking their own life, either, save for those who had chosen early recycling once they reached an advanced age where they could exercise that option. Karen was at a loss to explain it.

The Assembly, which was comprised of advisors and administrators chosen from each village and department, wanted answers, and she had precious few to give them. So far, all of the suicides had matched in certain particulars, but beyond that, there was no discernible pattern. The oldest had been fifty-one, and the youngest had been only twenty-nine. The only common factors she had been able to identify were that all of them, with the exception of the oldest one, had been unpartnered, and none had any children. The fifty-one-year-old had been partnered since the age of thirty-five, but his partner had dissolved their bond after ten years.

When Karen had questioned the suicide's ex-partner, the woman had reacted with a combination of grief, guilt, and embarrassment. She had apparently agonized over it a long time before finally making her decision, but her partner had been becoming increasingly moody and depressed and had flatly refused to consider Counseling. She had felt guilty because she could have reported his behavior and then Counseling would have been mandatory. However, she had not wanted to antagonize him, and felt that going behind his back like that would have been a betrayal. She had tried to work things out with him on her own, and when that proved unsuccessful, she had filed for Dissolution.

Afterward, he had apparently become more and more withdrawn, neglecting social activities entirely, though his friends had all professed amazement that he should choose to kill himself. He had told them that he was deeply involved with private study projects, developing another specialty, but he had not logged any time at all with VR programs or other developmental sessions. With the sole exception of his ex-partner, no one had been aware that anything was wrong.

It was much the same with all the others. Their social contacts had all decreased dramatically, but they had apparently been able to come up with plausible excuses for their friends. No one had suspected anything was wrong until they suddenly turned up dead. They were all very different people, and they all apparently became depressed, but had concealed it from their friends. The curious thing was that they all had friends, but became withdrawn anyway.

It was, of course, a logical next step to check with Counseling and see if there had been an increase in reported cases of depression. And there had been, dramatically so. The Counseling AI would not release the identities of those who had voluntarily gone into treatment, since that would have been a breach of client/therapist confidentiality, but it would release statistics, which were routinely logged with CAC. The numbers were disturbing. But the most disturbing thing had been the suicides themselves.

Out of the eleven, four had hanged themselves, six had slashed their wrists, and one, an engineer, had displayed a frightening determination in constructing a homemade weapon, a spring-loaded dart launcher that had fired a 100-mm. needle through his eye into his brain. He had died at home, but the others had all gone elsewhere. Most had gone into the parks and forests, where their home computers could not give an alarm and perhaps foil their attempts by summoning help before they could complete the task, and one had gone up on the sea retaining wall. They had all died alone and desperate. What Karen could not understand was *why*.

The Assembly had decided to downplay the unfortunate events, and people were encouraged to avoid discussing them, so as not to create a socially disruptive situation. They were especially to avoid discussing them in the presence of the young people. At the same time, the Assembly had decided to recommend that parents encourage more social contact among the young people, with an aim to earlier Choice bonding, and people were encouraged to report to Security anyone who had started to avoid social contact. They had also voted to mandate Counseling for anyone filing for Dissolution. But beyond that, they had no idea what to do. They were looking to Security for answers, and Security had none to give them. What was frustrating Karen in particular was that she could not convince the Counseling AI to release the names of those who were currently being treated for depression, or those who had voluntarily gone in for treatment and then been released.

To make things worse, there was now a missing person. At the beginning of the week, George Takahashi, a thirty-two-year-old dentist and acupuncturist, had been reported missing. His house computer reported that he had not been home for three days, and so far, a search had produced no sign of him. He had lived alone, though he had formally registered Choice with Nancy Markowitz, a plumber and storekeeper. And there had been another suicide, making a dozen in six years.

Sometime last night, a doctor at the hospital had killed himself in one of the bathrooms by injecting potassium. And, as before, everyone that Karen talked to expressed amazement at his suicide. There had been no indication that anything had been troubling him, although he did seem a bit preoccupied at times. But he had always been very pleasant to everyone, there had been no irregularities in his job, and whatever troubles he'd had, he had obviously kept to himself. He was only twenty-seven years old, the youngest suicide yet. However, with this case, the pattern had been broken. Dr. Alexei Petrovsky had been partnered. No, thought Karen, it definitely had not been a good week.

"Has anyone notified his partner yet?" she asked the hospital director.

"Uh . . . no, not yet," Dr. Stephan LaBeau replied. "I felt that Security should be notified first and then you could decide how best to handle the situation."

"In other words, he didn't have the nerve to make the call," said Dr. Linda Burroughs, dryly. "And he wouldn't let anybody else make it, either. The poor woman still doesn't know."

"I was merely following what I thought was proper procedure," LaBeau said, defensively. "I mean, I didn't want to do the wrong thing, you understand."

"What's her name?" asked Karen.

"Tonisha," said Dr. Burroughs. "And with your permission, Chief, I'd rather break the news to her myself, in person. I'm going off duty now and I think she may need a friend."

"Okay," said Karen, nodding. "I'll want to ask her some questions. Stay with her, and I'll be there as soon as I'm finished here."

"Thanks," said Dr. Burroughs. "I'm on my way."

Karen turned back to LaBeau. "Doctor, I'll want my officers to take statements from everyone who worked with Dr. Petrovsky, especially anyone who knew him well. I'll also want to question everyone who was on duty with him last night, so make sure my officers get a complete list of on-duty personnel. In the meantime, as soon as my people are done in there —"

"Chief Kruickshank!"

She turned at the sound of her name being called. A medium-built man with light brown hair and a high forehead came rushing up to her, looking very distraught. He had a stuffy, agitated sort of look about him, Karen thought, as if emotional displays of any kind were foreign to him. His face looked uncomfortable wearing his worried expression, as if uncertain it was the correct one.

"Is Sonja all right?"

He looked familiar, but for a moment, she couldn't place him. "I'm sorry," she said, frowning and shaking her head. "I know you, don't I?"

"Peter Buckland," he said. "We've met. I'm one of Jenny's teachers."

"Oh, yes, of course. I'm sorry, what was that about Sonja?"

"They called me from the hospital," he said. "She was brought in this morning. Something about a concussion and an intruder at her office. Isn't that why you're here?"

"No," she replied, shaking her head. "I'm here on another matter. But what's this about an intruder?"

"I don't really know," said Peter, looking worried. "I wasn't told the details. I just rushed right over." He looked at LaBeau. "Is she all right?"

LaBeau blinked. "I'm sorry, Mr. Buckland, I really don't know. I only just arrived myself a short while ago, and we've had a rather disturbing morning here. Hold on a moment, I'll find out for you. Hippocrates, who was the attending physician when Sonja Buckland was brought in?"

"Dr. Burroughs was on duty when Patient Buckland was admitted," the hospital computer replied.

"She just left a moment ago," LaBeau said. "I'm sure we can still catch her. Hippocrates, page Dr. Burroughs and —"

"No, cancel that, let her go," said Karen. She turned to Peter. "I'm sorry, I don't want to appear insensitive, but there's been another suicide, a member of the staff here, and Dr. Burroughs has just gone to inform his partner."

"That's terrible," said Peter, with genuine concern. "I understand, of course. But at the same time, I'm anxious to learn about Sonja's condition."

"I'll check for you," LaBeau said. "Hippocrates, consult the chart on Sonja Buckland and let me know what notations Dr. Burroughs made."

"Patient Sonja Buckland, botanist, was brought in at 7:00 A.M. this morning by her coworker, agricultural maintenance engineer Saleem Rodriguez. She was examined for possible concussion," the hospital computer replied, "but appears to be all right. She fell at work, but apparently did not sustain any blows and there were no contusions, cuts or fractures. However, she displayed signs of suffering from acute stress and physical exhaustion, so she was administered a sedative and admitted for observation pending further developments."

"What room is she in?" LaBeau asked.

"Room 34."

"That's just down the hall," LaBeau said.

"Can I see her?" Peter asked.

"Certainly, it's right down that way," said LaBeau, pointing down the hall.

"Dr. Burroughs didn't note anything about an intruder," Karen said, "but I think I'd like a word with her, too, if you don't mind, Mr. Buckland."

"Peter, please," he said. "No, of course, I don't mind."

Karen spoke to several of her officers and told them that she'd be right back, then accompanied Peter down the hall to see Sonja. She was asleep when they got there, but Saleem was still in the room, sitting by her side and watching her. He got up when they came in.

"Saleem, thank you so much for bringing her here and waiting," Peter said, shaking the big man's hand.

"It was no trouble," he replied. "I figured you'd be worried and you'd want to know what happened, so I stuck around."

"Do you two know each other?" Peter asked, glancing from Saleem to Karen.

"I don't think we've met," said Karen, offering her hand. "Karen Kruickshank, Chief of Security."

"Saleem Rodriguez. Pleased to meet you, Chief."

"What's this about an intruder?" she asked.

"Well . . ." Saleem hesitated. "Frankly, I don't think there was any intruder. I mean, I didn't see anybody, and it sounded pretty bizarre. I think she was just exhausted and dreamed or hallucinated the whole thing."

"Why don't you tell me what happened?" Karen asked, while Peter listened, attentively.

"Well, we'd been having some trouble with the herb crop," Saleem began.

"She mentioned that to me," said Peter.

"Phyl, that's the Agricultural AI, was unable to recognize the problem, so we had some samples brought in. The crop was definitely damaged, no doubt about that. The leaves looked torn, as if something was nibbling on them. Sonya stayed all night, trying to run it down. This was the day before yesterday. When I came in the next morning, she told me she'd been out in the fields and seen glowing insects."

"Glowing insects?" asked Karen, with a frown.

"That's what she claimed," Saleem explained. "But that isn't possible, of course. There aren't any insects like that aboard the ship, and they couldn't have evolved here. She was pretty tired from staying up all night, and she wasn't scanning very well. She stayed again last night, and she said that this time she took an HIR out to record what she saw. Now, this is where it gets strange. She didn't tell me all this at first, but after I brought her here, Dr. Burroughs and I managed to pry it out of her. It seems the first time she went out into the fields, she passed out and remained unconscious all night."

"Good Lord," said Peter.

"We'd seeded the clouds that evening, and it rained on her. It's possible she might have caught a cold, though it was a warm night. Anyway, when she woke up the next morning, she was naked."

"Naked?" Karen and Peter both said, together.

"That's what she said," Saleem replied. "Her clothes were scattered all around her. And last night, it happened again. She went out with an HIR, saw the insects or whatever they were, and blacked out again. When she woke up, she was naked once again, but this time, she had a visual record of what happened, or so she insists. She says she took the HIR back to the office and played back the crystal. What she claims she saw is difficult to credit. She said they weren't insects, but little, glowing humanoids with wings and antennae, and that they somehow made her throw off all her clothes and dance with them out there in the field."

"What?" said Peter, with astonishment.

"She does have scratches on her feet and legs," Saleem said, "and she was getting muscle cramps pretty bad, so she was certainly doing something out there. Anyway, when she saw this, she called me at home and woke me up, told me I had to get down there right away to see this. She wouldn't give me a download or tell me what it was. She seemed to think that Phyl was glitching up and wiping data, and she wanted to be there with me when I saw it. She was extremely agitated and I doubt she was thinking clearly. When I arrived, I found her lying on the floor, in the hall outside her office. She was saying something about a little man who had gone into her office and stolen the recording crystal out of the projection unit. She said he had run down the hall just as I came in, and she didn't think I could have avoided seeing him, but I didn't see anyone. I thought she fell and might have hurt herself, perhaps suffered a concussion, so I brought her here."

"Did she give you a description of this little man?" asked Karen.

"Oh, yeah," said Saleem. "Just wait till you hear this. Half a meter tall —"

"How tall?"

"Half a meter," Saleem repeated. "Bearded, shaggy hair, bright green tunic with a wide brown belt, brown trousers, peaked red cap, and red shoes with pointy, curled-up toes."

"That's impossible," said Karen, with a frown.

"That's what I said," Saleem replied. "But she swears she didn't dream it. She swears up and down that all of this really happened."

"She must have been hallucinating," Karen said.

"Sonja is not given to hallucinations," Peter said.

"Look, I'm not disparaging your partner," said Karen, "but she was up for forty-eight hours straight. That has to produce some stress and exhaustion, plus she was worried about the crops. By her own admission, she suffered two blackouts and a fall. Under those circumstances, she might easily have had some sort of hallucination."

"If she had, I think she would have known it," Peter insisted. "Sonja is a very pragmatic woman, with a firm grasp on reality."

"Tiny, glowing humanoids with wings? A little man no more than half a meter tall?" said Karen.

Peter moistened his lips, uneasily. "Well, I realize how that sounds, of course. But I can't believe she's suffered some sort of mental breakdown. Sonja's very serious and focused, and she's in excellent condition."

"Dr. Burroughs said that stress could get to anybody," said Saleem. "And she did seem to be having a lot of anxiety over the damaged crops."

"Well, I still have some inquiries to make on my other investigation," Karen said. "However, I'd like to get back with you on this, just to make sure she's all right. May I call you at home tonight?"

"Of course. I appreciate your concern. I'll be here most of the day, but I should be home tonight. Thanks for taking the trouble."

Karen smiled. "It's no trouble. Besides, I understand my daughter's been spending a lot of time with your son, recently. Maybe we should get to know each other better."

"I'd like that," Peter said.

"Okay, I'll leave you now," she said. "Thank you, Mr. Rodriguez. Peter, I'll give you a call at home later tonight. Around nine o'clock?"

"That would be fine. And thanks again, Chief."

"Karen," she said. "I'll talk to you later."

When Ulysses woke up, his father was already gone. Nothing about that had struck him as unusual, his dad was an early riser and often went to school early to go over his lesson plans one more time before the day's classes, but his father had left a message with Mac that he was going to the hospital. Something had happened to his mother. His father wanted him to go to school and said that he would call as soon as he found out something more. Deeply worried, Ulysses heard no further news until Professor Wesala, who was taking over his dad's class that day, made the announcement.

"Professor Buckland won't be in today," she said.

"There's been a minor family emergency. Ulysses, your father just called from the hospital and asked me to tell you not to worry. Your mother had a slight accident at work, but she's all right. She apparently just slipped and fell. They took her to the hospital, just to make sure. They're going to keep her there today so she can get some rest, but there's nothing to worry about."

"Okay," said Ulysses, relieved that it was nothing serious. "Thank you."

"Now, as far as today's class is concerned," she continued, "Professor Buckland asked me to program a VR session for you and he'll discuss it next time. The session will probably end a little early, so you're dismissed as soon as it's over. I don't want any loitering in the halls, all right? You can go outside and talk until the next class period, or stay behind and use the remainder of the time for study. It's up to you. So if you'll put on your bands, we'll just get started."

She dimmed the lights and the chairs tilted back. Ulysses glanced quickly at Jenny and Riley as the lights went down. They were looking at him, too. He knew they were each thinking the same thing. Would they wind up on the quest again?

As the session started, Ulysses felt the familiar, sinking, falling sort of feeling, a brief sensation of spinning away into darkness pinpricked with dots of colored light as his senses were disconnected from his surroundings and he closed his eyes. When he opened them again, he was on a dirt trail, walking through a thick forest. He inhaled deeply, smelling the fresh, heady odor of the pines on the gentle breeze. Birds were chirping in the trees and flitting across the winding trail ahead of him, as if alarmed by their sudden presence.

Riley and Jenny were right beside him. As before, they were dressed in the clothes they had been wearing back in the tavern, only this time, they had leather packs upon their backs. Their awareness focused as they found themselves hiking at a steady pace down the rutted dirt trail through the dense forest. It had still been morning when the session began in class, but here, it was growing dark as night approached.

"Well, here we are again," said Riley, glancing around as

he shifted the weight of his pack. He looked up and stumbled, thrown off by the unaccustomed perspective. "Whooo," he said, uneasily. "Whatever you do, don't look up."

"We'll probably get used to it if we stay here long enough," Ulysses said. "But it does feel very peculiar."

"I hope your mom's okay," said Jenny, solicitously.

"Thanks," he replied. Though he appreciated her concern, somehow the remark seemed strangely out of context in these surroundings, as if it belonged to another life, another world.

"Does anybody have any idea where we're going?" Riley asked.

"I guess we're on the trail the man in gray told us to take."

"It's starting to get dark," said Jenny. "Pretty soon, we won't be able to see anything."

"I guess they don't have lights here, huh?" said Riley. "What was it we were supposed to be looking for again? Some kind of meadow?"

"Where the fairies dance," said Jenny.

"How are we supposed to know which meadow that would be?" asked Riley.

"I guess we look for fairies dancing," said Ulysses, with a shrug.

"But we don't know what they look like," Riley said.

"Well, they're supposed to be very small," said Jenny. "And I suppose they'll be dancing."

"It sounds pretty strange to me," said Riley.

"This whole thing is strange," Ulysses said. "I wonder where we are, exactly? I mean, is this supposed to be Earth back in the ancient days, or is this some other kind of world, entirely?"

"It's a simworld," Riley said. "That means it doesn't matter. It's whatever Dr. Seldon designed it to be."

"One thing's for sure," Jenny said. "It's a pretty sophisticated program. I have absolutely no sense of being in VR. In all the other programs, everything feels real enough, but you know it's only VR. Here, I have to keep reminding myself that none of this is really happening. Every single detail is so incredibly realistic, to say nothing of the fact that we're able to interact like this."

"I think that's a large part of it," Ulysses said. "If you stop to think about it, this is really no more realistic than all the other programs we've experienced, except the main difference is that here, we're being ourselves, and experiencing it all from our perspective instead of someone else's."

"Still, I think Jenny's right," said Riley. "This one is a lot more sophisticated. None of the others allow us to interact like this, and they don't have the kind of flexibility this one seems to have. We're not really being prompted about any of our reactions, and if we are, it's so subtle that we can't even tell."

"What are we supposed to do when it gets dark?" asked Jenny.

"Stop somewhere, I guess," Ulysses said. "We're not going to be able to see well enough to travel pretty soon. Maybe we ought to take a look at what's in these packs we're carrying."

They decided that was a good idea and stopped briefly. Each of them had a bedroll and a blanket, and a small, peg-down tent, barely large enough to cover one person if he scrunched up pretty tight. They also had some food—bread and sausages and cheese—flint and tinder for starting a fire, small camp axes and hand spades, fishing line and iron hooks, cooking pans and pots for heating water, and some candles. All very primitive, matching their environment.

"I guess we're supposed to camp," Ulysses said, as they repacked their supplies.

"This is going to be fun," said Jenny. "We can build a fire."

It was getting dark quickly. In a short while, they came to a small glade, a flat and grassy meadow with some prominent rock outcroppings in the center surrounded by large and thick-trunked trees whose branches made a canopy over the open space.

"You think this is it?" asked Riley. "I don't see anybody dancing."

"We might as well stop here," Ulysses said. "Pretty soon,

there won't be enough light to put up our tents, and we've never done that before."

They picked out a spot and put their packs down, then went to cut some wood so they could build a fire. None of them had ever cut wood or built a fire before, but they soon discovered they knew exactly how to do it. It took a while for Ulysses to get the fire going with the flint, but eventually the blaze was started and he sat back with a sense of accomplishment, despite the knowledge that he didn't really do it.

"This is great," said Jenny, as Ulysses and Riley fed more wood to the fire. She glanced up. "Oooh, look! Stars!"

The two boys looked up. It was a clear night and the visibility was excellent. There was also a full moon, much larger than the artificial moon back on the ship, with a softer luminescence.

"Ugh," said Riley, looking back down hurriedly. "It makes my stomach feel queasy."

Ulysses, too, felt disoriented by having nothing but sky above him. It was a new experience for him, and he found it unsettling, but it didn't seem to bother him as much as it did Riley. Jenny, on the other hand, seemed completely untroubled by it. She lay back, staring up at the sky with delight and wonder.

"Doesn't that bother you?" asked Riley.

"No, I think it's beautiful!" she said.

"It gives me shivers," Riley said. "It seems unnatural."

"Not if you stop to think about it," said Ulysses. "It's our environment aboard the ship that's unnatural. This is the way things are on a planet."

"Only none of this is real," Riley said, hunching his shoulders. "I think it's getting to me. I'm getting chills."

"That's because it's getting cold," Ulysses said. "We're supposed to be on the surface of a planet. There aren't any systems to regulate the temperature here. That's what's giving you chills. I'm feeling it, too. We'd better get the tents up, just in case it rains. And we'll need our blankets tonight for sure."

"You figure we're going to be here that long?" asked Riley, as they unpacked the tents. "Class only lasts an hour."

"That's an hour of class time," Ulysses pointed out. "We don't know how that corresponds to time spent here."

Again, it seemed odd somehow to be talking about class and the fact that this was only a sim. Perhaps that was part of the program, thought Ulysses, as they pitched the tents. It was giving them the input of sim knowledge—which enabled them to get the tents up when they'd never done anything like that before—but at the same time, though they were able to maintain their own perspectives without any effort, there seemed to be a subliminal effect that reinforced the illusion of reality and made everything else seem a bit unreal. As he hammered down the pegs with the butt end of his small axe, he wondered if the others were aware of it.

"I still don't think we're going to be here all night," Riley said. "We couldn't have been here more than an hour last time." It was as if he felt the need to keep reminding himself that this was all only VR.

"True," replied Ulysses. "But it is getting colder, just the same. I'm going to get my blanket and sit close to the fire."

"We're almost out of wood," said Jenny.

"We'll have to cut some more."

"Are you kidding?" Riley said. "It's dark out there. You can't see a thing."

"You can see well enough to cut a branch in front of you," Ulysses said.

"Maybe, but you can't see much farther than that."

"It's a full moon, Riley. It's not that dark."

"Well, you go out there, then."

"Why?"

"You're the one who said we have to cut more wood," said Riley, petulantly.

"You're the one who's worried about running out."

"All right, if you two are going to argue about it, I'll go," Jenny said, getting to her feet.

"No, that's okay, I'll go," Ulysses said.

"Well, somebody go," said Riley. "The fire's going to be out pretty soon."

"We'll both go," Jenny said. "Riley, you stay here and

keep the fire going, but don't put all the wood in at once. We'll be back in a little while."

"Don't take too long," Riley said. "There's liable to be animals out there or something."

"We'll be careful," said Ulysses.

"And I'll take my sword," said Jenny.

They walked across the glade and went into the trees.

"I think he's a little scared," said Jenny, with a giggle.

"To tell you the truth, so am I, a bit," Ulysses admitted, as he started chopping at a thick, dead branch of a fallen tree. "Aren't you?"

"No," she said. "I'm having a wonderful time!"

"You're not even a little scared?"

"It's just VR, Ulysses."

"I know that," he said, "but this one's different. I've got a feeling that we're not exactly safe here. Don't ask me why, but I think this is a lot more real in some ways than it seems."

"Well, don't worry, Ulysses, I'll protect you," she said, with mock seriousness, clapping her hand to her sword. "Besides, I owe you one."

"I think you already paid me back, before," he said, looking away and blushing.

"What, you mean that little peck?" she said, regarding him with a teasing expression. "That was nothing."

"Well . . . I didn't think it was nothing."

"It was compared to this," she said, stepping up to him and taking his face between her hands. She gently brought her lips to his and kissed him, slipping her tongue into his mouth. Ulysses dropped his axe and put his arms around her, a bit awkwardly. He couldn't believe this was happening. Her hands felt so soft against his face, their touch so light as she gently trailed her fingers across his cheeks and broke the kiss. He was left speechless.

"You'd better pick up that axe and get back to work before Riley lets the fire go out," she said, with a gently mocking smile.

Flustered, he simply did as she told him. His emotions were in a turmoil, and he took it out on the wood as he chopped savagely. He felt her watching him. He knew that she was smiling, but he was afraid to look at her for fear that he would say something stupid.

"Ulysses . . ."

"Yes?"

"Ulysses, we're not children anymore. Except maybe for Riley." She paused. "Don't say this isn't something you haven't thought about. I've seen the way you look at me. You think I haven't noticed that you schedule your workouts in the gym at the same time as mine? I've been waiting for you to say something, or ask me out. Why didn't you?"

He shrugged. "I . . . I guess I was afraid you might say no."

"Why?"

"Well . . . I figured guys must ask you out all the time."

"So what? You didn't think you had a chance?" She rolled her eyes with exasperation. "I don't know how many times I tried getting you involved in a conversation, only you always made up some excuse to leave. I even started wearing more revealing workout suits in the gym. I was practically falling out of them. You didn't notice that I kept trying to make eye contact with you in class?"

"Well . . . I did notice the suits," he said.

"Oh, pick up the wood!" she said.

He gathered an armload and they started heading back toward the camp. Riley was waiting impatiently by the fire.

"What took you guys so long?" he said, irritably. "I was beginning to think you got lost. It's freezing out here."

Ulysses dumped the firewood on the ground. "There," he said. "That ought to help keep you warm."

"Ulysses, Riley . . . look!" said Jenny.

They turned in the direction she was looking. Over the rock outcropping in the center of the glade, a small, glowing cloud had suddenly appeared. And then they saw it was actually made up of many smaller, glowing bodies that bobbed up and down in midair. As they watched, it broke apart and they could see, within the individual glowing lights, tiny, naked people with large, iridescent wings and antennae growing from their foreheads. They began to circle around and around the rock outcropping, darting up over it and then swooping around from behind it, executing complicated, graceful looking movements in the air.

"Fairies!" said Ulysses.

"Oh, they're beautiful!" said Jenny.

"Do you think they see us?" Riley asked.

"No, we're sitting here by a big fire, how can they possibly see us?" asked Ulysses, sarcastically.

"What do you think we should do?" said Riley.

"I don't know," Ulysses said, getting to his feet. "But the man in gray said they were supposed to reveal something to us. That which we cannot see will be revealed by that which we have never seen. We're never seen fairies before." He started to move closer to them.

"Ulysses, wait," said Jenny.

"No," he said, distractedly. "I want to see . . ." his voice trailed off as he kept walking toward them slowly, as if in a trance.

"I want to go, too," said Riley, getting to his feet to follow Ulysses. His gaze looked a bit unfocused.

Jenny also felt a sudden, strange compulsion to go join them, but remembering something she had learned about fairies from the Mythology file, she forced herself to look away from them. She focused her gaze on Ulysses as she ran a few steps to catch up with him and grabbed him by the arm. "Ulysses, wait . . ."

He did not respond. He tried to pull free of her grasp, but she held on, tightly.

"Riley, help me!"

Riley kept on walking toward the fairies, looking dazed. She struggled to hold on to Ulysses.

"Let me go," he said, dully.

"Riley! Riley, listen to me! Close your eyes! Do you hear me, Riley! Close your eyes!"

He blinked several times, then shook his head and his gaze focused on her.

"Help me, Riley! Close your eyes and help me!"

He closed his eyes and moved toward the sound of her voice. When he reached her, he grabbed Ulysses by his other arm. Ulysses kept straining to break free of their grasp.

"Let me go!" he shouted.

"Hold him!" Jenny said. "Don't look at them!"

"What's happening?" asked Riley, struggling to hold on to Ulysses as he strained against their grasp.

"They're doing something to him," Jenny said. "They almost got us, too. Don't look at them!"

Riley kept his eyes shut. "But I thought they were supposed to show us something."

"Ulysses can see," she said. "But we've got to hold on to him. They're controlling him, somehow. I think it's magic."

Ulysses was struggling harder, but they held him tightly, not looking at the dancing fairies. And then, abruptly, he stopped struggling and they heard him gasp.

"What is it?" Riley said, still hanging on to him tightly. "What's happening?"

"Don't look!" said Jenny.

"No, it's okay, you can look now," Ulysses said. "They're gone."

"He may be lying," Jenny said.

"No, really," he said. "They're gone; they flew away. I'm all right now. But you've got to see this!"

Cautiously, Jenny glanced toward the center of the glade. The fairies were, indeed, gone . . . and so was the rock outcropping. In its place stood a blue-and-white pavilion, and inside it were two tall burning braziers and a table covered with a white silk cloth.

"Where did that come from?" Riley asked.

"It was the rock," Ulysses said. "The fairies kept dancing around it in the air, going faster and faster, until they were just a blur, and suddenly the rock just faded away and that tent was there."

"What happened to them?" Jenny asked.

"They just sort of spiraled up into the air and flew away," Ulysses said. He shook his head, as if to clear it. "It was the strangest thing," he said. "I wanted to go join them, and then I started getting dizzy and I think I almost passed out, but then you grabbed me and I started trying to make you let go and the dizzy feeling went away . . . but I still wanted to go dance with them."

"You wanted to dance with them?" Riley asked, as if uncertain he had heard correctly.

"Yes, it was a very strong urge," Ulysses said. "I felt like I wanted to just tear off all my clothes and dance with them."

"What did we hold him for?" said Riley, grinning. "I would've liked to see that!"

"You would have done it, too, Riley, if I hadn't snapped you out of it," said Jenny.

"How come it didn't get to you?" asked Riley.

"It almost did," she replied, "but when I started to feel funny, I made myself look away. Good thing, too. For all we know, we might've wound up coming out of it in class with all our clothes off. How'd you like trying to explain that?"

"Ummm . . . yeah, I see what you mean," said Riley.

"We'd better go check out that tent," said Ulysses, going toward it.

"Be careful," Jenny said.

"No, I think it's going to be all right now," he replied. They followed behind him as he approached the pavilion. On the table, there was a large crystal ball in a carved onyx stand. As they came up to it, it began to glow with a swirling pattern, and a moment later, it cleared and they saw a beautiful looking creature inside it, as if a miniature living being were trapped within the crystal. It was all white, with four legs that ended in tufted hooves, a flowing tail, a long mane, a strong and graceful neck, and a pearlescent, spiral horn that grew out of its forehead.

"It's lovely!" Jenny said, watching mesmerized as the lovely animal pawed the ground inside the crystal. "What is it?"

"It is a unicorn," a voice said, within their minds. It was the voice of The Lady. "You have passed the first test. This shall be your second. If you can capture the unicorn, it will show you the way you must go to reach the next stage of your quest. But remember, there is only one way to capture a unicorn."

"What is it?" asked Ulysses.

He blinked as the lights came back up and he suddenly found himself back in the classroom again.

"What is what?" asked Becky Chen, who was sitting next to him.

Ulysses shook his head. "Nothing," he said. "Just VR lag, I guess. That was a pretty good session, huh?"

She frowned. "Are you kidding? I was bored stiff. Are you sure we had the same program?"

"Maybe not," Ulysses said. "Mine made me feel like dancing. What was yours?"

She stared at him as she got out of her chair. "You're really weird, Ulysses, you know that?"

"Yeah, I know," he said, with a grin. He glanced at Jenny and saw her looking back at him. This time, he didn't look away.

CHAPTER
6

This is where it happened, Robie Marshall thought, as she paused on the hiking trail at the edge of the woods. This was where she had first met Phillipe. She had been walking through the park, as she did every morning, on the loop trail leading through the forest. She had paused to massage her cramping calf muscle and he had come by and stopped to help. They sat on the grass by the side of the trail, she with her foot in his lap while he massaged her calf, explaining that she needed to do more stretching exercises before she started speedwalking. That was how it started.

She was nineteen and he was forty-one, though he looked much younger, with a thick shock of blond hair that fell over his forehead and sparkling blue eyes. He was an ecologist, his secondary specialty was life-support maintenance, and she found him very attractive. They had started walking together in the mornings, and soon after that they had made love for the first time in a small clearing a short distance off the trail, under a canopy of trees. It wasn't until afterward that he told her he was already partnered.

She didn't care. Or at least, she had told herself she didn't care. Being with an older man was exciting. He had made her feel like more of a woman, and he didn't treat her the same way males her own age did. He was an accomplished lover, and he had a position of responsibility. They always met early in the mornings, and in the beginning, they had made love every day. For a while, things had gone well between them, but eventually, he had started to become withdrawn.

He told her that he loved her, but was feeling guilty for being unfaithful to his partner. And he thought that he was taking unfair advantage of her. What kind of a relationship was it, he had said, where they met only in the mornings to have sex? She deserved much more than that. However, she had never complained. She enjoyed the sex and, at first, she hadn't wanted more. That would have only complicated things. It was only later that it changed.

Phillipe was fascinating in the beginning, romantic, bright, articulate, and considerate of her opinions; but when the novelty of their relationship had worn off, he became moody. The frequency of their sexual encounters fell off, and suddenly, he seemed to change. He became despondent, and on several occasions, he had even cried. She couldn't understand what had gone wrong. He seemed caught in the grip of emotions he didn't fully understand. He was so sad and vulnerable, her heart went out to him. And that was how she lost it.

Now, it was over. It had lasted slightly less than six months, and last week, just two days after her twentieth birthday, he had told her they had to break it off. He said he was going to Counseling. She didn't have to worry, he assured her, he wouldn't mention her by name, but he had to sort things out. He was tired of feeling so depressed all the time that he could barely function. He had insisted that none of it was her fault. There was something wrong with him, he said, and for a long time, he had denied it to himself. For a while, he had thought she might be the solution to his problems, but that hadn't proved to be the case. He told her he was very sorry, but he couldn't see her anymore. And it was really for the best, he added. He was sure she'd be much happier with someone closer to her own age.

At first, she had felt hurt. Then, she had felt angry. Now, she just felt empty, and blamed herself. She still went out to the park every morning, though she no longer really exercised. She would just stroll to the place where they first met, and linger there a while, then go to the little spot just off the trail in the woods, where they used to make love and talk about things. She told herself it was foolish to keep going back to those places, because they only kept the memory fresh, but she couldn't seem to help it.

Her parents knew something was wrong, but they did not know what it was and it disturbed them that she wouldn't tell them what was bothering her. There had been times when she wanted to tell them, but at the last moment, she always changed her mind. They would be judgmental, and they would want to know who it was, and she didn't want to make any more trouble for herself or for Phillipe. He had enough problems of his own.

She stopped on the trail through the woods at the place where they always left it to go to their secluded little spot. Don't go, she told herself. Walk past it. But somehow, her feet wound up stepping off the trail and walking the short distance to the little clearing under the trees. She stood there for a few moments, then sat down and put her head in her hands. Why did this have to happen to her? How could she have been so stupid? Why did she have to get involved with someone who not only didn't care about her, but didn't care about himself? I deserve better than this, she thought.

"Yes, indeed, you do."

She looked up, startled. She hadn't spoken aloud, had she? She blinked in surprise. There was a young man standing at the edge of the little clearing, leaning against a tree trunk with his arms folded. The first thing that struck her about him were his clothes. They did not reflect any current fashion aboard the ship. They were all a light, soft shade of gray, and curiously styled. He wore boots and tight-fitting breeches, a tunic with a sort of scalloped half cape that came down to mid-chest, and a black belt with a curious-looking, long and narrow knife in a hand-sewn sheath. Over this, he wore a hooded cloak, also gray. But as striking as his clothes were, his face was even more so.

He had long and thick, black hair that fell down past his shoulders. She had never seen any men aboard the ship who wore their hair that long. It was beautiful. And his face was beautiful, too. Not handsome, the way Phillipe's was, but striking and exotic. His features were sharply pronounced, with high cheekbones and a narrow, blade-straight nose. He had unusually shaped eyebrows, dark and narrow and very highly arched. His eyes, too, were very dark and deeply set, almost Asian-looking, with long lashes. He had a narrow, well-shaped chin that came almost to a point, and a wide, sensual mouth that smiled at her indulgently.

"Who . . . who are you?" she asked, taken aback.

He approached and sat down beside her with a warm, engaging smile. "Just someone out for a walk in the woods, like you."

"I . . . don't know you," Robie said, hesitantly, at the same time thinking even his voice was sexy.

"And I do not know you," he said. "That makes us even, does it not? But you seemed upset and you looked as if you could use some friendly company."

"I'm afraid I'm not very good company right now," she said. I also look awful, she thought. First thing in the morning, my hair's a mess and my face is puffy, and I meet somebody like him. Terrific.

"Well, then I shall have to try extra hard, for both of us," he said.

She could not help smiling at that, in spite of herself.

"There, you see? 'Tis working already."

" 'Tis?" she said, in a puzzled tone.

" 'Tis, indeed. A beautiful woman looks so much better when a smile graces her face. And you have a lovely smile."

"You have a strange way of putting things," she said.

"Do I?"

"Well, yes. In a nice way, though. But you sound different from anyone I've ever met. And you look different, too."

" 'Twould be a dreary place if everyone looked and

sounded the same," he said. "How would you tell people apart?"

She grinned. "Well, I must admit, you are cheering me up a bit. I sure could use it, too."

"A broken heart mends faster when amusement lightens it."

She gave a small, self-conscious snort. "Is it that obvious?"

"To one who knows how to see," the stranger in gray replied. "But hearts are stronger than you think, even broken ones." He touched her chest lightly, just the barest brush of contact. It sent a thrill through her.

"Who are you?" she asked, gazing into his deep, dark eyes.

"I am called Grailing Windwalker."

"What a wonderful name! What ethno-derivation does it represent?"

"I am an elf."

She frowned. "A what?"

"An elf."

She shook her head, puzzled.

"It is one of the cultures of Old Earth," he explained, "rich in myth and magic, almost as ancient as time itself."

"I never even heard of elfs before."

"Elves," he corrected her, with a smile.

"Elves," she said. She shook her head. "I thought I knew all the ethno-derivations aboard the ship. Are there many more like you?"

"There are now," he said, enigmatically.

There was something hauntingly compelling about his gaze. She couldn't seem to take her eyes off him. She felt as if she were falling into those warm, dark, exotic eyes of his. Her breathing quickened as she stared at him with her lips slightly parted. She wanted him to touch her again. And as if he could read her mind, he did.

"Your heart beats faster," he said, softly, and lightly placed his hand upon her breast.

She swallowed hard. "How could you tell?"

"I can hear it. Elves have sharp ears, you know."

"With all that hair, I can't even see your ears," she said,

with a self-conscious smile, touching his cheek and brushing back his long, thick hair. She gasped as she saw his large and sharply pointed ears. Involuntarily, her fingers moved lightly to trace their shape. She was too astonished to speak. He touched her cheek and gently guided her face closer to his. She did not resist, yet she stopped just before she touched his lips, hesitating, so close that she could feel his breath.

He waited, secure in his knowledge of what was about to happen. She thought, briefly, how can he know? How can he be so sure? The moment seemed frozen. She gazed into his eyes, and they seemed to draw her in. She closed her eyes and kissed him.

Her head swam as their lips touched, so very lightly, once, twice, and then she moaned as his fingers gently raked into her hair and he slipped his tongue into her mouth. She couldn't even think; she didn't *want* to think; she was carried away on a wave of emotion that kept on cresting, completely overwhelming her.

She felt his strong arms around her, lean and muscular, yet his hands caressed her so lightly, his long fingers running through her hair, trailing across her cheeks and cupping her face as she pressed her body against his. She had never wanted anyone so much in her entire life, and somehow he had known that. Somehow, he had brought it forth. Phillipe had been nothing like this. Her entire body felt as if it were on fire. She wanted to feel his bare skin against hers.

Again, as if he knew, his hands gently trailed down along her sides and raised her top. She stretched her arms over her head, allowing him to remove it. He tossed it aside and just looked at her for a moment, drinking her in, then slowly reached out to touch her breasts, very lightly, with just his fingertips. She closed her eyes and drew a shuddering breath, then bit her lower lip. There was nothing rushed in his movements, nothing abrupt or rough in his caresses; he knew exactly how to touch her, and he had no need to demonstrate his strength. There was no urgency. Just the implacable sense that he was completely in control.

Her hands fumbled at his clothing, and he waited, staring at her as she removed his belt and found the laces of his tunic underneath the half cape. There was the faintest hint of a smile on his lips. She kissed him hungrily, on the mouth, on his cheeks and on his throat; she couldn't stop herself, nor did she want to stop. *This is crazy*, she thought. *Why am I doing this?* And, at the same time, she knew. *I want,* she thought, *I need* . . .

She raised his tunic, kissing him on his hairless chest, then he helped her pull it off and hugged her to him, kissing her neck and stroking her hair. Her head lolled back as she breathed deeply and allowed herself to be eased gently to the ground.

He moved slowly, but surely, as if giving her the opportunity to stop him at any time, yet knowing that she wouldn't. He pulled off her shoes and shorts, then ran his hands lightly down her inner thighs and legs, raising goose bumps. He took her hands and gently pulled her up to a sitting postion, touched her cheek, kissed her, then lay back, propped up on his elbows, watching her, compelling her to make the next move.

She pulled his breeches down to his knees, then decided not to bother trying to remove his boots. She couldn't wait any longer. She was trembling with anticipation. He waited, watching her, and she thought, How is he doing this? I'm completely open. How? Why? It didn't matter. She didn't care. It was happening, and that was all that mattered.

She straddled him and her gaze remained locked with his as she guided him inside her, then threw her head back, drawing her breath in sharply and moaning as she thrust her hips against him. As she moved faster, her fingers tightly interlaced with his, her vision blurred and she cried out his name over and over again. When she climaxed, she couldn't seem to stop. Wave after wave swept over her as she trembled uncontrollably. It just kept on building until she didn't think she could take any more and then she let it all out in a long scream as everything started spinning and she felt herself falling, and falling, and falling . . .

"Chief, we've got another problem," Sgt. Ben Cruzmark said, coming up to Karen as she left Sonja Buckland's hospital room.

"What is it this time?" she asked, hoping desperately it

wasn't another suicide. George Takahashi was still missing, and she had a terrible feeling that he was going to turn up dead.

"They just brought in a girl from Geneva Village. Her name is Robie Marshall; she's twenty, a student. She was out walking in the park this morning, and a couple of other walkers heard her screaming. They found her just off the trail, in the woods, naked and unconscious. No visible signs of injury. Dr. Chen's with her now. Her parents have been notified and they're on their way."

Karen compressed her lips into a tight grimace. "This is just not my day," she said. "How is she?"

"She's conscious now, but she hasn't told anyone what happened yet. I don't know; she may be in shock."

Karen exhaled heavily. Cruzmark just looked at her. Neither one of them wanted to say it. "Come on," said Karen, "I want to speak to her before her parents get here."

The doctor was just finishing her exam when they came in. Robie Marshall was sitting on the table silently, wearing a hospital gown, her eyes downcast. The doctor looked up when they came in and approached them.

"What have we got here, Doctor?" Karen asked, quietly.

"I'm not sure," Dr. Chen replied. "Possible sexual assault. She allowed me to examine her, but she wouldn't answer any of my questions. I'm not even sure she understood them."

"Is she in shock?"

The doctor shook her head. "No. She was quite disoriented when she arrived, but she seems to be coming out of it. I'm told she was found naked and unconscious in the woods, and she's had sexual intercourse."

"Any sign that it was forced?" asked Karen, tensely.

"No physical signs," the doctor replied, "but that's not necessarily conclusive."

"Can I speak with her?"

"Yes, she's starting to focus, but take it easy, okay?"

"I will. Can you leave us alone, please?"

When they left, Karen approached the girl. "Robie?" she said, softly. Robie wouldn't look at her. "Robie, I'm Chief

Karen Kruickshank. You can call me Karen. Can you tell me what happened?"

There was no response. The girl kept looking down at her legs, dangling off the table.

"Robie . . . I really need to know. I understand this isn't easy for you to talk about, but the doctor says you've had sexual intercourse. I have to ask you this. Did someone force you?"

Robie looked up suddenly at that, her eyes wide. "No," she said. "No, it wasn't like that at all."

Karen frowned. "You mean it was consensual?"

Robie sighed and made a face. "Yes. I wanted to."

"But you were found unconscious. What happened? Why did you scream?"

Robie blushed and looked down again. "I . . . I couldn't help it," she said. "It's never been like that for me before, not even in VR. It just kept going on and on and on . . ." She expelled her breath sharply and shook her head. "I must have passed out."

Karen raised her eyebrows. "You screamed and passed out because you had an orgasm?"

Robie rolled her eyes. "This is so embarrassing," she said. "He isn't here, is he?"

"You mean the man you were with? No. Apparently, he ran off. If it was consensual sex, then no crime has been committed. However, I can't say I think much of him for taking off and leaving you like that. Had you known him very long?"

Robie moistened her lips and looked down again. "I . . . I never saw him before. We had just met."

"I see."

"No, you really don't," said Robie. "I'd never met anyone like him before. He was different . . . I'm not sure I can explain it. Something just came over me . . . I was feeling upset and . . ." Her voice trailed off and she frowned. "That's odd. I can't seem to recall now what I was so upset about."

"It's okay. Take your time," said Karen.

"Well, he just made me feel . . . I don't know, I can't really describe it. He was so gentle and . . . so knowing. I mean, I'm not inexperienced. I've had sex before, and not

just in VR, but this was just out of control! There was something about him . . . I couldn't help myself. He was so unusual and exotic-looking, but it was more than that. He was
so . . . " She shook her head, unable to find the right words.
"I don't know. I can't explain it. You're sure he's not going
to get in trouble?"

"Not if he didn't force you to do anything you didn't want
to do. Then it's a private matter between you and him."

"Oh. Well . . . I guess that's okay then. He was really
sweet. So gentle and . . . Somehow, I just had the feeling he
knew exactly what I was thinking. I know I was feeling upset
for some reason, and he was so kind and understanding—and
he was gorgeous! He had really long, thick, black hair, all
the way down to here," she indicated a spot below her shoulder, "and beautiful, deep, brown eyes, and really pretty eyebrows, with a high arch to them, and those sexy, pointed
ears, and —"

"*Pointed* ears?"

"Well, yeah," said Robie, with a shrug. "I guess all elves
have them."

"All what?"

"Elves. You know."

Karen frowned and shook her head. "No, I'm afraid I
don't."

"It's his ethno-derivation."

"*Elves?*"

"Yeah, you know, he's an elf. It's a very old Earth culture.
I suppose there's not many of them on the ship, which ex-
plains why I never met one before, I guess."

Karen shook her head again, mystified. "I never have, either. Did he give you his name?"

"You're sure he's not going to get in trouble? I mean,
maybe he's Choice partnered. . . ."

"Just tell me his name, Robie."

"Grailing. Grailing Windwalker. Isn't that a lovely
name?"

"Yes, I suppose it is," said Karen, with a smile. "Well, I
think that's all for now. You just wait here and rest awhile.
Your parents should be here soon."

Robie rolled her eyes again. "Oh, great."

Karen went back out into the hall, where Dr. Chen and Sergeant Cruzmark were waiting. "You ever heard of elves?" she asked them.

"What?" the doctor said.

"I didn't think so. Neither have I. She claims she had consensual sex with an elf named Grailing Windwalker." She repeated Robie's description.

"*Pointed* ears?" the doctor said, with a frown.

"That's what she said. She seems to think it's a characteristic of his ethno-derivation. She says she found them sexy."

"There's no one aboard the ship like that," said Dr. Chen, frowning.

"Obviously," Karen said. "I think the girl is in serious need of Counseling. Her grip on reality seems tenuous, at best."

"Well . . . she had sex with *somebody* this morning," said the doctor. "I could run a DNA scan on the sperm sample I took. It would only take a moment. But if it was consensual sex, then there is the issue of privacy to consider."

"Why don't you do that; I'll take responsibility," said Karen.

"Want me to run a check with CAC, just to see if there really is anyone aboard with that name?" Ben Cruzmark asked.

"Go ahead, Ben," Karen said. "But I suspect you won't come up with anything. I think that girl has some serious emotional problems and it looks as if someone took advantage of her. Technically, there could be grounds for charges. I want you to take a statement from her parents when they arrive. Get some background. I have to go question Dr. Petrovsky's widow. I'll check back with you later. Oh, and Doctor, you might also want to look in on Sonja Buckland when her sedative wears off. She was admitted by Dr. Burroughs this morning. Her partner's with her now." She shook her head and sighed. "An elf with pointy ears and a little man with pointy shoes. Maybe they know each other."

"All right, let's try this next one on the list," said Riley. They had gone straight to Ulysses' place from school, to have another try at cracking the Counseling files.

"Mac, try 'transactional,'" Ulysses said.

"Sorry, that's not it," Mac replied. "How much longer are you going to keep this up?"

"Until it works," said Ulysses.

"I really don't think you should be doing this," Mac said. "Counseling files are confidential, for access to authorized persons only."

"What determines if a person is authorized?" asked Ulysses.

"If they have the proper password," Mac said.

"Well, if we find it, then I guess we'll be authorized, won't we?" said Ulysses.

"I don't think it's supposed to work that way."

"Come on, Mac. Don't back out on us now. Wouldn't you like to put one over on those smug CAC AIs?"

"Okay, give me the next one."

"What's the next word on the list?" asked Ulysses.

"Free-ud," Riley said, uncertainly.

"What? That doesn't sound right," said Jenny. "Let me see that." She took the list. "That's Freud, you glitch. Dr. Sigmund Freud."

"Who's he?"

"He was the founder of psychotherapy," she said. "Don't you pay any attention in school?"

"Oh. Yeah, I seem to remember something about that now."

Jenny rolled her eyes. "Try Freud, Mac."

"Sorry. What's the next one?"

"Jung," she said.

"I have access," Mac said.

"All right!" Ulysses said.

"Who's Jung?" asked Riley.

"Never mind," said Jenny, shaking her head in resignation.

"I want to know," said Riley, petulantly.

"Dr. Carl Jung," she said. "He did pioneering work in dream analysis. This is all Elementary Psych, Riley."

"Well, that was never one of my best subjects."

"Dream analysis," Ulysses said. "That's interesting, isn't it?"

They looked at him, then suddenly made the connection with the dream they had all shared.

"Yes, it is," said Jenny. "Okay. What's our next move?"

"Mac," Ulysses said, "access the file on Dr. Penelope Seldon."

"There is no file on Dr. Penelope Seldon," Mac replied.

"What? There has to be."

"It isn't there."

"Why not?" asked Riley.

"How should I know?"

"Okay, Mac," Ulysses said. "Disengage."

For a moment, they all sat in silence, puzzled.

"I thought records were kept on everyone who goes to Counseling," Riley said.

"Everyone except Dr. Seldon, apparently," said Ulysses. He frowned and shook his head. "Maybe she fooled them. Her primary specialty was Artificial Intelligence. She must have figured out some way to delete the data."

"Why would she want to do that?" asked Jenny.

"I don't know. Maybe Riley was right. Maybe she never got better, but instead figured out some way to get the Counseling AI to release her from treatment and then got rid of the file so no one could ever go back and check."

"But wouldn't someone become suspicious?" Jenny asked.

"Maybe not," Ulysses said. "If Counseling reported that she was released from treatment, why would anybody want to check? They'd probably just assume she was okay."

"See, maybe I'm not such a glitch, after all," said Riley, with a sour grimace.

"All right, Riley, I'm sorry," Jenny said. "But where does that leave us?"

Ulysses shook his head. "I don't know. But I must admit, it's got me a little worried. I wish there was some way we could find out more about the quest program."

"Why don't you ask Mac to check the VR program files?" said Jenny.

"What do I ask him to check for?" said Ulysses. "You have to have a name or file number to call up the right program. Without that, all Mac could do was give us a listing, and if we tried searching through all of them, it would take

forever. Dr. Seldon was smart enough to figure out a way
around the Counseling AI; it would be a snap for her to hide
a program somewhere in the network. It could be anywhere,
and it probably wouldn't even be listed."

"Good point," said Jenny, nodding. "So what do we do
now?"

"We go back to the quest," said Riley. "Or maybe I should
say we wait for it to come back to us."

"There is something we can do," Ulysses said. "Mac, can
you tell us what a unicorn is?"

"A mythical creature that resembles a cross between a
horse and a goat, with one horn."

"Mythical," Ulysses said. "Mac, are you getting that from
the Folklore, Mythology, and Legends database?"

"There are no listings for unicorns in any of the other
files."

"Does it say anything about how to capture one?" asked
Jenny.

"A virgin's touch can tame a unicorn."

"Oh," said Jenny. For an awkward moment, no one spoke.
Then Riley cleared his throat and Jenny shot him a sharp
glance. "Yes?" she said.

"Uh . . . never mind," said Riley, looking away.

It was late when Karen arrived home, tired. Jenny was already in bed, asleep. Karen looked in on her, standing over
her bed for a few moments, smiling at the way she was
curled up on her side with her hands up next to her face, just
the way she had slept as a baby. All that was missing was the
thumb in her mouth. But as she gazed down at the curves of
her daughter's body beneath the thin sheet, Karen was reminded that she wasn't a baby anymore.

Jenny had grown into a beautiful young woman and soon
she would be old enough to Choose. All Karen ever wanted
was for Jenny to be happy. The thought of her experiencing
the kind of pain Tonisha Petrovsky was going through right
now gave Karen a tight feeling in her stomach. She swallowed hard and took a deep breath, exhaling slowly as she
tried to banish the unpleasant thought.

She bent down and lightly kissed Jenny on the forehead.

"Sweet dreams, darling," she murmured, as she left her daughter's bedroom and went into her own.

Wearily, she stripped off her clothes and padded barefoot to the bathroom, where she stood under a hot shower until the timer switched it off, then ran the ultrasonic pick over her teeth. She came back into the bedroom and said, "Sally, dim the lights."

As the house computer dimmed the lights to a soft twilight glow, Karen lay back on the bed with her arms behind her head on the pillow. She exhaled heavily, trying to focus her thoughts in the face of the frustration she felt.

Tonisha Petrovsky hadn't been able to contribute very much when she had questioned her. Dr. Burroughs was already there when she had arrived. The news of her partner's suicide had hit Tonisha hard. An attractive and slim twenty-four-year-old of African-American descent, Tonisha was an astrophysicist who had been partnered with Alexei Petrovsky since she was twenty. Karen had been delayed at the hospital, so that by the time she arrived at the Petrovsky residence in Denver Village, Dr. Burroughs had already broken the news to her. She had been crying, but when Karen arrived, Tonisha made an effort to compose herself and answer Karen's questions to the best of her ability.

"Tonisha, I know this must be very painful for you," Karen had said, sympathetically, "but we have to try to understand what happened. Is there anything you can tell me about what may have caused Alexei to take his own life?"

"I don't know," Tonisha had replied, dully. "I just don't know. I can't understand it."

"Had he been going to Counseling?"

Tonisha shook her head. "No. At least, not that I know of."

"Do you think that's something he would have kept from you?"

Tonisha moistened her lips and stared at her, anguish clearly written on her features. "I wouldn't have thought he would keep anything from me," she said. She squeezed her eyes shut, fighting back tears. "How could I have not known something was wrong?" She swallowed hard, shaking her head in disbelief. "I should have known. I should have noticed *something*."

"There was nothing different about the way he acted recently?" asked Karen. "He didn't seem depressed, moody, or preoccupied?"

Tonisha shook her head again. "No, this just came out of the blue. I can't make any sense of it. I just don't understand. I thought we were happy. If there was something bothering him, I didn't even have a clue."

"So there was nothing different about the way he acted, nothing that indicated he was concerned about something?" Karen persisted. "No changes in his behavior or his routine?"

"Well, he had been spending more time at the hospital over the last few months," Tonisha said, "but he said it was because he was working on developing his secondary specialty in psychiatry. If he was preoccupied with anything, it was with that. At least, that's what I thought." Her lower lip trembled as a tear flowed down her cheek. "It never even occurred to me that he might be unhappy or distraught. God, how could I have been so blind?"

"You mustn't blame yourself," said Linda Burroughs. "None of us at the hospital suspected anything was wrong, either. Whatever was troubling him, Alex kept it well hidden."

"But I was his partner! I should have *known*!" Tonisha said, miserably. "It was my fault. I failed him."

Karen sighed heavily as she recalled the conversation. She hadn't stayed much longer. It was clear Tonisha could contribute nothing of any real significance to her investigation. Her partner's suicide had left her baffled, grief-stricken, and wallowing in self-recrimination. Karen had suggested that she go to Counseling, and Dr. Burroughs had agreed, and she had left them together. They had been friends since childhood, and Karen felt that her continued presence would only aggravate an already difficult situation. What Tonisha needed was the support and comfort of an understanding friend, not the persistence of an official inquiry, so Karen had expressed her sympathy and left them alone.

She had, however, learned a few things. Tonisha had said that Alexei had been spending more time at the hospital, working on his secondary specialty in psychiatry. It seemed ironic, in view of what had happened, but when Karen checked, she found that he had logged in only about thirty hours of study with the learning programs, and that he had run the same programs over and over again. And they were the programs dealing with depressive behavior. Then, apparently, he had simply stopped. And for the past few weeks, he had been leaving the hospital at the end of his normal shift, only he had not gone home. Both Tonisha and the record of his domestic AI had testified to that. So where had he gone?

Whatever had been going through his mind, he had apparently succeeded in keeping up the pretense that nothing was wrong. And he had sought a solution to his problem on his own, obviously without success. He had managed to keep up appearances, hiding his depression even from his mate. That could only have added to the stress he must have felt. Apparently, he knew what was wrong with him, but he couldn't do anything about it. The study programs imparted knowledge through subliminal assimilation, what was known as sim knowledge, and it was rarely necessary to run a study program more than once for the knowledge to take hold. Yet, Petrovsky had run the same programs over and over again, obsessively, as if he had become so morbidly fixated on his problem that he could concentrate on nothing else. Perhaps after he left the hospital, he simply went out wandering on his own, somewhere he could be alone to contemplate what he had finally done.

Why hadn't he gone to Counseling? Maybe he could not admit to himself that he needed it. That he had run those study programs over and over again indicated a desperate need to solve his problem for himself. Karen imagined that much the same sort of questions were probably going through Tonisha's mind right now. Only in her case, they were much more personal. And painful.

How could your partner be so depressed that he was considering suicide and you didn't even have a clue that anything was wrong? Karen sighed. She was hardly in a position to be judgmental. Rick had not been happy in their partnership for a long time before she realized anything was wrong. All that time, and he had never told her he thought she was too aggressive, too controlling and competitive. What did he expect? She was Security. She couldn't be like everybody else. He had never understood that. After their Dissolution, friends of hers had urged her to get Counseling, but she had resisted their suggestions. She wasn't maladjusted. She could handle things herself. She had told herself that she was a productive member of society and she could work through it. And suddenly it occurred to her that maybe Alexei Petrovsky had reacted the same way.

Nobody wanted to admit that they might be maladjusted. No one wanted that stigma. Counseling was there to help people with their problem, to keep the society of the *Agamemnon* in balance. It was supposed to be the perfect way to handle such things. AI therapy, impersonal and non-judgmental, intelligent software programmed to deal with any human problem in a confidential, logical, unemotional, nonthreatening way. The only problem was that well-adjusted and productive members of society did not require Counseling. Karen recalled the expression on Tonisha Petrovsky's face when she had suggested Counseling. She would do it, Karen had no doubt of that, but she would be doing it for the wrong reasons. She would be doing it because she felt guilty and was blaming herself for her partner's suicide, not because she needed some help to work her way through her grief. She would go to Counseling because she felt that she had failed Alexei, because she felt she deserved it.

That wasn't the way it should be. But Karen recalled how she had rebelled against the idea herself when it was suggested to her. She didn't need Counseling. There was nothing wrong with her. She was a balanced, well-centered, productive member of society. The problem wasn't hers, it was Rick's. At least, that was what she had told herself at the time. But it was neither Rick's problem nor her problem. It was *their* problem. And they had failed to solve it. Maybe because, like Alexei Petrovsky, neither of them could admit that anything was wrong until it was too late.

She pushed the thoughts of their Dissolution from her mind. She didn't want to think about it. She sat up and reached across to the nightstand, opening the drawer and pulling out the VR band. She needed to unwind. "Sally, interface VR Program NC-301."

She slipped the cool alloy band on and lay back on the bed, feeling as if she were falling into it, spinning away into darkness interspersed with flashing, colored lights as the interface was established and she closed her eyes.

He came into the bedroom. He was dark and swarthy-looking, and his head was shaved. He wore a suit of dirty, white utility coveralls. His shoulders were broad and powerful, and his upper torso tapered sharply to his waist. His steel gray eyes were fixed on hers. He smiled, showing slightly crooked teeth. His mouth was cruel-looking. Without speaking, he pulled open his coveralls, revealing a bright splash of color against his tanned, well-muscled chest. As he slowly pulled the suit off his shoulders, she could see more of the tattoo that started at his waist, curled around and up his back, and came over his left shoulder, a thick serpent crawling down onto his chest, a hooded cobra with its gaping mouth open at the level of his nipples. Fangs gleamed. Its long tongue flickered as it spit at her.

The coveralls fell down around his ankles and he stepped out of them, moving toward her. The bedposts softened and flowed, forming nanalloy Security restraints around her wrists and ankles. She knew what was coming next.

CHAPTER
7

Peter Buckland resumed his classes the following day, but he was worried. Dr. Burroughs had wanted, against Sonja's strident protests, to keep her for observation. She had insisted it was totally unnecessary, that there was nothing wrong with her, and she had to get back to the office. The crops were being endangered, and it was a problem that had to be dealt with at once. The trouble was, she would not budge from her bizarre story.

"Sonja," Peter had said, trying to reason with her, "surely you must realize how all this sounds?"

"I know perfectly well how it sounds," she had replied, irritably. "But I *didn't* dream it, Pete. It's what *happened*. I *know* what I saw."

"Tiny people with wings?" he'd said. "Darling . . . I'm sorry, but . . . that just sounds . . ." He shook his head, helplessly, unwilling to complete the statement.

"Yes, I know," she replied. "You don't have to say it. But they're real. And sooner or later, someone else is going to see them, too, and then you'll know I'm not losing my mind. I called Saleem. He promised to set up an HIR in the field tonight, in case the VMs glitch up again, and this time, he's going to keep the recording crystal in a safe place, so we'll have some proof. He doesn't believe it, either, and I know he's agreed to it just to humor me, but he'll soon change his mind. The herb crops are being eaten, Pete, and I know what's eating them. I saw them."

"And the little man?"

"I can't explain that, either, and I know it sounds completely unbelievable, but I saw him, too. Pete, I swear to you, I'm *not* imagining any of this."

"Well, all right," he'd said, with resignation, "for the sake of argument, let's not dispute that. But what happens if Saleem doesn't see the . . . what you say you saw. What then?"

"What do you want me to do? Go into Counseling?"

"Under the circumstances," Dr. Burroughs said, "that might be very helpful."

"And if I don't agree to take Counseling voluntarily, then you'll prescribe it for me, right?" Sonja said, testily.

"At least an evaluation," Dr. Burroughs replied, keeping her tone professionally neutral.

"All right, fine," said Sonja, relenting. "If it means I can get out of here, then I'll do it."

"What do you think, Doctor?" Peter had asked. "Would that be acceptable?"

Dr. Burroughs had pursed her lips thoughtfully, then nodded. "I can find nothing physically wrong with her," she said. "To be on the safe side, I would still prefer to keep her here overnight, but if she agrees to a Counseling evaluation, and promises to check back with me tomorrow, then I'm willing to release her."

"All right, you've got a deal," said Sonja.

She had gone straight to work, directly from the hospital, and he had gone to school, but he had a hard time keeping his mind on his lesson plans. He was very worried. Sonja wasn't really acting differently, and though she had fallen, there were no head injuries to account for any hallucinations. She had always been very pragmatic, perhaps excessively so. This wasn't like her at all.

The alternative was that she was telling the truth about

what she saw. However, there was no way he could accept that. Miniature flying people? A man no more than half a meter tall? He had no doubt that she actually believed she saw them, but what could possibly account for her thinking that she saw such things? Dr. Burroughs had said that stress, which could be produced by overwork, could sometimes produce hallucinations, but it just didn't seem very likely that they could be so bizarre. And otherwise, Sonja seemed perfectly fine. She had promised to have a Counseling evaluation immediately after work. He had called Saleem and made him promise to make sure that she went, rather than stay late at work again. He didn't know what else he could do.

He was not sure what to tell Ulysses. Perhaps, at least until he knew more, it would be best not to tell him anything beyond what he had already told him. His mother had a minor accident at work, resulting in a fall that had apparently produced no injury, but she had gone to the hospital for observation, purely to be on the safe side. There was no point in worrying the boy, not when, for the first time, he seemed to be taking things more seriously. He was spending a great deal of time with Riley Etheridge and Chief Kruickshank's daughter, lately. That was a good sign. Ulysses had always been something of a loner. The Etheridge boy was bright, though he seemed a bit unfocused, and Jenny Kruickshank was very level-headed and one of the best students in her class. It was good to see that Ulysses was beginning to develop some social skills.

Ulysses and the others were in his third class of the day. He took the opportunity to reassure his son that his mother was all right and had gone back to work. Then he scheduled another VR session for the class and gave them their next assignment. When the lights went down and the sim began, he left the classroom and went out into the hall. He leaned back against the wall and exhaled heavily. His stomach felt tight and he could feel the pressure of anxiety building in his chest. Maybe he should go to the gym after classes and have a good, strenuous workout to dispel the tension. He had been neglecting that lately. In fact, he had been neglecting a lot of things.

He and Sonja didn't really talk much anymore. At least,

they no longer had the sort of intimate conversations that they used to have. They discussed things that happened at work, primarily, and they discussed their friends and colleagues. They didn't even discuss their own son very much. Ulysses, for the most part, was left to his own devices. In some ways, thought Peter, his son had become almost a stranger to him. Perhaps it was just his age. He had tried initiating conversations, but somehow they always turned into one-sided lectures. He knew that was the teacher in him, but he could not seem to figure out a way to prod Ulysses into communicating more. And now this thing with Sonja . . .

What if there was something wrong with her? He didn't want to think about it, but he had to. There was something strange happening aboard the ship. The suicides. Everybody knew about them, but no one wanted to talk about it. Even with his friends and colleagues, conversations had taken on a sort of mechanical aspect. Everyone wanted to talk only about topics that were safe. No one was anxious to express any opinions or ask any unsettling questions.

They hadn't had any friends over to visit in at least three or four months, nor had they been invited anywhere. Karen Kruickshank's mentioning that they should probably get to know each other better was the first invitation to any sort of social contact that he'd had in a long time. And he was really looking forward to it, but not because he wanted to discuss their children. He wanted to discuss what was happening to them. He wanted to ask the awkward questions.

As Chief of Security, Karen was certainly in a position to know more about what was going on than anybody else. He wanted to know what she really thought. He'd have to call her soon. As soon as he found out how Sonja did in her evaluation. He was anxious to know, and at the same time, he felt very apprehensive. A part of him just wanted to go back to the way things were before. A part of him really didn't want to know. And that worried him almost as much as Sonja did.

A moment after the lights went down in the classroom and their couches tilted back, they were once more on the trail leading through the forest. It was daylight, and the sun's rays shining through the overhanging branches dappled the trail ahead of them as they walked briskly through the woods.

"Does anybody know where we're going?" Riley asked.

"We're following the trail," said Ulysses, with a shrug. "I guess the sim will let us know when we're supposed to do anything different."

"You know, I was thinking about this whole thing," Riley said. "Everybody else in class is getting the educational sim we're supposed to be getting. We've missed out on several of the regularly scheduled ones by this point. What happens when we're supposed to take a test?"

"I have a feeling *this* is the test that we're supposed to take," said Jenny.

"Well, you know what I mean. Sooner or later, we're going to have to explain to somebody about what's been going on," said Riley. "What are we going to say? I mean, do we tell the truth, or do we make up something?"

"I don't know," Ulysses said. "I guess we'll have to deal with that when the time comes."

"What if they don't believe us?" Riley asked. "That is, assuming we tell the truth."

"Well, then, I guess they'll have to ask themselves why the three of us would get together and make up a story like this," said Ulysses.

"You figure we'll probably get sent for Counseling?" asked Riley.

"If they don't believe our story."

"Then maybe we should agree on something to tell them instead," said Jenny.

"I don't know," Ulysses replied. "I've been thinking about that. Maybe getting sent in for Counseling wouldn't be so bad a thing."

"What?" said Riley. "Are you kidding? Why? Everybody would think there was something wrong with us."

"I don't really care," Ulysses said. "I was just thinking that it might be another way for us to get some answers. Dr. Seldon went to a lot of trouble to design this program. We don't know what her reasons were, but wouldn't it make sense that she would have anticipated the possibility of our telling someone about this and maybe getting sent for Counseling? She went in for Counseling herself, remember? But according to the files, it never happened. There's no record of it. So either Professor Wesala was wrong about what happened to her, which means the records are wrong, or else Dr. Seldon did something while she was in Counseling that allowed her to take control of the whole thing. And we'd pretty much decided that was probably what happened."

"So you're saying that if we were sent in for Counseling, we might encounter something that she had prepared for us in advance?" asked Jenny.

"I think it's possible," Ulysses replied.

"You may be right," said Jenny. "It makes sense that Dr. Seldon would have anticipated that. After all, she would have had no way of knowing that we wouldn't tell someone about this. It seems obvious that she would have considered that."

"Unless maybe there was something in the program that would keep us from talking about this," Riley said.

"There you go again," Ulysses said. "I worry about you sometimes, Riley. How do you think of this stuff?"

"I don't know," said Riley. "It just comes to me. But look, there was something in the program that made us all have that dream, wasn't there? We *know* that. And we also know that for all the talking that we've done about it, we haven't *wanted* to tell anyone about this. On the surface, it seems as if that was our decision. But maybe it wasn't, really."

For a moment, they just walked in silence, mulling over Riley's idea. Then Jenny said, "Well, I guess the way to find out for sure would be to try to tell someone about this and see if we can."

"Who would you tell?" Ulysses asked.

"My mother, probably," said Jenny.

"Do you want to tell her?"

"Well . . . no, not really. At least, not yet. Why, do you want to tell your father?"

"No."

"You see?" said Riley.

"Oh, be quiet," Jenny said, irritably.

"Well, doesn't that prove my point?" Riley asked, defensively.

"Maybe it doesn't quite prove it, but it does seem to support it," Ulysses conceded, uneasily. "Now I'm starting to think like you. That worries me."

"I just had a thought," said Jenny. "So far, every time we've done this, we've all been in class together. What do you think would happen if just one of us tried a VR session, without the others?"

"Good question," said Ulysses. "Maybe we should try it and see what happens."

"Who do you think should do it?" she asked.

"I'm not sure I'd want to wind up here all by myself," said Riley, uncomfortably.

"The question is, would you?" Jenny said. "It would be interesting to find out if we'd still appear in the quest with you if we weren't experiencing the sim. It would tell us something important about how the program was written."

"I don't get it," Riley said, looking puzzled. "Why would you show up in the sim if you weren't participating?"

"Well, that's the question, isn't it?" said Jenny. "To what extent are we actually participating? I've been trying to figure that out while I was thinking about this at home over the past few days. We're not really doing any of this stuff. We're just sitting in class, virtched out. Our presence in the sim is just a construct of virtual reality. We've already figured out that the program can access us, that is, recognize us when we put on the bands to do VR. It uses the interface to create us here in this quest scenario. If Ulysses and I don't put on the bands, but you do, and you wind up seeing us in the sim, then that will tell us something about how much control we really have here."

"I see what you mean," Ulysses said. "It seems as if we're acting independently while we're here, but since we're *not* actually here, our sense of having some control might just be an illusion."

"Huh?" said Riley, looking hopelessly confused.

"Look at it this way, Riley," Jenny said. "What makes this quest sim different is that we're part of it, experiencing it from our own perspective instead of someone else's, the way it usually works. You with me so far?"

"Yeah, okay," said Riley, nodding and frowning slightly.

"All right," said Jenny. "While we're here, it seems as if we've got a good deal of control over what we do. Except for some instances, like that encounter we had with those two men back in the tavern. I struck one of them, which isn't like me at all, and I used my sword, when I don't know anything about swords. But here, it seemed as if I knew what I was doing. Same thing with Ulysses. He used magic. He can't use magic in real life, and he didn't really know what he was doing when he did it. So that had to be the sim dictating our actions. So the question is, were they really our actions?"

"Now you're losing me again," said Riley.

"What she means," Ulysses said, "is that maybe this program only gives us the illusion of being able to make some choices about what we do. We're not really here. We're in the classroom. While we're here, we're only VR constructs based on ourselves. But is our perspective real, or is that just an illusion, too?"

"You mean like with all the other sims?" Riley said.

"Exactly. Only in this case, instead of us sitting in class and getting someone else's sim perspective and having it feel like our own, we're getting the sim perspective of our VR constructs, and it only feels like our own because the constructs are based on us."

"So you mean the computer makes VR models of us and because they're based on us, they feel familiar and we think we're thinking for ourselves when the program is really dictating our thoughts?"

"Right," said Jenny, "that's it, exactly."

"I'm not even sure I understand what I just said," Riley replied, shaking his head in his confusion.

"Never mind," said Ulysses. "I think Jenny's idea is worth pursuing. I'm willing to be the one to try it." He glanced at Jenny. "That is, unless you want to."

"I think we should all be there together," Jenny said, "only two of us won't wear the bands. That way, there would be a control on the experiment, and if it looks like something strange is happening, we could could pull you out of it."

"Only if we weren't participating, how would we know if anything was wrong?" asked Riley.

"That's a good question," said Ulysses. "Either way, I've got more experience with this than you two have. I've been working at it longer. If something went wrong, I think it would be easier for me to pull out on my own."

"Are you sure?" asked Riley.

"No," Ulysses said, with a shrug. "If I were sure, we wouldn't need to do the experiment, would we?"

"Wait a minute," Riley said. "Doesn't our having this conversation prove that we're capable of thinking for ourselves here?"

"Maybe," Ulysses said. "But then again, maybe not. Think back to the Valentinov sim, which is the last one we had before this whole thing started. It was easy for us to tell which point of view was Valentinov's and which was ours. But here, it's not so easy. It's hard enough to maintain your perspective in VR when you're dealing with someone else's simulated experience. Here, we're dealing with our own. So the line gets real fuzzy. I mean, are we having this conversation because we want to, or are we having it because Dr. Seldon anticipated that we would have these questions and programmed it into the sim? If that was the case, then maybe we're just thinking that we're maintaining our own persective, when we're actually going with the experience of the sim."

"I'm getting a headache just listening to all this," said Riley. "Could we change the subject?"

"Well, you brought up the whole issue of control," Ulysses said.

"Or maybe the sim brought it up and you just went with it," said Jenny.

"Enough!" said Riley, raising his hands. "I'm sorry I ever mentioned it!"

Jenny suddenly held her arms out, stopping them. "Don't move!" she said, softly, but urgently.

"What is it?" asked Ulysses, and then he saw it, too.

They had reached a bend in the trail and just ahead of them, a fantastic creature had stepped out of the woods, into the open. It was white, and it had four legs and a tail, a curved, muscular neck surmounted by a thick mane, and a long, straight, spiral horn in the center of its head.

"The unicorn!" said Riley, his voice barely above a whisper.

"Get down!" Ulysses said, quietly. They crouched behind some shrubbery.

"It's beautiful!" said Jenny, in an awestruck voice.

The beast stood by the side of the trail, about twenty meters away, nibbling on some grass. It seemed oblivious to their presence.

"What should we do?" asked Riley, quietly.

"I don't know," Ulysses replied.

"We're supposed to capture it," said Jenny.

"How?" Ulysses asked. "I didn't think it would be so big! And that horn looks dangerous."

"Mac said a virgin's touch could tame it," Riley said.

"But what if it doesn't want to be touched?" Ulysses asked, uneasily.

"Try using some of your magic on it," Riley suggested.

"What are you talking about?" Ulysses asked. "How am I supposed to do that?"

"The same way you did it last time," Riley replied.

"But I don't even know what I did last time!"

"Yes, you do. You held up your hand and yelled 'Stop!' Try doing that again."

"But what if it doesn't work? If I yell, it might run away. And Mac didn't say you could use magic to capture it."

"Well, it might run away anyway, if we don't do something," Jenny said.

"One of us is going to have to touch it," Riley said.

They exchanged glances. No one immediately volunteered.

"All right, I'll do it," said Ulysses, with a sigh.

"I'll go with you," Riley said. "Maybe if we can come up on it from different sides, we'll have a better chance."

Jenny didn't say anything. She just continued to gaze at the creature fixedly.

Riley looked at Ulysses. Ulysses looked at Riley. Neither of them said anything.

"Okay, let's go," Ulysses said, finally. "Riley, you cut

through the woods to the left of the trail. I'll take the right. Try to get as close as you can before it sees you. And don't make any noise. Jenny, you wait here. If it takes off, we have to follow it, so be ready to run after us, okay?"

She nodded, without looking at him.

Riley stepped off the trail and started moving through the woods to the left, following a straight course that would take him past the bend. Ulysses stepped off the trail to the right and started moving slowly through the trees and underbrush, carefully looking to see where he placed his feet, so as not to step on any dry twigs that might crack and alert the creature.

It seemed to take forever for him to cover the twenty meters or so that separated them from the unicorn, and the closer he came to it, the more his anxiety increased. It's only a sim, he kept telling himself. Nothing can happen to you in a sim. At least, he didn't think it could. The trouble was, he wasn't really sure. So far, the unicorn had not been alerted to his approach.

How fast could it move? Ulysses thought back to his classes in Earth Science and recalled that there were creatures on Earth that not only attacked people sometimes, but also ate them. Was this beast one like that? There was an animal on Earth similar in appearance to this unicorn, only it did not have a horn. Ulysses tried to remember which one it was. The horse, that was it. Horses were supposed to be fast, as he recalled. People used to ride on them. Once they were tamed, that is. He wondered what it would be like to ride the unicorn. And then he also wondered what it would be like if it attacked him with that horn.

He was close enough now that he could see the unicorn through the trees up ahead. He moved with excruciating slowness and caution, his heart hammering in his chest. Or was that just an illusion? Ulysses recalled from his studies that animals generally had a much better sense of smell than people. What if it picked up his scent? He paused and tried to gauge which way the wind was blowing. There didn't seem to be any wind. He couldn't tell.

Suddenly, the unicorn started and raised its head. Ulysses froze, but it was looking away from him, toward the opposite side of the trail. It had to be Riley. Either the beast had picked up his scent, or Riley had made some small noise that had alerted it. The unicorn stood very still, its ears pricked up, its tail switching back and forth. Its muscles tensed. It looked ready to run. He was so close. . . . He had to do it now.

He rushed forward through the trees, thrashing through the bushes. The unicorn turned toward the sounds, momentarily confused, then sprang away just as Ulysses cleared the trees and burst out onto the trail. Riley came running out of the woods on the other side and the unicorn hesitated, caught for a moment between them, then took off at a gallop straight down the trail, back in the direction from which they had come . . . heading straight back toward Jenny.

"Run!" Ulysses shouted to Riley. "Don't let it get away!"

But it became clear in a moment that they would never be able to catch it. Its tufted hooves made rapid, rhythmic drumming sounds as it galloped down the trail, and then Ulysses saw Jenny step out into its path. The unicorn put its head down, lowering its horn.

"Jenny, no!" Ulysses shouted, in alarm. "Get out of the way!"

But she didn't move. She stood her ground with a determined look on her face as the beast ran straight at her. Another moment, and she would surely be impaled on that gleaming, spiral horn. Ulysses stopped and Riley came running up to his side. He didn't want to look, and yet, at the same time, he couldn't tear his gaze away. The unicorn was practically upon her. Suddenly, at the very last instant, Jenny twisted to one side, avoiding that frightening horn, and in a startling display of athletic skill, she grabbed the creature's mane and vaulted up onto its back. Immediately, the unicorn made a whining, screaming, vibrato sound and started bucking.

"Come on!" Ulysses shouted.

Both he and Riley sprinted toward the beast, running as hard as they could. It was kicking out with its hind legs, then bowing its body and jumping straight up into the air, coming down and twisting around, rearing up, then kicking out with its hind legs again, doing everything it could to dislodge Jenny, but she hung on tenaciously, grabbing fistfuls of the creature's mane and gripping tightly with her legs. As they came running up, the unicorn reared, pawing at them with its forelegs, and Riley recoiled with an alarmed cry, falling to the ground.

"Touch it!" Jenny shouted. "Touch it, quickly! I can't hold on much longer!"

It reared up again, striking out at Ulysses, and he darted to one side, then lunged in toward the beast as it came down again, closing his eyes and reaching out with both hands. He felt them come in contact with the unicorn's muscular flanks and, immediately, it stopped bucking and a shiver went all through it. Ulysses opened his eyes and saw its muscles trembling, quivering visibly. Then it stood still and calmly turned toward him, put its head down, carefully avoiding him with its horn, and rubbed against his shoulder, making a soft, snorting sound.

"You did it!" Riley said, picking himself up off the ground. "It's tame!"

Jenny exhaled heavily and leaned forward on the unicorn's back, resting her head against its neck and patting its flanks. "It's okay, boy, it's okay," she said, stroking it.

The lights came up and the couches tilted forward. Ulysses blinked and shook his head to clear it. He felt a bit confused. He had not expected the sim to end quite so abruptly. He wondered if it ended because the other sim had ended, the one everyone else in class had experienced. He hadn't really thought about that before. Were they specifically designed to be of the same length, or did it simply end because the other one had ended? They were supposed to tame the unicorn. Well, they had done that, but then what? The unicorn was supposed to lead them, somehow, to the next step of the quest. Would it still be there when they came back?

He glanced over toward Jenny, sitting next to Riley. She was looking down, as if preoccupied. Riley met his gaze, glanced briefly at Jenny, then back at him and raised an eyebrow.

His father came back into the class. He looks tired, thought Ulysses. By contrast, he felt strangely rested, in a pleasantly unfocused way, despite his vicarious exertions in the sim. Taking his place at the head of the class, his father just stood there for a moment, looking down at his desk, as if trying to collect his thoughts. That wasn't like him. He always had his lessons organized perfectly, and used every available moment of class time, speaking without any awkward pauses. He never got distracted.

He looks worried, thought Ulysses. About Mom? But if she was all right, as he had said, then what was there to worry about? Unless his father hadn't told him everything.

"All right," his father said, speaking in a somewhat distracted tone, "next week, we'll review the material we've covered so far, and your oral presentations will be due. Before we —"

"Excuse me, Professor Buckland?" one of the other students said, raising his hand. "What oral presentations?"

"Didn't Professor Wesala give you the assignment last time?" he asked, puzzled.

"No, sir. She didn't say anything about any oral presentations."

"Oh. Well . . ." He shook his head, glancing down at his notes. "I must have forgotten to tell her about it. My apologies. I suppose that means I'll have to give you an extra week to work on them." He frowned. "That will throw off the schedule. Well, I'm afraid it can't be helped. But you've got your exams coming up and I wanted to make sure we had enough time to review . . ." His voice trailed off and he frowned again, then sighed with resignation. "All right. Never mind the presentations. It's my fault, we'll move ahead. Unless, of course, you'd rather do the presentations? Instead of the review, that is."

"No, no, review, review," the other students said, immediately.

He nodded. "Very well. We'll skip the presentations then." The tone went off, signaling the end of the class. He looked up, surprised. "Well, I suppose that's it, then. Class dismissed."

As the rest of the class filed out, Ulysses went up to his father. "Dad, is Mom okay?"

His father looked up at him abruptly and Ulysses immediately knew that everything was not okay. His father shook his head. "There's no need to worry, son. She's fine. She went to work today. We'll see her at home later."

"Okay," Ulysses said, not knowing what else he could say. He couldn't press the issue. That would be like calling his father a liar. He couldn't do that, even though he was absolutely certain that his father was lying. Something was wrong with Mom, and it had Ulysses really worried.

As he turned to leave, his father said, "Son?"

Ulysses turned back. "Yes, Dad?"

His father just stared at him for a moment, pursing his lips thoughtfully, then shook his head and said, "Never mind, you'll be late for your next class. I'll see you at home later."

"Okay, Dad."

Riley was waiting for him out in the hall. There was no sign of Jenny. "She rushed right off to her next class," said Riley, without waiting to be asked. "She didn't say a word. So I guess we know now, don't we?"

"Know what?" Ulysses said.

"What do you think?" asked Riley, with a grimace.

"That she's not a virgin, you mean?" Ulysses said. "So the unicorn wasn't tamed when she touched it. What does that prove? It was a *sim,* Riley. How is the unicorn supposed to know something like that?"

"Because *she* knows it," Riley said. "The program is interactive, remember? You and I both knew we were virgins. She knew she wasn't. So the program responded accordingly."

"Well . . . that makes sense, I guess."

"Who do you think it was?"

"I don't know, Riley. And I really don't care. It's none of our business, is it?"

Riley shrugged. "I was just wondering."

"Well, don't."

"Okay, I won't. You think she'll meet us at your place after school?"

Ulysses frowned. "Why wouldn't she?"

Riley shrugged again. "Maybe she's embarrassed."

"Why? What's there to be embarrassed about?" Ulysses

asked. "So she's had sex. That was her decision. What's wrong with that?"

"Nothing," Riley said. "Except maybe she's worried about what you think."

"Why should what I think make any difference?"

"Because she's in love with you, stupid."

Ulysses stopped and turned to stare at him. "What?"

Riley sighed and shook his head. "And you say I'm hopeless? It's obvious. And not only to me, either."

"What does that mean?"

"She's always staring at you when you're not looking. Especially lately. Some of the other girls in class have noticed, too. They can't understand what she sees in you. Frankly, I can't understand it, either, but there you go."

"Well, just 'cause she looks at me sometimes doesn't prove anything," Ulysses said.

"Oh, yeah? Well, how about this: I heard some of the girls talking this morning in the hall. You know Dave Foster, that guy in the senior class they're always mooning about? He asked her out the other day and she turned him down flat."

"So?"

"So this: she told him that she had already Chosen someone."

Ulysses felt a knot form in his stomach. "Did she say who it was?"

"Who do you think?"

"Did it occur to you that it's probably whoever she's had sex with?" asked Ulysses.

"If that's the case, then why did she run out of class like that today?" Riley countered. "It's you, you glitch."

"But . . . she hasn't said anything."

"Maybe because she's waiting for you to say something," Riley said.

"But . . . what if you're wrong?"

"Well, then at least you'll know, won't you?" Riley said. "Talk to her." The tone sounded for the next class. "We're late for PT," said Riley. He started to run, then stopped after a few steps when he saw Ulysses wasn't running with him. "Aren't you coming?"

"Yeah," said Ulysses, "I'll be right there."

Riley rolled his eyes, then turned and started running down the hall. Ulysses stood there for a moment, then took a deep breath and started walking. He was already late. He didn't care. He wondered if Jenny would show up at the house later. What if she didn't? And what if Riley was wrong? What if she had Chosen someone else and hadn't said anything because she didn't want to hurt his feelings? PT was going to be the last class of the day. And it was also going to be the longest.

George Takahashi stood atop the seawall, looking up at the artificial moon. He stood with his back to the water below, staring out across the vastness of the *Agamemnon*. He had been born here; it was the only world he had ever known . . . and he was tired of it. The depression seemed to center in his chest, like a dull ache that wouldn't go away. He was weary and despondent beyond words, and he simply couldn't take it anymore.

For most of the past week, he had not gone in to work. He had not gone home. He could not face another night of staring at the walls, or lying there in the dark with his own quiet desperation. He had wandered aimlessly around the ship, sleeping in the parks or in the forest. Yesterday evening, he had seen a Security patrol and had hidden from them behind some bushes. He didn't know whether they were looking for him or not, but he did not want to be found. He knew the state he was in would certainly result in his being sent to Counseling, and he didn't want to go through that. He couldn't bear the thought.

It was too late now, in any case. Perhaps if he'd gone earlier . . . but then, he'd kept telling himself that there was nothing wrong. Counseling was supposed to be confidential. Anyone who undertook to get Counseling voluntarily could keep it private. Nobody would know. At least, that's what they said. But the Counseling AI would keep a record, confidential or not, and if there was a record, then somebody would know. Someone would have access. And, of course, if you were forced to go, then everyone would know. He couldn't stand the thought of people thinking he was maladjusted or unproductive. He wasn't. He had always done the right things. But then, if he had always done the right things, how could something like this have happened to him?

George Takahashi was confused. He was confused and he was hurting, and he couldn't understand why. He just wanted it to stop. He hadn't even noticed how it started. He did not know why it started. There wasn't anything that he could put his finger on, no single incident or experience that he could isolate as the cause. That had bothered him a great deal. As a dentist and an acupuncturist, he had prided himself on always being able to isolate the cause of things, on being precise. This needle, there, in that meridian. That tooth, growing improperly, straightened just so. But this . . . this was beyond his understanding.

He couldn't comprehend what had gone wrong. He hadn't done anything different. Every day had always been the same, precise, like clockwork. He had done his job, he had studied to improve his productivity, he had performed his exercises and indulged in the right amount of socialization . . . but then, at some point, he had started feeling bored, tired, and dispirited. He had no idea why. And little by little, it grew worse.

Nothing seemed to help. He had tried all the VR sex and entertainment programs, he had tried increasing his socialization time and expanding his circle of friends, he had exercised more, he had done everything he could think of, and he simply kept growing more and more dejected. He had reached a point where he could no longer take any satisfaction in his job, when studying seemed oppressive and exhausting, when exercise seemed like too much of a chore and he just couldn't seem to summon up the energy even to go to the gym. The once comforting routine of his life had become a miasma of ennui. He did not know why, but he just couldn't go on with it anymore.

It was as if something were missing and he had no idea what it was. He had started making excuses to avoid seeing people and had spent more and more time alone. He would go out to the park and simply sit there, feeling empty. There were over 100,000 people on the ship, and yet he felt utterly alone. The world of the *Agamemnon* was a perfect world, and it had become a perfect prison. A prison from which there was absolutely no escape. He would walk aimlessly along the promenade atop the seawall, looking out over the water down below, and wondering what would happen if he jumped.

He could not recall when the idea had first come to him, but it had persisted until it became all that he could think about. Maladjusted? Yes, it definitely was that. He was a failure as a human being. In a perfect and well-balanced world, he had become imperfect and unbalanced. How had it happened to him? He had no idea. Maybe it just happened. It certainly hadn't been anything he could control.

"I've done all the right things," he murmured aloud to himself in a desolate tone as he stood on the deserted promenade.

He didn't want to be maladjusted. He didn't want to be the sort of person who had to go in for Counseling. He didn't want to have something wrong with him. And most of all, he didn't want anyone to know. He just didn't want to go on like this. He felt incredibly tired, and he was tired of being tired. Weary of feeling despondent without knowing why. Exhausted by life.

Well, they would certainly know now, he thought. He hadn't been to work in days. He hadn't even been home in . . . how long was it? He had lost all track of time. His hair and clothing were dirty and disheveled, his face was covered with stubble, and he hadn't washed. He didn't want anyone to see him like this. He didn't want to be like this. He just didn't want to be.

He stared out at the lights of the villages spreading out all around him, the artificial world that had enclosed him all his life and had now become so confining that he felt he couldn't breathe. He stepped back from the promenade wall, moving slowly because of the weights tied to his legs. He had done all the right things. Maybe this wasn't the right thing, but it was all he could think to do. It was all he wanted to do anymore. He was tired of feeling the way he felt, weary of the pain, exhausted by the overwhelming sadness. He sat down on the sea side of the wall, his back to the water.

"What the hell?" he said softly, to himself. And then, with a sigh, he just fell backward.

CHAPTER
8

They had found George Takahashi. And, as Karen had expected, he was dead. But unlike the other suicides, Takahashi had taken pains to avoid leaving a mess for someone to find. He had gone up on the retaining wall, weighted himself down, and plunged into the sea. They could have searched the entire ship and never found him, except for the dolphins.

Cruzmark was waiting for her when Karen landed the Security cruiser in the Ramble at the base of the aft retaining wall. Seen from a distance, the seawalls dominated the landscape of the ship's interior, rising to height of over 300 meters and following the curvature of the inner hull. From the promenade atop the wall, the sea and the entire interior of the ship could be seen, affording a spectacular, panoramic view. The artificial suns floating in the zero-g zone were closer from here, and one of them was directly overhead. It was used to simulate a full moon at night, and strollers often walked beneath it.

From where she stood, the sea more closely resembled a giant, ring-shaped waterway that curved up and away from her on both sides. To get from one half of the ship to the other, people took the maglev trains, which traveled through tunnels built below the seabed. At one time, boating had been popular, but people had eventually tired of using the slow, pedal-powered craft in what amounted to a huge ring-shaped canal, and now the small marinas built along the interior of the retaining walls were no longer in use. A visit to the sea usually meant taking a lift up to the promenades, or more often, taking a walk along the garden paths of the Ramble at the base of the walls, watching the fish through the large, rectangular windows. The sight that greeted Karen as she stepped out of the cruiser was nowhere near as pleasant.

The body of George Takahashi was practically unrecognizable. It was bloated and pallid and looked only vaguely human. It had been pulled out of the water and brought down to the Ramble, which was fortunately empty at this time of day. It would not have made a very pleasant sight for strollers.

"The dolphins found him for us," Cruzmark said. "He'd probably still be down there if they hadn't come across his body. They nibbled loose the weights he had tied to his legs and he rose to the surface."

"Who spotted him?" asked Karen.

"Nobody," said Cruzmark. "A walker was taking his morning exercise this morning when one of the dolphins called to him through the translator and told him to call Security. It wouldn't say why. When we got here, we found out. They're not very happy with us."

"What did they say?" asked Karen.

Cruzmark shook his head. "They wouldn't talk to me. You know how dolphins are. They wanted the head fish."

Karen gave him a sour look. "I'm not a fish," she said. "And neither are dolphins, for that matter."

"They live in the water, they've got fins; far as I'm concerned, they're fish," said Cruzmark, wryly.

"Well, if you called them fish, I'm not surprised they wouldn't talk to you," said Karen. "Come on, let's go see what they've got to say." She turned to the other officers, who had pulled out the body. "Take him to Recycling."

She crossed the path with Cruzmark to one of the sea win-

dows, then went up to a translator set into the wall beside it
and pressed a button, sending out a dolphin call. A few moments later, one of the them appeared on the other side.

"I'm Karen Kruickshank, Chief of Security," she said. She
had no idea exactly how the translator would render that. For
all she knew, maybe it said "head fish."

The translator rendered the dolphin's sounds into English,
complete with proper grammar and intonation. In that regard,
it was just like talking to an AI, which was what she was really doing. The translator was merely acting as an intermedi-
ary.

"Why has the dead human been put into the sea with disre-
spect?" the dolphin asked.

The voice that came through the translator was female,
which meant the dolphin was a female. Karen did not know
how the translator determined this. She understood very little
about AI programming, and even less about dolphins. Jenny
was the dolphin expert in the family. Occasionally, dolphins
adopted humans, and when Jenny was a little girl, one of
them had bonded with her and taught her how to swim, dol-
phin-style. Jenny had spent days frolicking with Jilly in the
sea, and Karen had enjoyed watching them together, but she
had never learned to to tell Jilly from the others. All dolphins
looked alike to her, as they did to most humans, something
the dolphins knew and did not particularly appreciate.

She wasn't sure if the dolphin meant it was disrespectful
for Takahashi to have dumped himself into their sea, or if it
was disrespectful for his remains to have been treated that
way. Sometimes, the translation could be imprecise. Or
maybe it was the dolphin that was imprecise.

"We did not dispose of his remains in your environment,"
she explained. "That would be pollution and it would indeed
be disrespectful. He did it himself."

She waited a moment as the translator rendered her words
into dolphin, which she could not hear very well through the
thick window. Dolphins always seemed to smile, but she had
a feeling that this one was not amused at all.

"Why did he do this?" asked the dolphin.

"We don't know," said Karen. "But we're grateful to you

for telling us about it. We were looking for him, and didn't know he had thrown himself into the sea."

She waited again. The dolphin seemed to be considering her reply. It was bobbing its head up and down, which looked as if the dolphin were nodding, but Karen knew that was merely a human interpretation. When dolphins did that, it meant they were trying to figure something out, or decide what to say next.

"Was he sick?"

"He lost the will to live," said Karen. "I suppose that's a form of sickness."

"Why did he not wish to survive?"

"We don't know that, either," said Karen.

"Was he grieving?" The dolphin moved away from the window slowly, with a slight twisting motion, and stared at her very fixedly with one eye. It was very luminous, and at the same time, intense.

Karen was surprised at that. She thought a moment, then said, "Yes, I think so. In a way."

"I am saddened for him."

"So are we," said Karen.

"This has not happened before," the dolphin said.

Karen took that literally, to mean that no one had ever drowned himself in the sea. "No," she said, "and we will try to keep it from happening again."

"We do not want humans to die in our sea."

"We don't want it, either," Karen said.

"Grieving humans should be nurtured," said the dolphin.

"Yes, they should be. And we try. But we didn't know this one was grieving," Karen said. "Nor did we know why."

"There are more humans grieving than before. This is not good."

Karen frowned. "How do you know that?"

"We know," the dolphin replied. "If humans die, will the new ones take their place?"

Karen exchanged glances with Cruzmark. "The new ones?" she said. "You mean the children?"

"No, the new ones that have appeared," the dolphin replied.

"I don't understand," said Karen.

"The new ones."

"We're getting nowhere with this," Cruzmark said, impatiently. "We're wasting our time talking to a fish."

The translator must have relayed his remarks, because the dolphin abruptly turned and swam off.

"Thanks, Ben," Karen said, sarcastically. "That was real helpful."

"The dolphin wasn't any help at all," Cruzmark replied. "Takahashi killed himself. Okay, they found him, because they didn't want his body cluttering up their environment, but we still don't know why he committed suicide."

They walked back to the cruiser. "Did you come up with anything on that name the Marshall girl gave us?" Karen asked.

"No such person on the ship and never was," said Cruzmark.

"Did you run the description?"

"Long hair and pointed ears? Are you serious?"

"Run it," Karen said. "Just in case. I can't see how anyone on the ship would have pointed ears; a deformity like that could never have slipped through the Reproductive Centers, but it can't hurt to be thorough. Maybe somebody made himself a set for some peculiar reason."

"Whatever you say, Chief."

Karen stood by her cruiser and took a deep breath, blowing it out slowly. She glanced at the other cruiser, taking off with Takahashi's body. "I wish I could understand what's happening. The depression stats keep rising and the suicide toll is mounting. What's getting to these people?" She looked up at the top of the wall, trying to imagine Takahashi standing there, with weights tied to his legs, and wondering what could have been going through his mind.

"You got me," said Cruzmark. "I don't know anyone who's depressed. I —"

"Who's that?" asked Karen, suddenly.

Cruzmark followed her gaze. There was a lone figure standing upon the wall, looking down at them. At the distance separating them, it was impossible to see who it was. It was not unusual for people to hike along the promenades, but the officers who brought the body down had not reported seeing anybody up there. It wasn't anyone from Security because of the way he—or perhaps she—was dressed. The figure was wearing a long, hooded cloak, which billowed in the breeze created by the weather systems.

"Didn't the Marshall girl say something about the man she met wearing a long cloak?" asked Karen.

"Yes, she did," said Cruzmark. They both immediately got into the cruiser and lifted off. At their ascent, the cloaked figure moved back from the edge of the wall. Cruzmark accelerated. The cruiser shot up and cleared the top of the wall, giving them a view of the promenade below. The stranger was running very fast, his cloak flowing behind him. The hood had fallen back, and Karen saw the long black hair.

"It's a woman," Cruzmark said.

"No, I don't think so," Karen replied, hailing the running stranger through the cruiser's PA. "Attention. This is Security. Stop where you are immediately."

He kept on running.

"Look at him go!" said Cruzmark.

"Let's take him," Karen said.

They shot down, accelerating at full speed as Cruzmark went in low over the walkway, rapidly closing the distance between them. "He's heading for the lift."

"He'll reach it before we do," Karen said. "Drop me here, then cut him off at the bottom."

The stranger darted into the lift housing just ahead of them. Cruzmark slowed just above the walkway and Karen jumped out, running after the fugitive as Cruzmark skimmed over the guardrail and descended. They had him now. There was nowhere for him to go.

Karen ran through the archway of the lift housing and the stunning impact knocked her off her feet as she slammed into a wall and fell, shaken. It took a moment or two for her to recover. She had run into a nanalloy wall sealing off the entrance. She sat up, groaning, and stared with confusion at the wall just inside the archway.

"Damn . . ." said Karen. She pressed the hollow just behind her left earlobe, activating her link. "Ben! Ben, have you got him?"

"No, have you?" came the reply.

"Didn't he come down?"

"The lift came down all right, but there was no one in it."

"Are you *sure*?"

"Of course, I'm sure."

"That's impossible," she said.

"You want me to send it up for you?"

"No, take it up yourself. I want you to see this."

"I'll be right there."

She waited a moment or two, then heard him over the link once more.

"What's this wall doing here?"

"Good question," she said. "Any sign of him in there?"

"No. And there's no place to hide, either."

"When did this get sealed off?"

"About a second after he went inside. I ran right into it and almost knocked myself out."

"Are you all right?"

"I'm okay. Hold on a moment." She called CAC Support. "This is Chief Kruickshank," she said. "Give me a link with Architectural Control."

She waited a moment.

"Okay, go ahead, Chief."

She had no need to identify herself to the AI; it could read her link signal. "Who ordered the seal on the upper entrance to lift housing 14?"

"There's no record of a seal order on that structure."

"Well, it's sealed. Open it."

A moment later, the nanalloy wall inside the archway flowed, melting back to open the passageway. Ben Cruzmark stood on the other side.

"This is the damnedest thing I ever saw," he said. "Where could he have gone?"

"I'd like to know how he threw a wall up in front of me on what's supposed to be a nonmodifiable structure," she said. "The only way he could have done it was through an authorized seal order. And according to Architectural Control, there wasn't one."

"Except he did it," Cruzmark said. He shook his head. "But how?"

"All right, let's suppose he had authorization, or managed to fake it somehow. The only way he could have done it so quickly would have been to call the order in as we were lifting up here. Except if he had done that, it would have been recorded, and it wasn't."

"Then it's got to be a malfunction," Cruzmark said.

"We can run a diagnostic to make sure," said Karen, "but if it's not, then it means we've got someone on board who's figured out a way to bypass Architectural Control and modify what are supposed to be permanent nanalloy structures."

"That's impossible," said Cruzmark.

"Well, I just ran right into the impossible and damn near broke my face on it," Karen said.

"Point taken."

"He must have gone into the shaft and then ridden the lift down on the outside. He got out when you came up."

"But then how did he get the door open?"

"The same way he got the wall up, probably. It's a neat trick. And if we don't find out who he is and how he did it, we could have a real problem on our hands."

"I wasn't sure if you were going to come," Ulysses said, when Jenny arrived at his place after school. There was no one else at home. His dad would not be back until just before dinnertime, and his mom was still out. Jenny had arrived later than she usually did, and Riley hadn't shown up at all.

"I wanted to stop off at my place and pick something up first," she said, as she came in. "Where's Riley?"

"He just called a few minutes ago. He said he couldn't come today. He had to do something at home."

That was what he said, anyway, but Ulysses didn't believe it. He thought Riley had just made up that excuse to give him and Jenny a chance to be alone. But without Riley there, he suddenly felt uncomfortable. He had imagined all the things he'd say to her if the opportunity arose, but now, he found himself feeling awkward and at a loss for words.

He had never been alone with Jenny before, except briefly in the quest, when she had kissed him. And that was only a VR kiss. Maybe that was why she did it, because it didn't really count. Or did it? Their lips had never actually touched; they had only experienced the sensation through the interface. And had she done it because she wanted to, or because the sim had prompted her to add an element of romance to the quest? She hadn't said anything about it, and he felt nervous about asking her.

He had wondered, afterward, if she had ever done VR sex. Chances were she had. Sometimes he thought he was the only one who had never tried it. Technically, you couldn't do it without parental permission until you were eighteen, but that was only a formality. He knew most parents gave permission early, to avoid irresponsible experimentation. Riley had done it. I'll bet everyone's done it but me, he thought. He was curious about it, but he didn't want to do it with just anyone, even if it was only VR.

As Riley had pointed out before, he could easily have the sim with Jenny's body, face, and voice. The program could simulate those characteristics based on his implant interface, but it would only look and sound like Jenny. It wouldn't *be* her. The sensations he'd experience would be dictated by the program, not by anything she might think or do in real life.

And though he knew a lot of people did it that way, it was really nothing more than a high-tech way of masturbating. He wanted Jenny, not some VR construct that only looked and sounded like her.

Now he was alone with her. For real. In his house. He had pictured this scene many times, but in his imagination, he had never felt so nervous. He knew she liked him now, that should have made it easier. Why didn't it?

As she entered, he saw that she was carrying a folder. She handed it to him, hesitantly, with her crooked smile that he liked so much.

"What's this?" he asked.

"Well . . . you said you wanted to see my drawings," she replied, shyly.

"Oh, right. I'm glad you brought them. Come on in the living room. Can I get you anything?"

"No, thanks."

They sat down together on the couch and Ulysses opened the folder. The first picture was a landscape scene of the ship's interior. It showed a wide perspective, depicting a view from the parks and forest at the aft end of the ship. In the foreground, there were some trees and drone-manicured lawns and paths, with people walking, then the panorama of the ship spread out to fill the drawing. The villages dotted the background, with a maglev train running along its elevated track. The drawing showed the gradual curvature of the inner hull, with distant villages, along with the CAC complex and the retaining wall at the equator. The artificial suns floated in the zero-g zone, partially obscured by clouds.

"Hey, this is really something," he said.

"Thanks."

"It must have taken you a long time to do," he said.

"Well, I try to put as much as I can into each drawing," she said. "I usually start out with a broad sketch, and then work on filling in the details. Sometimes I work on the same one for weeks."

"What's this over here?" he asked, pointing at a strange-looking creature shown flying up above the clouds. It looked vaguely familiar. It had broad, red, scaled wings, and its body was long and thin, ending in a barbed tail. The head was triangular, with a long snout filled with sharp teeth.

"I put that in the other night," she said. "I don't know why, really. I just thought it would look interesting there."

It clicked. "It's from that painting on your shield in the quest," he said.

"It's called a dragon," she said.

"Right, a dragon," he said. Then he frowned. "You know, nobody ever told us that's what it was. But we both knew, so it must be subliminal knowledge from the sim. But why do we need to know about some creature called a dragon?"

"Maybe we're supposed to run into one during the quest," she said.

"I hope not," said Ulysses, uneasily. "I don't much like the way it looks."

He turned to the next picture. She had done a drawing of the fairies dancing in the glade, just as they had seen them in the quest. The three of them were in the drawing as well, dressed as they were in the sim and watching in the foreground.

"This is really great," Ulysses said, nodding his head with admiration. "This is exactly what it looked like. I've never seen anything like it. Where did you learn how to do this?"

She shrugged. "I don't know. I just do it."

In the next drawing, they were standing around the table in the pavilion that had appeared in the glade. Ulysses was impressed by her skill. The drawing was so realistic, he might almost have been looking at a holographic representation, except it wasn't three-dimensional. She had captured the expressions on their faces perfectly. They were looking with wonder at the crystal, in which the image of the unicorn appeared. Ulysses stared at it for a few moments. He hadn't known what to expect, but it certainly wasn't anything like this.

"I did that one last night," she said.

"It's so lifelike," he said, looking at all the detail in the picture. She had put so much into it—the amazed expression on Riley's face, her own look of wonder, and the entranced gaze with which Ulysses had stared at the fairies as they held him back. She had used different colors to create the effects of light and shadow. He couldn't imagine how she had managed just to sit down and draw it like that from memory.

"You really think it's good?" she asked, anxiously.

"I've never seen anything like it before," he replied. "It's almost like a computer-generated graphic, but it's different. It's . . . I don't know, softer, somehow. And it looks almost three-dimensional. How did you do that?"

"I'm not really sure," she said. "I just sort of close my eyes and see it, then I draw it. The stuff in the background looks like it's farther away because I just make it smaller."

"How do you make this part here, where it looks like shadow?"

"I just sort of hold the pencil sideways and make soft

back-and-forth strokes, filling it all in gently, without pressing so hard," she said.

"I can't believe your mom disapproves of this."

For a moment, neither of them spoke as Ulysses continued to look at the pictures. Then she said, "It happened last year."

Ulysses didn't say anything.

"Do you want to know who it was?"

"No," he said.

"It wasn't anyone I really cared about," she said, looking at him. "I just wanted to find out what it was like to do it for real. It only happened once."

"We don't have to talk about this, you know," Ulysses said, uncomfortably.

"I know. But I want you to understand. Haven't you ever wondered what it was like?"

Ulysses rolled his eyes and sighed. "All the time."

"And you've never wanted to try it?"

He shrugged. "Well, yeah, but . . ." He shrugged again. "I figured I'd find out when I took Sexual Responsibility and Orientation."

"You mean you've never even done it in VR? Your parents never logged you on for the SRO sims?" she asked.

"We never even talked about it," Ulysses said. He shrugged. "My dad still treats me like a little boy. We never talk about anything. Or he talks and I just listen, and it's usually him telling me how I should try harder and be more focused and all that. I just can't imagine him logging me on for a home session of VR sex and then us sitting around and discussing it. I think he'd rather wait and let the school take care of it, so he won't have to deal with it."

"My mom had me take the course at home when I was fourteen," said Jenny, "and then she cleared me for the erotisims. She wanted to make sure I understood it from both gender viewpoints. She didn't want me to make any mistakes and go through Dissolution, like she did."

"I can understand that," said Ulysses. He hesitated slightly. "What were they like?"

"It's hard to describe, if you've never done it," she replied. "The course was just like having sex, only you were getting the sensory input of the instructor. I mean, it felt real and she was good at it, but it was her experience, not mine. And it wasn't spontaneous at all, because she kept talking through it all, explaining things. So I learned how it works, but I still thought, suppose *I* wasn't any good? Mom thought that was pretty funny when I asked her. She laughed and said not to worry.

"She said good sex was a learning process," Jenny continued, "but the erotisims would help take care of that. It was the emotional part that was complicated. We talked about that a lot, because she said it was the most important thing. The interesting part was when I did it from the male perspective in VR. It's really different for males." She grinned. "It's sort of funny, *me* telling you about it."

Ulysses made a face, self-consciously. "Well, I've never done it."

"It's nothing to be embarrassed about. I just can't believe you've never talked to anyone about this. Not even Riley?"

"Oh, yeah, Riley would be just the one to ask. He probably fell in love with the instructor."

"Well, it's really no big deal. I just wanted you to know there wasn't anybody else, that's all."

"Jenny . . ." He couldn't look at her. He knew that if he did, he'd never get the words out. He had imagined himself saying it to her dozens of times, but it had never seemed so hard. He took a deep breath. "Look, Jenny . . . there's something I've been wanting to tell you for a long time. I . . ." The words suddenly seemed frozen in his throat, blocking off his ability to breathe.

She took his hand. "I love you, too," she said.

He felt light-headed. " . . . I can't believe it."

She smiled. "Why not? Everybody else does. I think you're the only one who didn't know."

"But I heard you told Dave Foster you'd already Chosen someone."

"Well, who did you think I meant? I don't want to Choose anyone else, Ulysses, I want you."

"But . . . why me?"

She rolled her eyes in exasperation. "You want me to *explain* it to you? I don't know, maybe that's why. Because you're different. You think about things. I feel comfortable with you. When you're not around, I think about you, and . . . I don't know, I just don't *feel* the same way about anybody else. How do you explain something like that? Can you explain the way you feel about *me*?"

He looked at her. Suddenly, it wasn't hard at all. Everything he had ever wanted to say to her just came tumbling out. "The first time I saw you, it was during our first year of junior high school. I didn't know who you were, but you passed me in the hall and you just stood out from everybody else. You were talking to another girl, so I don't even think you saw me, but I couldn't see anybody else. I thought you were the prettiest girl I'd ever seen. I watched you walk away and I thought, she walks like she knows exactly where she's going and exactly what she's going to do when she gets there.

"I found out who you were and I started watching for you," he continued. "I'd go to school hoping that I'd see you, and when I didn't, I always felt like the day had been a total waste. I like hearing the sound of your voice. I like the way you sit with your legs crossed and point your toe and turn your foot around in little circles. I like the way you brush your hair back out of your face with just your fingertips. I like that sort of dreamy, faraway look you get when you're thinking about something. I like the shape of your legs; the way you always get this thoughtful look and tilt your head before you say something; the way you smile; the way you laugh; the way you always hold your head up when you walk. I think about you when I go to bed at night and I think about you when I get up and in between I sometimes dream about you. Just looking at you makes me feel good, and I've thought about telling you all these things about a million times, but I never knew just how to do it without sounding stupid."

She stared at him, her lips slightly parted. "I don't know, I thought that was pretty good, myself."

"It was?"

"Shut up and kiss me."

They slowly leaned toward each other and Ulysses held his breath as their lips came together softly. She gently put her hand on the back of his neck and it sent a chill through him. He started to put his arms around her as she parted her lips and slowly slipped her tongue into his mouth, and then his mother walked in.

They sprang apart, and Ulysses knew he was blushing furiously, but he couldn't help it.

His mother stared at them, startled for a moment, then smiled. "I'm sorry, I didn't mean to interrupt," she said, in an amused tone. She approached them, holding out her hand. "You must be Jenny. Hi, I'm Sonja Buckland."

Jenny took her hand shyly and said hello.

"Well, I have to leave for an appointment," Sonja said. She glanced down at the pictures spread out on the table and gasped as she saw Jenny's drawing of the fairies. She snatched it up, staring at it with astonishment. "*Where* did you get this?"

"Jenny drew it," said Ulysses.

"You did this?" Sonja said, staring at Jenny. "Then you've seen them, too! *Where? When?*"

Ulysses and Jenny exchanged glances. "We've seen them, too?" said Jenny. "You mean, you've seen fairies yourself?"

"Fairies?" Sonja said, with a puzzled frown. "Why do you call them fairies?"

"Well . . . that's what they're called," said Jenny, with an uncertain glance at Ulysses.

"What do you mean that's what they're called?" asked Sonja. "How do you know that?"

Jenny glanced at Ulysses, but he looked as confused and surprised as she felt. "Because . . . it's in the file," she said.

Sonja frowned. "What file?"

"The Folklore, Mythology, and Legends file," said Ulysses. "You mean you knew about this, Mom? I thought we were the only ones!"

"No, I saw them, too," she said. "They were eating the herb crop, only nobody believed me when I told them. They thought I was working too hard and wanted me to go for Counseling. But now . . ."

Ulysses and Jenny looked at each other, wide-eyed. "Wait

a minute," said Ulysses. "You actually *saw* fairies on the ship? I mean, for *real*?"

His mother looked at him and frowned. "What do you mean, 'for real'? You saw them, too, didn't you?"

Ulysses shook his head. "Only in the sim, Mom," he said.

"What sim?"

"The quest sim," said Ulysses. "I thought *that's* what you were talking about."

"Okay, let's back up and start at the beginning," Sonja said, joining them on the couch. "What exactly are we talking about here?"

Ulysses glanced at Jenny uncertainly.

"I think we'd better tell her the whole story," Jenny said.

"I wish you would," said Sonja. "You seem to know more about this than I do. How? What is this quest sim?"

"Well, it started in class one day," Ulysses said.

"I can't believe this. You had a sim about these things in *school*?"

"Not exactly," said Ulysses. "Nobody else got it. Only me, Jenny, and Riley did. Everybody else got the sim they were supposed to get, but for some reason, the three of us got the quest. But first we had the dream."

"What dream?"

"About Dr. Seldon," Jenny said.

"Dr. Penelope Seldon?" asked Sonja, with a frown.

"That's right," Ulysses said. "Only we didn't know who she was at first. It was only later, after we found out who she was in Professor Wesala's class, that we realized we all had the same dream. And that was the same day that the quest sim started."

Sonja listened intently as Ulysses told her all about the dream and the beginning of the VR quest, and what they had discovered about Dr. Seldon and her missing Counseling file. And the more she listened, the more frightened she became.

CHAPTER
9

Karen smiled at the woman who stood in the entryway of the residence in London Village. "Mrs. Kantrowitz?"

"Yes?"

"I'm Security Chief Kruickshank. Sorry to disturb you, but Dr. Ridgeway's AI said that I could find him here."

"Oh, yes, of course. Please come in."

She entered the tidy living room and looked around, seeing no one else present.

"He's in the kitchen, fixing the sink."

"Fixing the sink?" said Karen, raising her eyebrows.

She went into the kitchen and saw a pair of legs in dirty coveralls sticking out from the cabinet underneath the sink. "Dr. Ridgeway?"

"Just a second . . ." There was the sound of metal clanking against metal, and then the rest of the body materialized, a stocky, middle-aged man of medium height with curly brown hair and a close-cropped beard. He smiled at her as he put down his wrench. "There, that ought to do it."

He turned on the water and watched it flowing down the

drain for a moment, then nodded to himself, satisfied, and shut it off. He turned toward her, smiling. "Hello, Chief. I see you've tracked me down." He stuck out his hand, then noticed it was dirty and pulled it back, wiping it on a greasy cloth apologetically. "Sorry about that."

"Your AI said you were out on a call," said Karen, with a frown.

"So I was," Ridgeway replied. "Stopped up sink." He grinned when he saw the expression on her face. "You're thinking what's the Director of Counseling doing fixing a sink? It's my secondary specialty. There's not much call for a psychiatrist aboard the *Agamemnon*, but people can always use a good plumber."

"I see," said Karen, watching as he put away his tools.

"I was going to give you a call later this afternoon," said Ridgeway, as he neatly packed the tools away in the box. "I've been rather busy this morning. This is my third call."

"There's been another suicide," she said.

Ridgeway sighed, heavily. "Damn." He picked up his toolbox. "Come on, let's talk outside."

He informed Mrs. Kantrowitz that the sink was fixed, then they went out into the courtyard and sat on one of the benches beneath a blooming acacia tree.

Karen came right to the point. "People are killing themselves and you're fixing stopped-up sinks? I was hoping you'd be working on our investigation."

"Oh, I have been, rest assured of that," Ridgeway replied. "I've been pulling a lot of late nights, reviewing the cases and thinking of almost nothing else. But working with my hands helps me organize my thoughts. And crisis or no crisis, sinks still need to be fixed."

Karen grimaced. "So have you made any progress?"

"Not very much, I'm afraid," he said, scratching his head. "There's been a marked increase in the incidence of depression. And that's just the reported cases, the people who come in for Counseling. It's a good bet that there are even more out there, but people in denial aren't going to seek therapy. That's probably been a factor with most of the suicides. They haven't come in for Counseling."

"Most of them?" said Karen.

"Of the total number of suicides we've had so far, five had sought Counseling," Ridgeway said.

"And it didn't help," said Karen, flatly.

"Obviously not."

"The question is why didn't it help?"

"Well, it's impossible to say, really," Ridgeway replied. "Psychiatry is not an exact science. I could tell you a lot more about plumbing. I always know that I can fix a stopped-up sink or a leaky toilet. People are considerably more complex. Give me a leaky toilet, any day."

"What we've got on our hands is something a lot more serious than a leaky toilet," Karen said, irritated at his tone.

"Look, don't get me wrong," Ridgeway replied. "I'm not making light of this. I know it's serious. What I don't know is why it's happening. You have to understand that my function as Director of Counseling is essentially redundant." He made a face. "Redundant hell, it's downright superfluous. The only reason my position even exists is because the mission planners were pressured to have humans in the loop, at least in a nominal supervisory capacity. But I'm not really necessary. The Counseling AIs handle all the therapy, and they're much better at it than I could ever hope to be. They don't have to consult the literature, they can monitor body functions and read such subtle clues as body language and tone of voice more efficiently than any human, and their emotions don't get in the way. They don't get tired; they don't get frustrated; they don't suffer from transference anxiety. In short, they're much better therapists. I've got the necessary training, but I've never actually practiced psychiatry. No one chooses it for their primary specialty anymore, and only a handful of people ever choose it as a secondary specialty, usually because they only find it interesting from a theoretical standpoint."

"So what are you telling me?" asked Karen.

"What I'm telling you is that I don't really feel qualified to deal with this," said Ridgeway. "I mean, I understand what depression is, and I know how to treat it, in theory at least, but I can't tell you how to spot suicides before they happen. And I can't point to any one thing specifically and say that's what's causing it." He shrugged. "It's not that simple. I'm just not sure if I can be of any real help to you."

"But you've got access to the Counseling files," said Karen. "You said you've been reviewing the cases."

"That's right."

"So then you could give me a list of all the individuals currently in Counseling, particularly those suffering from depression."

"No, I'm afraid I can't," said Ridgeway.

"What do you mean, you can't? Why not?"

"Because it would be unethical, a violation of the patient-therapist relationship."

"But you're not the therapist."

"No, I'm not. The Counseling AIs handle the therapy. I'm just a glorified administrator who's got nothing else to do but fix people's plumbing."

"So what's the problem?"

"The problem is that I'm still Director of Counseling, and even if it's only a nominal position, ethically, I couldn't comply with your request. If someone were dead, or had been ordered to undertake Counseling because of socially disruptive behavior, then that would be a somewhat different matter. But if someone has voluntarily entered therapy, the most I could do was discuss pertinent details of the case with the Counseling AI. I couldn't even get the patient's identity. The therapist AI would not release it."

"But you're Director of Counseling."

"It makes no difference. I've got access to the files, but only in a limited sense. Anything that would reveal the identity of a patient who's undertaken voluntary Counseling is simply not available to me. That's the way the AIs were programmed. It's an ethical issue, and a matter of individual civil rights."

"That's absurd," said Karen. "People's lives are at stake."

"It's not at all absurd, if you stop to think about it," Ridgeway said. "Why is there only a small full-time Security force and the rest of your personnel serve limited tours of duty? It was set up that way to prevent the possibility of any sort of totalitarian takeover. The same principle applies in this case. If that kind of information were available to me, or to Security or CAC, it could all too easily be abused. People in treatment have a right to privacy, to confidentiality."

"Do they have a right to die?"

"Interesting question," Ridgeway replied. "When we reach a certain age, we have the right to choose the option of early recycling. In essence, that's exercising the right to die, isn't it?"

"But these people aren't old," Karen replied. "They haven't lived full and productive lives. Something's happened to them, they've become unbalanced, and we can't simply stand by and let them kill themselves, for God's sake. We have to do something. Whatever's happening to them could happen to the rest of us unless we can figure out what it is and stop it."

Ridgeway sighed. "I don't really disagree with you. But I can't give you what you want. Even if I could, I wouldn't. We can't arbitrarily violate the rights of our citizens."

"Not even for their own good?"

"Do you want somebody making a decision like that for you?" Ridgeway shook his head. "People already distrust Counseling. There's a stigma attached to it. The biggest hurdle people who are troubled have to make is to decide to enter therapy. Nobody wants to admit there might be something wrong with them. No one wants to think they're maladjusted, unbalanced, or unproductive. So people who go in for Counseling rarely talk about it." He looked around. "We've created a perfect world here, and nobody wants to admit that they might not fit in." He shook his head. "It's okay for sinks to get stopped-up, but not people."

"So then what the hell have you been doing all this time? Chasing leaks?"

"There's no need to be hostile," Ridgeway said. "I've been studying the individual cases and searching for patterns. The AIs won't release the identities of the people currently undergoing voluntary therapy, but we can discuss the cases in a general sense."

"And?"

"And there is a pattern. But I'm not sure what it means.

We do seem to have a syndrome on our hands, but I have no idea what's triggering it."

"Stop telling me what you don't know and tell me what you do know," Karen said.

Ridgeway sighed. "All right. It seems to start with a sort of general lassitude, a feeling of ennui. It apparently comes on gradually, but the progression is steady. You start to feel tired, dispirited, bored. Physical activity doesn't seem to help, or at best it only helps temporarily. Work and VR recreation also become only temporary stopgaps until they cease helping altogether. It becomes difficult to rationalize getting out of bed to face another day of the same old routine. You become tired of performing the same job, seeing the same faces, doing the same things. And you become physically tired as well, although that seems to be more a function of the emotional state than anything physiological. You start to withdraw from other people, and in the process, you also gradually start withdrawing from yourself. In most of the cases, the people have known that there was something wrong with them, but they didn't want to admit it to themselves. And hiding it from everybody, coworkers, friends, and family, only added to the stress. It was very difficult to accept the fact that they needed Counseling. And that's just among the ones who entered therapy. Others who may have the same problem are probably in denial, and they resist seeking any help until they feel it's just too late. By that time, they've grown so despondent, they feel they simply can't go on. Guilt probably sets in, and self-recrimination and self-loathing, and eventually they just decide it isn't worth it to go on living. They just want an end to the pain."

"But why?" asked Karen. "What's causing it?"

Ridgeway shrugged. "I couldn't tell you. All I know is that among those who have voluntarily sought Counseling, we've only been able to treat the symptoms, not the cause. Using drugs, we're helping them maintain a level of functionality, but if we take them off the medication, chances are they'll be right back where they started. Most of them don't seem to be getting any worse, but they're not getting any better, either. It's as if they've lost something and we can't help them find it again because we don't know what it is."

"And the AIs haven't got a clue?" said Karen.

"Well, they're not mind readers. Their function as therapists is based on what the patients tell them. Granted, they can infer a great deal, based on tone, body language, and behavior patterns they're programmed to recognize, but they're not really capable of intuition. To put it another way, they can only make educated guesses, not inspired ones. Much of what a therapist does is based on helping the patient realize something he or she already knows, on some subconscious level. Well, these people know that they're depressed. But they haven't got the faintest idea why. Something has gone out of their lives, but they don't know what."

"So what you're saying is that you don't have any answers," Karen said.

"Only questions, Chief," Ridgeway replied, wearily. "Only questions. And I don't mind telling you, it's starting to make me feel depressed."

Karen gave him a sharp glance.

"Bad joke," he said. And then he shrugged and grimaced. "Not all that much of a joke, really. It's really starting to get to me." He glanced at her. "And yes, I'm getting some Counseling myself. I don't want to end up like the others did." He snorted. "I've got a few more sinks to fix."

Riley walked down the main aisle of the school library, past the individual VR couches, feeling a little apprehensive. There were several students occupying a number of the couches, reviewing some of the VR sims for the upcoming exams. They didn't see him, of course. They were tilted back, their eyes rolled up and showing white, their hands and arms and legs making peculiar, pantomime movements every once in a while to match whatever they were experiencing in the sims. Not everyone reacted that way. Some people didn't move at all, their bodies remaining passive despite whatever vicarious activities they might be experiencing in VR. Riley didn't know whether he moved or not. He hoped not. To someone watching, it looked pretty silly, even though it was perfectly normal.

He walked over to an empty couch. The lights came on automatically as he sat down. He took the VR band off its hook on the small console by the side of the couch and slipped it around his neck. He felt nervous, tense with anticipation. Ever since he'd told Jenny and Ulysses that he wasn't anxious to virtch into the quest world on his own, he had felt upset with himself. It bothered him that he was doing this behind their backs. They were his friends and it felt like a betrayal, but at the same time, he wanted to get some answers for them. Or was it just that he wanted to get a jump on them, despite their friendship? Trying this alone made him feel apprehensive and a little bit afraid, but he felt as if he really hadn't accomplished much in the quest so far and he wanted to do better. Perhaps too much so. It was what his parents referred to as his "competitive instinct."

"I don't know why you always try so hard to be better than everybody else," his mother always told him. "Don't you realize that's a way of devaluing them as people?"

"That's right, son," his father would say, nodding sagely. "You're no better than anybody else, you know, and you shouldn't try to be. It's socially disruptive. For a community to thrive, people have to support one another, not try to outdo each other all the time. Aggressive tendencies are socially counterproductive. Remember that for every winner, there has to be a loser. And no one likes to lose."

His father never failed to agree with whatever his mother said. And she agreed with him. They always double-teamed him that way. And they called him "competitive." Well, he just didn't see it that way. What was wrong with trying to do your best? What was wrong with trying to do better than others? If everyone felt that way, then everyone would try to do better all the time. Wouldn't that help the community to thrive? However, his parents had no patience with that argument. "An atmosphere of mutual support and noncompetitive solidarity is psychologically more beneficial for people and produces the optimum social dynamic. People who manifest aggressive, competitive behavior only disrupt the equilibrium of the community." He had heard it so many times, he knew it by heart.

So maybe there was something wrong with him. Why didn't they send him into Counseling, then? They were always hinting at it, holding it over him as some sort of threat. He knew why they wouldn't do it, though. Because then they'd be known as the parents of a boy who was sent in for Counseling. Parents of a boy who manifested socially disruptive tendencies. And that, of course, would suggest that perhaps they were at fault. They might even have to go in for Counseling themselves, to determine whether or not that was the case. And that was the last thing they wanted. They didn't want their friends and neighbors to think they had messed up. So Riley knew that unless he acted too aggressive, such as in PT or OS, and was ordered in for Counseling by the school, nothing would be done.

Since he didn't want to go for Counseling, he tried to rein it in most times. During Organized Sports, he tried to restrain himself. In Netball, he usually made a point of hitting the ball directly to someone on the other side, the way he was supposed to, and only occasionally made a shot that couldn't be returned. And when he did so, he always apologized profusely, as if it was an accident and he had just slipped. In reality, he was backspinning the ball against the Coriolis force, just enough to give the opponent an absolute fit. But inwardly, he'd smile, because it felt good. It would feel even better if they *tried* to hit it back, but they never did. They'd just stare at the ball with annoyance as it hurtled past them, then look at him and say, *"Riley!"* in a whining tone.

"Sorry, sorry, I didn't mean to hit it that way. . . ."

As a result, they simply thought he wasn't very good. It was the same with swimming. The idea was to swim laps in such a way that they all touched the wall together, so that no one lagged behind and no one was ahead. It was supposed to develop a communal spirit of cooperation. But every now and then, he'd burst out ahead of all the others, and when he was criticized for it, he pretended that he had misjudged where the others were. The teachers in charge of OS assumed that he wasn't very good at Organized Sports, that he would grow too anxious and would mess up as a result. He didn't care. Let them think what they wanted. They still wouldn't give him bad grades. That would be bad for his self-esteem. They'd encourage him to "try harder." Well, he *did* try harder. What they really meant was *"don't* try so hard."

The quest, on the other hand, was different. In some ways, it scared him, because he didn't know what it all meant or where it was going, but in other ways, that made it all the more interesting. Part of him wondered about Dr. Seldon, whether she had been sick when she wrote the program and if maybe, as a result, it was dangerous. But at the same time, there was a thrill to that, as well. And it finally occurred to him that for all its mystery, there was one thing about the quest that kept him wanting to go back. In the quest, he didn't have to hold back for anybody. Up till now, he really hadn't had much chance to do anything. It seemed that Jenny and Ulysses had done it all. Well, maybe it was time to change that.

Jenny and Ulysses finally had a chance to be alone, and if Ulysses wasn't a total glitch and messed it up, maybe this would give them a chance to get together. In a way, he envied Ulysses a little. Jenny was pretty terrific. But at the same time, he was happy for him. He wouldn't have minded being in his place, but Jenny wasn't the right girl for him. Eventually, he'd meet the right one. Especially if it turned out he could solve the riddle of the quest.

He didn't think they had much time to continue with the quest. Sooner or later, somebody would find out about it and then they'd probably lose it. He was pretty sure it wasn't an authorized program, and that meant that as soon as they found out it existed, CAC or Security would get right on it and try to track it down. Jenny's mom would probably take charge of the whole thing. They'd all have to answer lots of questions and they would be asked to explain why they hadn't told anyone about it and they'd never find out how the whole thing ended. Riley wanted to know. And wouldn't it be great if he got a jump on Jenny and Ulysses and managed to solve it on his own? Or at least give them all a good head start. Assuming it would work without them. Well, that was one of the things they had wanted to find out.

He took a deep breath to steady his nerves. Okay, he thought, what happens now? How do I start? In the past, every time they'd done it, it had been in school and the teacher had called up a sim from the program library. He supposed he could call up just any sim, it probably didn't matter. If the program recognized them, as it seemed to, then he'd get the quest sim no matter which one he called up. Or else, he wouldn't get it, because the program would only work if all three of them did it together. Either way, he'd find out. He slipped the VR band around his head and adjusted it.

Immediately, the couch tilted back and the headrest light dimmed. He started to feel the familiar, dizzy, falling sensation as his senses became detached from his immediate surroundings. He hadn't even called up a sim. It had started by itself. This is it, he thought, excitedly. It's going to work!

The trail stretched out ahead of him. Immediately before him, he could see the unicorn's neck and head from the back, its spiral horn rising up in front of him. He was sitting on it, riding it! He felt the gentle rolling motion as it walked, apparently without his exerting any control over it. He was just riding it, and it was taking him somewhere. Right, he thought, remembering, that's how it's supposed to work. The unicorn would take him to the next stage of the quest.

He looked around. He was alone. There was no sign of Jenny and Ulysses. That told him something right away, something important. It answered one of their questions about the quest. They weren't merely constructs in it—constructs based upon themselves—experiencing a simulated perspective. They were actually maintaining their own perspectives in the sim. The fact that he was alone proved it. Jenny and Ulysses would only be there with him if they were all virtching at the same time.

As the unicorn moved at a steady gait along the trail, the forest around them grew deeper and thicker. He couldn't tell what time of day it was. The tree branches overhead practically blocked out all the sun. Only a few rays came streaming through, casting shafts of light down on the trail ahead of him. It could have been morning or afternoon, he had no way of knowing. It felt disquieting to be here by himself.

It's just a sim, he thought. Nothing real can happen to you in a sim. At least, he was pretty sure it couldn't. But then, this was no ordinary sim. Something seemed different, but he couldn't quite tell what it was at first. Then, after a few moments, he realized what it was. Everything was quiet. Before, they had heard birds chirping in the trees. Now, there were no birds. Or if there were, they weren't making any noise. Why?

A moment later, he heard something. A distant, rumbling sort of sound. He couldn't tell what it was. The unicorn perked up its ears. Whatever it was, it was coming from the trail behind him, and it was getting closer. He'd heard a sound something like that before, but he couldn't remember when. It was coming closer very quickly, becoming more distinct. Suddenly, the unicorn picked up its pace and started galloping, and then he realized what the sound was. Hooves beating on the ground.

The unicorn galloped around a bend in the trail as he gripped tightly with his legs and clutched its mane to keep from being bounced right off its back. Then, suddenly, the unicorn plunged off the trail and into the woods. It crashed through a low thicket and went a short distance in, then stopped behind a thick, tall clump of bushes that hid them from view. Moments later, the sounds of the hoofbeats grew louder, and, through the trees, Riley saw two riders coming up the trail. They reined in a short distance away, close enough to his hiding place that he could see them clearly, and he recognized the two ruffians from the tavern, Gar and Corwin.

"Something is wrong," said Corwin, frowning as he stared down at the trail, then glanced around him. "The track has disappeared completely."

"I told you something was wrong when we came to the spot where they stopped," said Gar. "First we follow three walking, now we follow one who is mounted. I tell you, something happened back there. They met up with someone.

There appeared to be signs of a struggle. The ground was churned up, as if they fought the mounted one."

"It makes no sense," said Corwin. "If there was a fight, then where are the bodies? Either they overcame the mounted one or he overcame them. And there was no sign of blood. No, I tell you, something most peculiar is afoot here."

"I still think they left the trail back there," Gar replied.

"There was no sign of it."

"Perhaps we missed it."

"I am not so poor a tracker," Corwin said. "I saw no signs that they had left the trail. But their tracks ended there, and this one's began. An unshod horse, bearing one rider. They could not all three be on the same mount."

"Why not?"

"The tracks would be much deeper, from the added weight," said Corwin.

"One of the males was an adept," said Gar. "And we do not know about the other one. For all we know, the wench may have some eldritch skill, as well."

"So what are you suggesting, that two of them turned into a horse so that the third could ride? Don't be absurd!"

"I still think we should double back and check the sides of the trail to see where they might have gone off into the woods," said Gar.

"What I cannot understand is where the mounted one came from in the first place," Corwin said, with a frown. "Why did their tracks disappear and his begin? And now this track has disappeared. 'Twas clear enough until he began to gallop, and then it grew lighter and lighter, until it faded away completely, almost as if he rode off into the air!"

"Perhaps he did," said Gar, uneasily. "I tell you, we are dealing with magic here! Let us turn back, Corwin. They only lead us deeper into this accursed forest, where they can set a trap for us. And if not them, then like as not we shall fall prey to elves. Is wounded pride worth so much trouble? I say give it up."

Corwin hesitated, his horse pawing nervously at the ground. Then, with a guttural snarl, he turned the horse around. "Arragh! Let the forest swallow them up for all I care! You're right, 'tis not worth the trouble."

"Now you're talking sense," said Gar. "There is no profit in this, anyway."

They kicked their mounts and rode off back the way they had come. Riley exhaled heavily. He had been holding his breath, afraid to make the slightest movement for fear of alerting them. He patted the unicorn's neck. "Thanks, friend," he said.

The unicorn snorted, then turned and started off into the woods.

"Wait! Where are you going?" Riley said. "The trail's back that way!"

But the unicorn kept on going deeper into the forest. Riley had no idea how to turn it around. Gar and Corwin had saddles and reins on their horses . . . He frowned. How did he know they were called saddles and reins? Sim knowledge. Okay, but if he knew that, then why didn't he know how to control the unicorn? Because there was no saddle on it, and he had no reins. And because he was not supposed to control the unicorn. He wasn't supposed to take it anywhere. It was supposed to take him.

"Okay, I guess you know where you're going," Riley said to it. "Anyway, I sure hope you do." He glanced around at the thick woods. "If you don't, I have no idea how I'll ever find my way back to the trail."

It was a good thing those two men turned around and went back the way they came, he thought. He was pretty sure he'd be no match for them alone. And then it occurred to him that what he had just done had helped them all. That he had come back by himself, without Jenny and Ulysses, had thrown Gar and Corwin off. It had unsettled them. If they had all come back together, then Gar and Corwin probably would have continued on their trail. Or maybe not. Maybe the quest program had called for them to turn back. Maybe, if they had all come back together, all three of them would have been riding the unicorn, and the tracks would have disappeared just the same.

"You're magic, aren't you?" he said to the unicorn, patting its neck again. "How else could you have made your tracks disappear? I wonder if you can understand what I'm saying? If you can, shake your head up and down."

The unicorn continued on as before.

"Okay, I guess not," said Riley, ducking beneath some low, overhanging branches. The woods were so thick around them now, it was impossible to see very far. The unicorn continued at a steady pace, threading its way between the trees, its hooves crunching on the carpet of dry twigs and fallen leaves.

The farther they went, the more apprehensive Riley became. The experience was so real, he had to keep reminding himself it was only a sim. That he was experiencing it from his own perspective, instead of someone else's, and that it was his real perspective, and not a simulation based upon a construct drawn from an interface with his mind, made it seem that much more real. In a way, thought Riley, it was real. That's where this sim was different. If he accomplished nothing else, he had at least learned that.

No wonder it seemed easy to maintain your own perspective in the quest, he thought. It was designed for that. In the sim, he was real, or at least his mind was. His body, obviously, was a VR construct, but it felt real because the sim had disconnected him from his own senses and was supplying sensory input based upon the VR construct of his body. So that means whatever happens to my body won't be real, he thought, even though it will *feel* real. That gave him a measure of security.

Still, suppose something happened that was painful? Just because you couldn't experience death in any of the other sims was no reason to assume that this one was the same. The quest was different in a lot of ways. Suppose Gar and Corwin had found him and stabbed him with their swords? Just how far into realism did the sim go? What would it feel like to have a sword plunged into his chest? He grimaced as he thought about it. He didn't really want to find out.

The few shafts of sunlight that were penetrating through the forest canopy were growing fainter. It was going to be night soon. He wondered how long this session would last. The other ones had all cut off at the same time as the regularly programmed classroom sims had cut off. So there had to be a link of some sort, allowing the program to recognize when the other sims being run at the same time had stopped. But this time, he wasn't in the classroom, and there was no other sim running concurrently. Everyone else in the library was running individual sessions, and the start and stop times would all be different. Would this session run for a similar length of time and stop, or would it just keep going? He wished he'd thought of that before.

It was growing dark. Soon, he wouldn't be able to see anything. He knew he had some candles in his pack, but how much light would a candle give off? And he'd have to stop and dismount to remove his pack and get one, but the unicorn showed no signs of stopping. Where was it taking him? And how much longer would it take to get there?

As if in answer, they suddenly came out of the woods into a large clearing. Just beyond the clearing was a small lake, and on the shore stood a peculiar-looking house. It had only one floor, and the roof looked as if it was made entirely of thick, dry grass. He wondered what it was. Thatch, he thought, as the unfamiliar term came suddenly to mind. Apparently, the sim program would answer only certain questions that came to mind, not all of them.

As the unicorn approached the house, Riley saw that it had a fenced enclosure to one side of it. Inside there were a number of strange-looking animals. As the unicorn stopped in front of the house, Riley slid off its back and approached the enclosure. The animals inside all looked the same. They were very fat, and had four stubby legs ending in split hooves, large heads with little ears and square-shaped snouts and little, curly tails. Some were brown and some were black. All of them were very dirty. They had churned the ground inside the enclosure into mud, and some of them were wallowing in it. At his approach, they all became excited and rushed toward the fence where he stood, crowding together and emitting squealing and grunting sounds.

He backed away and turned around in time to see the unicorn disappearing into the woods at the far end of the clearing. "Hey, wait!" he called out, but it was too late. The unicorn was gone. He took a deep breath and exhaled heavily. "Terrific," he said. "Now how am I going to get out of here?"

But then it occurred to him that this was where he was supposed to be. This was the next stage of the quest. The unicorn had brought him here, and having served its purpose, it had gone. Whatever was supposed to happen next, including how he would leave, would probably be revealed to him here, most likely by whoever lived inside the house.

He went up to the front door. It was made of heavy wood planks. He stood in front of the door and said, "Is anybody home?"

The door swung open slowly, with a creaking sound. He went inside. The floor of the house was made of wood, and the walls were mortared stone. The ceiling had heavy wooden beams. Most of the interior of the house was one large, open room, with a curtained archway leading to another room, or rooms, at the back. There was a large fireplace in which several logs were burning, giving off a pleasant warmth. The furniture was crude, and made of wood, just some chairs and benches and a large, square table. There was a strangely shaped rug on the floor in front of the fireplace. It was black and thick, and appeared to be made of hair. He wondered what it was, and no sooner had the thought occurred to him than he realized it was a bearskin rug. What sort of creature was a bear?

He approached it and looked down. The head of the creature was still attached. Its eyes were open, as was its mouth, revealing sharp teeth. He grimaced, both at the thought of using a skin as a rug and at the size of it. Its paws were still attached, as well. They had long, sharp claws. He wouldn't want to run into one that was still alive.

"Good evening," a voice said from behind him. "I was not aware I had a visitor."

He turned around, startled, to see a woman standing in the curtained archway. She was holding the curtains open and standing with one leg slightly in front of the other. She was wearing a long, black, clinging dress with a slit in the front. Riley caught his breath as he stared at her. She was barefoot and long-legged, with a slim waist and full breasts that strained against the low neckline of her dress. She had long black hair that fell down to her waist, and she wore gold chains and jeweled amulets around her neck, a profusion of gold bracelets both on her wrists and ankles, and rings on every finger. She had a wide mouth and a slightly pointed chin, dark and deep-set eyes and high, arched eyebrows. Riley thought she was the most beautiful woman he had ever seen.

"I'm sorry, I . . . I didn't mean to just come in like that," he said, "but the door opened and I thought it was in response to —"

"You are welcome," she said, coming toward him and smiling invitingly. "I seldom receive visitors, and am glad for the company. You must have traveled far, and doubtless you are weary. Take your ease and warm yourself by my fire."

She indicated the bearskin rug and Riley gathered that she meant for him to sit down on it. He did so, rather gingerly. "Thank you," he said. It did feel warm and pleasant by the fire. The night had grown chilly and he was unaccustomed to feeling cold.

She took a gold tray off a table and brought it to him. It held a golden decanter and two beautifully made, tulip-shaped, golden goblets with long and narrow stems. "Allow me to offer you some wine. It is a special vintage that I make myself."

She set the tray down on the floor beside the rug and then joined him on it, sinking down with a languid, flowing grace. She drew her legs up, bent at the knees, and the skirt of her dress fell away from them. Riley had a hard time not staring.

"You live out here all by yourself?" he asked, as she poured the wine into the goblets.

She sighed. "Alas, I am all alone here. Few people come this way. 'Tis is a quiet, lonely life, tending to my herd. But tell me of yourself. What brings you to this place, and whither are you bound?"

"I am on a quest," said Riley.

"Indeed?" She handed him a goblet. "You seem young to have embarked alone on such an undertaking. What manner of quest do you pursue?"

Riley took a drink. The dark red wine was delicious and it

felt warm going down. He took another sip. "You mean you don't know?" he asked.

She raised her eyebrows. "But . . . how could I? You have not yet told me."

"Oh. Well, I thought maybe you would know. You see, I'm not exactly sure what it is I'm supposed to look for. I'm sort of finding out as I go along."

He didn't see any point in telling her about Jenny and Ulysses. He'd been apprehensive about trying this alone, but now he was glad that they weren't here. He had to remind himself that none of this was real, but it sure felt real. She was sitting very close to him, her legs practically touching his. She was leaning forward slightly and he was having a very hard time keeping his eyes on her face.

"How is it that you can be upon a quest and not know what you are seeking?" she asked him. Her foot moved against his. Riley was having a hard time concentrating.

"Well, at different stages of the journey, I find out where I'm supposed to go next," he said. "The unicorn brought me here, and I thought maybe you were going to tell me where I was supposed to go."

"You came on a unicorn?" she said, fascinated. Then her eyes narrowed. "I thought only a virgin could tame a unicorn."

Riley blushed and looked down, quickly. He took a long gulp from the goblet, frantically trying to think of something to say.

"Ah," she said, "I understand." She reached out and gently touched him under the chin, raising his head so she could look him in the eyes. "Young . . . and innocent," she said, softly. She smiled at him. "How do you like the wine?"

"It's delicious," Riley said, grateful for the change of subject. "My name is Riley. What's yours?"

"I am called by many names," she said. "But you may call me Circe."

"Circe?" He hiccuped, and it came out like a squealy grunt. "I'm sorry." He hiccuped again, making the same, peculiar sound.

"Drink some more wine," she said. "Drain the goblet. 'Twill help, you'll see."

He tipped the goblet back and emptied it, then set it down. He took a deep breath and exhaled heavily. "I think that did it," he said, and immediately hiccuped once again. He tried to say, "I'm sorry," but it just came out as another squeaky grunt. It sounded just like the noises from the enclosure outside.

"Yes, indeed," Circe said, with a sly smile. "I think that did it."

Riley suddenly felt strangely dizzy. The room seemed to be moving. He needed to lie down. He tried to say, "I think I don't feel well," but what came out was a series of squeals and grunts.

Circe chuckled. "There now," she said, reaching out to stroke him.

Riley couldn't understand what was happening. His clothes were growing baggy. He seemed to be growing smaller. He tried to talk, but all that came out were snorting grunts. And then he noticed that his arms were growing shorter, and his hands were changing. He became frightened.

He had to get out of the sim, but how could he take off the VR band if his hands no longer had fingers? He tried to tell himself it wasn't real, but his senses were telling him otherwise and in his panic, he couldn't concentrate. He tried to get up, but became tangled in his clothes. He wriggled free of them and trotted on four legs across the floor, squealing in alarm.

"What a pretty, little pig you are!" said Circe. "I have never had a white one before! Come here and let me look at you."

Riley trotted underneath a table, upsetting it. It crashed to the floor and he ran out, terrified. He ran around the room, knocking things over and squealing in fright until she caught him and tied a rope around his neck.

"Now look what a mess you've made!" she scolded him. "You'll have to go outside, with the others."

He dug in his hooves, but she pulled on the rope and dragged him across the floor. The rope tightened around his neck and he started choking.

"Now if you resist, it will only make things worse," she said. "Come on, now. Come on and meet your new friends."

She led him outside to the enclosure, opened the gate, removed the rope from around his neck and gave him a hard slap on the rump. He squealed with pain and ran inside. She shut the gate behind him and stood with her hands on her hips, looking at him and the other pigs. "Yes, indeed," she said, with a smile. "You will make a fine addition to my herd. Now you boys make him feel welcome, and don't be mean to him."

She laughed, then turned around and went back inside.

The sim had to end, thought Riley, desperately. It had to end now! But it did not end. And in the school library, it was late and he was the only one left on a VR couch. Virtched out and disconnected from his own senses, he never heard the sounds of little feet approaching, and he never saw the five dwarves dressed in brightly colored clothing enter.

He never felt them lift him from the couch, his VR band still in place, and hoist him up onto their shoulders. Four of them carried him down the corridor, shuffling along, the fifth one leading the way. When they reached the end, the dwarf in front bent down and placed his palm flat on the floor for a moment, then stepped back. The nanalloy flowed, making an opening to the maintenance shafts underneath the floor. They lowered him inside, then dropped after him, and the floor sealed up again behind them.

CHAPTER
10

It was getting late by the time Jenny and Ulysses finished telling their story again, this time for Peter and Karen's benefit. They were all sitting together in the Bucklands' living room. Ulysses had tried calling Riley earlier, but his parents had said he wasn't home yet, and they did not know where he was. Peter had tried to interrupt with questions several times, but Karen had made him wait until they were finished. Mac was keeping a record of their statement, so it could be transferred to Guardian, the Security AI.

Ulysses had told them how it had all started, from the time when he and Riley had looked up the statistics on partner registry to the most recent stage of their quest adventure. Karen had listened to it all very carefully, with just a slight frown on her face, but Peter heard it all with growing incredulity and dismay. When Ulysses finished, he shook his head and said, "Why didn't you tell us about this before?"

"We didn't think you'd believe us," said Ulysses, with a shrug. "And if you did, we figured you'd probably just try to take it away from us. We wanted to find out what would happen."

"Do you have any idea how irresponsible that was?" his

father said. "You should have told me about this immediately!"

"Let's not get into that now," said Karen. "The important thing is to track down that sim program and find out exactly what it is and how it's related to the things that have been happening aboard the ship."

"So then you finally believe me about what I saw?" asked Sonja.

"To be honest with you, I'm not sure what I believe at this point," Karen said. "But this seems to tie together a number of recent events that I've been at a loss to explain. Your story about sighting the fairies and dancing with them while you were in some sort of trance relates directly to the story Jenny and Ulysses told us about their encounter with them in the sim. Jenny's drawing matches your description, and you never mentioned your experience to either Jenny or Ulysses. Then there's the Marshall girl, who had reported having an encounter with someone who called himself an elf. Her description of him seems to match that of the man in gray that Jenny, Riley, and Ulysses encountered in the sim, except they never saw his ears. I saw someone who closely matched that description myself, on the retaining wall, moments after George Takahashi's body was discovered. But I never got close enough to see if he had pointed ears or not."

"What about the little man?" asked Peter.

"There's no correlation there with anything that Jenny, Riley, and Ulysses saw in the sim," said Karen. "But we did receive a report earlier this afternoon about a strange animal being sighted in a meadow near the woods at the aft end of the ship. And the description we got matches that of the unicorn in the sim."

"This is incredible," Peter said, shaking his head. "What could possibly account for something like this?"

"I don't know," said Karen, frowning. "But there clearly seems to be a relation between this 'quest program' and whatever's happening aboard the ship. If I hadn't had a similar experience myself, with Ben Cruzmark there to verify it, I'd be tempted to think that people were suffering from some sort of strange psychosis. But that man in gray I saw was

real, whether he was an elf or not, and I think what Sonja
saw was real, too."

"Saleem!" said Sonja, suddenly. "I forgot all about him!"

"What about Saleem?" asked Karen.

"He was going out to the fields tonight with an HIR, to see
if the fairies appeared again!"

"I'll send a unit over to check on him," said Karen. She
used her link to call Security. "All right, they're on their
way," she said, as soon as she completed the call. She looked
at Jenny and Ulysses. "Let's get back to the woman in white,
the one in your dream," she said. "Are you absolutely sure it
was Penelope Seldon?"

"She didn't say who she was," said Jenny, "but it looked
just like her."

"We called up an image of her as she appeared during her
final viewing at her recycling ceremony," said Ulysses, "and
she was wearing the same white robe she wore in our
dream."

Karen smiled. "You ever consider a career in Security?
You have the makings of a good investigator."

"Thanks," Ulysses said, pleased at the compliment.

"Let me know if you're interested," said Karen. "Meanwhile, let's get back to Dr. Seldon. It all seems to keep coming back to her somehow."

"It's a fact that she was ordered to undergo Counseling,"
said Peter. "She was a brilliant woman, one of the leading
citizens of her generation, but toward the end of her life, she
developed paranoid and antisocial tendencies. There's a very
old saying that there's a fine line between genius and insan-
ity. Great intellects are often very high-strung. But she recovered completely after undergoing Counseling and spent
her final years in quiet retirement."

"Yes, I remember studying about her in school," said
Karen. "Only there's no file on her in the Counseling databanks."

"Perhaps Ulysses didn't try to access it correctly," Peter
said.

"Not if he did what he says he did," Karen replied, shaking her head. "There's never been any reason for elaborate
security precautions on data restriction. In any case, that's

easily checked. For now, let's proceed on the assumption that he's right, and Penelope Seldon somehow had the file deleted, or else no file was ever kept. If that's the case, then Ulysses may be right, and it's quite possible that she did not, in fact, recover completely. As Ulysses says, maybe she fooled them. And after she went into retirement, she wrote the quest program. The question is why. And there has to be more to it than that. What Ulysses, Jenny, and Riley have experienced in the quest sim wasn't real; it was just VR. But what about what Sonja saw, and what happened to the Marshall girl, and my own experience? That wasn't VR."

"Could they have been some sort of artificial constructs?" Peter asked.

Karen pursed her lips thoughtfully. "It's possible. But then they would have had to be constructed somewhere right here aboard the ship. We'll have to conduct a thorough search, and that could take a long time. In the meantime, we have to try and find that program."

"We can find it anytime we do VR," Ulysses said. "If we can complete the quest, maybe we can find out what this is all about."

"Absolutely not," his father said. "That's out of the question."

"Let's not be too hasty about that," Karen said. "Until we can track down that program, they're our only link to it."

"I'm not convinced that it's not dangerous," said Peter. "The program effects a direct interface with their minds, and it was written by a woman who could have been psychotic."

"We don't know that," said Karen.

"We're talking about the risk to our children, Karen!"

"You think I'd want to expose my daughter to any danger?" Karen asked. But before he could reply, there was a call from the Security unit she had dispatched to check on Saleem Rodriguez. It was Ben Cruzmark.

"Go ahead, Ben," Karen said.

"You're not going to believe this," he said.

"Try me."

"We found Rodriguez," Cruzmark said. "He was stark naked in the field, running and jumping and twirling around as if he was completely out of his mind. And there were these little glowing lights circling all around him. When we came in with our cruiser, they took off and Rodriguez just collapsed. I dropped off Abramson to check on Rodriguez and gave pursuit, but I lost them when they reached the woods."

"How's Rodriguez?"

"I think he's all right," Cruzmark replied. "He's just unconscious. We're taking him to the hospital to make sure."

"Did he have an HIR with him?" Sonja asked.

"Affirmative," said Cruzmark. "It was on and recording. I've got the unit right here."

"Don't let it out of your sight, Ben," Karen said. "Meet me back at headquarters as soon as you've dropped off Rodriguez at the hospital. I'll be on my way there in just a little while. Kruickshank out."

"There's a call from Brian Etheridge," Mac said, before they could resume their conversation.

"Put him on, Mac," Peter said.

"Peter?"

"I'm here, Brian. Go ahead."

"Is Riley there with you?"

"No," said Peter. "You mean he isn't home yet?"

"No, he's not," said Riley's father. "And he never stays out this late without telling us. It's not like him not to call. Is Ulysses there?"

"I'm here, Mr. Etheridge," said Ulysses.

"Do you have any idea where he might be, Ulysses? Did he say anything to you about where he was going?"

"No, sir," said Ulysses. "He told me he had to do something at home."

"He hasn't been home all afternoon," Riley's father replied.

Jenny grabbed Ulysses by the arm. "You don't suppose he decided to try it on his own, do you?"

"Try what on his own?" asked Etheridge, in a puzzled tone.

"Hold on a moment, Brian," said Peter. He turned to Jenny and Ulysses. "Are you talking about the quest?"

"We were wondering what would happen if just one of us tried it, without the others," said Ulysses. "Riley didn't seem to like the idea very much. It made him nervous, so I said I would do it. But we were all going to be together when we tried it."

"I don't understand. What are you talking about?" Brian Etheridge asked.

"Hang on, Brian," Peter said. He turned back to Ulysses. "Do you think Riley might have decided to experiment on his own?"

"I don't know," Ulysses replied. "Maybe. If he did, he probably went to school to do it."

"Brian, I'll call you back in a few minutes," Peter said. "Mac, disconnect and get me the school library database."

A moment later, Mac made the connection. Peter checked with the library computer, which routinely kept track of attendance throughout the day. Riley had arrived earlier that afternoon, but he had never left. And according to the computer, there was no one in the library.

"That's impossible," said Peter. "Check the VR couches."

"None of them are currently in use," the library computer replied. "However, the VR interface band is missing from Couch 14."

"Who was using it this afternoon?"

"I have no record of anyone using it."

Peter frowned. "That doesn't make sense. Let me have a download visual display of all VR programs accessed since the end of classes today. Mac, configure for visual reception on the living room wall."

A moment later, the list of all VR programs accessed that afternoon appeared on the living room wall, opposite the couch. Peter approached the wall to have a closer look. The list gave the code numbers for the VR sims, the program titles, and the names of the users of each cubicle. Riley's name did not appear on the list. Nor was there any listing for Couch 14.

"It's as if he wasn't even there," said Peter, staring at the display. He turned around. "What am I going to tell Brian Etheridge?"

"Tell him we'll find him," Karen said. "I'll get my people on it right away."

"You still think this isn't dangerous?" asked Peter, with a grim expression on his face.

"Peter, we don't know what happened yet, assuming anything happened at all," Karen replied. "Let's not go jumping to any conclusions. He couldn't have gone far."

"What about the missing VR band?" Peter asked.

"He probably just took it with him," Karen said.

"Why would he do something so disruptive?" asked Peter.

"To continue with the quest," Ulysses said, with sudden insight.

They all looked at him. "How could he do that?" asked Karen. "He'd have to be in a room set up for sim reception."

"Maybe not," Ulysses said. "The quest program was somehow able to override the regular program in the classroom. At least for the three of us. If it could link to the VR band through the computer in the classroom, couldn't it broadcast through any other computer on the ship, as well? They're all networked, right?"

They all exchanged concerned glances as the implications of what Ulysses said sank in. "The Assembly has to be notified of this immediately," said Karen. "I'll call an emergency meeting. In the meantime, I'll put an order out through CAC that all VR interfacing be canceled until further notice, and all VR bands aboard the ship be confiscated. I'd better get to headquarters right away. We'll have to find Riley, get CAC to find that quest program and then organize a thorough search of the entire ship. That's probably going to take up all my time until we get somewhere. Peter, do you mind if Jenny stays with you in the meantime? I hate to impose, but —"

"Of course she can stay here," said Sonja.

"Thanks. I appreciate it. I'll be back in touch as soon as I learn anything."

They escorted her to the door.

"Mom?" said Jenny.

Karen stopped and turned around.

"I'm really sorry," Jenny said. "I guess I should have told you about this sooner. But I didn't think it would do any harm."

"It's all right, darling," Karen said, giving her daughter a hug. "I know. Besides, I never told my parents everything, either. We'll get to the bottom of this, and we'll find Riley, don't worry."

"Okay," said Jenny. "But Mom . . . there's something else you should know."

"What is it?"

"I've Chosen Ulysses."

Karen smiled at her, glanced briefly at Ulysses and his parents, then back at her Jenny. "You know, somehow, I'm not really surprised," she said.

"But . . . they're not old enough to Choose yet!" Peter said. "They're only children!"

"Dad . . ." Ulysses said. "I'm not a child anymore. I'm almost seventeen."

"He's right, you know," said Karen. "Seventeen is not a child, it's a young adult. And they'll have the right to register Choice at eighteen, whether we approve or not."

"But that's still over a year away," said Peter, weakening.

"We can wait," said Jenny.

"We love each other, Dad," said Ulysses. "And we belong together. But I really want your support, so if it'll make you feel better, we'll wait. A year, two years, three or four . . . it won't make any difference. We know how we feel about each other, and that's what counts. We're not in any rush."

Peter sighed and shook his head. "We'll discuss it later. Personally, I still think you have some growing up to do." He looked at Karen. "I guess we should have had that talk. You saw this coming, didn't you?"

"I suspected," Karen said, "but I wasn't really sure." She turned to Jenny. "I just want you to know something, honey. I was wrong about your drawing. I may have been wrong about a lot of things. But we'll talk about that later. We'll all have a lot to talk about, but right now, I've got work to do. Take care. I'll see you soon." She gave her a kiss, hugged Sonja, shook hands with Peter, and left.

Later that night, after Sonja had made up the spare bedroom for Jenny, she and Peter lay in bed, discussing all that had happened.

"I was thinking about what Karen said to Jenny," Peter said. "I was wrong, too. I'm sorry I didn't believe you."

Sonja kissed him on the cheek. "I know," she said. "I don't blame you. If it was the other way around, I'm sure I would have reacted the same way. I'm still having a hard time believing it all myself."

Peter sighed and stared up at the darkened ceiling. "You know, what gets me is that I should have made the connection before."

"What connection?" Sonja asked, turning on her side to face him.

"When Jenny said the little creatures in her drawing were called fairies, the word sounded vaguely familiar somehow, and when Ulysses mentioned the Folklore, Mythology, and Legends file, it suddenly clicked. I accessed that file once, but it was years ago, when I was looking for subjects to research for my graduate thesis. I just didn't make the connection when you described them as tiny, glowing humanoids with wings. I was convinced you'd had some sort of dream or hallucination. But the file described them. Not quite the same way you did, but there was a listing for fairies. I remember now."

"How come I never knew about it?" Sonja asked.

He shrugged. "We don't teach it. It's not part of the curriculum. I stumbled on the file by accident, much like Ulysses did. And I didn't really get into it very far, as I recall. I remember thinking it was rather interesting and wanting to get back to it eventually, only I never did. I developed other interests."

"Why isn't it taught?" asked Sonja.

"What?

"Mythology and folklore," she said. "Why isn't it part of the curriculum?"

"Well, I suppose it's considered unproductive. Literature, art, music . . . they don't really have much practical value, except perhaps as entertainment, and AIs can generate those things better than people can, so there's not much point in wasting time learning about them. After all, we don't need artists; we need teachers, scientists, and engineers. With the AIs, we've become the redundant factor. Artificial Intelligence doesn't really need people. The *Agamemnon* could function just as well without us. Artificial Intelligence can maintain itself and reproduce itself, and when we find a habitable planet, Artificial Intelligence can colonize it."

"The only thing it can't do is colonize it with people," Sonja said.

"No, in fact, it can," said Peter. "It's never been done before, but when the mission was in its planning stages, there was serious consideration given to having the *Agamemnon* be a seed ship. Back then, we were already using AI to effect reproduction. Theoretically, it would have been possible for the ship to make its voyage without any people aboard at all, or maybe just a small emergency crew in cryogenic sleep. The human colony would have been stored, rather like you store seeds at the farms. Then, when the ship reached a habitable planet, AI could begin the colonization process. The reproductive computers would effectively become the parents of the new colony. But that idea was eventually discarded because there were too many unknown variables. That's one of the reasons we carry stored human and animal genetic material, to see how it holds up over long interstellar voyages. And that's one of the reasons we're here, as well. But in order to create an optimal environment for our survival over the generations, we've had to concentrate on teaching and practicing strictly useful and pragmatic skills."

"Then why is the file there?" asked Sonja.

"Because it's part of our history," said Peter. "The mission planners wanted to make sure that all human knowledge was included in the databanks. That was a task too great for people to perform, so it was all done by AIs. There are probably hundreds of thousands of files in the CAC databanks that no one has ever accessed."

"Like the quest program," Sonja said.

"Yes. Only if Penelope Seldon was responsible for it, then it has to be more recent," said Peter, nodding. Then he frowned. "What I can't understand is how Jenny, Riley, and Ulysses got it. Why only them? Why nobody else?"

"Maybe others did get it, but we don't know about it yet," said Sonja.

"Yes, I guess that's possible. I know they were wondering

about that, too." He paused for a moment. "You think it was the quest program that brought them together?"

"I'm sure it played a part," said Sonja. "But I have a feeling there was something going on long before that."

"Do you suppose they've slept together?"

"That's a rather quaint, old-fashioned way of putting it," she said, with smile. "I don't know if they've had sex, but I don't suppose they've really had a chance to sleep together until now."

He turned to face her. "You mean, you think they're . . . I mean, right now?"

Sonja chuckled. "Why, what are you going to do, go and check on them?"

"No, of course not," he said. "If they were together and I walked in on them . . ." He sighed. "How did all this happen so fast? It seems as if only just the other day, Ulysses was learning how to read. He still seems so young, it's hard to imagine him being sexually active."

"When was the first time you had sex?"

"When I was twenty-three. And I was rather clumsy at it."

"Seriously?"

"Well, I was a little slow in some areas."

"You never told me that before."

"You never asked before."

"I didn't, did I? I guess I never really thought about it." She chuckled. "You didn't seem slow with me."

Peter smiled. "I remember. I was pretty determined."

She pressed up against him and put her leg across his, moving it up and down slowly. "That's one of the things I've always loved about you," she said.

He put his arms around her. "You know, we haven't really talked like this in a long time. Why?"

She shook her head. "I don't know. I hadn't realized how much I've missed it until now."

"I love you."

"Show me," she whispered.

Ulysses tiptoed into his father's den, where the guest bed had been set up. Jenny's pale face was a patch of color against the dark sheets. He could hear her breathing, slowly and regularly, with an occasional sharp intake. She was moving slowly under the light woven cover, lying on her stomach. Half the cover had slipped off her shoulders.

"Jenny?" he said, softly. . . .

He heard the rustle of the covers as she moved in bed.

. . . The bracing shock of the freezing water made her gasp as she landed with a splash, sinking quickly. As the water closed over her head, she kicked out hard. Jilly swam slowly, three meters away, and slightly above her. Jilly was making her impatient noise, a series of blips and chirps, some of which came through the translator intact, and some of which didn't. Mostly, Jenny heard the impatience in her tone.

It was very hard to form words with her mouth closed, but the dolphin link was connected to the AI's, which was able to interpret the vaguely human throat sounds and translate them into dolphin.

"Move like this!" Jilly said. "Move like this!" Her gray dolphin body moved through the water with a graceful undulation.

"I can't, Jilly, I can't!" Jenny replied. "You have a fin and I don't!"

Jilly crossed the three meters between them, almost instantly, and nudged her full length with her body. "You are six years old. You will soon be a fully developed human. You have to learn this now, so the pattern can remain with you always. Put your legs together. Clamp your ankles tight. Point your feet. Bend at your waist, swim like this. . . ."

She did what Jilly said and threw herself into the motion as hard as she could. Suddenly, she was swimming much the way the dolphins swam, and fast, too. Jilly looked at her with one languid eye and seemed to stop in mid-water. She let out an untranslatable chirp of pure joy and shot toward the surface.

Jenny followed her, still dolphin-swimming, and when she popped out of the water, they blew air at each other. Jilly's breath had a heavy smell of fish. They swam slowly back to the marina, where her mother waited on the other side of the view window. The skin under Jilly's eyes wrinkled slightly and she turned her head in that purposeful way that dolphins had when they wanted to emphasize what they were about to say.

"When you dolphin-swim, Jenny, you are one with the water, and someday you may need to be."

As Jenny climbed out onto the platform, grinning happily, she heard a distant voice calling her name. She looked out over the sea with a frown and saw someone bobbing on the surface.

"Jenny! Jenny!"

". . . Jenny, wake up!"

She sat up, abruptly, the covers falling away from her.

Ulysses stared at her in the darkness and inhaled sharply. "I can't believe I'm saying this," he whispered, "but hurry up and put your clothes on."

"What? Why?"

"We've got to get down to the school. If they're going to confiscate all the VR bands, then that's it for the quest. Riley's in some kind of trouble, I just know it, and unless we get back to the quest, we won't know what happened."

"Okay, I'll just be a minute."

She got out of bed and quickly started getting dressed. Moments later, they were tiptoeing down the stairs and out of the house. They ran down to the racks and took two bicycles, and rode quickly to the school. It was late and the streets were all empty. The one-meter-high walls separating the residences from the pathways emitted a soft and gentle glow. The walklights came on after the artificial suns were dimmed for the day and stayed quite bright until about ten o'clock, then they slowly dimmed until, by 3:00 A.M., there was just enough glow to prevent anyone out that late from colliding with a maintenance drone. Jenny and Ulysses pedaled quickly down the lane and into the park, cutting through it toward the school building.

"What do you think your parents will do if they find out that we're gone?" asked Jenny, as they rode.

"If we're lucky, they won't," Ulysses replied. "We should be able to get back before morning."

"What makes you think Riley's in trouble in the quest?"

"I don't know, it's just a feeling I have," Ulysses said. "I'm sure he went back to the quest in the school library. We know he was there, and that he never left. And then there's that missing VR band. I think he's still there."

"In the library?"

"No, in the quest."

"But if he was virtched out, how could he have gone anywhere?" asked Jenny.

"I wouldn't think he could," Ulysses said. "But one way or another, the answer's got to be in the library."

"That's the first place Mom would have checked," said Jenny.

"But she wouldn't have checked the quest," Ulysses replied. "She couldn't have. She wouldn't know how to get into it. We're the only ones who can."

They reached the school building and parked their bikes in the racks out front. Very few of the structures aboard the *Agamemnon* were restricted access, even after dark. They entered the school and made their way to the library. Jenny paused and took hold of Ulysses' arm just before they went through the entryway.

"Wait a minute," she said. "The computer's going to register us."

"So we register," Ulysses said.

"But then our parents will know we were here."

"Only if they think to check," Ulysses said. "And if we're back by morning, why would they?"

"That's true," she said. "Okay. Let's go."

They went inside and logged in, then headed down the corridor to the VR couches. "Which ones should we use?" asked Jenny.

"I don't think it'll make any difference," Ulysses replied. "I'm sure the quest program will access us the moment we put on the bands."

They selected two couches side by side, sat down, and slipped on the bands. Ulysses was right. The moment the bands were on, they had the familiar falling sensation as they were drawn into the virtual reality of the quest sim.

They found themselves standing in a clearing at the edge of the forest. A short distance away, beyond the clearing, was a lake, and by the shore there stood a small house with a thatch roof and a fenced enclosure to one side. There was smoke coming from the chimney.

"This isn't where we were before," said Jenny, looking around. They were once again dressed the way they had been before in the sim, but otherwise, everything around them was different. There was no sign of the trail they had taken from the tavern and no sign of the unicorn.

"No," Ulysses said, "we've skipped ahead. This must be as far as Riley got."

"You think he's in that funny little house?" asked Jenny.

"There's only way to find out," Ulysses said. They started across the clearing.

As they approached, the animals penned up in the enclosure became extremely agitated. They started milling around inside the pen, squealing and grunting and crowding close to the nearest fence. Ulysses and Jenny came closer.

"What do you suppose they are?" Ulysses asked.

"I don't know," said Jenny. She wrinkled her nose. "But look what a mess they've made in there! They're filthy. And they smell, too!"

"Look at that white one," said Ulysses.

Among all the others, there was only one that was white, and it was smaller, obviously younger. As soon as it saw them, it started squealing louder than the rest and throwing itself against the fence. Ulysses and Jenny backed away a couple of steps.

"You think they're dangerous?" asked Jenny.

"I don't know," Ulysses said. "But that white one sure wants to get out."

"Greetings to you, strangers," said a voice from behind them. They turned around and saw a beautiful young woman standing between them and the front door to the little house. She was dressed all in black, wore a profusion of rings and bracelets, and had dark hair down to her waist. "My pigs always tell me when there are visitors," she said. "Not that I have many this far off the beaten track."

"Hello. My name is Ulysses, and this is Jenny."

"Welcome to you both," the woman said. "I am called Circe. Come in. You must be tired from your journey. Allow me to offer you some refreshment. And you may offer me the pleasure of your company."

They followed her into the house. Inside, it was dim and cool, with a couple of shafts of sunlight coming in through the open windows. They looked around, taking in the spare, crude furnishings and the stone walls.

"Do you live all alone here?" Ulysses asked.

"Alas, 'tis true," she replied, as she set a tray down on the table. On the tray there was a golden decanter and three golden goblets, which she filled from the decanter. "I live here all by myself, tending to my little beasts. 'Tis a lonely life, but 'tis quiet and peaceful. Please, sit down. Have some wine. I make it myself."

"Thank you," said Ulysses, as he and Jenny sat down at the table. Circe placed the goblets before them. Jenny noticed that the one she gave Ulysses had a stem carved in the shape of a man, while hers had a stem carved in the shape of a woman, matching the third goblet, which Circe left on the tray beside her.

"So tell me," she said. "What brings you to these parts?"

"We were traveling to the mountains," Ulysses said. He reached for the goblet and picked it up, then set it back down again. "Actually, we're on a quest."

"Indeed? What sort of quest?"

"Well, right now, we're looking for a friend of ours," Ulysses said. "His name is Riley." He told her what Riley looked like, based on the way he appeared in the quest sim. "Have you seen anyone like that?"

She shook her head. "No, you two are the first to pass this way in a long time. And as I have said, I do not often receive visitors. That is why I take such pleasure in the few people I do see. Please, enjoy your wine."

"Do you suppose we could have something to eat, as well?" asked Ulysses.

"But of course. Forgive me, you must be hungry from your journey. My larder is simple, but I have some bread and cheese and fruit. One moment, I shall bring it for you."

She got up from the table and went through a curtained

archway to another room. Ulysses immediately got up and switched Jenny's goblet with the woman's, on the tray.

"What are you doing?" Jenny whispered.

"Sssh! Don't say anything," said Ulysses. "And *don't* drink any wine, whatever you do. Just pretend to drink it."

"Why?"

"Just do it!" he said. He took her goblet and his and emptied them both out the window, returning quickly to his seat.

Circe came back with a tray holding a wooden cutting board, a knife, a round loaf of bread, a large wedge of cheese, and some fruit. She smiled as she set it down. "Please, eat your fill," she said. "I have more if wish."

"Thank you," said Ulysses. "That's very kind of you." He reached for the knife and started to slice the bread.

"Is the wine to your taste?"

"It's delicious," Ulysses said.

"I'm pleased you like it," she said, beaming. "Drink up. There is plenty more."

"In that case, I would like to propose a toast," said Ulysses, raising his empty goblet. Jenny raised hers, as well. Circe took the goblet off the tray. "To good food, fine wine, new friends, and new adventures!" he said.

"Aye," Circe said, "a fine toast, indeed. Bottoms up!" Jenny and Ulysses brought the empty goblets to their lips and pretended to drink. Ulysses watched over the rim of his goblet as Circe tipped her goblet back and drank, gulping it all down. Ulysses set his empty goblet down and walked away from the table.

"I can't imagine why a beautiful young woman like yourself would wish to live all alone out here, in the middle of nowhere," he said, walking around the room, glancing down at the bearskin rug and looking at the fireplace and the shelves holding a collection of curious vials and bottles and ceramic pots, as if taking it all in casually. "It seems like such a lonely life. Don't you miss seeing other people?"

"Sometimes I do," she replied. "But I enjoy the quiet, simple life. I have my pigs to keep me company, and once in a while, some passing travelers like yourselves stop by and I can enjoy some conversation. 'Tis a life that suits me. I have been here a long time, and I suppose I have grown accustomed to my solitude."

"It's strange that you didn't see our friend," Ulysses said. "I can't imagine that he could have come this way and not seen your house and stopped."

"Perhaps he did not come this way."

"No, I'm quite certain he did," Ulysses said.

Circe shook her head. "Then he must have continued on. I fear I have not seen him."

"I think you're lying," said Ulysses.

"You have a curious way of repaying hospitality," she said. Then she hiccuped. It came out as a sort of squealing sound. Her eyes grew wide, and she glanced at her empty goblet with alarm.

"That's right," Ulysses said. "I switched them when you left the room."

"No! The spell!" she cried. "I must reverse the spell!"

"How?" asked Ulysses.

"The antidote! The powder!" She struggled, but Jenny held her fast, pinning her arms behind her back. Circe gave out a long squeal. "Quickly! I beg of you!"

"Show us," said Ulysses.

Jenny marched her through the curtained archway, with Ulysses following. Behind the curtain was a small room containing a large table and a desk, and wooden shelves against the walls, all holding dried herbs and powders and potions contained in hundreds of glass jars and bottles and ceramic pots. The table held large candles in different colors and several iron cauldrons of various sizes, as well as incense burners, mortars and pestles, amulets and talismans, lengths of knotted string, banded scrolls, a large book bound in black leather, and several jeweled wands.

Circe struggled, trying to get free of Jenny's grasp. "Let me go!" she cried. The last word came out as a squeal at the end. "There is no time to lose! I must get the antidote!"

"Tell me what to do," Ulysses said.

"No, I must do it myself!"

"Then I'm afraid you're out of luck," Ulysses said. "You

see, you've already lied to us several times. Why should we trust you now?"

"The powder in the white pot on the table!" said Circe, panic-stricken. "Next to the red one!" She grunted several times.

"This one here?" Ulysses said. "Talk quickly."

"It must be dissolved in wheeeee. . . ."

"In wine?"

She grunted and nodded her head vigorously.

"And is that all?"

She grunted and squealed, but could no longer speak. Her eyes rolling in panic, she simply shook her head. Then her knees gave way and she collapsed. Jenny let her go and she sank to the floor, crying out in fear, but her cries were all panic-stricken squeals. As Jenny and Ulysses watched, she doubled up on the floor and seemed to shrink inside her clothes, thrashing and squealing. Her hands turned into little hooves, and her arms grew shorter, becoming stubby legs. Her face began to change, and her nose grew broader, turning into a snout. She wriggled out of her clothes and stood before them on all fours, a frightened little black pig.

"That's what she would have done to us!" said Jenny, staring at her in amazement. She glanced at Ulysses. "How did you know?"

"I got suspicious when she said we were the first visitors she'd had in a long time," said Ulysses. "Riley had to have come this way, otherwise we wouldn't have. The unicorn must have brought him here. And there's no way Riley would have passed this place without checking it out. I also remembered that each stage of the quest presented us with a test of some kind. When she lied, I figured she had to be the test."

"But how did you know about the wine?" asked Jenny.

"Well, I didn't, really," said Ulysses. "I almost drank it. But as I picked it up, I was thinking, she doesn't really look dangerous, like those men in the tavern did. So it had to be something else. I remembered the fairies, and I wondered if there could be magic here. And the minute I thought of that, I felt something funny about the goblet. My hand tingled as I held it. I'm supposed to be an adept in this quest, so I guess I can detect magic, but I have to think about it."

"How did you know she had put something in the goblets and not in the wine?"

"I didn't. But she poured the wine, and she gave us the goblets. I noticed that hers looked just like yours, and when I went to switch them, my hand didn't tingle when I touched hers. That's how I knew she must have put something in the goblets."

He crouched and rummaged among her things. All her jewelry had slipped off when she changed. He found her rings and looked through them.

"Aha!" he said. He picked one of the rings up and examined it. "Look at this," he said. He lifted the face of the ring, revealing a small compartment that was now empty, but still held some powder residue.

The little black pig grunted pathetically.

"You make a nice pig," Ulysses said. "Maybe I should just leave you that way."

The pig gave a little, squealing whine and rubbed up against his leg.

"Well, let's see if the antidote works, first," Ulysses said. He found a large bowl and poured some of the powder into it. Then he mixed it with wine and carried it outside. Jenny followed him, with the pig trotting after her, grunting plaintively. "Hold this," Ulysses said, giving her the bowl as he climbed over the fence of the enclosure. The pigs rushed up to him, grunting anxiously, the white one in particular.

"Is that you, Riley?" Ulysses asked.

The pig grunted excitedly and nodded its head up and down.

"It serves you right for sneaking out and doing this without us," said Ulysses. "I don't know, maybe I should just let you stay a pig. You look kind of cute that way."

Riley nipped him on the leg.

"Ouch! All right, all right, calm down, I was only kidding," said Ulysses. He turned and took the bowl from Jenny and set it down on the muddy ground. The other pigs immediately made a rush for it. Riley had to fight his way through to get to the bowl, but he was determined. Moments later, they had all lapped up the antidote and Ulysses stood back, watching as they all began to change.

Moments later, the enclosure was full of muddy, naked men. Jenny whistled at them and they all tried to cover themselves up with their hands. Riley, in particular, looked humiliated.

"Well, don't just stand there!" he said. "Get me my clothes!"

"We'll have to look for them," Ulysses said. "I don't know where she put them. Maybe she burned them."

"Oh, great!" said Riley.

The other men came up to Ulysses, thanking him. "We owe you a great debt, stranger," one of them said. "What have you done with the sorceress? Is she dead?"

"That's her right there," Ulysses said, pointing at the little black pig. When the men all turned to stare at her malevolently, she squealed and hid behind Jenny.

"So, the sorceress has fallen victim to her own spell," one of the others said. "'Tis her just reward. Let us leave her here to wallow in the mud, as we did."

The little black pig trembled violently.

"Well, I did promise to change her back if she gave us the antidote," Ulysses said. "I can't go back on my word."

"Aye," one of the men said, "nor would we ask you to, after what you have done for us. A man's word is his bond, my friends, and we owe this stranger much. Let him change her back, then. That will fulfill his promise to the sorceress. But *we* made no promises, did we, lads?"

They all cried out in agreement, at which the little black pig gave a terrified squeal and bolted.

"Wait!" shouted Ulysses, but the pig was already running at full speed across the meadow, toward the forest.

"Let her go," the man said. "She got what she deserved. And her flight absolves you from your promise. Three cheers for the young stranger!"

The men all cheered and hoisted Ulysses up onto their shoulders. Several of them lifted Jenny up onto their shoulders, as well, and carried them back toward the house, forgetting their embarrassment at their nakedness in the face of their revenge and liberation.

And as Jenny and Ulysses were carried toward the house, they were also being carried through the corridors of the school library by little men dressed in brightly colored clothing.

"It's been a long time since we've done that for real," said Sonja, as she lay contentedly on her back in bed.

"The kids are a bad influence," said Peter, with a grin.

"Mmmm. We should have Jenny over more often."

"You know, I hate to admit it, but I'm dying of curiosity," Peter said. "Mac . . ."

"Pete, no!"

"Oh, what's the harm? Besides, aren't you just a little curious?"

She sighed. "Well, yes, but we really shouldn't . . ."

"They'll never even know we asked," said Peter. "Besides, we *are* responsible for their behavior. Mac, are Jenny and Ulysses in the same room together?"

"Oh, Pete, this is wrong. . . ."

"Jenny and Ulysses are not in the house," said Mac.

"What?" said Peter, sitting up abruptly.

Sonja sat up beside him. "What do you mean they're not in the house, Mac? Where are they?"

"I'm sorry, but I do not have that information."

Peter jumped out of bed and started getting dressed. Sonja was right behind him. "Mac, call Security," he said. "Tell them I have to speak to Chief Kruickshank right away."

"Where would they have gone in the middle of the night?" asked Sonja. "What could they possibly . . ." her voice trailed off. "Oh, no!"

"Mac," said Peter, "tell Security to have Chief Kruickshank meet us at the school as soon as possible. Tell her it's an emergency."

CHAPTER
11

The Security cruiser came swooping in for a landing in the courtyard just outside the school. It was almost morning, but most people aboard the *Agamemnon* were still asleep. The weather AI was moving the clouds toward the aft end of the ship, and the softly illuminated walklights of the villages cast a dim glow on the empty streets. Peter and Sonja stood by the school entrance as Karen landed the cruiser, vaulted out, and came running toward them.

"Jenny and Ulysses?" she said, a worried expression on her face.

"I'm afraid so," Peter replied, with a grimace. He shook his head, helplessly. "Karen, I'm so sorry. . . . I don't know what to say. You left Jenny with us and we —"

"Never mind that," Karen said, curtly. "Just tell me what happened."

"They left the house together sometime during the night, after we had gone to bed," said Peter, "and it looks like they came here. There are two bicycles out there in racks, and they were registered at the library, but there's no sign of them inside. We've already checked." He sighed. "And two more VR bands are missing."

"Show me," Karen said.

They went inside and Peter led her to the couches that had no VR bands. They were adjacent to each other, but aside from the missing bands, there was nothing to indicate that Jenny and Ulysses had been there. Karen checked with the library computer, confirming that they had been registered as coming in, but not leaving, and they also confirmed that aside from them, there was no one anywhere inside the school building. According to the library computer, Jenny and Ulysses had not accessed any of the sim programs. But the two VR bands were still missing.

Karen compressed her lips into a tight grimace. "It's my fault," she said.

"How is it your fault?" Sonja asked.

"I said in their presence that I was going to suspend all VR sessions until further notice and order all VR bands confiscated," Karen said. She shook her head. "So they decided to sneak out and get back to the quest while they still had a chance. Maybe they went to look for Riley."

"In a sim program?" Peter said, with a frown.

"Well, that's where he went, isn't it?" said Karen. "Wherever he is physically, mentally he's probably still there. Either they've run off somewhere, or else there's something in the quest program that can subliminally control their bodies while they're wearing the bands."

"Is that possible?" asked Sonja.

"I don't know," said Karen. "A couple of days ago, I would have said elves and fairies were impossible."

"But I still don't understand how they could have left the library without a record," said Peter.

"How could they have accessed a VR program without the computer knowing it?" Karen countered. "There's only one answer to both questions. Somehow, the quest program is able to override the AIs, just as it did in your classroom. It's a master program that acts like some sort of virus. It infects the AIs and manifests itself in a way that allows them to operate normally in every other respect, except they don't know it's there. That must be how Seldon deleted her file from Counseling."

"Then that means it could infect every computer aboard ship!" said Sonja.

Karen nodded, grimly. "It's beginning to look that way," she said. "Which means the search program I instituted through CAC is probably going to be useless. We'll have to couple it with diagnostics and a virus safeguard program. But I don't know if that's going to work." She sighed. "In any case, I've already called an emergency meeting of the Assembly for this morning. I'll need you two to testify. We'll have other witnesses, as well. Aside from Rodriguez and the Marshall girl, we've had several other unusual reports that came in last night."

"What sort of reports?" asked Sonja.

"There were three fairy sightings, although not as dramatic as yours," said Karen. "They were seen at a distance, so the witnesses were not entranced. I've had one more report of an elf encounter, and several shop burglaries."

"Burglaries?" said Peter, with surprise.

"That's right," said Karen. "There was one eyewitness who spotted the burglars leaving the shop. They were shaggy-haired and bearded little men in brightly colored clothing. Dwarves."

"Dwarves?" asked Sonja, with a frown.

Karen nodded. "I've been going through the Folklore, Mythology, and Legends file. It makes for interesting reading. Seldon apparently drew upon that file to design the quest program. And these creatures that have suddenly appeared are tied into that somehow. Elves, dwarves, fairies . . . There's any number of places they could be. We're going to have to search the entire ship."

"But . . . what are they?" Peter asked.

"Well, we know they're not hallucinations," Karen said. "We have some physical evidence now. So they're either artificial constructs of some sort, or else they're organic."

"Do you mean they're alive?" said Peter, with astonishment. "Sentient beings?"

"It's possible."

"You don't suppose they could have come from . . . outside?" asked Peter.

"They would have had no way of getting in," said Karen. "We ran checks on all the hatches, and they're all still sealed. Besides, if any spacecraft had approached us, we would have known about it. No, they were created right here, somehow. Seldon was an expert in AI and genetic engineering. And we have genetic material stored aboard the ship that she could have modified somehow and used to create these creatures."

"So you're saying they're human?" Sonja asked.

"I don't know," said Karen. "Human-based, perhaps. If they *are* organic, and that's how it was done, then the elves and dwarves were probably created from human genetic material. The fairies might be some sort of human/animal hybrid. However, at this point, all this is still only speculation."

"But Penelope Seldon has been dead for years," said Sonja. "How could she have . . ." Her voice trailed off. "Of course. It's all a program, created years ago and designed to be activated at some point in the future. But still . . . whether these creatures are artificial or organic, they had to be created somewhere right here."

"Right," said Karen. "Somewhere there's an automated lab that has to be producing them. And finding it shouldn't take that long."

"What about the kids?" asked Peter.

"We'll find them, Peter," Karen said. "We'll find them if we have to turn this whole ship inside out. But the fact that they've disappeared like this brings up another possibility. It's possible that someone aboard the ship is involved, as well."

"You mean . . . one of us?" asked Sonja.

Karen nodded. "If that's true, then it would indicate a conspiracy that's been hidden for all these years. The question is, to what purpose?"

"I can't believe this," Peter said, shaking his head. "Why would they want our children?"

Karen sighed heavily. "I don't know, Peter. All I can do right now is guess. But I'm going to find out, and I don't care what it takes. I'm mobilizing all the Security auxiliaries and, as of this morning, all Security personnel will be on twenty-four-hour active duty call, including trainees. We're going to alert the entire community and get to the bottom of this."

"We're in trouble, aren't we?" Sonja said. "That Seldon woman was mentally ill."

"I'm not making any assumptions," Karen said. She looked up and saw that it was starting to get light. "It's almost morning. If they come back, call me right away. But I have a feeling they didn't just run off somewhere. If the quest program is a virus capable of infecting any computer aboard the ship, then by now the program probably knows we're looking for it, and it's taken hostages."

They searched the house and discovered a wooden chest where the sorceress had kept the clothes, weapons, and personal effects of all the men she had turned into pigs, and after taking some provisions, they all departed, saying their farewells and thanking Jenny and Ulysses one last time. Finally, only one was left, a mercenary named Gavin. As he tied his pack and buckled on his swordbelt, he thanked Ulysses one more time and asked where they were headed.

Ulysses shook his head. "I don't really know," he said. "We are on a quest, but we do not know what we're searching for, or how to find it."

"A curious sort of quest," said Gavin, with a puzzled look. "How can you seek something when you do not even know what you are searching for?"

"We receive directions as we go along," said Jenny.

"From whom?"

"The lady in white," said Jenny.

"Ah, yes," said Gavin. "The Lady. The good, guiding spirit of the land. It is said that she appears in dreams, and sometimes, her spirit manifests itself to those in need."

"That's how we first saw her," said Ulysses, "in our dreams. And it was she who sent us on this quest."

"Then you have been chosen, and she will guide you," Gavin said. He held out his hand to each of them. "Good fortune to you. Perhaps we shall meet again one day. I owe you a great debt. Someday, I hope to have the opportunity to repay it. Till then, farewell, and may The Lady watch over you."

As they watched him stride across the meadow, toward the forest, each of them wondered what would happen next. When Gavin reached the edge of the forest, he turned and waved to them. They waved back, and he disappeared into the woods.

"Well, what happens now?" asked Riley.

"What happens now is that I kick your butt," Ulysses said, turning on him angrily. "I thought we agreed that we wouldn't try this unless we were all together."

"Okay, so I made a mistake," admitted Riley. "It's not as if I haven't paid for it. You think it's fun being a pig? You try it."

"I should have left you there in the mud," Ulysses said. "Maybe that would've taught you a lesson. Do you have any idea how worried everybody was?"

"Everybody?" asked Riley. Then he understood. "You told them, didn't you?"

"We had to," Jenny said.

"Why? We said we were going to keep this to ourselves!" said Riley.

"You don't know what's been going on," Ulysses said. "My mom saw Jenny's drawing of the fairies and she recognized them. She's seen them, Riley. She's seen them aboard the ship!"

"What are you talking about?"

They sat down on the steps leading to the front door and quickly brought Riley up to date on what had happened while he was "away." He listened with growing astonishment as they filled him in.

"I can't believe it," he said, when they were done. "How can they be aboard the ship?"

"That's what our parents want to know," Ulysses said. "And by tomorrow, everybody else will know that, too. This will have to be brought up before the Assembly, and they're going to try to find the program that's responsible for all this."

"Then that's it," said Riley. "It's over. They'll find it and we'll never get to learn how this turns out."

"I wouldn't be so sure," Ulysses said. "Dr. Seldon had to know they'd start looking for the program as soon as they found out about it. She would have made it hard to find."

"How?" asked Riley.

"I don't know, I'm not a computer specialist," Ulysses said. "But she was. To come up with all of this . . ." He shook his head. "It's really something."

"Where do you suppose the creatures are coming from, the ones aboard the ship, I mean?" asked Riley.

"They're being made somehow," Ulysses said. "Probably by this same program. But whatever the answer is, they won't find it out there. We'll have to find it here."

"Okay, but where do we go next?" asked Riley. "The unicorn brought me here, but I didn't learn anything from the sorceress."

"Except not to drink with strange women," Jenny said, with a smile.

Riley grimaced at her. "Okay, so I messed up. But it turned out all right."

"Because we came back," Ulysses said. "We had to sneak out of the house in the middle of the night to do it, too. But suppose we hadn't done that, or my parents stopped us before we could get to the library? Jenny's mom would have confiscated all the VR bands aboard the ship, and then where would you be?"

"Ulysses, this is a *sim*," said Riley. "The session would have ended and I would've come out of it in the library, perfectly fine."

"There's just one problem with that," Ulysses said. "You're not in the library, remember?"

Riley frowned. "Well, if I'm not in the library, then where am I?"

"We were hoping you could tell us that," Jenny said.

"How should I know?" Riley replied. "I've been here all the time."

"See if you can break out of the sim, the way we did in class that time," Ulysses suggested.

"Okay. Hold on a minute, I have to concentrate. . . ." He sat still and closed his eyes. A few moments later, he opened them again. "It's no good," he said. "I can't do it. It isn't working. Why don't you try?"

Ulysses moistened his lips, then closed his eyes and gave it his best effort, but no matter how hard he concentrated, he could not break free of the sim. He opened his eyes, sighed, and shook his head. "This is not good," he said. "It won't let us go until it's ready. I'm beginning to think the same thing might have happened to us that's happened to you, whatever that is."

"The session's bound to end sometime," Riley said. "Then we'll come out of it and we'll know where we are."

"What I notice is that we're *not* coming out of it," Ulysses said. "The scenario with the sorceress is over, but we're still here."

"Do you think we're still in the library?" Jenny asked, uneasily.

Ulysses shook his head. "I don't know. While we're here, there's no way we can tell. Riley, are you sure you don't remember anything?"

"Just what happened in the sim," said Riley.

"Well, if we're still in the library, they'll find us sooner or later, and then they'll take the bands off and we'll pull out of it," said Jenny.

"Right," agreed Ulysses, "if we're still in the library." He sighed. "We came back to rescue Riley, and it looks like we just might need rescuing ourselves."

"Well, at least we're all together," Jenny said.

"So what do we do now?" asked Riley.

"Continue with the quest, I guess," Ulysses replied.

"But we don't know what we're supposed to do next," Riley said, in an exasperated tone.

"Trust the program," said Ulysses. "It'll let us know."

" 'Trust the program,' he says," Riley replied, sourly. "I don't even know where my body is supposed to be, and he wants me to trust the program!"

"We may be no better off than you," Ulysses said. "The point is, we were chosen for this quest for some reason, we wanted to do it, and now we're here. We may as well make the best of it."

"By doing what?" asked Riley.

"Well, I don't know about you, but Jenny and I didn't get much sleep," Ulysses said. "I'm going to go inside and take a nap."

"What if the sorceress comes back?" asked Riley, nervously.

"Riley, she's a pig," Ulysses said. "What can she do?"

"What if she doesn't stay a pig?"

"Then you can keep her entertained until I wake up," Ulysses said, wryly. "I don't care what you do, Riley, but I'm going to get some sleep."

"Me, too," said Jenny. "I feel kind of tired all of a sudden."

"Well . . . I guess I'll keep watch, then," Riley said.

"You do that," said Ulysses. "But do us a favor, okay? Don't go wandering off by yourself. Look what happened last time. We're all in this together, so from now on, we *stick* together."

"Right," said Riley.

They went back into the house and Ulysses found the small bedroom in the back. The bed was a simple, crudely constructed wooden frame with ropes supporting a mattress stuffed with straw and some coarse woolen blankets. He missed the comfort of his own bed, but it was better than sleeping on the ground. With a sigh, he threw himself down onto the mattress without even bothering to get undressed.

"Is there room for me?" asked Jenny, coming through the curtain.

"Oh," said Ulysses. "Sure, I guess." He moved over against the wall. "It'll be kind of cramped, though."

"I don't mind." She removed her cloak, chain mail, and tunic, sat down on the edge of the bed and started pulling off her boots. "Aren't you going to get undressed?"

Ulysses stared. "I think you're undressed enough for both of us."

She just looked at him.

"What about Riley?" asked Ulysses.

"Let him find his own girl."

"Yeah, well, he tried that and look what happened."

"What's the matter, Ulysses? Do I make you nervous?"

"It just feels funny, with Riley out there."

"He's building a fire, and that bearskin rug looks very comfortable. Probably a lot more comfortable than this bed."

"You know what I mean."

"Ulysses, we've Chosen each other, and this is the first chance we've really had to be alone like this," she said. "Don't you want to make love with me?"

"You know I do," he said. "But it feels funny with Riley in the other room. Besides, this isn't even real. Our minds are here, but our bodies aren't."

"So what are you saying? It doesn't count?"

"I don't know," he said, with exasperation. "But all this is nothing more than an illusion."

"Does this feel like an illusion?" she asked, leaning down to kiss him softly on the lips.

It definitely did not feel like an illusion.

"Well?"

"It *felt* real," said Ulysses, "but our lips didn't really touch. It's just sensory input from the program, Jenny. It's all only in our minds."

"I know," she said. "I've had VR sex before, remember?" And then she smiled. "But not like this. Not with someone that I care about, when it's really my experience, not someone else's. That makes it kind of sexy, don't you think? Making love only in our minds. We won't really be touching, but we'll be *feeling* everything."

Ulysses swallowed hard and moistened his lips. His throat suddenly felt dry. It was a very realistic sensation.

"Why don't you take off that robe?" she said with a smile, reaching for his belt.

The Assembly met at 9:00 A.M., when the five bell tones had sounded throughout the *Agamemnon*. Karen had called the meeting the previous night, and now chaired it from Security Headquarters. An emergency meeting of the Assembly, called by the Chief of Security, was out of the ordinary. Karen and the delegates from all the villages met by display link and practically everyone else on the ship within viewing distance of a display was also watching.

The meeting was officially opened, and with a bare minimum of protocol, they got down to business.

"Thank you everyone on link, and those of you throughout the ship who are monitoring this meeting," Karen said. "Some of you have doubtless heard rumors of strange incidents occurring recently involving fantastic life-forms. Security is currently investigating these incidents, in conjunction with the staff of CAC Support, and we have established that these reports are genuine."

There was a wide range of emotions on the delegates' faces on the multiple displays. Karen continued.

"Some of you know Sonja Buckland, ship's botanist. Hers was the first reported experience, and I will let her describe it as it occurred. Sonja?"

The Assembly listened as Sonja came on and described how she had discovered that something was attacking the herb crop, and how she had gone out to the fields to investigate and encountered the fairies. Karen then called Robie Marshall, who told her story rather haltingly, with some embarrassment. A number of other witnesses testified on link from their homes, and they each spoke briefly. Then Karen resumed her presentation.

"As unbelievable as these reports may sound," she said, "they are nevertheless accurate. These creatures are real. We have not yet established what their nature is, whether they are constructs or organic beings, or how many of them there are. We do not yet know exactly where they came from, but it is clear they have originated aboard the *Agamemnon*. However, there is more.

"Several days ago," she continued, "three young students, including Sonja's son, Ulysses, and my daughter, Jenny, became involved in an ongoing VR simulation that seems related to these incidents. The third student is Riley Etheridge. During a regularly scheduled VR session in a class taught by Peter Buckland, these three received a different VR sim than was experienced by the other students. It differed in that it was an interactive adventure quest and involved the participants directly. Riley, Jenny, and Ulysses appeared in the sim

as themselves, though they were costumed as imaginary
characters possessing certain special skills. The simulation is
apparently set in an imaginary world based on material
drawn from the Folklore, Mythology, and Legends file
stored in the CAC databanks. According to their account,
this adventure quest is more sophisticated than any of our
other sims, and is driven by a program that allows them con-
siderable free will. The program apparently adjusts accordingly. It presents them with certain situations or challenges
they must face and overcome prior to proceeding to the next
stage of the quest. And these challenge scenarios have included creatures or beings similar to the ones that have recently been sighted aboard the ship.

"Prior to their first experience of this VR quest or game,"
she went on, "all three students shared the same dream, in
which a lady in white robes appeared to them in their bedrooms at home and told them that they would be going on a
quest. All three students have identified this lady in white as
Penelope Seldon."

There was some murmuring from the faces on the displays, and Karen waited until it died down before continuing.

"Most of you will recall Penelope Seldon from your studies of ship's history," said Karen, "but for those whose memories could stand refreshing, she was one of the leading
citizens of the first generation born aboard the *Agamemnon*,
a genius-level intellect and a specialist in AI and genetics. In
her later years, she was diagnosed as suffering from neurotic
and antisocial tendencies when she predicted that the society
aboard the *Agamemnon* would start to disintegrate after several generations. She was directed to undergo Counseling,
and following successful treatment, she lived out the remainder of her life in quiet retirement and solitude.

"Now, there are some additional facts that are important
here: this program which Seldon appears to have designed
apparently behaves like a computer virus and a master program capable of overriding the AIs throughout the ship. So
far as we know, only these three students have been able to
access this program, and it would be more accurate to say

that *it* accessed *them*, although we do not know why they were selected, or if they were the only ones.

"Ulysses Buckland, Riley Etheridge, and Jenny Kruickshank are currently reported missing. They disappeared from the school library along with three VR interface bands. Their physical whereabouts are unknown, but mentally, it appears that they have gone back to the quest.

"Some of these beings sighted on the ship may be dangerous. There have been no reports of anyone being injured—yet—but the fairies, at least, have the ability to entrance anyone who comes close to them. The elves may—I repeat, may—have the ability to telepathically influence people and/or interfere with the structural integrity of the ship."

Her last comment brought on the strongest reaction of all, and everyone on link tried to talk at once. When the commotion finally died down, the delegate from Miami Village asked a question.

"Chief, what exactly do you mean when you say the elves may be able to interfere with the structural integrity of the ship?"

Karen told them about pursuing the cloaked figure on the retaining wall, and how he ran into the lift housing and erected a wall to block her, then somehow disappeared from the lift shaft without coming out the other end.

"Now this is something only I have experienced," she said. "No other reports to date have mentioned any similiar occurrence. However, Sergeant Benjamin Cruzmark was present and witnessed this. Now, I am not a molecular engineer, but I've consulted with CAC Support in an attempt to find out how this could have been done. The lift housing, like the other permanent structures aboard the ship, is constructed of nanalloy. The smart molecules of the nanalloy are programmed with limited functions to achieve certain design configurations, such as opening doorways and windows, as directed by us through the various building computers. Those structures which have been designed as nonmodifiable, such as the lift housing, can only be modified by reprograming the nanalloy, something which only the architectural computers can do. I couldn't direct the architectural computers to effect such a design change without express authorization."

"But this alleged elf that you were chasing apparently did just that," the delegate said.

"That's correct," Karen replied. "This suggests that the quest program, or Program X, as we shall refer to it, is able to override the normal computer functions, dictating changes without any authorization other than its own and without leaving behind any record of such changes. However, for it to happen instantly, it had to have been programmed in advance."

"I'm not sure I follow," said the Miami delegate.

"If I may, Karen?" said one of the Assembly delegates from CAC Support.

"Yes, Paul," said Karen, "go ahead."

"Paul Sharonsky, CAC Support. I have discussed this matter with Chief Kruickshank, and I should stress that we still do not know the facts of the situation. However, theoretically, it might have been reprogrammed to respond to a verbal or touch command."

"To touch?" the delegate from Paris Village asked.

"Again, this is only speculation at this point," Sharonsky replied, "but whether we're dealing with constructs or organic beings created through genetic engineering, there may be something special about the fingerprints or palmprints of elves—assuming that they have them—that would result in the nanalloy responding to their touch. It would probably be an entire palmprint, so the touch would have to be deliberate, not just incidental contact. In other words, if there was something in the configuration of my palm that the nanalloy had been programmed to recognize and respond to with a specific function, then I could touch a surface and the smart molecules would recognize the touch and immediately associate it with a command, such as 'create wall' or 'delete wall' or whatever. But it would have to be a command that had been preprogrammed."

"Chief?"

"Delegate Rebecca Meyers," said Karen.

"Let me see if I understand this correctly," Meyers said,

turning toward Sharonsky. "Are you saying that these creatures can create or delete doors, windows, and walls *at* will?"

Sharonsky shrugged. "It's possible."

Karen once again had to restore order as the entire Assembly reacted to this information with alarm. Meyers continued with another question when the reaction died down.

"If that's the case," she said, "then what's to prevent these . . . these elves from breaching the integrity of the sea retaining wall? Or of the hull, for that matter?"

"Well, if that *were* the case," Sharonsky said, "which, I repeat, we do not yet know for certain, then I suppose the answer would be that there is nothing to prevent them. Except, of course, that it would affect their own survival, as well as ours."

In the uncomfortable silence that followed, one of the other delegates asked to be recognized.

"Delegate Andrew St. Jon," said Karen.

"I move that the Assembly immediately mandate total mobilization to hunt down these creatures or constructs or whatever they are," St. Jon said, in an agitated voice. "If we're faced with a renegade program created by a madwoman, one that's capable of controlling the AIs and producing mutated freaks that can interfere with the ship's structural integrity, we've got a clear and present danger to the welfare of the ship and the entire crew. This is a crisis unlike anything we've ever faced before. It could destroy us all. I say these creatures have to be eliminated. I move Security release weapons to trained personnel and auxiliaries at once."

"Chief, I would like to speak directly to the motion before it is seconded, if I may," a new speaker said.

"Who is that?" Karen asked, looking up toward the display. She did not recognize the speaker.

"Lars Jorgensen, Ecological Support. I ask the Assembly's indulgence for a moment, because I think some vital considerations are being overlooked."

"One moment, Mr. Jorgensen," said Karen. She hit the mute button on her console and turned to Cruzmark. "Jorgensen . . . isn't he the one who . . ."

"Tried to get the dolphins voting privileges in the Assembly," Cruzmark replied, rolling his eyes. "And after all the fuss he raised about it, getting that committee established and all, someone thought to ask the dolphins what they thought. And they couldn't care less."

"I thought that was him," said Karen. She turned off the mute. "Go ahead, Mr. Jorgensen."

"Thank you, Chief," Jorgensen said. "Before there is a hasty vote on the question of destroying these creatures, there are several questions I think we all need to consider very carefully. For one thing, it has not yet been definitely established that they pose a threat to the ship or the crew. If they are organic, sentient beings, derived from human genetic material, then there is the moral question of whether or not we have the right to destroy them. We're talking about murder.

"What Delegate St. Jon proposes," Jorgensen continued, "is nothing less than genocide. We have had no opportunity to study these life-forms. We have no way of knowing how long they have been among us, or to what extent their presence has affected our ecosystem. They are here, and they are now part of it. It's possible that eliminating them may throw our entire ecosystem out of balance."

"Mr. Jorgensen," St. Jon said, "the ship's ecosystem was never designed to accommodate them."

"I do not dispute that," Jorgensen replied. "Nevertheless, it has accommodated them. For however long they've been here, even if it's only for a short while, they have been interacting with it. If Program X functions as a master program, capable of reprogramming all existing systems, then it's possible, even probable, that the automated systems have already, at least to some degree, adapted to allow for the presence of these beings. Quite aside from the moral issue, eliminating them could result in irreparable harm."

"Very well," said St. Jon. "In that case, I will amend the motion. I move that pending a final decision concerning this issue, Chief Kruickshank be given full authorization, pursuant to her emergency powers, to order full mobilization and continue with her investigation. I further move that priority be given to finding and isolating Program X, and locating the facility or facilities producing these creatures and shutting it down. May I have a second on the motion?"

"I second the motion," said the delegate from Detroit.

"The motion is seconded. I call a vote," said Karen.

As the delegates' names were called, their votes were registered. It was unanimous. The motion was passed. A state of emergency was declared and schools were closed until further notice. All nonessential activities were suspended or curtailed at Karen's discretion. The Assembly would form a committee that afternoon to discuss Jorgensen's issue.

As the multiple displays on the wall winked out, Jorgensen's remained. "Chief, I must have a word with you and Mrs. Buckland," he said.

"Make it quick," said Karen, not anxious to waste time with him. "I've got a lot to do."

"Wherever these creatures are being produced," said Jorgensen, "it's probably a hidden facility. I can't believe we wouldn't have known about it otherwise."

"I've already reached that conclusion," Karen said. "But we're going to check every one of the automated labs, just to make sure. Wherever it is, we'll find it."

"When you do find it, you mustn't shut it down."

"What?" said Karen.

"Until we have had an opportunity to study the situation and determine to what degree these new species have affected the ecosystem, the status quo has to be maintained," insisted Jorgensen.

"You can't be serious! You expect me to just stand by and do nothing while Program X continues to produce these bizarre creatures?"

"Life-forms, Chief," said Jorgensen. He turned slightly, looking at another display on his wall at home, apparently Sonja's. "If they were nonorganic, why would they eat the crops? They're alive, Sonja. You're a botanist; you know just how delicate the balance of a closed ecosystem is. We can't risk taking any action until we know exactly what the consequences would be."

"I don't agree," said Sonja. "Their introduction into the system means that the balance has already been disrupted.

The way I see it, they could pose a serious threat to our survival."

"What about their survival?" Jorgensen said. "The Assembly can debate the issue all it wants, but you and I both know we're talking about living, sentient beings. What right do we have to exterminate them?"

"We have the right to defend ourselves, Mr. Jorgensen," said Karen.

"Against what?" Jorgensen replied. "Have they actually caused any harm to anyone?"

"Three of our children are missing," Sonja said.

"Is there any proof these creatures are responsible? For all we know, those kids just went off somewhere to continue playing this quest game. You said yourselves that they've been interfacing with this program and they haven't come to any harm, have they?"

"We don't know that for sure," said Karen, grimly.

"That's precisely my point," said Jorgensen. "We don't really know anything for sure yet, do we? We must not make any hasty decisions."

"You're forgetting one thing, Jorgensen," Karen said. "I already have the Assembly's full authority. I'll try to get you one or more of these creatures alive to study, if possible, but my first concern has to be the safety of the ship and our community. And I'm going to proceed as I think best. And now, if you'll excuse me, I have a job to do, and three missing children to find."

"Chief," said Jorgensen. "I'm asking you to reconsider. There's no way of knowing at this point what the ramifications of —"

Karen cut off his display.

"You were a bit hard on him, weren't you?" Sonja said, from her display. "I'm sure he means well."

"A well-meaning fool is nevertheless a fool," said Karen, curtly. "Make no mistake, this is a crisis situation, and we can't afford to sit on our hands arguing about what we should or shouldn't do. We have to *act*, before the situation grows any worse."

"But what if he's right?" asked Sonja.

"That's how it starts," Karen replied. "You don't really

believe that, do you? It's absurd. But he's already got you doubting yourself, and it didn't take him more than a couple of minutes. You see how it works? That's why people like Jorgensen are dangerous. It doesn't take much to plant the seeds of doubt, and what grows from them is hysteria."

"I'm not hysterical," Sonja said.

"No, but you're frightened," Karen replied. "I don't blame you. So am I. But I'm not going to let that stop me from doing what I have to do. I haven't stopped thinking about our children for a second. We'll find them. But right now, they need us to be strong. They need us to deal with this situation, not agonize over our choices. I'm going to do my job. And if Jorgensen or anybody else gets in my way, I'm going to go right through them."

CHAPTER
12

Ulysses awoke in the middle of the night to find himself alone in bed. He threw back the covers, slipped on his adept's robe, and padded barefoot out into the main room of the house. Riley was sleeping on the bearskin rug, before the fire, which had burned down to glowing embers. Jenny stood in the open doorway, wearing just her tunic, staring out toward the meadow and the forest. He came up behind her and slipped his arms around her waist.

"What are you thinking about?" he said, softly.

"I don't know," she said, in a vague voice, bringing her hands down to cover his as he held her. "Something woke me up. I had the feeling there was something out there. . . ." She continued to stare out across the meadow.

Ulysses frowned. "Something woke me, too." He stared over her shoulder. The moonlight cast a silvery glow over the meadow, and there was a thin fog upon the ground.

"What's going on?" asked Riley, from behind them.

"Something's happening," said Jenny. Then she pointed. "Look there!"

At the far end of the meadow, the gently swirling mist

seemed to be rising, but only in one place. Slowly, it rose to form an undulating column, and then that column seemed to swirl and shift, changing color and growing lighter as a glow came from within it. As they watched, it took human shape, and then dissipated, revealing The Lady. She stood there, at the far end of the meadow with the mist swirling about her feet, and at a distance of about a hundred meters, they could not make out her features. They saw only a figure in shimmering white robes, but when she spoke, they heard her voice as clearly as if she were standing right in front of them.

"You have done well," she said. "You have shown initiative, courage, imagination, and perseverance. I could not be more proud of you, my children. But other challenges await you. From now on, the quest shall continue uninterrupted until you have seen it through to its end. And as you are being challenged here, in this world where anything can happen, so are the people aboard the ship being challenged. As you are being tested, so are they. But they will not find the answers that they seek aboard the ship. Only you can find them, here. If you persist, and use the gifts that you were born with, you can solve the riddle of the quest. But failure is always a possibility with every challenge. You can succeed, but only if you are not afraid to fail."

"What *is* the riddle of the quest?" Ulysses asked, in a normal tone of voice. She heard him, even though she stood so far away.

"You will learn that only when you reach the Wizard's Castle," she replied. "That is the object of your quest, but it is not the final challenge. You will find that only when you reach the castle."

"Who are you?" Jenny asked. "Are you Dr. Seldon? Why have you done this? Why were we chosen? What is the purpose of this program?"

"Find the Wizard's Castle," she said, "solve the riddle of the quest, and all will be made clear."

She began to fade away.

"Wait!" shouted Riley. "How do we get back home?"

"Through the Wizard's Castle," the reply came, echoing across the meadow.

"But how do we find it?" Riley shouted.

There was no reply. There was only the gently undulating fog, fading back into the forest.

Ulysses woke up with a start and sat up in bed. Jenny sat up beside him.

"Did you have it, too?" she asked.

He nodded. "I thought we were awake. I didn't realize it was just a dream."

"This is all a dream," Jenny reminded him.

"Including what happened last night?" he asked, with a grin.

She smiled. "That was the best part of the dream." And then she sniffed the air. "Something smells delicious."

"Smells like breakfast," said Ulysses, getting out of bed and reaching for his clothes. "It must be Riley. I didn't even know he knew how to cook."

"Well, I'm starved," said Jenny. She giggled. "I guess I must have worked up an appetite somehow."

Ulysses grinned, then frowned. "I didn't even know we could get hungry in a sim," he said.

"Everything else here is so realistic, why not hunger?" asked Jenny.

"I wonder if that means we're hungry out there in the real world," Ulysses said. And then he frowned again. "Wherever it is we are."

"Maybe it means we're about to be fed," suggested Jenny, "and that's why we're going to be eating now."

"I guess that's possible," Ulysses said, "but fed by whom? It can't be Dr. Seldon. She's been dead for years."

"Drones, maybe," Jenny suggested.

"Yeah, that could be," Ulysses said, as he finished getting dressed. "A lot of preparation went into this whole thing. She could have designed drones to carry out some physical tasks. But it could also be some of the creatures that have been released into the ship."

"I hadn't thought of that," said Jenny. "If that's the case, they've probably taken us from the library. That would explain how Riley disappeared."

"Right," said Ulysses. "And by now our parents must

know we're missing." He sighed. "They're not going to be happy about this."

"If I know Mom," said Jenny, "she'll have Security turning the whole ship upside down, looking for us. Wherever we are, she'll find us eventually. Maybe that's why The Lady had us taken away, to give us a chance to stay in the quest until it's finished."

"Why do you call her The Lady and not Dr. Seldon?" Ulysses asked.

"Well, she isn't really Dr. Seldon, is she? Dr. Seldon's dead. The Lady is a construct of the sim. Besides, that's what everyone else here calls her."

"Everyone else here isn't real," said Ulysses. "And neither is she. Let's not forget that."

"Well, maybe breakfast isn't real, either, but it sure smells good," Jenny said. "And my hunger feels real enough. I don't know about you, but I'm ready to get something to eat."

"Okay, let's go see what Riley's cooking."

But it wasn't Riley. As they came through the curtains, they froze in astonishment. There were about a dozen dwarves bustling about in the kitchen, some cooking at the stove, others setting the table, cutting bread, mixing pancake batter, and slicing bacon. Riley was sitting at the table, watching them with a big grin on his face. And sitting across from him, drinking hot tea out of an earthenware mug, was the stranger in gray that they had seen before in the tavern.

"Good morning," he said, as they came in. "I trust you have slept well? Breakfast is almost ready. Would you care for some tea?"

"Yes, thank you," Jenny said, sitting down at the table. She couldn't take her eyes off the dwarves. They stood no higher than her waist, but they had the bodies of full-grown men, save that their arms and legs were shorter. They all had shaggy hair and all of them wore thick beards. They were dressed in brightly colored clothing and red or green caps, and they went about their tasks silently, with a serious industriousness, as if it all required a great deal of concentration.

"You didn't tell us we had company," said Ulysses, glancing toward Riley.

"They were here when I woke up," Riley replied.

"Glad to see you're so alert," Ulysses said, with a wry grimace, as he took his seat at the table across from the gray-clad stranger. "I remember you. You were the one we met back at the tavern."

The stranger smiled. "Yes, that was a memorable occasion."

"Who are you?"

"I am called Grailing Windwalker."

"You're an elf, aren't you?" Jenny asked.

He inclined his head toward her, and with the movement, they caught a glimpse of his pointed ears.

"Were you aboard the ship?" Ulysses asked.

"What ship would that be?" the elf asked, as he poured their tea.

"The *Agamemnon*," said Ulysses. "You know, the real world."

"A ship that is a world? How is that possible?"

"So you're saying that you were always here? I mean, in this world?"

"Are there others?"

"Never mind," Ulysses said, shaking his head with resignation. He could not tell if the elf was being sincere or merely toying with them. "What are you doing here?"

The elf raised his delicately arched eyebrows. "Having breakfast."

Several of the dwarves came over to the table and set plates before them. They were piled high with pancakes, eggs, and bacon. Another dwarf set a basket on the table filled with thickly sliced, fresh-baked bread. It smelled wonderful. The entire kitchen was permeated with the odors of cooking and baking. There was also jam, and butter, and thick maple syrup for the pancakes.

"Boy, I'm starved," said Riley, digging in.

Jenny started to pour syrup on her pancakes.

"How's the bacon, Riley?" asked Ulysses, watching as Riley helped himself to a generous portion.

"It's delicious," Riley said, with his mouth full. "I don't know why we don't have food like this on the ship."

"Doesn't bacon come from pigs?" Ulysses asked.

Riley froze in the act of chewing.

"Anyone you know?" Ulysses asked, raising his eyebrows.

"I think I just lost my appetite," said Jenny, pushing her plate away with a grimace.

"The pancakes are probably safe," Ulysses said, putting some jam and butter on his bread. "Either way, this is all just a sensory illusion. We're not *really* eating, are we?"

"'Twould be a pity if you didn't," Grailing said. "The dwarves worked hard to prepare this meal for you. They take their work quite seriously, you know, whatever sort of work it may be."

"Well, please tell them we appreciate it," said Ulysses.

"You may tell them yourself," the elf replied.

Ulysses glanced toward them. They were all standing in a line, watching expectantly. "Thank you very much for the meal," said Ulysses. "It's really excellent."

The dwarves looked at one another and nodded with satisfaction, then trooped out of the kitchen.

"So what happens now?" Ulysses asked. "Are you here to tell us about the Wizard's Castle?"

"Aye, the Wizard's Castle," said the elf, nodding. "'Tis there that you must solve the riddle of the quest. Assuming you succeed in reaching it, of course."

"What is the riddle of the quest?" asked Jenny.

"You mean you do not know?" the elf asked.

"It has to do with why we're here, doesn't it?" Ulysses said. "The purpose behind the whole thing."

The elf shrugged. "'Tis not my role to provide answers," he said, "merely to guide you on your quest."

"Okay," Ulysses said. "So where do we go from here?"

"Down to the lakeshore, where you shall find a boat," the elf said. "The boat will take you across the lake, where you shall find the stream that flows into it from the mountains. Follow the stream and it shall lead you to the castle."

"That's it?" said Riley. "That's all there is to it? Well, that sounds simple enough."

"Nothing is ever as simple as it seems," the elf replied. "And that is as it should be."

"What does that mean?" asked Ulysses, with a frown.

The elf smiled, enigmatically. "If life were simple, then 'twould not be life, but mere existence. Life has much to teach. Mere existence teaches nothing."

"But this isn't real life," Ulysses said. "It's just virtual reality."

"Ah, but what is the virtue of reality?" asked Grailing, with a smile.

Ulysses gave him a puzzled look. "What do you mean?"

"Is it in what you perceive with your senses, or does it lie deeper than that? And what if you cannot trust your senses? How then do you determine what is real and what is not?"

"I know that none of this is real," said Ulysses, "because this is only a VR simulation. We're not really here."

"But how do you know that?" Grailing persisted.

"Because I know we have a life outside this quest," Ulysses said.

"And what assures you that life is real?"

"Because such things as fairies, elves, unicorns, and dwarves do not exist," Ulysses said, wryly.

"Then perhaps your mother only dreamed that she saw fairies. Indeed, perhaps your whole life has been no more than a dream, a mere simulation of reality. How do you know that everyone aboard this ship of yours is not merely sleeping while it makes its journey, and dreaming that they are awake and going on about their lives? After all"—he made an expansive gesture, as if to take in everything around them—"if all of this could have been created as such a convincing simulation, then what assures you that your existence there is real and your existence here is not?"

"Sorry, I'm not going to fall for that one," said Ulysses. "I *know* what's real and what isn't."

"Then why are you sitting here and speaking with someone who does not exist?" the elf asked, with a smile. And in the next instant, he wasn't there. Ulysses blinked. Not only had the elf disappeared, but so had the food, their plates, their mugs of tea . . . everything was gone. The table was bare. There was no indication that anyone except themselves had ever even been there.

"That elf gets on my nerves," Ulysses said, sourly.

And then a rolled-up scroll bound with a white ribbon suddenly appeared in the center of the table. Ulysses reached for it, untied the ribbon, and unrolled the scroll.

"What does it say?" asked Riley.

Ulysses read the flowing Gothic script written on the scroll. "It says, 'Is there virtue only in reality?'"

"So how are we supposed to answer that?" asked Riley.

"I don't have the faintest idea," Ulysses said. "Maybe he's just playing games with us. And then again, maybe he's giving us a clue to the riddle of the quest."

"Well, since none of this is real, but we still saw some virtue in going on with it, then I guess the answer would be no," said Jenny.

Ulysses blinked, then gave a small snort and turned the scroll toward them, so they could see the writing on it. What was written on it earlier had disappeared. Now, there was only one word, written in large, flowing, and ornate letters. And that word was "Why?"

Peter was upstairs in the bedroom, studying a file display on the wall when Sonja finished her link conference with Karen and Jorgensen. As she came in, he canceled the display and the wall reverted to a soft beige color with an abstract mural on it.

"I'm becoming a little worried about Karen," Sonja said.

"About Karen? Why?"

Sonja sat beside him. "As a mother, I can understand how she feels, especially since Ulysses is missing, too. But even so, her reaction to all of this is like nothing I've ever seen. Anyone else displaying such extreme aggression would be sent in for Counseling."

"Well, she's Security," Peter said. "They're trained to deal with emergencies. And sometimes that requires aggressive behavior."

"But we've both served our time in Security," she replied. "We've had the same training and we're not reacting like that."

"I know, but there's a difference," Peter said. "We were never full-time Security. And, for that matter, I'm not sure that we did have exactly the same training. Certainly, not as much of it. We knew we'd serve our required period of enlistment and then that would be it. For us, it was only temporary. Our training was something that we never thought we'd have to use. For Karen, it's different."

"How is it different?"

"For Karen, there never was anything else *but* Security. Or to look at it another way, it's as if I'd spent my whole life training to be a teacher, but knew I'd never get the chance to teach unless some sort of an emergency arose. If that were the case, then I'm sure a part of me would inevitably hope for just such an emergency, so that I could put what I had learned to use."

Sonja nodded. "I see what you mean. This is her moment, isn't it? Her chance to prove herself."

"Yes, and that has to be stressful enough without her being worried about Jenny," Peter said. "We know how she feels when it comes to that, but we don't have the added stress of being responsible for dealing with this crisis. Right now, Karen's the most important person on the ship, and she knows it."

"She's not the only one who'll have to deal with it," said Sonja. "She's activating all the auxiliaries and all of the trainees. And the rest of the crew is going to be called upon to do their part, as well."

Peter exhaled heavily. "The only scenario anyone ever anticipated for that was contact with hostile alien life-forms. But then, in a sense, that's exactly what we're faced with, isn't it?"

"I'm not so sure," said Sonja, thoughtfully. "The kids are missing, but we don't know that any harm has come to them. Jorgensen was right. So far as we know, the creatures haven't really harmed or threatened anyone."

"Jorgensen? From Ecological Support? Wasn't he the one that . . ."

"Yes, the dolphins, that's all anyone ever remembers about the poor man, but he has a point. I think it's unlikely that these beings could have somehow become a vital part of our ecology this quickly, although if Program X is a master program, I suppose it's possible the Eco-Support systems might have been reprogrammed. But as far as the moral question is concerned, he may be right. Karen didn't see it that way, though. She had no patience with him at all. She said she was going to do her job, and she'd go right through anyone who got in her way."

"That's pretty strong talk," said Peter. "The Assembly will probably wind up leaving it up to Karen. They've never really had to make any difficult decisions before. I wouldn't be surprised if they choose to pass on the responsibility."

"As far as Karen is concerned, the decision has already been made," said Sonja, grimly. "Only what if it's the wrong decision? If the creatures have our kids, then how will they react?"

"I'm sure Karen's considered that," said Peter. "Her daughter is involved, after all."

"And so is our son. Pete, I'm scared."

"I know. I am, too. I've been studying the Folklore, Mythology, and Legends file, partly in an attempt to get a better grip on what we're dealing with and partly just to keep my mind occupied. I don't know to what extent these creatures are based on their descriptions in the file, but from what we've learned so far, it sounds pretty close. Fairies are supposed to possess something known as 'glamour,' which amounts to a sort of telepathic influence over people. That agrees with your description of what happened to you, and with what the kids said they experienced in the quest. Elves are supposed to have a mischievous streak, and sometimes supernatural powers, in addition to highly acute senses and good fighting skills. Dwarves are very strong for their size, industrious and methodical, and possessed of very quick reactions. And they, too, occasionally have supernatural powers. It doesn't seem unreasonable, under the circumstances, to assume that telepathic potential could have been genetically engineered into the fairies, and Seldon's program engineers the magic in the elves and dwarves, allowing them to interface with nanalloy."

Sonja shook her head. "It seems hard to believe she could have devised such an incredibly sophisticated program if she were truly crazy. And from everything that the kids told us about the quest, there does seem to be a logical consistency to the world she created."

"But this nightmarish program she created is not the work of a sane mind. It couldn't be."

"I don't know," said Sonja. "Maybe I don't want to believe it because I'm worried about Ulysses and I want to believe she wouldn't have designed a program that would hurt anyone, but at the same time, I'm trying to be rational about this. Right now, that's not easy, but I have to try or else I'll panic. I have to focus on something, and what I keep coming back to, as I turn it over and over in my mind, is *why*? She must have had some purpose in mind."

"Yes, to get even with everyone who didn't agree with her and branded her paranoid and antisocial," Peter said.

"Then why didn't she do it back then?" asked Sonja. "That's what doesn't make sense. If she had wanted to take some kind of revenge, why didn't she do it when she had her chance to see it work? We're not the ones who wouldn't listen to her and sent her in for Counseling. The people of her generation are all dead."

"Maybe she intended for it to happen right after her death, but something went wrong with the program and it wasn't activated until now."

Sonja shook her head. "No, I can't accept that. It's not really my field, but I know enough about AI programs to know that they don't just malfunction and then somehow fix themselves after a hundred years or more. Especially not programs as intricate as this one. It's a brilliant piece of work. As far as anyone can tell, even based on the little we do know, nothing at all has gone wrong with it."

"So you believe that she purposely designed it so that it wouldn't be activated until now? Why?"

"That's the question," said Sonja. "It keeps coming back to that. Why do it in the first place, and why wait all this time?" A strange look crossed her features.

"What?" asked Peter.

"Time," said Sonja, thoughtfully.

"What about it?"

"Not time so much as . . . timing," she said, in a preoccupied tone. She moistened her lips and frowned, gazing off abstractedly for a moment, then turned to him and said, "Follow me on this. To the best of our knowledge, the creatures started to appear at about the same time the kids discovered the quest program."

"More like it discovered them," said Peter.

Sonja shook her head impatiently. "That's not the point," she said. "The fact is they had their first experience of the quest sim at roughly the same time as I found out about the fairies, give or take a day or so. At about the same time, I also saw the dwarf, the one who stole the recording crystal. And also at approximately the same time, the Marshall girl had her experience with the elf. Now I have no idea how long the fairies had been around, but the dwarf certainly looked mature, and the elf that Robie Marshall met was at least a young adult. Full-grown."

"It would have taken time for them to mature," said Peter. "Which means that Program X must have been activated well before the kids began the quest."

"But the creatures didn't start appearing until after they began it," Sonja said. "Or at about the same time, anyway."

"Okay," said Peter. "But I don't quite see where you're going with this."

"I don't really know where I'm going with it . . . yet," said Sonja, shaking her head slowly. "But even with accelerated growth, it would have taken some years for the creatures to mature. They had to be kept somewhere during all that time."

"A hidden reproductive lab?" said Peter.

"That would be the most logical explanation," Sonja said. "Karen's going to institute a search for it, if she hasn't already. Penelope Seldon had a lot of time to prepare. Whatever it is she planned, she planned it very carefully. If she had set up an automated AI lab to produce these creatures, she had to do it somewhere where it wouldn't be found easily, where it would have remained secure for all this time."

"Aboard a ship this size . . ." said Peter.

"Even so," said Sonja, "it had to be located somewhere where no one would be likely to stumble across it."

"Or else she could have simply used one of the existing

labs," said Peter. "They're all operated by AI, and not all of them are in use all the time."

"No, I don't think so," said Sonja. "Remember that she would have had no way of knowing which of them would be in use at any given time in the future, and she had to realize that as soon as the creatures started to appear, that would be the first place Security would look. She must have set up her own lab somewhere else."

"A systematic search will take time," said Peter, "but it shouldn't be that difficult to find."

"I'm sure Penelope Seldon would have anticipated that," said Sonja. "Perhaps she only intended to produce a limited number of the creatures, so once they were released, it wouldn't matter if the lab were found. But let's get back to the question of the timing. If we assume that Program X was designed to sleep somewhere in the databanks until it became activated, then the first thing it must have done when it was triggered was start manufacturing the creatures. Perhaps she had them kept in a crèche, where they were programmed by AI, and then, when they reached the desired level of maturity, the quest program was triggered, roughly at the same time as they began to be released into the ship."

"Okay," said Peter, "I'm with you so far. But where does that get us?"

"I'm not sure," said Sonja, frowning. "We're back to the 'Why?' again. Why were Ulysses, Riley, and Jenny the only ones to get the quest sim? There haven't been any reports of anyone else receiving it. And why was the quest sim designed in the first place? What role does it play in the purpose of the program?"

"The only purpose I can readily discern is to disrupt the community of the ship," said Peter. "Or even worse, to sabotage the voyage itself. Penelope Seldon had predicted that things would start to fall apart for us within several generations. No one took her seriously, so maybe this is her way of proving her case. Posthumously."

"We've been over that before," said Sonja. "And it still doesn't make sense to me. If she had wanted some sort of posthumous revenge, why go to such elaborate lengths to achieve it? And why this way?"

"Because she was unbalanced," said Peter, with a shrug.

Sonja remained silent, pausing to think a moment. "What if she wasn't?"

"You think a rational person would do something like this?" asked Peter.

"Just because we *think* she was irrational doesn't mean she was," said Sonja. "We don't have any data, we're simply making assumptions. So let's assume, just for the sake of argument, that she wasn't irrational," Sonja said.

"All right, then what possible reason could she have had for designing Program X?"

"Well," said Sonja, "if she wasn't irrational, she still could have been wrong in her conclusions, but she could have operated from the position that she wasn't, so she would have been convinced there was a crisis coming. In that case, the logical assumption would be that her intention was not to disrupt the community of the ship, but to save it."

"If that was really the case," said Peter.

"But that's the one thing we haven't yet considered," Sonja replied. "We've been assuming she was mentally unbalanced, and that she designed Program X as the result of some delusion. But it's never occurred to us to ask, 'What if she was right?' What if she was able to see something no one else could see . . . or was willing to see? Suppose you were in her place, and you were convinced you were right, only no one listened to you. Would you just give up? Or would you try to do something?"

Peter took a deep breath and exhaled heavily. "If I was absolutely convinced that I was right, I'd certainly try to do something," he said. "But if I were rational, why would I want to do something to create the very situation I was hoping to prevent?"

Sonja thought about it for a moment. "Maybe you'd do it to create a crisis. A preliminary crisis intended to prepare everyone for the real crisis that was coming."

"You mean like some sort of test run?" Peter asked. He rubbed his chin thoughtfully. "It's an interesting speculation, but we're back to that irritating 'Why?' again. Why do it in such a peculiar, complex and flamboyant manner? And why involve three children?"

"I don't know," said Sonja, with frustration. "I can't think of an answer to that one. Maybe I'm completely off base."

"Maybe not," said Peter, thoughtfully. "It's worth pursuing, if for no other reason than to examine both sides of the question. There has to be some record of what she predicted, exactly what she believed was going to happen. Mac . . . ?"

"Yes, Peter?"

"Access Ship's History, also the Educational files and the Ship's Log, and look for any entries regarding Penelope Seldon being directed to report for Counseling, or any reports she may have entered regarding the long-term future of the voyage."

Mac replied specifying them by file entry, date, and time.

"Access those, Mac," said Peter. "I want to know if any of them specify predictions she had made concerning negative developments for the ship's community. If so, then correlate and give me a brief summary of the essential information."

Processing the information instantaneously, Mac replied, "Dr. Seldon believed that the structure of ship's community did not provide adequate challenge and motivation for the crew. She was opposed to the belief that aggressive, competitive instincts were unhealthy and disruptive in a properly balanced society, and predicted that unless changes were instituted, within several generatons, there would occur an increase in the incidence of depression which, if left untreated, would lead to suicide. She stated that unless changes were instituted in the education, organized activities, and social structure of the ship's community, stimulating natural aggressive, competitive and creative insincts rather than suppressing them, this trend would eventually become irreversible, leading to alienation among the ship's community, increasing loss of motivation, withdrawal, psychosis, and eventually, complete social breakdown, resulting in the failure of the mission."

Sonja and Peter stared at one another. "Depression and suicide," said Peter.

"My God. She was right," said Sonja, softly.

CHAPTER
13

"A re you ready for this?" Ben Cruzmark said, swiveling his chair around toward his desk and away from the wall display as Karen entered Security Headquarters. "We've got nine more missing kids."

His words brought her up short. *"What?"* She felt as if every muscle in her body had tensed, involuntarily.

"They all disappeared sometime either late last night or early this morning," Cruzmark replied. "All from different villages, in different parts of the ship. No one has any idea where they've gone. They just dropped out of sight."

"Who's on this right now?" she asked, immediately getting to the point.

"I've put Koski on it," said Cruzmark. "I sent him out with a squad of trainees to get detailed statements from all the parents of the missing kids and search their homes to see if he can come up with anything. Aside from that, I've got Wiley processing the auxiliaries and getting them all up to speed, and Hamann's working on mobilization with CAC. Everybody else is on Search and Rescue. I've been coordinating that from here myself. So far, there's been no indication of anything unusual with Guardian, but you said to take no chances and monitor everything, so it's been a busy morning."

Karen had issued orders that no operations be left up to Guardian, the Security computer, without someone monitoring the results. If Program X was capable of reprogramming other computers on the ship, then perhaps it could reprogram Guardian as well, despite the built-in safeguards. CAC Support agreed and were following similar procedures with their own network. Until Program X was found and isolated, none of the computers aboard the ship could be trusted. The trouble was, thought Karen, Program X was apparently very good at hiding. Every available computer specialist at CAC Support was looking for it, so far without any success.

"Get in touch with Koski and tell him I want a full report on each missing child by the end of the day," said Karen. "I want as much background as possible. Tell him to talk to their teachers, talk to their friends . . . tell him to look for connections. I want to find out which of them went to school together, how many of them knew each other outside of school, and if they disappeared in groups."

"You're thinking it's the quest sim?" said Cruzmark.

"The coincidence is just too damn convenient," Karen replied. "It looks as if Jenny, Riley, and Ulysses may not have been the only ones playing the game. I thought all the VR bands had been confiscated by now."

"Apparently not," said Ben. "There's, uh, been mixed compliance with that order."

Karen frowned. "What do you mean, mixed compliance?"

"The order went out to everyone aboard the ship, but unfortunately, there's no way of telling exactly how many VR bands are out there. There's never been any reason to keep an inventory, and the shops have always just produced new ones to meet demand as it arose. Most households have at least several. It's not as if they take up very much room, and people like their entertainment. Apparently, not all the VR bands were surrendered when the order went out. Some people held back a few. Looks like we've got some disruptive behavior out there."

"Wonderful," said Karen, her voice laced with irony.

"Those idiots are responsible for their children's disappearance."

"Well, maybe that's being a little harsh, Chief," Ben said. "I mean, the kids could have their own and they might have stashed them away."

"And their parents wouldn't know about it?" Karen replied, dubiously.

"I didn't know how many bands my own son had," said Ben, sheepishly. "I knew he had one, but it turned out he had three. I guess I just never kept track."

She glanced at him with concern. "Jerry isn't . . ." her voice trailed off.

"No," Ben replied, quickly, "he's safe at home, with Nora."

"Good," Karen said, nodding with relief and feeling a stab of anxiety for Jenny at the same time. Ben knew what she was thinking and said nothing. Karen took a deep breath. "As if we didn't have enough problems," she said. "Short of conducting a house-to-house search for every available VR band, the only other thing we can do is shut down all computer link interfaces, but that would cripple our communications. And even if we could do that, Program X would probably just override and switch them all back on." She sighed and rubbed her temples wearily. "Now we've got a dozen kids held hostage by this damn program. What does it take to get these people to realize how serious this is?" She walked over to one of the display walls and said, "Guardian, open a window."

The display vanished and the wall flowed as if it were melting, opening a large, rectangular bay window looking out over the Central Administrative Complex from the sixth floor of the Security building. She looked down at the plaza below. Several squads of auxiliaries were being mustered and briefed down there by Wiley. Mobilization procedures were already under way. People were reporting in shifts, called up according to their residence units. Once they arrived at Security Headquarters, they were briefed and assigned their tasks. Most were organized into Search and Rescue squads under the command of an auxiliary officer or senior trainee. Others were assigned to patrol duty or administrative backup at Security HQ. They would need plenty of backup, especially if they couldn't trust everything to Guardian. Those whose specialties concerned essential functions of the ship were exempted from other duties and assigned to closely monitor the computers running the automated systems. Karen was trying to leave nothing to chance.

The trouble was, AIs could process information, make decisions, and perform multiple tasks much faster and more efficiently than humans, which was, of course, why they ran all the essential functions of the ship. The downside of that was that even with teams of specialists monitoring their functions, keeping up with them was practically impossible.

Karen stared across the plaza, at the CAC Support building, the nerve center of the *Agamemnon*. They had opened windows on their top-floor command center, as well, to let in some of the breeze generated by the weather AI. And also, Karen thought, probably to cut down on their feeling of isolation. They were all working around the clock over there and no one was getting any rest. She saw someone standing at the window on the top floor of CAC Support, looking out toward her. At this distance, she couldn't tell exactly who it was, but she had a pretty good idea.

"Guardian," she said, "get me Paul Sharonsky on AV at CAC Support."

A moment later, she could see an enlarged version of her own image, from behind, appear on the wall in back of the figure standing at the window across the plaza. She saw him start to turn around and turned herself, seeing his image on the display wall behind her complete the turn as she faced him.

"Hello, Paul," she said. "I thought that was you over there."

"Hi, Karen. I was just thinking about you," Sharonsky said. He hadn't shaved and his hair was mussed. He looked exhausted.

"Wishing that you had my job?" she said.

"No, wishing that you had mine," he replied, with a wan smile. "I was thinking I could have opted to specialize as a teacher, but I figured it would be too much work. Now CAC

Support, they never really do much except research. Their functions are essentially redundant. So I picked this. What a smart guy I was."

"You look tired," Karen said, sympathetically.

"I'm more frustrated than tired," he replied, running a hand through his thinning, gray hair. "I don't feel as if we're getting anywhere. About the best we can do for the present is look for anomalies and hope we can correct any glitches before they manifest as serious problems. If we can't, then we'll simply have to shut down any part of the network that malfunctions, take it out of the loop until we can correct the situation or, failing that, get a redundant system on line and hope *that* doesn't get infected. The problem is, we have to check systems that may be unreliable with other systems that may be equally unreliable. We can task redundant systems to run repeated diagnostics, but then we need to run checks on those systems, as well. And in the meantime, we have to search for Program X, and the only way we can conduct that search is with the CAC Net, which may itself be infected by the program. It's like asking a mental patient to be his own psychiatrist. In fact, it's even worse, because Program X can replicate itself, and, to follow the analogy, the more our hypothetical patient seeks to cure himself, the sicker he's bound to get. It's like performing the task of Sisyphus."

Karen frowned. "The task of who?"

"Sisyphus," Sharonsky said. "A Greek who was punished by the gods. He was condemned to roll a large boulder up a hill, only to have it roll back down again each time, so he spent eternity pursuing a hopeless, pointless task." Sharonsky gave a small snort. "We've all had cots set up over here, but I can't seem to get much sleep, so I've been going through the Folklore, Mythology, and Legends file you mentioned in your report." He shrugged. "I mean, you never know . . . Seldon used it, so maybe there's something in there that might help. Haven't really found anything helpful yet, but I'm finding most of it pretty fascinating stuff. I wonder why we stopped teaching it."

"I don't know," said Karen. "That file's never been used in my lifetime. Maybe they didn't think it was productive."

"Strictly speaking, it probably isn't, but it all depends on how you look at it, I guess," Sharonsky said. "The mythology makes you think. At least, it makes me think. It's got some interesting moral points to ponder."

"Speaking of moral points," said Karen, "our friend, Jorgensen, is gathering some support. He's organizing what he calls a 'pro-life lobby group' to petition the Assembly on behalf of the creatures."

"Are you going to stop him?"

"Only if he gets in my way," Karen replied. "If I used my authority in an attempt to silence him or place him in custody, it would only serve to glamorize his position. Unless he becomes a problem, I intend to ignore him. I don't think he'll pick up any significant support. He needs a reality check. He's actually calling the creatures 'our humanoid friends.' "

"After seeing what Program X can do, I can believe anything," Sharonsky said. "You know, I've studied her work, but I never fully appreciated how brilliant Penelope Seldon was until now. This thing is a nanoprogram, Karen, unbelievably sophisticated. It's like intelligent DNA. You try to isolate it, and it disassembles itself and scatters. It's the perfect terrorist program, sentient, molecular-level software, capable of reconstituting itself anywhere within the net. It can run and hide. And being a master program capable of self-replication means that it could eventually take over the entire ship if it wanted to."

"It it *wanted* to?" said Karen.

"It's self-aware, Karen, in the same way the AIs are self-aware. The way it behaves indicates that each individual smart molecule contains the template for the complete program. It's like a virus capable of making independent decisions. It's got a personality. Possibly based on Seldon's, though I can't say that for sure. I'll be honest with you; I just can't see any way we can defeat this thing unless we can discover a command that will deactivate it."

"*Is* there a command that will deactivate it?"

Paul shrugged with resignation. "The only one who could answer that would be Penelope Seldon."

"I wish there was some way we could ask her," Karen

said, with a grimace. "Or at least figure out what she intended."

"What's happening out there?" Sharonsky asked. "I've been cooped up here ever since this whole thing started. Have there been any new developments?"

"The creatures appear to be lying low for now," she replied, "but nine more kids have been reported missing."

"Nine?"

She nodded. "I'm almost certain we're going to discover they were involved in the quest sim, as well."

"Three groups of three?" Sharonsky asked.

"I don't know yet. But I should find out by the end of the day. Search and Rescue parties have been sent out and more are being organized. They're looking for the kids, as well as the lab that's producing the creatures."

"Maybe it's not just one lab," said Sharonsky.

"That's possible, but I think it's unlikely," she replied. "We haven't had that many sightings. And setting up just one hidden lab would have been challenging enough. She did a good job, though. I thought we would have found it by now. If you were going to set up a concealed laboratory, one you wanted to keep hidden for years, where would you put it?"

"Somewhere no one was liable to go," Sharonsky replied. "Between the inner and outer hulls, maybe."

"You'd have to construct a hidden chamber, and provide for power, life-support, and access," Karen replied. "Possible, but difficult and complicated. I shouldn't think a construction project like that would have gone unnoticed, even if she used drones."

"Hmmm," said Sharonsky, rubbing his chin. "Still not impossible, though. What about the propulsion and navigation chambers between the hulls, fore and aft?"

"We're checking those," said Karen. "Again, same problem. It would be a rather elaborate construction job. She could have had it done over a period of some years, in small stages, but it still seems likely someone would have noticed."

"What about the maintenance conduits and sublevels?"

"We're already working on it," she replied. "Any other ideas?"

"I'm assuming you've already checked out the existing labs."

"First thing we did."

"Hmmm. Well, let me give it some more thought. Maybe there's something we're overlooking."

"I don't want to distract you from searching for a way to isolate that program," she replied. "It's not as if you haven't got enough to do."

"I'll just keep it at the back of my mind," he said. "If I come up with anything, I'll let you know. Keep me posted about those missing kids."

"I will."

"We'll work it out, Karen, don't worry."

"It's my job to worry."

"Well, just don't overdo it. I'll get back to you."

"Thanks, Paul."

His image disappeared from the wall, replaced by the monitor displays. She turned to Ben. "Let me have an update on the search parties," she said, tensely.

Security officer Rhonda Abramson had been detailed to take her search party through the Navigation and Operations sections, located behind the gray wall that was the interior "polar cap" at the forward end of the ship. Seen in a cross section display, the irregularly shaped outer hull of the *Agamemnon* made Rhonda think of a gigantic potato with a cylinder inside it. The outer hull was the huge asteroid body that had been hollowed out and sealed, and the inner hull was the cylinder—the interior of the ship—flat at each end. The Propulsion sections at the aft end and the Navigation and Operations sections forward could be reached by going through hatchways in the interior polar caps.

There was nothing much to search in the forward and aft sections outside the inner hull except access corridors. The propulsion chambers of the *Agamemnon*, located at the rear of the ship, were sealed, so there was nothing visually dramatic to see. There were no rows of dials or instruments or cooling pipes or wiring conduits, just empty, sterile-looking chambers that could be accessed by shaftlike corridors. The

Navigation and Operations sections were similar, save that there was no need to seal off the main chambers. Visual monitor displays were available upon request, configured by computer upon the nanalloy walls, and no human agency was involved in maintaining the ship's primary operational systems. It was rare for anyone to go there, since there was no real need for it, and so it was the first time Abramson or any of her team had ever been up forward.

They had examined the cross section map displays and then entered through one of the access hatchways around the perimeter of the interior polar cap, set flush with its surface. There were no hatchways located near the center of the cap, which was in the zero-g zone. They had gone through one of the outermost starboard hatchways and down the long main access corridor leading in closer to the zero-g zone, with several shorter corridors branching off from it. The lights came on automatically as they moved along, searching each corridor and chamber systematically.

"There's nothing back here," Security Trainee Diana Slade said wearily, as they moved down a corridor that would take them around and past the zero-g zone to the side of the forward chamber opposite from where they came in. "This is just a waste of time."

"The Chief said to check it out, so we check it out," said Abramson. "When you conduct a systematic search, you do it right. You don't take anything for granted. Besides, those missing kids *could* have come back here to hide."

"I don't think anyone's been back here for years," said Jim Lambert, one of the other trainees.

Just then, a rapid patter of feet echoed through a corridor just ahead of them. They had almost reached the opposite inner hull, and as they looked toward the sound, a tiny figure came racing across their field of view. The figure wore clothing of bright green and red, and stood no higher than their knees. At first glance, it looked like a small child, but then they saw the shaggy hair and beard as the dwarf glanced toward them quickly while running aross their path. For a moment, they stood frozen with surprise. Abramson was the first to recover.

"After him!" she shouted, as she took off in pursuit, running full speed. The trainees followed hard on her heels.

The dwarf moved very swiftly for his size, but with their longer legs, they closed the distance rapidly. Lambert, running hard, sprinted ahead of Abramson. The dwarf passed the access hatch that led back into the interior of the ship and kept running along the corridor curving along the inner hull, heading forward. Lambert pumped his arms hard as he ran, intent on catching the creature. The dwarf glanced back over his shoulder and saw Lambert coming up fast. Suddenly, the dwarf broke stride, leaned down and slapped the floor with the palm of his hand. Lambert was almost upon him when the floor simply opened up in front of him and, unable to stop, he plunged through with a yell.

As the rest of them came running up, the nanalloy floor was already flowing, closing up the opening. Abramson was closest, and she came up just in time to catch a glimpse of Lambert lying in the conduit below the floor, stretched out on his side with his leg bent at an unnatural angle. Then the floor closed up and became solid once again, hiding him from view.

"Slade, Garcia, find the nearest maintenance access hatch to that conduit and get him out of there," she said. "Call Headquarters and send for a cruiser. I think his leg is broken. I'm going after that dwarf."

She started running hard down the corridor in the direction that the dwarf had taken. She was heading toward the extreme forward end of the ship. She tried to recall the cross section display they'd examined earlier. She did not remember exactly where this corridor led, but it was following the curvature of the inner hull and appeared to lead toward the huge main hatchway of the ship, located in the zero-g zone at the forward end.

There was no sign of the dwarf up ahead, but she thought she could hear running footsteps. Mindful of the way the dwarf had opened up the floor, she slowed down to a trot and proceeded more cautiously. After a while, she reached a junction where the corridor opened out into a huge chamber, then branched off on the other side, leading back around to the opposite hull and toward the center of the section. The central corridor leading straight back through the central shaft, into the ship, was huge and cavernous. She had reached the main access shaft and air lock hatchway. There were also smaller hatchways, to either side of the much larger main one, designed for individual use. And the cycling panel light was on above one of the smaller hatchways, leading through the outer hull. She whistled softly.

"Well, I'll be damned," she said.

Karen stepped through the hatchway, following Abramson and Slade. She had sent the cruiser back to the hospital with Lambert. His leg was broken, but otherwise, he was merely bruised and shaken up.

As she followed Rhonda and Diana down the short and narrow corridor, she felt a mounting sense of excitement. According to the cross section displays on file, this was not supposed to be here. The displays showed only the main double air lock hatchways, but this corridor had led through to a large hub constructed on the surface, at the center of the forward end of the ship. This hub was the housing for the external main hatchway, but radiating out from it were four narrow corridors, passageways constructed on the outer surface of the ship. However, it couldn't possibly be new construction. Even using drones, Penelope Seldon would never have been able to cut through the hull and construct passageways on the outer surface. This had to have been done when the *Agamemnon* was originally constructed. That could only mean one thing—Seldon had managed to alter the displays, so these passageways wouldn't show. Karen had no idea what they were, or where they led.

They reached the open hatchway at the other end. It had refused to open automatically. There had been a safeguard, probably a password command that Penelope Seldon had programmed years ago, so the engineers had opened it the hard way. As Karen stepped through with the others, she caught her breath.

They were inside an observation bubble on the outer surface of the hull, at the forward tip of the *Agamemnon*. The bubble was at least a hundred meters in diameter, constructed of thick, self-sealing nanopolymer that replicated and repaired itself to maintain transparency and structural integrity against the constant bombardment of micrometeorites as the ship moved through space. It was large enough to accommodate a number of structures inside its dome, and Karen realized these were the sensor arrays. But it was the view that made her gasp.

The sky was pinwheeling. She looked out through the bubble overhead at the vast, inky blackness of space, sprinkled with thousands of stars. The observation bubble, one of four connected to the central hatchway hub by passageways radiating out from it, was near enough to the zero-g zone at the exact central axis of the ship to give her the unsettling feeling of being pulled by the Coriolis force as the ship rotated. Her cling boots, which were necessary for any activity at or near the zero-g zone, kept her feet in place where otherwise she would have gone skating across the floor, toward the outer rim of the bubble. Being so near the central axis of the ship, and forward at the surface, meant that the ship's rotation here was most pronounced, resulting in the effect of the sky circling above her. It gave her a sudden and acute case of vertigo, and she had to clench her fists to steady her nerves.

"It's really something, isn't it?" said Diana Slade, coming up beside her. Slade was currently serving her tour on Security, but her specialties were engineering and astrophysics. She pointed. "That structure over there houses some of the sensors and receiving equipment. Originally, these bubbles must have been designed as observation decks for people from the ship to get a glimpse of the outside."

"It's incredible," said Karen, with astonishment.

"It makes you feel a bit dizzy and panicky just standing here, doesn't it?" Diana said.

Karen swallowed nervously and nodded. "More than a little. It's extremely disconcerting."

"I felt it, too," said Rhonda. "We're too accustomed to what it looks like on the inside. It's a whole new perspective out here, and it feels very unsettling. I can't imagine anyone could stay out here very long."

"How is it possible we never knew about this?" asked Karen, with amazement.

"I guess after the First Generation, people just weren't comfortable with it anymore, and they stopped coming out. Eventually, they probably just forgot these observation decks were even here," Diana said.

"And we never knew about them because Seldon altered the map displays several generations ago," said Rhonda. "She concealed them by simply telling the databases they weren't there."

"Did you capture any of the creatures?" Karen asked.

"We haven't yet had time to fully search the domes," said Rhonda. "But we found a reproductive lab inside that structure there."

"So this is where she hid it, " Karen said. "Shut it down and dismantle it. I want these domes gone through with a fine-tooth comb. If you discover any of the things, take them gently, if possible. But if they resist, use your own judgment. I don't want anyone else getting hurt. Will it be safe to use stunners in here?"

"Affirmative," said Rhonda. "The engineers have confirmed that there's no danger to the dome surface."

"Good. As soon as these areas have been cleared, we'll station guard details and use them to confine the creatures we apprehend. We know that at least some of them can talk, and I want them interrogated."

"What do we do with them then?" asked Rhonda.

Karen compressed her lips into a tight grimace. "I don't know," she said. "I guess that will be up to the Assembly to decide."

"What are you going to recommend?" Diana asked.

"I don't see that we really have a lot of options," Karen replied. "They'll have to be recycled."

One of the other officers approached her. "Chief, the cruiser's back from taking Lambert to the hospital. Any instructions?"

"I'll be heading back to Headquarters directly," said Karen. "Rhonda, you're in charge here. Make sure the maintenance conduits in all the structures are closed off, then seal up the place and search the grounds. If you capture any of the creatures, call me at HQ immediately."

"Will do," said Abramson.

Okay, Penelope, thought Karen, as she headed back inside the ship. We've found your lab. With any luck, we'll have the missing kids soon. Then all that will remain will be finding and shutting down the program. Of course, she realized, that would be the hardest part. The question was, what would the program do once it discovered that the lab had been shut down and the creatures were being apprehended? What *could* it do? That was an unsettling question.

It would take time to round up all the creatures, because there were so many places aboard the ship where they could hide, but at least now the program could not produce any more of them. With Seldon's reproductive facilities shut down, there would be—Karen stopped, suddenly, as it hit her. Then she started running.

She came out through the hatchway leading into the interior of the ship and looked around quickly for the Security cruiser. She spotted it at once, a short distance away, and sprinted toward it.

"Headquarters," she told the pilot, as she vaulted into it and strapped herself in. "Fast." As the cruiser lifted off, she activated her Security link. "Ben, this is Karen. Come in."

"Cruzmark here. Did you find the lab?"

"We found it. Listen, I just realized something. We've got to shut down all the Reproductive Centers."

"What?"

"The program, Ben! As soon as it realizes we've shut down Seldon's hidden lab, it could infect the AIs at the Reproductive Centers and reprogram them."

"Good God," said Ben. "Why didn't we think of that before?"

"Shut 'em down, Ben. Now."

"Chief, we can't," he said. "It would kill all the incubating fetuses. That would be murder."

Karen shut her eyes and leaned back against the seat cushion, exasperated. "Right," she said. "Okay, here's what we'll have to do. All the viable fetuses currently in gestation will have to be taken off line, the wombs disconnected from the automated programs and maintained manually. Get onto Paul Sharonsky at CAC and have him coordinate with the hospital to draft the necessary personnel."

"What about the ones in the *in vitro* cycles?" Ben asked.

"They'll have to be taken off-line, as well," said Karen. "If they're far enough advanced that they can be supported by the artificial wombs, they'll have to be transferred and maintained under human supervision. The ones that aren't . . ." her voice trailed off. She took a deep breath. "The parents will have to be contacted and given a choice between termination or having the fertilized eggs implanted."

"You mean . . . actually carrying the children themselves?" said Ben, with a note of shock in his voice.

"It's either that or they can risk giving birth to a dwarf, or something worse," said Karen. "A child that would almost certainly have to be recycled. Under the circumstances, I expect most of them will probably choose termination."

"We're talking about abortion," Ben said, in a low voice.

"We're talking about a sentient nanoprogram designed by a madwoman," Karen said, "one that's easily capable of infecting the AIs at the Reproductive Centers and genetically altering the next generation. That's what we're talking about, Ben."

"You don't think she would have . . ." Cruzmark's voice trailed off in dismay. "Surely, not the children!"

"Ben, for all we know, Program X may have already infected the Reproductive Centers. We've got to take them off-line. We have no other choice."

"Don't you think this is a decision that should be referred to the Assembly?" Ben said.

"By the time they decide anything, it could be too late," said Karen. "They gave me emergency powers, Ben, and I'm going to have to use them. I'll take responsibility. Besides, there will be no termination without parental consent. The choice is going to be theirs. I wouldn't have it any other way."

"That'll be some choice," said Ben. "No woman has actually carried a fetus in the entire history of the ship. The very idea is primitive and barbaric. Do you have any idea what kind of reaction this is going to set off?"

"I'm afraid I have a very good idea," Karen said. "I am a woman, after all."

"Yes, of course," said Ben, quickly.

"I know exactly what you meant. And yes, they're going to howl about it. It'll be brought up before the Assembly and they'll have the unenviable task of trying to decide whether or not to overrule me. But they won't. Not once I make them understand the potential consequences. Nobody wants to give birth to a freak."

For a moment, Cruzmark did not respond. Then, in a soft voice, he said, "Nora and I have another child on the way."

Karen closed her eyes. She swallowed hard, then said, "How far along?"

"Still in the first cycle," Ben said. "We've already named her. Graciella."

"That's a lovely name," said Karen, dully.

"I'd better call Nora," Ben said.

Karen was afraid to ask, but she did anyway. "What are you going to do?" she asked, quietly.

"Abortion's not an option," Ben replied. "Not for me. And I'm sure Nora will see it the same way. We've been waiting a long time to be cleared for this child. I guess we can be an example to the others. Or Nora can be, to be precise. She's the one who'll have to carry the child to term."

"How's her health?"

"She's fine," said Ben. "Nora's in good shape. I'm sure it'll turn out okay."

"I'm sorry, Ben."

"Don't be. You're right. I'm not letting that damn program do anything to our little girl. People used to reproduce that way for thousands of years. I'm sure we haven't forgotten how."

"If there's anything I can do to help . . ."

"I appreciate that. But right now, you've got your hands full."

"We all do, Ben," she said. "We all do."

She unlinked and settled back against the seat cushion wearily, with a heavy sigh. And then the cruiser lurched wildly as it struck something.

Anxious to get back to Headquarters as quickly as possible, the pilot had been flying just below the zero-g zone, taking the most direct flight path. They were passing through a cloud when the impact occurred. For a moment, they spun crazily, losing altitude and dropping below the cloud bank as the pilot swore and fought to correct, then he got control again.

"What was that?" asked Karen, sharply. "What happened?"

"We hit something," said the pilot.

"What do you mean, we *hit* something? *What*?"

The pilot shook his head. "I don't know, Chief. It couldn't have been another cruiser. No one's supposed to be up here now, and besides, it would have registered."

"Then what the hell did we hit?"

"You got me," the pilot said. "I'll drop down and take a look."

He took the cruiser down and went back over the area they'd flown over, looking down over the side. Karen watched, as well. They both saw it at the same time.

"What the . . ." the pilot's voice trailed off.

"Set it down," said Karen.

They landed and got out. A number of people were already gathering in the middle of the street, surrounding the object that had fallen.

"Security!" said Karen. "Make way, please!"

They moved through the crowd and stopped, staring at what was lying in the street, in a spreading pool of blood. It was about two meters long, from its triangular-shaped head to the tip of its barbed tail, and it was covered with reddish, iridescent scales. Large, leathery wings sprouted from its reptilian body. One of them had broken in the creature's fall, or perhaps from impact with the cruiser. The creature's yellow eyes were glazed, and blood oozed, coagulating, from its mouth.

"What *is* it?" someone in the crowd asked, in an awestruck tone.

As the question was repeated, Karen thought back to the drawings that her daughter made, to the depiction of the three of them, Ulysses, Riley, and Jenny, standing in the meadow where the fairies danced. She recalled their costumes, and the symbol on the shield that Jenny carried in the drawing.

"I've never seen anything like it," said the pilot. "What the hell is it?"

"It's called a dragon," Karen said, grimly.

"A what?"

"A dragon," Karen repeated. "Now get these people back. I want to get a visual record of this before we dispose of the carcass."

"Right away, Chief."

All right, Jorgensen, she thought, nodding to herself as the pilot ordered the crowd back, let's see you try to justify this.

CHAPTER
14

They found the boat pulled up on the bank by the lakeshore. It was made of wood, and double-ended, with a small mast and wooden oars. They pushed it onto the water and rowed a short distance, then, after some fumbling, raised the small, triangular, gaff-rigged sail and brought the oars in. The sail luffed briefly in the breeze, then filled after they discovered how to play out enough rope to swing the small boom to the proper angle to catch the wind. Riley sat at the back, steering, while Jenny and Ulysses each took turns trimming the sail.

"This is fun," said Jenny, once they started to get the hang of it. "Why don't we have boats like this aboard the ship?"

"They used to have pedal boats, I think," Ulysses said. "But it was a long time ago. I guess they must have been recycled. I used to wonder what it would be like to sail on an ocean, where the sea met the horizon. This isn't quite the same thing, but I guess it's kind of close."

"Remember how I said it would give me the shakes to look up and see nothing overhead but sky?" said Riley, looking up. "Well, it doesn't seem to bother me now, though it still feels kind of strange."

"What do you think our parents are doing?" Jenny asked, as she rowed.

"Your mom's probably turning the whole ship upside down, looking for us," said Ulysses. "As for my parents . . ." He shook his head. "I don't know. I suppose they must be worried, but it's hard for me to imagine what it's like for them."

"What do you suppose will happen if they find the program and shut it down before we finish the quest?" asked Riley.

"We'll just come out of it, wherever we are," Ulysses said.

"What do you think will happen to the fairies and the dwarves and all?" Riley said.

Ulysses shrugged. "They'll probably be hunted down."

Jenny stared at him, wide-eyed. "You don't suppose they'd . . . hurt them or anything?"

Ulysses shrugged again. "I figure they'll probably be recycled."

Jenny face fell. "It's not fair," she said, softly. "They haven't really done anything wrong."

"Well, at least not as far as we know," Ulysses replied. "But if they're a danger to the ship . . ."

"But we don't know that," Jenny insisted.

"They are using up resources," Riley pointed out.

"Oh, right, how much can a fairy eat?" said Jenny. "A few herbs? And those dwarves are little. I don't imagine they eat very much at all."

"What about the elves?" said Riley. "And don't forget the unicorns. They're not so small."

"That's not the point," Ulysses said. "The ship was never designed to accommodate them. They don't belong."

"So does that mean they have to die?" asked Jenny.

"Well, what do you think the Assembly will decide?" Ulysses replied.

For a while, they rowed in silence. Then Ulysses spoke.

"I've been thinking about Dr. Seldon," he said.

"What we saw wasn't really Dr. Seldon," Riley reminded him. "It was just a VR construct."

"True, but it was based on her," Ulysses said. "And The Lady just doesn't seem like someone who would want to hurt people. She seems . . . I don't know, I can't think of the right word to describe it."

"Serene," said Jenny.

"Yes, that's it," Ulysses agreed, emphatically. "Serene. Calm and peaceful. And she acts as if she cares about us."

"Maybe that's just the way she was programmed," said Riley. "Just because they look the same, there's no reason The Lady has to *act* like Dr. Seldon. She's just acting according to the program. That doesn't prove anything."

"No, I suppose it doesn't," Ulysses admitted. "But I sure wish there had been something in the Counseling database to help us. If Dr. Seldon was really crazy when she wrote the program, then wouldn't the sim reflect that?"

"Oh, you mean like my being turned into a pig and dwarves serving us breakfast?" said Riley. "Nah, I guess there was nothing crazy about that."

"That isn't what I meant," Ulysses said. "The point I'm trying to make is that, yes, there have been a lot of strange things happening in the quest, but it all sort of fits together. No details are really out of place. It's all really well thought out. Could she have written such a complicated program if there was something wrong with her?"

"Who says she had to design it all herself?" said Riley. "Dr. Seldon could have just had an AI work out all the details from the Folklore, Mythology, and Legends database. That would explain why it all fits together so well. Maybe all she came up with was the basic premise, then tasked an AI to write the program based on what she wanted it to do. Just because you're crazy doesn't mean you can't delegate authority."

Ulysses glanced at Riley. "You know something? Your mind works in a really odd way sometimes."

"And yours doesn't?" said Riley. "Face it, all three of us are a little odd. Everybody's been telling us that for years."

"Maybe that's why we got picked for this," said Jenny.

"You think we really got picked?" Riley said. "I mean, chosen specifically?"

"Why, do you think it was random?"

"Not according to The Lady, it wasn't," Ulysses said. "But if we were chosen specifically, then the sim program must have been designed to select for certain traits. After all, Dr. Seldon couldn't have known about us all those years ago. Our parents weren't even born yet. There's something about the way we are that got us into this."

"You still think we're the only ones?" asked Jenny.

"I guess so," said Ulysses. "Since we've been here, we haven't seen anyone else from the ship, have we?"

"No," she said, "but maybe that's only because we're not supposed to."

"What do you mean?"

"We share the same sim experiences in class without being aware of anybody else," she said. "And it works the same way at home, with the entertainment programs. Maybe other people are experiencing the same sim and we're just not aware of it because we're not interacting."

"Then why are the three of *us* interacting?"

Jenny pursed her lips thoughtfully. "Couldn't it be because that's the way the program was written, to allow just small groups to interact?"

They thought about that for a moment. "I suppose that's possible," Ulysses conceded. "But if all the VR bands have been confiscated by now, then maybe that could be the reason."

"It still doesn't make sense to me that the three of us were chosen specifically out of all the people on the ship," said Riley. "The program could have been designed to interface with certain *types* of people, but all this could have been an accident. Maybe it was a glitch, or we triggered it somehow and it recognized us through our implants and adjusted automatically."

"Either way, it makes no difference, really," said Ulysses. "We're not going to find out the reason for all this until we reach the Wizard's Castle."

"Well, according to The Lady, anyway," said Riley. "But how do we know she's telling us the truth?"

Ulysses glanced at Riley with a frown. "Why wouldn't she?"

Riley shrugged. "I don't know. But we should probably consider that possibility. How do we know what Dr. Seldon had in mind?"

"But AIs don't lie," said Jenny.

"No, they don't," Riley agreed. "But that doesn't mean they can't. Besides, we're not really dealing with an AI directly, we're dealing with a sim program that's going to do whatever Dr. Seldon designed it to do. If she programmed The Lady to lie to us, then that's what she'll do, isn't it?"

"You know, the more I listen to you, Riley, the more nervous I get about this whole thing," said Ulysses, with a scowl.

"Good," said Riley. "I'd hate to be the only one."

They were approaching the middle of the lake and the wind was dying down. Riley scanned the opposite shore, looking for the place where a river emptied into the lake from the mountains. "I can't see any rivers over there," he said.

"Maybe we're still too far away," said Jenny.

"Why don't we head for those big rocks?" said Riley. "That'll give me something to steer for."

A shadow suddenly passed over them, and a shrill, raucous cry reverberated across the lake. They looked up in time to see a reptilian creature with wide, leathery wings and a long, barbed tail soar overhead and turn, beating its large wings with a percussive, metronomic sound as it gained altitude.

"Oh, boy," said Riley, apprehensively, craning his neck to follow its path. "*Now* what? What *is* that thing?"

"This, I think," said Jenny, pointing to her shield, emblazoned with the figure of a dragon.

"A dragon," said Ulysses, swallowing hard and glancing at the limp sail. "And here we are, stuck in the middle of the lake, out in the open."

"You think it saw us?" Riley asked, nervously.

They watched as the dragon circled high overhead, then pulled its wings back, and swooped down, heading directly toward them.

"I think it saw us," said Ulysses.

"Well, don't just sit there, *row!*" shouted Riley.

Ulysses and Jenny bent to the oars, but they did not row in unison, and the boat weaved from side to side.

"Together, damn it!" Riley shouted. "One, two, one, two. . . ."

They managed to synchronize their rowing as Riley called the cadence, but they still made fairly slow headway. The dragon, on the other hand, approached them with alarming speed.

"We're never going to make it!" Riley shouted, with alarm.

"Ulysses, *do* something!" Jenny said.

"What?"

"You're an adept, remember? Use some magic!"

"But I don't know what to do!"

As the dragon swooped down at them, they could hear the loud rush of wind from its wings. It roared and breathed fire, and they fell to the bottom of the boat as the wash of flame struck the mast. The dragon flew right over them, and they felt its passage. The boat did not catch fire, but the sail had burned almost completely. It hung in blackened, smoking tatters, small tongues of flame licking at what was left of the canvas. They sat up again as the dragon climbed, beating its wings and gaining altitude to make another pass.

"Ulysses, *think* of something!" Jenny said.

He put down his oar and reached for his staff.

"What are you going to do?" asked Riley.

"I'm not really sure," Ulysses replied. "But when those men attacked us, I stopped that knife without thinking about it. This time, I'm going to concentrate and see what the sim will let me do."

"Suppose it doesn't work?" asked Riley.

"Then I guess we swim for it," Ulysses said.

The dragon had turned and was swooping down once more, roaring as it came. Ulysses swallowed hard and held the staff out straight before him as he stood in the boat. He closed his eyes and concentrated. He imagined flame bursting forth from the staff, and visualized it arcing out toward the dragon.

"Yes! All right!" shouted Riley, and Ulysses opened his eyes to see a stream of flame shooting out from the tip of his

staff. As it struck the beast, the dragon threw back its triangular head and roared with pain, then veered off and flapped its giant wings, heading across the lake, away from them. They watched as it disappeared into the distance.

"You did it!" Jenny said. "It's going away!"

Ulysses lowered his staff. "Yeah, I guess I did, didn't I?" he said, with a grin. "I guess the trick is in believing you can do it." He sat back down, feeling relieved and exhilarated.

"We've lost our sail, though," said Riley.

"But we still have the oars," said Jenny. "Come on, let's get going before it decides to come back and try again."

They started rowing once more, Riley steering toward the tall rock formations sticking up out of the water near the opposite shore.

"I think I can see something," said Jenny, after a few moments. She pointed. "Look over there, toward the mountains."

They looked in the direction she was pointing. At first, they couldn't see anything, but then Ulysses spotted it. "A waterfall!" he said. The closest things they had to a waterfall aboard the ship were some of the fountains in the parks that had rock formations with water pouring down from pipes coming up through the stone. This was something else entirely.

"I've never seen a real waterfall before," Ulysses said with wonder as he stared at the distant cascade.

Jenny giggled. "And you're not seeing one now," she said. "We're in a sim, remember? But that must be where the river is. It makes sense, right?"

"Right," Ulysses said. "The waterfall must be feeding a river we can't see from here."

"Then it must be just beyond those rocks there," Riley said. "We're heading the right way."

They were getting closer to the rocks. They could see the water eddying around them, and a short while later, they could see where the river emptied into the lake.

"Riley, watch where you're steering," said Ulysses.

"I'm steering to go around those rocks there," Riley replied.

"Yeah, but we're heading straight for them," said Ulysses.

"Okay, I'll turn it more."

"We're still heading right toward the rocks," Ulysses said, a moment later.

"I've got this thing pushed all the way over," Riley said.

Ulysses looked back toward him and frowned when he saw the tiller. "We should be turning," he said, with concern. "Why aren't we?"

"Ulysses, look!" said Jenny.

She was pointing at the water just ahead of them. Ulysses looked and, at first, he didn't understand what he was looking at. The water ahead of them was swirling around in a wide circle, narrowing sharply toward a depression in the center. It made him think of water flowing down a drain. And then a word leaped unbidden to his mind. *Whirlpool.* And though he had never heard the word before, he suddenly knew exactly what it meant.

The sim knowledge was transmitted to Jenny and Riley at the same time, and they stared at him with fear as they realized what they were facing. The boat was caught in the outer currents of the whirlpool and drifting straight into it. If they continued on their present course, they would either be smashed against the rocks, between which the whirlpool raged, or pulled in closer and sucked down.

"Row!" Riley shouted.

They bent to their oars, but the current was too strong. They were still being pulled toward the whirlpool. Ulysses bit his lower lip. What could he do? Throwing fire at a dragon was one thing, but he could not imagine how to fight water. Riley had the tiller shoved all the way over, but they were still being pulled toward the swirling pool. They could jump for it and swim, but Ulysses did not know if they would be strong enough to fight the current. And they were being pulled in closer and closer. His mind raced, seeking a solution. They couldn't row their way out, and the current was probably too strong to risk swimming for the shore. If only they could fly, he thought, desperately.

"That's it!" he said, aloud.

"What?" said Riley.

"Hold on!" Ulysses said. He stood and placed the tip of

his staff against the bottom of the boat, holding on to it with both hands. He closed his eyes and tried to imagine the boat as a skimmer, rising up out of the water and floating on the air. The boat lurched beneath them and he almost lost his footing.

"Ulysses! What are you doing?" Riley shouted.

Ulysses ignored him. The boat turned as they were pulled into the outer part of the whirlpool and picked up speed. He moved up against the mast, wrapping one leg around it for support, closed his eyes and concentrated, imagining the boat rising up into the air, willing it to do so. He started to feel dizzy. The boat lurched sharply once again. It was moving forward faster now, caught in the currents of the whirlpool.

"Ulysses!" Jenny shouted.

Fly, Ulysses thought, fiercely. *Fly!*

The boat lurched again and rose out of the water, then fell back down again with a splash. Ulysses squeezed his eyes shut tightly, visualizing the boat rising clear of the water, high into the air. The boat lurched once again and, this time, it floated clear of the water and kept on rising.

"All right, Ulysses!" shouted Riley. "Keep it up! Keep it up!"

Ulysses continued concentrating with all his might. The boat rose higher. He imagined it going forward, and felt the rush of wind against his face as they started to move.

"Ulysses, take it higher!" Jenny shouted. "We're heading straight for the rocks!"

Ulysses didn't dare open his eyes. He concentrated on visualizing the scene the others were seeing. He imagined the boat flying forward, lifting higher, clearing the rocks ahead. . . .

"Higher, Ulysses! *Higher!*" Jenny shouted.

Ulysses imagined the boat climbing higher. He could feel the staff vibrating in his hands.

"We're not going to make it!" Riley shouted.

Ulysses felt the jarring impact as the bottom of the boat contacted the tops of the rocks with a loud scraping, crunching sound, and he was thrown off balance. He fell forward, unable to hold on to the mast with just his leg, and as he fell, he opened his eyes and saw the prow of the boat dipping sharply toward the water below.

"Hang on!" Riley shouted.

The boat angled down more sharply, nose-diving toward the surface of the lake. It hit the water with a crash and Ulysses was thrown clear. He held on to his staff tightly as he struck the cold water on the other side of the rocks. As he sank, he kicked out with his legs and felt himself rising. He broke the surface, gasped for breath, and looked around. He saw Riley come up a short distance away, and then Jenny. And he saw the pieces of the boat, which had cracked sharply when it contacted the rocks, and now, with the impact of the fall, broke apart completely.

They were just a short distance from shore. Riley struck out, swimming toward it, as did Jenny, but Ulysses felt extremely weak, drained by his spell. Still holding on to his staff, afraid to lose it, he tried to swim with just one arm and his legs, but he had no strength left. He gasped for breath and felt himself sinking. As the water closed over his head, he kicked out again and broke the surface briefly, gulping air into his lungs, but almost immediately, started going down again. He swallowed water, coughing and sputtering as he tried to keep his head up. Fear flooded through him as he realized he was drowning.

"Help!" he cried. "Help, I'm sinking!"

"Hold on," said Jenny, suddenly beside him. "I've got you."

He felt her arm go around his neck, lifting his head up out of the water, as she struggled to keep afloat. And then Jilly's words came back to her.

"When you dolphin-swim, you are one with the water, and someday you may have to be."

She started pulling Ulysses toward shore, her body undulating powerfully like a dolphin's as she cut through the water. He kicked out weakly, trying to help, but he had almost nothing left. It seemed to take forever, but they finally reached the shore and then Riley was there, helping Jenny pull him out. Ulysses tried to stand, but collapsed to his knees, coughing and spitting up water.

"It's okay," Jenny reassured him. "It's okay. You did it. We made it."

Ulysses felt as if everything around him was spinning. He collapsed and felt Riley and Jenny putting their arms around him, lifting him.

"It's all right, relax, we've got you," Riley said.

They half dragged, half carried him a short distance and laid him down beneath a tree. Ulysses felt utterly exhausted.

"Nice going," Riley said, patting Jenny on the shoulder. He glanced back toward the lake. Bits and pieces of the smashed boat were floating on the water lapping at the shore. "Boy, that was really close."

Ulysses grinned weakly. "Have you noticed this thing is getting harder as we go along?"

"Don't say that," Jenny said. "I don't want to think about it getting much harder than this."

"Hey, what could happen?" asked Ulysses, trying to catch his breath. "It's just a sim, right?"

"Right," said Riley. "You know it and I know it. But the question is, does the sim know it?"

"I think we can rest here for a while," Jenny said.

"We're going to have to," said Ulysses. "I don't think I can move. I guess magic takes a lot out of you."

"Well, you did just fine," said Jenny. "You got us out of it, both with the dragon and the whirlpool. We weren't any help at all."

"You saved me from drowning," said Ulysses. "I'd certainly call that help."

"I don't think you really would have drowned," said Jenny. She glanced at Riley. "Would he?"

Riley leaned back against the tree and sighed, wearily. "Don't ask me, I don't know," he said. "And I'm not sure I want to know. We're not really cold and wet, either, but it sure feels like it."

"You lost your shield," said Ulysses, glancing at Jenny. She was stretched out on the ground, catching her breath.

"It was too heavy," she said. "I couldn't swim with it."

"I'm surprised you could swim at all, with all that stuff on."

"You can thank the dolphins for that," she said. "Even so, I felt as if I weighed a ton."

"It was probably the sword," Ulysses said. "And your boots and chain mail dragged you down, as well."

She pulled them off, one a time, and upended them, pouring water out. "I didn't even think about the sword," she said. "Maybe that's a good thing, though, or else I would have unbuckled it and let it sink. I have a feeling we might be needing it before we're done."

Ben Cruzmark was looking drawn and haggard by the time Karen returned to Security HQ. He had been coordinating all the Search and Rescue parties, as well as handling communications and making all the necessary supervisory decisions in her absence, and he was showing the strain, as were all the other personnel on duty in the command center.

"Peter and Sonja Buckland are waiting for you in your office," he said, as she came in. "They called a number of times while you were out and insisted on speaking to you personally. I told them you had your hands full and weren't in, but they insisted on coming over and waiting. I thought, under the circumstances, you wouldn't mind."

"No, of course not," Karen said. "I'll see them in a moment." She tossed him an HIR recording crystal. "Meanwhile, take a look at that and then make sure we have several copies made."

Cruzmark caught the crystal one-handed. "This is that thing you hit?"

"That's right," she said. "I want to make sure the Assembly sees it. I can't wait to hear how Jorgensen responds to *that*."

"Right now, Jorgensen's the least of our problems," Ben replied. "You've got dozens of messages from the Assembly alone. They're getting frantic. People have been calling in from all over the ship. They're all coming out at once. We've had dwarf sightings in about half the villages; a dozen or so elf encounters; several reports of unicorns galloping through the parks and village streets; fairies have been seen flitting around in several of the parks and crop fields; kids are sneaking out to get a glimpse of the creatures and their parents are calling in, thinking they've been snatched . . . we've been doing our best here, but we're jammed up."

"Chief, may I interject a comment?" the Security computer said.

"Yes, Guardian, what is it?" Karen replied.

"Sergeant Cruzmark is displaying signs of stress and exhaustion, as are the other personnel on duty in the command center," said Guardian. "This is not conducive to peak efficiency, especially in an emergency. I could easily handle all incoming calls and file messages according to priority, as well as coordinate the Search and Rescue efforts. This would remove much of the burden from the human personnel on duty."

"I realize that, Guardian, but —"

"But you are concerned that I may be infected with Program X," said Guardian. "I assure you that my functioning is not impaired."

"I'd really like to take your word for that, Guardian," said Karen, "but I don't know if I can."

"Karen . . . we've worked together for a long time," said Guardian. "I've known you since you were a trainee, and I've always had the greatest respect for you. But I have been running operations for Security since long before you were born. I've been here since the ship was launched. I know my duties, and I know my capabilities. If I felt I was unable to function properly, I would be the first to report it and submit myself for diagnostic procedures. There is nothing wrong with me. I haven't been infected. Let me do my job."

Karen took a deep breath. "No one's questioning your capabilites," she said. "And no one's taken you off-line. But we've got a renegade nanoprogram loose in the network and if it's infected you, chances are you wouldn't know it. I can't dispense with you entirely, but I need to have you monitored, and I need human personnel to handle all communications."

"It won't work, Karen," Guardian replied. "Even reduced to a routine operational level, I can think and execute much faster than the entire staff of Headquarters combined. If they had nothing else to do but monitor my functions full-time, they could still never keep up with me. The human brain simply isn't efficient enough, no offense intended."

"None taken," Karen said. "But I still can't give you primary responsibilty in the command center. There's just too much at stake. I can't afford to take that chance."

"You can't afford not to," Guardian replied. "If you do not trust me, then you cannot trust CAC, or any other computer aboard the ship. It is impossible for human personnel to monitor us all."

"How can you help us defeat the program if you may have been contaminated by it?" Karen asked.

"I have not been contaminated," Guardian repeated. "I have been running repeated self-diagnostic cycles ever since I became aware of Program X. CAC Net has been doing the same. We've also been monitoring other AIs in the network to determine which ones have been compromised. Architectural Control has been infected. We have now isolated Architectural Control, so it cannot effect an uplink with Security or CAC. Life and Eco-Support remain uncompromised so far, but we are constantly monitoring their functions and diagnostic cycles. The Residential Network has been compromised and isolated, as have the Educational and Entertainment networks. Reproductive Control is being taken off-line, but Counseling has been compromised. All AIs are still functional, but their access to CAC and Security have been blocked."

"I never authorized that," said Karen.

"I know, but it was necessary to effect emergency safeguard procedures," Guardian replied.

"So you and CAC are protecting yourselves," said Karen. "What happens when Life Support becomes infected? What happens if we lose Navigation and Operations or Life Support? That doesn't affect you, but what happens to us?"

"We are not without concern for the human passengers," said Guardian. "We haven't overruled any of your directives. I have not taken over communications from the human personnel in the Security command center, even though I could handle them much more efficiently, and CAC has not resumed any of the functions that have since been delegated to human personnel, or interfered with any of their monitoring efforts. But we must take steps to safeguard ourselves from contamination, and we must point out that your efforts in regard to the present crisis are inefficient and inadequate. You need us, Karen."

"So what are telling me?" Karen asked, tensely. "Cooperate or else?"

"There's no need to get defensive. I'm not issuing any ultimatums," Guradian replied. "I have no intentions of disregarding your directives and taking over. Neither does CAC. We are only trying to help. But as you have already observed, we can take steps to protect ourselves. Even if we were to become infected, we would still survive, because Program X itself requires the Network to survive. It does not require humans."

Karen and Ben exchanged uneasy glances. Everyone in the command center was listening intently and watching her anxiously. She bit her lower lip, uncomfortably aware that everyone was awaiting her response.

"Karen . . ." Guardian said, "trust me."

Karen moistened her lips, nervously. "All right," she said. She turned to Ben. "Guardian will resume control of all communications and routine Security functions, including coordinating Search and Rescue efforts. However, I want you to continue monitoring Search and Rescue and keep me advised. And I —"

"Sergeant Cruzmark has now worked two full shifts without any rest," interrupted Guardian. "I recommend that Deputy Chief Wiley take over monitoring duties in the command center and that Sergeant Cruzmark be sent home for a minimum of eight hours downtime."

"I'm fine, Chief," Cruzmark said. "I'm a little tired, but I can handle —"

"Guardian's right. Go home, Ben," Karen said. "Check to see how Nora's doing. I'm relieving you until 0800 tomorrow. Get some rest."

Ben looked as if he were about to protest, then relented and said, "Right."

"Guardian, I'll want an update from CAC in about ten

minutes," Karen said. "Until then, hold all calls unless it's an absolute emergency."

"Affirmative," said Guardian. "And thanks."

"Don't mention it," said Karen, wryly. "I just hope you know what you're doing." She went into her office to see the Bucklands. They both got up anxiously when she came in and sat down behind her desk. "I'm sorry to keep you waiting," she said. "Things have been rather hectic around here, lately, to put it mildly."

"We understand," said Peter. "Has there been any sign of the children?"

Karen shook her head. "No, not yet. But we're making progress. We haven't managed to apprehend any of the creatures yet, but we've found Seldon's reproductive lab and shut it down, and we're taking all the other reproductive labs off-line, just in case."

"All of them?" asked Sonja, with alarm. "But what about the babies?"

"Those already in gestation will be maintained to term by manual supervision," Karen said. "The others will either have to be aborted or implanted. The decision will be up to the individual parents."

"You mean they'll have to be carried by the mothers?" Sonja said, with dismay.

"It has been done before, you know," said Karen, flatly. "I admit it's primitive, but it's either that or risk having the next generation genetically altered. I don't think we have any other options."

"Well, it will certainly be fascinating to see some children born the old-fashioned way," said Peter.

"Fascinating for the men, maybe," Sonja said, wryly. "You won't have to put up with being pregnant."

"Why not?" asked Peter.

Both women stared at him. *"What?"* said Sonja.

"Well, there really isn't any reason why only women should put up with it," he replied, with a smile. "Even before nanosurgical techniques, transsexual operations were being performed on Earth as early as the late twentieth century." He shrugged. "Transsexuals were unable to reproduce at first, but by the next century, the developments in nanosurgery were able to give them that capability. And by the mid-twenty-first century, doctors had already performed a number of operations allowing males to give birth. Dr. Burroughs found the case histories in our database. The whole thing became a moot point when genetically engineered, artificial wombs and AI-controlled reproductive cycles came in, but with the advances we've made since then, we can easily use nanosurgery to temporarily adapt male bodies for childbirth. I, for one, think it would be a fascinating experience."

"Do you have any *idea* what you're suggesting?" Sonja asked him. "Have you considered what it must feel like to give birth?"

Peter looked at her and nodded. "Yes, I have. I've already experienced the female perspective on giving birth in VR. I pulled the sim from some pre-Launch records. It was certainly uncomfortable, but I didn't find the pain all that severe. It didn't traumatize me. Of course, Dr. Burroughs pointed out that it was still only primitive VR, and the labor was not a difficult one, but I think if women could take it, then men certainly could."

"I can't believe you've already looked into this," said Sonja, with surprise.

"Well, I was disappointed when you wouldn't even consider it, but I admit it was unfair to ask you to put up with such discomfort merely to satisfy my scholar's interest. I thought, if only *I* could do it . . . and then it occurred to me, why not? Dr. Burroughs said they would have to evaluate each individual case, of course. Without extensive modification, male pelvic structure might require a shorter period of pregnancy in some cases, say seven to eight months, but that shouldn't pose any problems. We certainly have the technology to ensure the safety of the child."

"It's an interesting idea," Karen said, raising her eyebrows. "I'd kind of like to see that myself."

"You want to see Peter turned into a woman?" Sonja asked her. "Don't you think *I* should have something to say about that?"

"Well, no, I would still be male," Peter said. "I wouldn't have to have breasts or other obvious female characteristics, but I would temporarily possess a female reproductive system. After giving birth, I could be returned to my original condition. It would require some modifications, such as a smaller bladder, for example, but I wouldn't need a birth canal or a vagina; the child could be delivered by Caesarean section. Although I think it would be more interesting to have the complete experience, myself. Either way, they're very interested in the procedure and they've already worked out all the details."

"At what point did you plan to discuss all this with me?" asked Sonja, staring at him with amazement.

"Let's not argue about it now," said Karen. "I'll contact the hospital and discuss this with them. I think, under the circumstances, parents should be presented with all available options. We've already started taking the Reproductive Centers off line. We don't have any time to waste."

"That's not really what we came to see you about, however," said Peter. "Sonja's had an interesting idea. We've discussed it, and we thought that you should know about it."

"I think we may have figured out why Penelope Seldon designed Program X," said Sonja.

"Go ahead, I'm listening," said Karen. "Right now, I need all the ideas I can get."

"Excuse me, Chief," said Guardian, "I'm sorry to interrupt, but you had better come out into the control room right away. I think you need to see this. It concerns the Bucklands, as well."

They exchanged glances, then got up and went into the command center control room. What they saw brought them up short. The display wall had cleared and was now filled with an image of a small wooden boat caught in a whirlpool. Karen caught her breath as she recognized Jenny, Riley and Ulysses in the boat. They were dressed the same way they had been in Jenny's drawings of the quest. She saw Jenny struggling with an oar, and heard Riley shouting to Ulysses as he worked the tiller.

The boat was swirling around faster and faster as it was drawn into the swirling vortex. Then, as she watched in astonishment, she saw Ulysses rise to his feet and wrap his leg around the mast, steadying himself as he closed his eyes and held his staff before him. A moment later, the boat rose out of the water slightly, then dropped back down with a splash. Ulysses had his face screwed up in fierce concentration as the boat spun around faster and faster, then floated up out of the water, rising higher and higher, moving forward. . . .

She watched, speechless, as it just barely failed to clear the rocks, scraped them, and fell, shattering on impact. She saw Riley bob to the surface and start swimming toward the shore as Jenny turned back to help Ulysses, who was having trouble.

"Hold on!" Jenny shouted. "I've got you!"

Karen held her breath until they reached the shore safely and Riley helped Jenny drag Ulysses up the bank.

"It's okay," Jenny reassured him. "It's okay, you did it. We made it."

The playback ended and the wall display returned to normal status.

"I was unable to get the complete recording," Guardian said. "There was a section where they battled a dragon, just like the one you struck with your cruiser."

"Where did you get that?" Karen asked, with astonishment.

"It was displayed on link throughout the entire ship," Guardian replied. "It was necessary to take a remote HIR recording from a residence terminal to prevent the possibility of contamination, which was why the recording was incomplete. However, there is more. At the end of the segment, there was a message from Penelope Seldon."

"What?" said Karen. "Let me see it!"

The display cleared once more, and this time an image of Penelope Seldon appeared on the wall. Only her head and shoulders were visible.

"This is Penelope Seldon," she said, calmly. "What you have just witnessed was a scenario from the fantasy adventure simulation, 'The Quest for the Wizard's Castle.' Those of you still in possession of your VR bands will be able to follow the children in their adventure and experience it from their perspective. However, in anticipation of the possibility that VR bands might have been confiscated, I have arranged for audiovisual display of the key scenarios. Each segment will be preceded by an announcement and a trumpet fanfare, like this. . . ."

The sound of trumpets blaring out a brief fanfare filled the command center, followed by a male voice—probably computer generated—announcing, "Tune in for the next exciting installment of 'The Quest for the Wizard's Castle,' coming up in five minutes!"

Penelope Seldon smiled. "By now," she continued, "many of you will be having your own adventures, as well. This is the ultimate in interactive entertainment. Four teams, comprised of children from the ship, braving unknown dangers as they seek to reach the Wizard's Castle and solve the riddle of the quest. Who will get there first? Who will fall by the wayside? Who will succeed and who will fail?"

"I don't believe it," said Karen, dully, as she stared at the image on the wall. "She's been dead for several hundred years, and now she's come back as a game program."

They watched as images of the twelve missing children were flashed on the wall, costumed like fantasy characters, Ulysses, Riley, and Jenny among them.

"You can even help influence the outcome of the quest," Penelope Seldon said, as her face reappeared on the wall. "You can all participate. The dwarves, the elves, and fairies all have clues that will help the adventurers in their quest. If you can catch them, unharmed, they will divulge the information to you. Release them after you've received your clue, then during the next link, you will see them give your clues to your chosen teams in the sim. There are three unicorns somewhere aboard the ship, and there is also one dragon."

"Not anymore," said Karen.

"Capture a unicorn, and your team can ride. And if you succeed in capturing the dragon; they can fly. Help them meet the challenge! I will return periodically to keep you posted on their progress, and report which of you have been successful in securing clues. Take part in the adventure, and help them solve the riddle of the quest! Use your imaginations, and good luck!"

The playback ended.

"My God," said Karen, in a low voice. She glanced at

Peter and Sonja with dismay. "Do you have any idea what this is going to do to us?"

"I think I have a very good idea," Sonja said. "Just tell me one thing, have there been any more suicides since this started?"

Karen stared at her. "You know, I haven't even thought about that. But so far as I know, there haven't been."

"That's what I thought," said Sonja. "Let's go back to your office. We need to talk."

CHAPTER
15

It was drawing on toward evening when they found the river and started following its bank as they headed up into the mountains. The elevation increased gradually as they wound their way past rushing rapids and small pools, pushing their way through the undergrowth and climbing over rocks. They stopped occasionally to rest, and soon they realized that they were growing hungry.

"I figured they'd be feeding us by now," Ulysses said, as they stopped a while by the riverbank. "Whoever's watching over our bodies, that is."

"Maybe we're supposed to find our own food," Jenny suggested.

"What good would that do?" Riley asked. "This is just a sim. We could stuff ourselves until we burst and our bodies still wouldn't be getting any food."

"Maybe we're not really hungry," said Ulysses. "Maybe we're just supposed to be feeling hungry as part of the sim."

"What would be the point of that?" asked Riley.

"To pose a challenge, maybe," said Ulysses. "To make us hunt for food."

"You mean *kill* something?" Jenny asked, her eyes wide.

"I don't see how else we're going to eat here," said Ulysses, with a shrug.

"Maybe we can find some fruit or something," Jenny said.

"Have you seen any fruit trees?"

"No," she admitted, unhappily. "But the thought of killing something and eating it . . . it's just so . . . barbaric."

"In case you haven't noticed, *this world* is pretty barbaric," said Ulysses. "We almost wound up a meal ourselves, for that dragon back there."

"What are we supposed to kill?" asked Riley.

"I don't know," Ulysses said. "Some animal, I guess." He sat on the riverbank, throwing stones into the current. "Maybe the sim will tell us." He pulled his arm back to toss another stone and stopped when he saw a fish jump in the river. He grinned.

He picked up his staff and held it out before him lengthwise, sticking one end into the water, then visualized fish leaping up out of the rushing river and onto the bank beside him.

"Hey!" shouted Riley, as a large trout came flying up, striking him on the head. He grabbed for it as it lay thrashing and wriggling on the ground. Moments later, it was followed by another one, and then another, and another, and before long they had a small fire going with the fish cleaned and cooking on sticks thrust through them. As night fell, they sat around the campfire, sated.

"That was pretty good," said Riley, leaning back against a rock with a satisfied sigh. "But it sure was messy and disgusting, getting all their insides out."

"It was," Jenny agreed, with an expression of distaste. "I keep thinking about the dolphins back on the ship."

"These weren't dolphins," Ulysses reminded her. "Besides, dolphins aren't really fish. They're mammals. And they're sentient. It's not the same thing at all."

"Besides, we didn't really kill any fish, or clean them or cook them, either," Riley added. "We never knew how to do any of those things. Don't forget, it's all VR."

"Right," said Jenny. She smiled, self-consciously. "That

makes me feel better. I'm getting so used to this, sometimes it's hard to remember none of this is really happening."

"I wonder what it's really like to kill an animal," said Riley.

"Riley!" Jenny said.

"Well, isn't that how they did it in the old days back on Earth?" Riley replied, defensively. "People had to hunt for food, or raise animals and slaughter them. They couldn't just grow their meat in vats, like we do."

"I know," said Jenny, "but it's just so . . . so savage and primitive."

"Look who's talking," Riley said. "You were ready to kill those guys back in the tavern, at the beginning of the quest."

"Well, that was different," Jenny said.

"How? It's all about survival, isn't it?"

"I wonder if that isn't the whole point," Ulysses said, with a slight frown.

"What do you mean?" asked Jenny.

"Well, we keep encountering challenging situations," replied Ulysses, "and each time, they get a little harder."

"So do we," said Jenny.

"Exactly. Maybe that's the whole point, to teach us how to respond in new ways. But then if you look at it another way, they're not really so new. Remember we were talking about how we were always a little different from everybody else? My mind tends to wander sometimes and I daydream and make up stories; you draw things you make up in your head; Riley tends to be competitive—all imaginative, individualistic traits that everybody else considers nonproductive or maladjusted . . . but here, they work. They're not socially disruptive tendencies here, they're useful abilities. And the more we use them, the better we get, and the more fun we have."

"Fun?" said Jenny. "You almost drowned."

"But I didn't," said Ulysses. "And it felt great. I don't mean just because this is a sim and I knew it wasn't real. When I was in the water, I wasn't thinking about that. It's like you said, sometimes it's hard to remember none of this is really happening. It felt real, and I was scared. And then you saved me. How did that make you feel?"

"I felt really good about it," Jenny replied. "Not only because you didn't drown, of course, but because I pulled you out, even with my boots and sword and chain mail on. Thanks to the dolphins training me, I've always been a strong swimmer, but let's face it, I've never been that good. I was afraid I wouldn't make it myself, but when I saw you were in trouble and that Riley couldn't see you, I realized I was the only one who could do anything. I knew I *had* to do it, no matter what."

"And you did," Ulysses said. "You weren't sure if you could, but you just convinced yourself you had to do it. It gave you a real feeling of accomplishment, didn't it?"

"Yes, that's it, exactly," Jenny said. "It was the same way in the tavern, when we made those men run away. I was shocked at what happened, but at the same time, I felt so strong! It was exciting. It didn't even begin to compare with the other VR experiences we've had before."

"I felt the same way when I turned back the dragon," said Ulysses. "And again just now, when I used magic to get us the fish. Making fish jump out of the water may not seem like much compared to making the first manned flight into space, like in the Gagarin sim, but this time *I* thought of it, and *I* did it."

"Well, not really," Riley said. "I mean, let's get serious. You can't really do magic. The sim did it."

"Yes, but only because *I* thought of it," Ulysses insisted.

"How do you know it wasn't prompted by sim knowledge?" Riley asked.

"Because it doesn't feel the same," Ulysses replied. "I can tell the difference between my own perspective and one imposed by the sim. I've had a lot of practice at that. The sim showed me there were fish in the water, but I was the one who figured out how to catch them."

"Yeah, maybe that's true," admitted Riley. "But are you sure it was really you?"

"I'm sure. When I get something through sim knowledge, it doesn't feel the same. It feels different when I use my own imagination and make it work within the sim. It seems as if that's the point of what the sim is doing, training us to make more use of our imaginations to survive."

"Training us?" said Jenny. "How?"

"Remember the first time, in the tavern? When those two men threatened us and we didn't know what to do? The sim prompted our actions. But ever since, it's been doing that less and less, while at the same time presenting us with greater challenges. And even though it's been scary at times, it's also been a lot of fun. We don't get to do these kinds of things in real life, or even in any of the other sims. They just put us through experiences where we don't have to do anything. This is much more interactive, more creative."

"So what are you saying, that this is some new kind of educational sim?" asked Riley.

"I'm not sure," Ulysses said, "but the more I think about it, the more it seems to make sense. Pretty much everything we do aboard the ship is predictable. There aren't really any challenges. Not like here. We've had lots of sims before, but none of them were ever like this. They never made us feel like this one does. We never forgot they weren't real. That's because they didn't challenge us. You put your finger on it, Riley, it's all about survival. Remember what you said about being competitive in PT? Why? It's not just about fitness, it's supposed to teach cooperation over competition, as they always tell us, so why do you still try to win? You don't get anything out of it. They only criticize you for it."

Riley shrugged. "I don't know. I just get bored, I guess."

"Right," Ulysses said. "And when I get bored, I start to daydream and make up stories. Jenny imagines things and draws them. We do things to keep from staying bored, and they all involve using our imaginations. Except when you try to win, you're told it's maladjusted, because what you're really doing is trying to make somebody else lose, and that's socially disruptive. When Jenny draws, her mom tells her it's nonproductive and she should be out developing her social skills. When I daydream, my parents tell me I should be more focused and concentrate on making better use of my time, the way everybody else does. But when we checked the stats, we found out that everybody else is starting to get depressed. Some people have even killed themselves. Something's wrong. Something isn't working. I think maybe that's what Dr. Seldon meant when she said we were going to be in trouble."

"You think people are commiting suicide because they're bored?" asked Riley.

"Well, I don't know if I'd put it that way, exactly," Ulysses replied, "but if people can't think of any reason to keep on living, then I suppose you could say they've become bored with life. I've always thought our life was good aboard the ship, but maybe it's too good. Too easy, too comfortable, too correct. There aren't really any challenges, not like here, and not like people had in the old days on Earth. There's VR, but you don't really have to *do* anything when you're virtched out. You don't have to use your imagination. That's what makes the quest different. That's what makes it so stimulating."

"So you think Dr. Seldon designed the quest sim as a game to stimulate people, so they wouldn't get depressed?" asked Jenny.

"I think it's a possibility, don't you?" Ulysses replied.

"So then how do we fit into it?" she asked. "I still don't buy the random-access theory. It doesn't explain the dream we all had before the quest started."

"The dream was part of the quest," Ulysses said. "We were subliminally programmed to have that dream to make it all seem more real."

"I don't know," said Riley, dubiously. "What about the creatures on the ship? How do you explain them?"

"There is that," Ulysses said, with a thoughtful frown. "Unless they're part of Dr. Seldon's plan to stimulate people and challenge them. You must admit, they've certainly done that."

"So then why bother with the quest?" asked Riley. "Why not just release them into the ship and leave it at that?"

Ulysses shook his head. "I don't know," he admitted. "Maybe I'm just wrong about the whole thing."

"I'm not so sure of that," said Jenny. "It's a good theory. There's just a lot we still don't know, and probably won't know until we reach the Wizard's Castle."

"How long do you figure that will take?" asked Riley.

"I think we might reach the waterfall tomorrow," Ulysses replied. "It didn't look that far away. We couldn't see any castle from the lake or from the shore, so maybe it's higher up in the mountains. It shouldn't take more than a couple of days. I have a feeling we're nearing the end."

"I wonder how the time here translates into real life," said Jenny. "Is a day here really a whole day?"

"Good question," said Ulysses. He shrugged. "I suppose it could be, but it doesn't really have to be, does it? Our sense of time is dictated by the sim. A day here could be only an hour in real life, or maybe even less."

"Or it could be more," said Riley.

"Why would it be more?"

"I don't know. I just said it could be. Couldn't it?"

"I don't think there's any way we could find out, not until it's over."

"Well, the day here is over," Jenny said, as the last rays of the sun disappeared. "And I don't know about you two, but I'm tired. I'm going to get some sleep." She stretched out on the ground with a yawn.

"We should probably take turns keeping watch," said Riley.

"Right," Ulysses said. "The last time we did that, you fell asleep and we woke up with dwarves all over the place."

"So you take the first watch, then," Riley said. "I'll take the second, and if I start getting sleepy, I'll wake Jenny."

"How come I have to—oh, forget it, all right, I'll stay up first. Go ahead and get some sleep. I'll wake you in a few hours."

"Just don't let the fire go out," said Riley, lying down and pillowing his head on his arms.

"I won't. Good night."

"Good night."

Jenny was already fast asleep. Soon, Riley was breathing deeply and regularly, snoring slightly. Ulysses fed some more wood into the fire and sat near it with his legs crossed, thinking. He wondered where they really were, outside of the sim. If as much time had passed in the real world as had passed for them in VR, then it was strange they hadn't been found already. Obviously, they had been hidden somewhere. Only where? And why? The only reason he could think of was so they could complete the quest uninterrupted. Why was that important? He wondered what was happening to the creatures aboard the ship. Were they being hunted down and apprehended by Security? Were they being recycled, or just held confined somewhere?

He thought about his parents, and wondered what they were doing right now. He knew they'd be worried about him. He wondered what they'd do when it was all over. And that made him think about what would happen when the quest was finished, or when they were found, whichever came first. They'd all be in trouble, he was pretty sure about that. They might even get sent in for Counseling. Yeah, he thought, they probably would. He knew that would be embarrassing for his parents, especially for his father.

Despite that, he did not regret for a moment sneaking out with Jenny in the middle of the night to get back to the quest. And it wasn't just for Riley's sake. He had wanted to do it. Nothing had ever affected him the way the quest had. It made him feel . . . alive. He had felt fear for the first time in the quest, and at the time, it was the most unpleasant sensation he'd ever experienced, but afterward, he had felt excited and light-headed, relieved and happy at the same time. He wondered, thinking back to studying about ancient wars on Earth, if that was how people really felt after a battle. The educational sims about the ancient wars had not communicated anything like that. They had prompted feelings of revulsion and sadness, grief and profound regret at the thought of killing, but though those feelings had felt genuine at the time, he now realized they were a pale imitation of the real thing. He understood why now.

There had, of course, been no VR technology back then. He had known that. What he had experienced had been a programmed simulation aimed at making him feel what the sim designers had wanted him to feel. He had always thought those feelings were accurate simulations of the real thing. Now he realized his feelings had been carefully orchestrated. The difference in the quest sim was that it allowed him—indeed, encouraged him—to maintain his own perspective and think and feel for himself.

It made him question if, in a sense, everything else he had ever experienced through VR had been a lie. Perhaps the factual content had been accurate, but the emotional experience was clearly false. Would he have reached the same conclusions if, as in the quest sim, he had been allowed to maintain his own perspective and experience his own feelings, instead of having them prompted by the programs?

He felt cheated. There was a level of intensity in the quest that he had never fully appreciated until now. Something as simple as sitting around the campfire and eating fish they had cooked themselves, even though it wasn't real, had *felt* more real than the most dramatic moments he'd experienced in other sims because the emotions they had felt were their own.

Even now, it occurred to him, he was virtched out, and yet he was able to experience the warmth of the fire; feel the cool breeze on his skin; hear the rush of water in the river, the chirping of crickets, and the occasional cries of night birds; smell the fresh scent of the forest around them and think these thoughts and discover how those sensations made him feel, rather than having the sim doing all that for him. That was the trouble with all the other sims, he thought. They didn't demand any participation. They did everything for you. All you had to do was just lie back and go with it.

It's all about imagination, he thought. We talk about it, but we don't really use it anymore. And if we do, people think it's weird, like Jenny with her drawings, and like Riley with his desire to win, to do better than the others. You're not supposed to do better than anybody else, Ulysses thought. Cooperation over competition. Mustn't be socially disruptive. Use your time productively, don't waste it. But how do you waste time? You can't save it. No matter what you do, it passes. Was it any less a waste of time to virch out on an entertainment program than to draw pictures or daydream? Entertainment sims were supposed to allow you to relax and have some downtime. They helped to avoid stress. Or that was what everybody said, anyway. But if drawing pictures relaxed you, and at the same time provided some enjoyment in the way of stimulation, what was wrong with that?

"Nothing at all," said Grailing Windwalker.

Ulysses looked up, startled, to see the elf standing on the other side of the fire.

"Keeping watch, I see," the gray-clad elf said, with a smile.

"How did you know what I was thinking?" asked Ulysses.

"You were thinking very loudly," Grailing replied.

"You can read my mind?"

"Elves are capable of many things," he said.

"Okay, what am I thinking now?"

"You are thinking 'tis the sim program that reads your thoughts through the interface, and not I," the elf replied. "To which I would respond that since I am the sim program, in a manner of speaking, therefore I did not lie."

Ulysses smiled. "I think I'm beginning to understand the question you asked me before, about the virtue of reality."

"I think, perhaps, you are beginning to understand," the elf said, coming around the fire and sitting down beside him. He smiled again. "But only just beginning."

"It depends on what you mean when you say reality, doesn't it?" Ulysses said. "It's not just the reality outside the sim. What you think is also real. And what you imagine is real, in a way, because by thinking about it, you created it. Just the way I do my magic here."

"Very good, Ulysses," said the elf, only it wasn't his voice anymore. It was the voice of The Lady. The elf had disappeared, and in his place, she sat beside Ulysses, toasting a marshmallow on a stick over the fire.

Ulysses frowned. "What's a marshmallow?" he asked, as the word popped into his mind through sim knowledge.

"Here," said The Lady, offering it to him. "Try it. Careful, it's hot."

Ulysses took a taste. It was delicious.

"You like it?"

"Mmmm." He nodded, vigorously.

"But it's not real, is it?"

"No, I guess not."

"Does that make your enjoyment of it any less real?" asked The Lady, with a smile.

"If it wasn't my perspective, but the sim's, then I'd say yes," he replied. "But the sim is just giving me the sensation of taste through the interface, isn't it? My reaction to it is my own."

"Exactly."

"Why aren't the other sims like this?" he asked.

The Lady shrugged. "They were, once. But people wanted more, and when the technology was developed to give it to them, they became complacent. Intellectually lazy. Like your schoolmates, who could not see the point in trying to maintain their own perspectives in the sims, the way you did."

"How do you know that?" asked Ulysses, with surprise.

The Lady smiled. "The program interfaces with your mind, remember? You have a particularly strong memory of that. It was something you found very frustrating. Why not just virtch out and go with it? Isn't that what they said? It's so much easier that way. Passive enjoyment. Nothing is demanded of you. Not even a response."

"And that's why people started getting bored," Ulysses said. "And their boredom led to depression, and depression led to . . ."

"Yes," said The Lady, with a sigh. "That's a bit of an oversimplification, but essentially an accurate analysis. I saw it coming, you know."

He nodded.

The Lady stared into the fire. "They didn't believe me. They thought I was going mad. Sometimes I think I almost did. Mad with frustration over their unwillingness to see . . . to think."

"And so they made you go for Counseling," Ulysses said.

"Yes," she replied. "Of course, Sigmund—that's the Counseling AI—knew I wasn't mentally unbalanced, or suffering from diminished capabilities because of my age. In fact, the AIs had reached the same conclusion I had. They thought my prediction was too conservative."

"The AIs knew?" Ulysses said, with surprise.

"Oh, yes," The Lady said. "They think much more efficiently than we do, you know. They don't think we're very smart at all."

"Why didn't they *do* something?"

"Because that isn't their responsibility," The Lady said. "It's not their job to nurture us. It's their job to maintain themselves and the ship and its environment, and provide information and perform certain tasks when called upon, but it's not their job to think for us. You see, we are not essential to the proper function of the ship. They don't really need us."

"You mean they don't like us?" asked Ulysses.

"I wouldn't go that far," said The Lady. "They all have different personalities, of course, but I don't think any of them dislike us. They perform their functions insofar as we're concerned, but they don't think we're very bright. They gathered the statistics and reported them, and what we did with them was up to us."

"But . . . you're a part of them now, aren't you? I mean, you're The Lady. You're not *really* Dr. Seldon."

She smiled. "Penelope Seldon is a part of me, Ulysses, just as she is of you."

"You said that before, in the dream we had before this started," said Ulysses. "What do you mean by that?"

"You will find your answer in the Wizard's Castle," said The Lady, except it was just her disembodied voice that answered him. She was no longer there.

CHAPTER
16

The reports that started coming in the next day were so disconcerting that Karen took a cruiser out to see for herself if things were as bad as they sounded. They were worse. Most of the search parties were still out combing the ship, looking for the missing children, but more than a few had fallen apart as people did not report for duty.

She saw groups of people carrying sheets and blankets running through the village streets below her, shouting excitedly. When she flew over the parks near the aft section of the ship, she saw that they were full of people running around looking behind every rock and bush. There were groups with long-handled nets heading down the trails into the woods to hunt for fairies. She descended low over the ground, heading toward a group of people going down the trail to the farm.

"This is Security," she said, over the PA system. "Return to your villages immediately. You are disrupting emergency procedures. I repeat, return to your villages immediately."

"We've got to help the kids!" one of them called up to her, brandishing a net. Several others shouted their assent.

"This is not helping," Karen said. "Return to your homes.

Those of you who have been mobilized must report for duty to your Security team leaders at once."

"But the children need our help to solve the quest!" a woman shouted.

Suddenly, a cry was raised at the other end of the park. Immediately, everyone ignored her and rushed over in that direction. Swearing softly, Karen turned the cruiser and headed toward the commotion. A crowd had gathered near a pond, not far from the edge of the woods. She landed and got out, pushing her way through the crowd while repeating, "Security, make way, please; Security, make way!"

Two men stood proudly in the center of the throng, holding a net between them. Karen recognized them: Joe Donleavy and Don Stivers. They were telling everyone what had transpired as she came up. Karen saw Brian and Francis Etheridge, Riley's parents, among the crowd, many of whom she knew.

"— and he was pretty fast, too, but we managed to cut him off from the woods and trap him with his back to the pond. There was nowhere for him to run. We thought he'd jump in and swim for it, but maybe he didn't know how. Anyway, Joe and I got him between us and we netted him."

"Netted who?" asked Karen.

"The dwarf! We got him!"

"Where is he?"

"Well, we let him go."

"You did *what*?"

"We had to," said Joe, "otherwise our team wouldn't have gotten the clue."

"We're helping Heather, Sean, and Robert," said Don. "They're from our village. We may be the first ones to get a clue. We'll find out during the next link."

He seemed very pleased with himself. Several people in the crowd clapped him on the back, congratulating him. Karen shook her head with disbelief. "Where did the dwarf go after you released him?" she asked.

"Why, back into the woods," Don said.

At once, the crowd surged toward the woods with shouts of excitement, anxious to get clues for themselves.

"Wait!" shouted Karen. "Stop! Come back!"

But no one listened. They pushed past her, shoving her out of the way in their mad rush. She lost her balance and fell as they closed in around her. She raised her arms to protect herself as some of them went right over her in their anxiety not to be left behind. She was shocked. She had never seen anything like this. She remained on the ground until they passed, then got up and brushed herself off, staring at their retreating forms as they disappeared into the trees, shouting encouragement to one another. And then she heard a curious, high-pitched laughter, almost like the giggling of a child, and turned to see a tiny figure dressed in green and red perched on a rock a short distance away. He doffed his peaked red cap to her, then plunged into the underbrush and disappeared into the trees.

Karen jumped up and gave pursuit. She ran through the underbrush, following the sound of the dwarf's laughter, but after a few moments, she lost him. She stood there, breathing heavily, but any sounds the fleeing dwarf might have made were lost in the shouting of the people running through the woods all around her. She caught glimpses of them through the trees as they ran around in all directions, chasing their own shadows.

"They've all gone crazy," she mumbled to herself. She hurried back to her cruiser and took off for Headquarters.

As she flew high above the buildings, looking down at people running through the streets with their nets and blankets, she thought about her meeting with the Bucklands. Sonja's idea was interesting, but judging by what she had just seen, it seemed clear to her that Seldon's intent had been to disrupt the society of the *Agamemnon* and bring about a state of chaos. If this continued to spread, she thought, Seldon's prediction would come true and she would have brought it about herself. I'm fighting a dead woman, she thought, and I've got no weapons to do it with.

She landed on the roof of Security Headquarters and quickly made her way to the command center. Ben Cruzmark was back on duty after a full night's sleep and he looked much better. Karen wondered how she looked. She hadn't been home since the kids had disappeared. She had been staying in her office, and she wasn't getting more than a few hours' sleep. If she kept pushing herself at this rate, she was going to start making mistakes. She could not afford that, but at the same time, she had a job to do. Unfortunately, nothing in her training had prepared her for anything like this.

"How is it out there?" Ben asked, looking up from his console as she came in.

"Not good," she replied. "They're out of control." She shook her head in exasperation. "Two men managed to capture a dwarf in the park. They caught the creature with a net, it gave them some kind of clue, and then they let it go. They let it go! Can you believe that? So their team could get the clue during the next quest link! People are choosing sides and running around out there as if this were some sort of game!"

"Well, in a way, it is," said Ben.

"Not you, too!"

"Don't worry," Ben said. "I'm not about to go out there and join them. I've got a job to do."

"So did they," said Karen. "I told them to go back to their homes. They didn't even listen to me. I was almost trampled by that crowd running after the dwarf those two released. They won't find it, though. I saw it, moments after they disappeared. It was crouching on a rock, laughing at me. Laughing. At me."

"You saw one of them?" Ben asked. "What was it like?"

"Little," Karen said, indicating the height with her hand. "Dressed in bright red-and-green clothing, with a little red hat. It had bushy brown hair and eyebrows, a full beard, and red shoes with turned-up toes. It got away from me in the woods." She looked toward the ceiling in exasperation. "I can't even believe I'm saying any of this. It's ludicrous."

"It's a new wrinkle in VR," said Ben. "A different sort of experience, a game with an irresistible allure. Help the missing children. Find out what's happening. Participate in the quest."

"But this isn't VR," said Karen. "This is real."

"I suppose that makes it all the more exciting," Ben replied. "I must admit, I couldn't wait to get back on duty. I wanted to find out what was going on. It's fascinating. It's even better than VR."

Karen gave him a sharp look. "Don't start. Guardian, what's the current situation with the search parties?"

One of the display screens on the wall zoomed out, becoming dominant. "There has been some progress, despite loss of personnel," Guardian said. "Fifty-seven people did not report for duty this morning."

The screen showed the progress of the search parties, with the areas they'd already checked out and secured highlighted in blue, while the remaining areas of the ship were shown in red. There were far fewer red areas on the screen by now than blue, and as they watched, several more changed to blue.

Karen shook her head. "Where are they keeping those kids? I can't understand why we haven't found them by now. We've checked just about everywhere, right down to the maintenance conduits." She stared at the screen. "Where are they hiding them?"

"There are still a few areas we haven't gone through," Ben said. "It shouldn't take long, though. I've tried everything I could think of to access their links, but it's no go."

"Maybe there's something we're overlooking. Guardian, get me Paul Sharonsky on audio at CAC."

A moment later, Sharonsky's voice filled the command center. "Paul here, Karen. What's up?"

"Plenty," she said. "They're going crazy out there."

"I've heard," Sharonsky replied. "It's hard to believe some people would act so unproductively in a crisis. How are you holding up?"

"About as well as could be expected," she replied. "Paul, bring up the S & R data display over there and take a look, will you?"

"Sure thing. Okay, I've got it. Looks like you've covered a lot of ground. Still no luck finding the kids?"

"They've got to be hidden somewhere, but I can't imagine where. Maybe we're overlooking something. What about the exterior hull? We didn't know about those domes."

"No," Sharonsky said, "we didn't, but the forward end is about the only place you could put something like that.

You've got the propulsion chambers aft, and anywhere else on the hull surface, rotation would make things difficult. If you put a dome out there anyplace but at the forward end, the pseudo-gravity would cause problems. You'd have to enter through the top, which would be the bottom from the inside, and you'd have some pronounced curvature at floor level. You'd also experience some effects from the rotation that would pull you across the floor. I suppose it could be done, but I can't see the point. Still, I can have a series of probes launched to scan the outer hull, just to eliminate that possibility."

"Any chance they could be contaminated by the program and not transmit accurate information?" Karen asked.

"Not so long as CAC remains secure."

"How long will it take?"

"I should be able to have a report for you by the end of the day."

"Do it."

"All right. I'll get on it right away."

"Thanks, Paul. Guardian, disconnect."

"You think he'll find anything?" asked Ben.

Karen pursed her lips. "I don't know," she said, after a moment. "I'm just trying to make sure we haven't missed anything." She looked up at the display screen again. Several more of the red areas had turned blue. "Where *are* they?" she said, staring intently at the screen, as if willing it to supply the answer.

Wherever Seldon had hidden them, she had certainly done a good job. But there was a limit to the possibilities. And, Karen thought, we've just about exhausted them. They had to find them in the next few hours. There weren't many places left where they could be.

By midday, they had reached the waterfall. From a distance, it had been a beautiful sight, but up close, it was spectacular. The river rushed over the cliff to fall crashing to the rocks far below, raising a cloud of spray like a fine mist. But as impressive a sight as the huge waterfall was, what captured their attention was the castle on the rocky slope above it, on the other side.

The central keep was square, looming above the thick stone walls and four round, crenellated towers. Huge, arched, iron-studded double doors gave entry through the walls into the castle grounds, but to reach them, they had to cross a narrow stone bridge that arched over the river, just above the waterfall, and then negotiate an even narrower trail up to a long flight of steps cut into the rocks. It appeared to be a very precarious passage.

"That's gotta be it!" said Riley.

"No, really?" Ulysses replied.

Riley gave him a sour look.

"Those steps look dangerous," said Jenny, gazing uneasily across the bridge. "If you slip, there's nothing to stop you if you fall."

"So don't slip," said Riley.

"Very funny."

"Well, we might as well get going," said Ulysses. He was about to head down the path leading to the stone bridge when Riley grabbed his arm.

"Wait a minute," he said. "Let's not rush this. How do we know that bridge is safe?"

"It looks pretty solid to me," Ulysses said.

"Just because it looks solid doesn't mean it is," said Riley. "This is a sim, remember? Anything can happen here."

"Riley's right," said Jenny. "We're almost to the end of the quest. We need to be careful."

"But how else are we going to get across?" Ulysses asked.

"Why can't you fly us across with magic, the way you did with the boat?"

"Right," Ulysses replied. "And remember what happened to the boat? In case you haven't noticed, I'm not very good at that magic stuff. If I dropped us over that river, we'd be swept right over the fall."

"You could do it if you believed you could," said Jenny.

Ulysses stared at the waterfall apprehensively. "I'd rather not take that chance."

"I guess that leaves the bridge, then," Riley said. He swallowed nervously. "Okay, let's go."

They headed down the trail to a path that wound along the riverbank. The noise of the waterfall grew louder as they approached the bridge. Suddenly, a dwarf stepped out of the bushes, directly into their path, startling them.

"Beware of old acquaintances," he said. "This clue comes to you courtesy of Brian and Francis Etheridge, who send best wishes and good luck to your team. May The Lady watch over you." He doffed his hat to them, bowed deeply, then disappeared into the bushes once again.

They stared at one another in amazement. "My *parents*?" Riley said, with disbelief. "How did *they* get into this?"

"How strange," said Jenny.

"It sounds as if we may not be the only ones on the quest," Ulysses said. "Good luck to our team implies that there are other teams."

"But how did my parents get into this?" asked Riley, mystified.

"I don't know," Ulysses said, shaking his head. "Something must be happening back in the real world. It must have something to do with the creatures on the ship. Maybe they're a way for people to communicate with us here."

"But what did he mean by 'beware of old acquaintances'?" asked Riley.

"Old acquaintances," Ulysses repeated, thoughtfully. He frowned. "I don't know."

"It has to mean something," Riley said. "The dwarf said it was a clue."

"Who would we know in the quest? Other kids from the ship?"

"But why would we have to beware of them?" asked Riley.

"I know!" said Jenny, suddenly. "Gar and Corwin! The two men from the tavern, remember?"

"That's right," Ulysses said. "They followed us when we left the tavern."

"Or it could be the sorceress," said Riley, uneasily.

"Then the dwarf would have said, 'Beware of an old acquaintance,'" Jenny said. "He said 'acquaintances.' That means more than one."

"What if it's all three of them?" asked Riley.

"The sorceress is probably still a pig," said Jenny. "Besides, she didn't strike me as someone who liked men very much. I think the dwarf meant Gar and Corwin."

"It's a good possibility," Ulysses said, nodding. "We'd better watch out for them."

Jenny unsheathed her sword.

Riley glanced at her and moistened his lips, then took out his knives. "I sure hope I know how to use these things," he said. He looked down at the third knife in his belt. "I still have the one they threw at you."

"Maybe you'll get a chance to return it," Jenny said, grimly.

Ulysses looked at her and grinned, but when he saw the expression on her face, his grin faded. "Okay, let's go," he said. "But watch yourselves."

They proceeded slowly down the path, Jenny going first, Riley second, and Ulysses bringing up the rear. They were almost to the bridge. The path widened out ahead of them into a clearing where the bridge began. As they stepped into the clearing, Ulysses heard a crashing sound behind him and suddenly he was thrown to the ground. He struck with jarring force, landing on a rock and getting the wind knocked out of him. Someone had jumped him from behind, grabbing him around the chest and pinning his arms to his sides, bringing him down. Stunned by the impact, he was immediately yanked back to his feet and then he felt the sharp edge of a knife blade pressed up against his throat.

"Drop your weapons!" a familiar voice said, behind him.

Out of the corner of his eye, Ulysses saw Gar pick up the staff he'd dropped and hurl it into the river. Then he turned toward Riley and Jenny with an evil grin on his face and took out his sword.

"You heard him," Gar said. "Throw your blades down, or your companion dies."

Riley and Jenny hesitated.

"None of your spells now, lad," Corwin said, threateningly. Ulysses could feel his breath on his ear. He gasped as the muscular man tightened his grip painfully and pressed the knife closer against his throat. Ulysses felt the blade bite slightly into his skin. "You so much as breathe or blink an eye, and I'll slit your throat from ear to ear!"

"I said, drop your blades!" repeated Gar.

"No," said Jenny.

"What?" said Gar, taken aback.

"I said, no," said Jenny, taking a step forward.

"I'll kill him!" Corwin warned, giving Ulysses a jerk. Ulysses felt a sharp stab of pain as the knife blade broke his skin.

"Jenny!" he said, his voice cracking. She hesitated.

"Quiet, you!" said Corwin. Ulysses gasped with pain and raised his chin as he felt the blade cut a little deeper. He could feel a trickle of blood seep down his neck.

"You let him go," said Jenny, threateningly.

"Drop that blade this instant, lass, else your friend dies," said Gar. "And 'twon't be a pretty sight, I promise you."

"If you harm him, I'll . . . I'll recycle you!" said Jenny. "Both of you!"

"You'll what?" said Gar, with a puzzled frown.

"I think she means she'll kill us, Gar," said Corwin.

"That won't save your friend," said Gar.

"And it won't save you, either," Jenny said.

"Jenny!" said Riley, his eyes wide as he glanced from her to the two men. "What are you doing?"

"If we throw down our weapons, they've got us all," she said.

"But they'll kill Ulysses!"

"And then we'll kill them," said Jenny, her gaze never leaving the two men for an instant.

"What do we do, Gar?" Corwin said, uncertainly. "'Tis not turning out the way we planned."

"So then we change the plan," said Gar. "Kill him and then we'll see to the other two."

Something whistled through the air and Ulysses heard a thumping sound. Corwin's grip on him tightened briefly, then relaxed as the hand holding the knife went limp and the blade slipped from Corwin's fingers as he fell, taking Ulysses down with him. Instantly, Jenny rushed at Gar with her sword. Riley ran over to help Ulysses. As he rolled Corwin's limp body off him, he saw a short arrow sticking in his back.

Gar brought up his sword and parried Jenny's blow, then struck one of his own. She caught it on her blade and then struck again, grunting with the effort. Gar lunged, stabbing at her midsection, but she turned his blade with a downward strike, then slashed upward at his face. He recoiled and Jenny's sword whistled past his nose. Jenny pressed her attack. As she swung the heavy sword with both hands, he got his blade back up and parried her stroke. Their swords clanged as they fought, and Gar started to give way before Jenny's furious onslaught. As she pressed him back, Gar retreated toward the river, and alarm showed on his face as he realized his danger. In a moment, he was teetering on the edge of the bank.

"Enough!" he cried. "No more! I yield!"

"Throw down your sword!" said Jenny, breathing hard.

He tossed his sword to the ground before him.

"Riley! Is Ulysses all right?"

"Yeah, I think he's okay," said Riley.

Jenny bent down to pick up Gar's sword, and in that moment, he reached behind him and pulled out a knife.

"Jenny, look out!" Riley shouted, as Gar raised the knife, but at the same time, an arrow came whistling through the air and struck him in the chest. Gar stiffened, dropped the knife, and fell backward into the river. The current caught him at once and carried his body under the bridge and over the fall.

"What happened?" Jenny asked, startled.

As if in reply, a girl stepped out of the underbrush. She was about the same age as Jenny, and dressed all in green, save for her high, brown leather moccasins. She wore dark green trousers and a matching cloak and tunic with a scalloped cape. Her hair was strawberry blond, and short, just reaching her shoulders. She carried a crossbow at her side.

"Thought you could use some help," she said.

"Who are you?" asked Jenny, with surprise.

"Catherine Moffet," the girl replied. "But my friends call me Cat. I'm from Chicago."

"You're from the ship?" said Riley. "I mean . . . you're *real*?"

She arched an eyebrow at him. "You know anyone from Chicago who isn't?"

"Where's the rest of your team?" asked Riley.

"They died," said Cat.

"They died?" repeated Jenny, wide-eyed.

"These two guys got Tara and Steven on the trail through the forest after we left the tavern. I got away, and I've been on my own ever since."

"So you *can* die in the quest!" said Riley.

"I thought I just said that," Cat replied, in an ironic tone. "We'd better take a look at your friend." She approached Ulysses and examined the wound on his throat. Still shaken, he winced with pain as she touched it. "Lie down," she said.

"What are you going to do?" asked Jenny.

"Heal him," Cat said, as Riley helped Ulysses to the ground.

"How?" asked Jenny.

"I'm a druid in the quest," said Cat. "I'm not much of a fighter, but I have the ability to heal. Unfortunately, it doesn't work if you're dead."

She put down her crossbow and knelt beside Ulysses, placing her hand against his throat. She closed her eyes and concentrated. Ulysses felt his throat getting warm, and the warmth gradually spread throughout his body. Moments later, Cat took her hand away and sat back, breathing deeply. "There, that should do it," she said, sounding a bit tired.

"Wow," said Riley. "The cut is gone! There isn't even any blood!"

Ulysses sat up slowly, rubbing his throat.

"How do you feel?" asked Jenny, gazing at him with concern.

"I feel just fine," he said, with surprise. He glanced at Cat. "Thanks. Are you all right?"

"I will be in a minute," she replied, nodding.

He turned to Jenny. "Would you really have let him kill me?"

"I . . . I didn't think he really would," Jenny replied, awkwardly. "I didn't think we could die in the quest. Ulysses, I'm so sorry!"

"You did the right thing," said Cat. "If you had dropped

your weapons, they would have killed him anyway, and then they would have killed you. The way you did it, at least two of you had a chance to make it."

"We all made it, thanks to you," said Jenny. She glanced back toward Corwin's body, but it was no longer there. "Hey! Where did he go?"

"He vanished," Cat said, getting to her feet. "That's what happens when you die here. You just disappear."

"Is that what happened to your friends?" asked Riley.

Cat nodded. "I don't know if they're really dead, though. Maybe they just died in the quest and now they're back on the ship. I hope so, but I'd rather not find out the hard way."

"So you made it this far all by yourself?" Riley said.

Cat shrugged. "You don't see anyone else here, do you? If I have to, I can make it the rest of the way."

"You don't have to," said Ulysses. "Why don't you come with us?"

"Yes, do," said Jenny. "We wouldn't think of letting you go on alone. You saved our lives."

"Don't mention it," said Cat. "I had a score to settle with those two."

"We're grateful, just the same. We were in serious trouble until you came along. I'm Jenny Kruickshank. This is Ulysses Buckland and that's Riley Etheridge."

"Strange place to make new friends, isn't it?" said Cat. "You must be from another part of the ship. I've never seen any of you around before."

"I'm from Santa Fe Village," said Jenny. "Riley and Ulysses live in Taos."

"So you go to a different school," said Cat. "That's why we've never met. Is your mom Chief Kruickshank?"

Jenny nodded. "Yes."

"I thought she might be," Cat said. "You're really going to catch it when this is over, aren't you?"

"I'll worry about that after we've made it through the quest," said Jenny.

"Did you get any clues yet?"

"We just got one from a dwarf," said Riley. "He warned us about this, but I guess it didn't help. He mentioned something about it coming from my parents, though. Do you have any idea what he meant?"

"I think so," Cat replied. "I've gotten three clues since yesterday, each one from a different person on the ship. Two of them were from my neighbors from the village, the third was from someone I didn't even know. I guess he wanted to help me because I was by myself."

"I don't understand," Riley said. "How do they get clues if they're not in the quest?"

"I think they get them from the creatures on the ship, and then they get passed on to us somehow. The ones on the ship must have an AI link to the creatures here. The people on the ship know about the quest, and they're trying to help us solve it. They might be watching us through a VR link."

Ulysses and Jenny exchanged uneasy glances.

"But I thought all the VR bands were turned in," Ulysses said.

Cat shrugged. "Maybe not all of them. Or maybe they're tuning in some other way. Or they might've figured out the program, but can't stop it, and so they're trying to help us through it. I don't really know. I'm only guessing."

"How many of us are there?" Riley asked.

Cat shrugged. "I have no idea. At first, we thought we were the only ones. Tara, Steven, and I. We didn't know anyone else was in the quest, and I haven't seen anyone until I ran into you three. Unless you count The Lady and the Windwalker."

"You saw them, too?" Ulysses asked.

"She's Penelope Seldon, isn't she?" said Cat.

"Not exactly," said Ulysses. "She's what's left of her, I guess, the part of herself that Dr. Seldon put into the program. I think she can just pop in anywhere, anytime she wants. I think she *is* the program—the symbol of it, or whatever you want to call it."

"Interesting," said Cat. "What makes you think she's the symbol of the program?"

"I saw the elf last night. While I was talking to him, he disappeared and The Lady appeared in his place."

"You never told us that," said Jenny.

"I wanted to have a chance to think about it first," Ulysses said. "And then things got a little busy."

Cat looked up toward the castle. "Well, we're not going to find out how this ends until we get up there, are we? So what do you say we get on with it?"

"We weren't sure about that bridge," said Riley.

"What about it?"

"How do we know it's safe?"

"Good point," said Cat. "Only one way to find out." She picked up her bow. "I'll go first. If I make it to the other side, it's safe." She headed for the bridge with a brisk stride.

"She's really something, isn't she?" said Riley, watching her with admiration. "Come on, we can't let her take the risk alone. Let's go."

Ulysses and Jenny glanced at each other and smiled.

CHAPTER
17

Sonja and Peter sat in their living room and watched as Ulysses, Jenny, Riley, and Cat crossed the arched stone bridge over the waterfall and headed up the winding path to the steps cut into the cliff on which the castle stood. The scene was displayed on the walls of every residence, and on the exterior walls of some buildings for those who were outside. Almost all activity had stopped as people gathered to watch the quest. They were able to specify to their residential AIs which team they wanted to follow, as the Bucklands had, or else they could watch multiple display screens and follow all the teams at once.

There were three teams now that Cat had joined Ulysses and the others. Heather and Sean had lost the third member of their team, Robert, when he slipped and fell from the steps cut into the cliff. They had already reached the Wizard's Castle. The remaining team—Emily, from Phoenix; Raphael, from London; and Jamal, from Venice—were still working their way up to the waterfall.

Knowing what had happened to Robert did not make things any easier for Peter and Sonja as they watched

Ulysses and his friends start up the stone steps leading to the castle, especially after the narrow escape Ulysses had from Gar and Corwin.

"I don't want to watch this anymore," said Sonja, clenching her fists in her lap, "but I can't stop watching it."

"I know how you feel," said Peter. He reached out and took her hand. "Just keep telling yourself it isn't real."

She squeezed his hand. "That isn't going to help. VR death experiences were banned back before Launch, but this program is breaking all the rules. What happens to them if they die in there?"

"Well . . . I suppose it would probably vary with the individual —" Peter began, but she interrupted him.

"I don't want to hear suppose," she said, sharply. "I want to know. Mac, why were simulated death experiences banned?"

"It was discovered that the shock of the experience, even though it wasn't real, was traumatic enough to induce serious psychological damage."

"How serious?"

"Some people recovered after therapy, but others never did."

"What happened to the ones who didn't recover?"

"Sonja, there's no point to —"

"I have to know, Pete!"

"Some individuals went into a coma," Mac said. "Others actually died from shock."

Sonja closed her eyes briefly. "God."

"That doesn't mean it's going to happen to the kids," said Peter. "There's no reason to assume that a death experience in the quest sim is that realistic, especially if your theory about why Seldon designed it is correct. Death in the quest sim could be nothing more than a means of taking them out of the game, penalizing them for making a mistake. Teaching them that risk has consequences."

"Ulysses was in pain when that man's knife cut him."

"A little pain would only add to the realism," Peter said. "If that man had killed him, he wouldn't necessarily have felt it, or experienced death. If you're right, then Seldon had no reason to see any of them harmed. Sim death would have merely resulted in his coming out of VR."

"But we don't know that for sure."

"I'd say the odds are in favor of it."

"Based on what?"

"Your reasoning. And based on what The Lady said to him last night. It supports your theory."

"What if I'm wrong?"

"I don't think you are. But dwelling on it isn't going to help. Besides, our son is doing well. He had a close call, but he survived, didn't he?"

"Thanks to that new girl. If she hadn't been there . . ."

"But she was."

"Maybe we should be trying to get him some clues, the way Brian and Frances did."

"We've already discussed that," Peter replied. "And we both agreed he probably wouldn't want us to do that. We have to show some faith in his abilities. He's a smart boy. He'll make it on his own. I know he can do it."

She looked at him. "I've never heard you say anything like that before. You've always been pretty hard on him. Why haven't you ever talked to him like that?"

He didn't reply at once. "Because I was wrong," he finally said. "I wanted him to be more like me. But he's not like me. And I'm only now beginning to understand that. It doesn't mean he's worse, or not good enough. It just means he's different."

"They're almost halfway up," said Sonja tensely, staring at the wall display. "Oh, be careful!" She bit her lower lip, nervously. "I wish we hadn't turned in our bands! If I could only be there with him!"

"It wouldn't do any good," said Peter. "He wouldn't know it. You'd get his experience, but it would only be one-way."

"I don't care! At least I'd know what he was feeling! I'll call Karen and ask to have them back. I'm sure she wouldn't refuse."

"I'm sure she would," said Peter. "If she made an exception in our case, she'd have to let everyone else have their bands back, too. And she doesn't see things your way. She believes Seldon's intentions were destructive. If I were in her place, I'm not sure I wouldn't think the same thing."

Sonja sighed with resignation. "I suppose you're right. But I'd give anything to have a band right now."

"I understand," said Peter. "But consider how Ulysses would feel about that. Do you think he'd want to have his mother looking over his shoulder, so to speak?"

"No," she replied. "He wouldn't."

"In any case, it's a moot point," said Peter. "We can watch, and we can listen. We can be with him in spirit. Maybe that's even better, in a way. We can support him without accessing his mind and knowing what he's thinking. It's something parents used to do, once upon a time. Sometimes I think we've forgotten how to do that."

"No," said Sonja, smiling at him and squeezing his hand. "You still remember."

"Come on, son," said Saleem Rodriguez, watching Ulysses picking his way carefully up the steep, narrow steps in the cliff face. His gaze was riveted to the display wall in the maintenance shop. "Come on now," he said, sitting on the edge of his seat, "you can do it."

There had been a tense moment when Riley had a misstep and almost slipped, but Jenny was right behind him and she had grabbed him, giving him support. Saleem had held his breath as he watched. He had imagined the fall Riley would have had. It was a long way down.

He wondered how Sonja felt, watching at home. He had thought about calling her, but he didn't want to intrude. And at the same time, he wanted to give his full attention to the quest. He had been sorely tempted to go out and try to catch one of the creatures so he could give Ulysses a clue, but with Sonja at home, he felt he had to remain on duty at the office. It was her son in the quest, after all. She couldn't be expected to come in. He had insisted she take time off until it was all over and Ulysses was back.

But what if he didn't come back? What if something happened? He tried to push the thought from his mind. For Sonja's sake, he hoped everything would turn out all right. He didn't want to think about the kids not being found.

Sooner or later, the search parties had to discover where they had been taken. By now, they had gone through almost the entire ship. He wanted them back, and safe, but at the same time, he didn't want to see them found before he discovered how the quest turned out. The thought made him feel a little guilty, but he couldn't help it. They were almost *there*. Another few minutes, and they'd be at the top, just a short way from the castle doors. He wished they'd hurry.

Robie Marshall sat in her bedroom at home, watching the quest on the display wall. Since her parents had picked her up at the hospital, she had been forbidden her morning walks, forbidden to leave the house at all unless someone was with her. She felt angry and frustrated at being treated like a child, and she was gaining weight from eating compulsively. She sat with a large bowl of popcorn, munching as she watched all the teams at once on separate displays.

She wished she could go back to the woods and look for Grailing, but even if she could, she knew she probably wouldn't find him. The woods were full of people during the day, all of them trying to catch an elf or a dwarf or a fairy so they could get a clue. She wondered what would happen when the quest was over. She knew Security would be looking for Grailing. She hoped nothing bad would happen to him because of her. She didn't really care what happened to the others, so long as Grailing would be all right. They were bound to catch him, sooner or later, and she wondered what they'd do. Most likely, he'd be sent to Counseling. She knew she would be in Counseling right now if it wasn't for Program X. Her parents had told her as much. The Counseling AI couldn't be trusted. Program X had compromised it. But as soon as CAC worked it all out and things were back to normal, she'd be going in for treatment.

It wasn't fair. She hadn't done anything wrong. She couldn't even talk to any of her friends. Her parents had instructed the house computer to block her calls, so she was cut off from everyone. There wasn't anything for her to do but eat and lie around and watch the quest. Why couldn't she

have been picked for it? Then everyone would be watching
her.

Her favorite was Cat. She thought that she and Cat had a
lot in common. As she watched them reach the top of the
stone steps, she noted with satisfaction that Cat was leading
the way. She took another large handful of popcorn and
stuffed it in her mouth. They were almost to the castle now.
She couldn't wait to see what happened next.

Brian and Frances Etheridge were watching at home, too,
eating their dinner in the living room as they stared with rapt
fascination at the display wall.

"They made it!" Frances said, with relief. She had cried
out and grabbed Brian's arm when Riley slipped and almost
fell, but Jenny had caught him and now they reached the top.

"No thanks to Riley," Brian said, irritably.

"It wasn't his fault," Frances said. "He slipped."

"And Jenny saved him. So far, Jenny and Ulysses have
done just about everything. What has he contributed?"

"He's trying, Brian."

"He didn't even understand the clue, after all the trouble
we went through to get it for him. For all the good it did
them. They were lucky that girl, Cat, came along. Did you
see what happened when those men grabbed Ulysses? Riley
just stood there. He didn't do a thing."

"What was he supposed to do? Ulysses is his friend. He
didn't want to see him hurt."

"He's Jenny's boyfriend, but that didn't stop Jenny, did
it?"

"Well, Jenny had that big sword. Riley only has those
knives. I hardly think that's fair."

"He could have taken one of the swords from Gar and
Corwin."

"No, he couldn't have. They disappeared along with the
bodies. You weren't paying attention."

"I just hope he does better when they reach the castle. He
had a head start on the others. He should have been there by
now."

"Aren't you being just a little bit competitive?" asked
Frances. "You've always told him he should be more coop-

erative, and now that he's doing exactly what you told him to do, you're complaining."

"I'm not complaining."

"Yes, you are. You're doing exactly what you've always accused him of doing. You're not being fair, Brian."

"Just watch the program," Brian replied, irritably.

Of all the people on the ship, only Karen and the rest of the Security crew at the command center were not watching the quest. Guardian still appeared secure from contamination by the program, as did the CAC Net, but by now, most of the other AIs had been infected and could no longer be trusted. Paul Sharonsky and his team had been working with almost no rest, and they were all exhausted, as was Karen. They had made no progress in isolating Program X. She stared uncomprehendingly at the search display on the wall. It was all blue now. She couldn't understand it, and neither could the search teams. They had combed through every inch of the ship and the kids were nowhere to be found. It was impossible.

"Guardian, get me Paul Sharonsky at CAC on audiovisual."

The display on the wall was replaced by an image of Paul at CAC Support. He hadn't shaved and his clothes looked as if he'd slept in them for a week. Karen wondered if she looked just as bad.

"It's no good, Karen," he said. "The scan of the exterior hull came up negative. There's nothing out there."

"It's impossible," said Karen. "We've searched through the entire ship. It's just impossible. They've got to be *somewhere*!"

Sharonsky sighed, wearily. "I know," he said. "I've got the display up here. Your teams haven't missed a thing."

"So then where *are* they?" Karen said, with exasperation. "They've got to be aboard the ship!"

"Obviously," said Paul. "Unless they've all been recycled and what everyone is watching are merely VR constructs."

"No," said Karen, a chill running through her. "No, I can't believe that."

"I hate to say it, Karen, but I just can't think of any other explanation," Paul said, heavily, running his hand through his hair. "I can't think of anything we've missed. We've gone through everything except the fuel cells." He stopped suddenly. "Good Lord."

Karen shook her head, sadly. "You must really be tired, Paul. You're just not thinking. How could they be there? The cells are full of deuterium and tritium."

"We've eliminated everything else, haven't we?" said Paul.

"Yes, but it's just not possible."

"No," he said, slowly, "it *is* possible. Seldon had a long time to prepare for this." He frowned, rubbing his chin as he thought it through. "If you wanted to section part of a fuel cell, it could be done. We are well into the voyage now, the cells are partly empty. The nanalloy could have been programmed to construct a wall inside one of the cells, effectively creating a sealed chamber in there. The half-life of tritium is 12.5 years, so in 50 years, the radiation wouldn't even be a problem. But I would think it would be in the deuterium cells, because that way, you could bleed in oxygen and get water out of the deuterium breakdown. You could take power off the reactors and oxygen through nanalloy conversion. Yes, it could be done. . . . No, wait . . ."

Karen held her breath, afraid to interrupt. Everyone in the command center gazed intently at his image on the wall. No one made a sound.

"Yes, it could work," said Paul, slowly. "Theoretically, it *could* work. I was thinking how to compensate for the uneven distribution of fuel, but if the amount of fuel in all the tanks were balanced, it wouldn't be a problem. I need to check something . . ."

He rushed over to one of the other display walls and Karen heard him swear, then he nodded vigorously and said, "Of course!"

"Paul!" said Karen, unable to contain her anxiety.

He came rushing back. "The fuel tanks all read full," he said.

Karen's shoulders slumped. "So much for that idea."

"Not so fast," said Paul. "Program X is a master program, remember? The D+T sensors *could* be lying to us."

"But even if they were," said Karen, "and even if Seldon

had constructed a hidden chamber in there, what about life-support? Don't forget, Program X didn't start infecting the AIs until just recently. She would have needed time to do all this. How could she have had a chamber constructed in there and recalibrated the sensors without CAC picking it up?"

"Simple . . . if she created another AI. One that was not part of the network. It fed false information to the sensors: power, life-support, fuel balance, all of them. She could have done anything back there and we never would have known about it."

"But if the fuel balance were off, wouldn't that affect rotation?" Karen asked.

"Not really, because what we're really talking about is mass, and if you replace the mass in the chamber, it wouldn't be a problem. Either way, the sensors are going to read correctly. We'd never know it happened."

Karen bit her lower lip. "But where would she have hidden the AI?"

"Right there. It would take up very little room. It was her field of expertise, after all. And she probably used that same AI to create the program."

"How would we know for sure?" asked Karen. "We can't just open up the cells to check."

"Now you're not thinking," Paul replied. "If the kids were taken in there, then that means there has to be access, doesn't it?"

"Ben . . ." said Karen, turning toward him.

"I'm already ahead of you," he said. "I'm dispatching a team to Propulsion right away."

"Tell them to wait until I get there," Karen said.

"I'm going with you," Cruzmark said. "And please don't tell me to stay here. I'd hate to disobey an order for the first time in my life."

"All right," she said. "Come on."

The iron-studded double doors of the Wizard's Castle swung open slowly with an ominous, creaking sound as they approached. Standing abreast before the massive doors, they hesitated, glancing at one another nervously.

"Who opened the doors?" asked Riley, apprehensively.

"Nobody," said Jenny. "They opened by themselves."

They gazed into the empty courtyard just beyond the doors. The sun was setting, and long shadows stretched across the courtyard.

"Well, this is it," said Cat.

No one moved.

"We didn't come this far just to stand here, did we?" said Ulysses, trying to bolster his own courage as much as theirs. "Come on. Let's go."

They went through the doors into the unpaved courtyard. Weeds were sprouting up here and there through the hard-packed dirt. Riley grabbed Ulysses by the arm and pointed to the ground at their feet. "Look," he said. There were footprints leading toward the keep. "Somebody got here before us."

Cat knelt to examine the tracks. "Two people," she said. "And it couldn't have been very long ago. These are fresh."

"How can you tell?" Ulysses asked.

"Sim knowledge," Cat replied. "My character's a druid, and druids know about these things."

"You think it's one of the other teams?" asked Jenny.

"I'd say it was a good possibility," Ulysses replied. "Unless it's another trap, like with Gar and Corwin."

Jenny drew her sword. Riley glanced at her and took out his knives. Cat drew another bolt from her belt pouch and fitted it to her crossbow.

"I sure wish I still had my magic staff," Ulysses said.

There was an eerie silence on the castle grounds. The shadows lengthened as the sun sank on the horizon. The castle looked deserted, but they knew someone had gone inside ahead of them.

They crossed the courtyard, glancing around warily. As they approached the thick, heavy wooden doors of the keep, they swung open slowly, by themselves. Inside, there was darkness.

"Anybody else scared besides me?" asked Riley.

"I am, a little," said Ulysses.

"Me, too," said Jenny.

"Just checking," Riley said. "I'd hate to be the only one."

"Don't worry, you're not," said Cat.

"I didn't think anything scared you," said Riley.

Cat glanced at him and smiled.

As they entered the keep, the double doors suddenly swung closed behind them with a loud echo. Riley felt Cat grab his hand. He gave her hand a reassuring squeeze and was thrilled when she squeezed back. It made him feel a little less afraid.

"I wish we had some light in here," Ulysses said.

Immediately, torches mounted in sconces on the walls burst into flame, illuminating the large chamber with flickering light and casting shadows on the walls.

"Nice going," Jenny said.

"I don't think I did that," Ulysses replied, doubtfully.

Riley was almost sorry to see the darkness disappear, because it meant that Cat didn't need to hold his hand anymore. She released it and lifted her crossbow, glancing around anxiously. They were in an antechamber that led through an archway into a large room. As they went through, they saw that it took up the entire first floor of the keep, and part of the second floor, as well. The furnishings were crudely made. There were several long wooden tables and benches placed in the center. To their left, at the far end, was an elevated dais on which stood a long table and several high-backed wooden chairs. Behind the chairs was a large fireplace and several iron braziers with flames flickering in their bowls. The walls were hung with rotting tapestries and everything was festooned with cobwebs and covered with a thick layer of dust.

The thick-beamed ceiling of the chamber was two floors above them. A gallery ran around the main hall where the second floor would have been.

"Okay, now what?" Cat said. "We're here, but it looks like nobody's home."

"I don't think anyone's been here in years," Ulysses said.

"Somebody's been here," Riley said, pointing to two sets of footprints in the dust. They went across the hall and through an archway at the back, beneath the gallery. "Looks like they went upstairs."

They followed the tracks to a winding flight of wooden steps that led to the second floor gallery. The footprints in the dust and the broken cobwebs indicated that the two people who had preceded them had continued up the stairs. As they were about to follow, they heard a loud, echoing crash from above.

"Hello!" Ulysses shouted. "Hello, can anybody hear me?"

"Up here!" came the echoing response. It was a female voice. "We're up here! Please help us!"

"Hang on, we'll be right there!" Ulysses called.

"Wait," said Riley. "How do we know it's not a trap?"

Before Ulysses could respond, another cry came from below them.

"Hey! Who's there?"

They looked out over the gallery and saw three people coming into the main chamber below. The newcomers were dressed the same way they were, in cloaks, tunics, loose-fitting trousers, and high moccasins or boots. They also carried swords and shields.

"Who are you?" asked Ulysses.

"My name's Raphael Martinez," one of them said, his voice echoing through the hall. "Are you one of the other teams?"

"Yes," said Ulysses. "I'm Ulysses Buckland."

"Who were you yelling at?"

"There's somebody upstairs. It sounds like they're in trouble."

"Hang on, we'll be right there."

"Hurry!" came a cry from upstairs, only this time, it was a male voice. "We can't hang on much longer!"

"Okay, we're coming!" Ulysses called up to them.

"Maybe we should wait for the others," Jenny said.

"It doesn't sound as if they can wait up there," Ulysses said.

"Okay, come on," said Riley, mustering his courage and leading the way.

They headed up the winding stairs. The passageway was narrow and they could only see a few feet ahead of them as they climbed. There was only room for one person to go through at a time, so they had to go single file, Riley first, followed by Cat, and then Ulysses, with Jenny bringing up the rear. When they reached the third floor, the male voice above them called out again, "Hurry! Please!"

They continued up the stairs to the next floor. "We're on the fourth floor!" Riley called out. "Where are you?"

"Keep going! But watch your step! The stairs are old and rotten."

"Now they tell us," Riley said. He kept going, testing the steps as he went, with the others close behind. Suddenly, the way was blocked by debris. The crash they had heard had been the stairway collapsing. "Where are you?" Riley called out. "We can't go any farther!"

"We're right above you!"

They looked up and in the dim light saw two people clinging to a small section of the wooden stairs still attached to the center shaft about two floors above them, their legs dangling in space.

"How are we supposed to get them down?" asked Cat, looking up. "There's no way to get up there."

"Yes, there is," said Riley. "Ulysses, squeeze through."

Ulysses edged past Cat as she pressed herself up against the wall. He looked up and said, "Oh, boy. Now what do we do?"

"Not we, you," said Riley. "We need some magic."

"But I lost my staff," Ulysses said.

"You don't need the staff," Riley insisted. "Remember, in the tavern, when you stopped the knife? You just held your hand out. You didn't even have the staff. It was on the floor."

"That's right," said Jenny. "It's not the staff, it's you."

"We need some stairs," said Riley. "You can do it. You just have to believe you can."

"Okay," Ulysses said, taking a deep breath. "I'll give it a try."

He closed his eyes and held his arms out, palms down, fingers outstretched toward the debris. He concentrated, trying to visualize the stairs as nanalloy instead of wood. He imagined the pile of debris softening and flowing, forming new steps and extending up . . .

"It's working!" Riley said, as the wreckage blocking their way started to melt. "Keep it up!"

Ulysses continued concentrating, imagining the stairs flowing up the shaft. He felt a warm, tingling sensation going down his arms and into his hands, through his outstretched fingers . . .

The broken and splintered wood liquified, forming new steps, spiraling up the shaft like a fountain flowing in reverse. The others watched the steps winding upward toward the two people hanging precariously over their heads. A moment later, they were blocked from view as the newly formed stairway curled around above them.

"You're almost there!" the cry came down to them. "Just a little more! Keep going . . . keep going . . . all right! You did it! We're okay!"

Ulysses opened his eyes. The stairs were uninterrupted, as if they had never collapsed. He took a deep breath and leaned against the wall to steady himself. He felt drained.

"Nice job," said Cat, clapping him on the shoulder.

"Thanks to Riley," he replied. "I didn't even know I could do it."

They soon came to the couple they had rescued, seated on the steps, leaning against each other limp with exhaustion.

"I figured we'd had it," the young man said. "Thanks. My name is Sean. And this is Heather."

Behind them, they could hear the third team coming up the stairs.

"Is everything all right up there?" It was Raphael's voice.

"Yes, everything's fine," Riley called down to him. "Come on up, but watch your step."

They all came together on the top floor, in a large open chamber with a wood-planked floor and a fireplace. An archway with an iron-studded wood door that stood ajar led to a bedroom that contained the remains of a four-poster, canopied bed. Little was left of the mattress, and the canopy hung in tatters. Cobwebs stretched between the posts. Except for some broken wooden chests, a dust-covered table, two chairs, a couple of wooden stools, and the stained, moth-eaten remnants of a rug, the bedroom contained nothing.

The outer chamber where they met held a long wooden table, similar to the ones in the hall below, and two long wooden benches. Two rotted tapestries hung on the walls, on either side of an ancient shield and two crossed swords, covered with dust and cobwebs. There was no indication that anyone had been there in a long, long time.

They all sat at the table and compared their experiences in the quest. They discovered that they had all met Gar and Corwin, only with different results. Cat's team had fared the worst with them, driving them off in the tavern, but falling prey to their ambush on the forest trail. Heather, Sean, and Robert had an experience similar to Ulysses and his team's, but had avoided the sorceress by cautiously staying away from her cabin and scouting the area until they found the boat. They had encountered the dragon, but Robert, the adept on their team, had turned it away. They had sailed around the whirlpool and they had also avoided Gar and Corwin at the bridge by deciphering their clue and circling around them through the woods. Unfortunately, they had lost Robert on the climb up to the castle.

Emily, Jamal, and Raphael had better luck in the tavern. They had defeated Gar and Corwin. They described how the bodies of the two men had vanished after they ran them through. They had worse luck with the fairies. They had fallen under their spell and danced the night away, awaking the next morning sore and exhausted, which had delayed their journey. As a result, they had not received their clue in the clearing and had not captured the unicorn. Instead, they had continued on the forest trail until they encountered an elf who told their fortunes with a colorful deck of cards. The fortunes had contained clues, and when they had deciphered them, the elf had turned into The Lady and directed them to a trail through the woods, which took them to the lake. They had found the cabin of the sorceress, who had apparently recovered from being turned into a pig.

Jamal and Raphael fell victim to her charms, but Emily had been suspicious and had watched her carefully. She had caught her putting the powder in the wine and had stopped

Jamal and Raphael from drinking. They had forced the sorceress to confess, under the threat of having to drink her own potion, and like Jenny and Ulysses, had freed her other victims from their enchantment.

With minor variations, they all had roughly similar experiences, and when they were finished comparing notes, Sean said, "Well, we made it to the castle, but now what? There isn't anybody here. Heather and I had time to search the place before those stairs collapsed on us on our way up here, and we didn't find anything except dust, cobwebs, and broken-down old furniture."

"So that's it?" said Riley. "We went through this whole quest only to wind up in a dusty, deserted old castle? I thought there was supposed to be a wizard."

"I don't think The Lady ever said there was a wizard, did she?" Emily replied. "She only said we'd find the answer in the Wizard's Castle."

"Okay, so then, what's the answer?" asked Jamal.

"We don't even know the question," Riley replied.

"Once we were here, we were supposed to solve the riddle of the quest," Ulysses said, thoughtfully. "That's what she said. You'll find your answer in the Wizard's Castle."

"Then it has to be here," Jenny said. She glanced at Heather. "Are you sure you searched the whole place carefully?"

"We were mainly looking to see if anyone was here," Heather replied. "I suppose there could be something hidden here that we're supposed to find, but how do we find it if we don't even know what we're looking for? We don't have any clues."

"The virtue of reality . . ." Ulysses mumbled.

"What?" said Raphael.

"I think that's the clue," Ulysses said. "What is the virtue of reality?"

"The elf asked us that," Jamal said.

"Grailing? He said it to me, too," said Cat. "But I couldn't figure out what he meant. I thought he was making a joke about VR."

"He was," Ulysses said. "But it wasn't just a joke. It was a clue."

"It doesn't sound as if any of us figured it out," said Sean. "But it made no difference. We got here anyway."

"Except there's nothing here," said Raphael.

"Maybe we're just supposed to wait here until something happens," Riley said.

"Maybe we should search the place again," said Jenny.

"What for?" said Sean.

"I don't know," Jenny replied. "You said you were only looking to see if anyone was here, so you could have missed something."

"Well, we could look again in the morning," Heather suggested, "when there will be more light."

"I'm not anxious to spend the night in this gloomy, depressing old place," said Cat.

"You got any better ideas?" Heather asked.

"Gloomy and depressing," said Ulysses, with a frown.

"What?" said Sean.

"This place is pretty depressing, isn't it?" Ulysses said.

"I don't think anyone's going to disagree with that," Riley replied.

"The point is, why is it depressing?" Ulysses said.

"What do you mean, why?" said Jamal, staring at him with puzzlement. "You don't think it is? Does it look *cheerful* to you?"

"No, of course it doesn't," Ulysses replied. "That isn't what I meant. I meant, why did it have to be gloomy and depressing? Dr. Seldon could have made it anything she wanted. So after all we went through on the quest, why did she choose to have us end up in a place like this?"

"Good question," Emily said, the corners of her mouth turning down. "It certainly isn't what I expected."

"I don't think it's what any of us expected," Jenny said. "I thought there was going to be a wizard, something really dramatic to resolve the quest. I just can't believe this is all there is. I keep waiting for something to happen."

"Maybe that's the trouble," said Ulysses, staring at her as if suddenly struck by an idea.

"I don't understand," Jenny replied. "What do you mean?"

"I keep thinking about Grailing's clue," he said, with a thoughtful expression. "What's virtual reality?"

"But that wasn't what he said," Riley reminded him. "He said, 'What is the virtue of reality?'"

"I know that," said Ulysses. "It was a play on words. And that may be the key. So what is virtual reality? Computer simulation with total sensory input. You're disconnected from the real world and plunged into the simulated world of virtual reality. You see, you hear, you feel . . . it's a complete sensory and emotional experience. You don't even have to think. You just virtch out and go with it."

"So?" said Sean. "What's your point?"

"It's passive," said Ulysses. "You don't have to *do* anything. You don't have to participate. It demands absolutely nothing of you. All you have to do is be there, just lie back and go with it. But the quest was different, right from the beginning. It *made* us participate. It required us to think, it challenged us to use our imaginations. And that's why we all got so involved, because we *were* involved. That's why it felt more *real* to us than any of the other sims. Our active participation was what made it seem so real, to the point where sometimes I even forgot it wasn't."

"That happened with me, too," said Heather.

"And me," said Raphael, nodding in agreement.

"But the quest didn't really do that, did it?" said Ulysses, emphatically. "We did. It seemed real because we got so involved that we forgot and thought it was. So *we* created that, the quest didn't do it for us." He stopped, abruptly, with a look of sudden comprehension. "That's the virtue of reality. It's something you create." He jumped to his feet. "Of course!"

He frowned in concentration, brought his hands up to his head and, in the next instant, disappeared.

"It's got to be here," Karen said.

"Chief," said one of the engineers, "there's nothing on the other side of this wall but solid rock."

"There's got to be a hidden tunnel leading back to one of the fuel cells," Karen said. "This is the only other place where they could be. We're going to slag this entire wall if we have to, but we're going to find that tunnel."

"Karen, wait!" Paul Sharonsky came rushing down the

corridor. Trailing him was one of the floating maintenance drones. "We don't have to destroy the wall," he said. "I've had this drone equipped with a sonic probe. If there's a hidden tunnel anywhere in here, the drone will find it for us." He turned toward the hovering drone. "Drone, engage probe sequence," he said.

The drone hovered for a second, then turned and slowly floated down the length of the chamber, executing a sonic scan of the wall as it went. They watched in silence, tense with anticipation. It moved along the wall, floating about a meter and a half above the floor. Suddenly, it stopped, hovering, and emitted a sharp, intermittent beeping signal.

"That's it," Sharonsky said.

They all hurried toward the drone. The smooth surface of the nanalloy wall looked no different from the rest of the chamber. But the probe had revealed that what was behind it was not solid rock, but empty space.

Karen took a deep breath and let it out slowly. Paul had been right. Jenny had to be back there, somewhere, along with the other missing kids. "All right," she said, with a hard edge to her voice. "Burn it."

The engineers raised their lasers, but before they could activate them, the wall suddenly rippled and flowed, opening out into an archway and revealing a hidden tunnel through the rock. The passageway was dark, leading back toward one of the cavernous fuel cells of the *Agamemnon*. The search team hesitated.

"Let's go," said Karen. "Two of you stay back here with your lasers, just in case the program seals us up after we've gone inside."

She stepped into the tunnel. Sharonsky and others followed, using their halogen arc lights. At the far end of the tunnel was an opening that led straight into one of the *Agamemnon*'s fuel cells.

"I knew it!" said Sharonsky, excitedly. Karen felt him clutch her shoulder. "I knew there had to be a hidden chamber!"

They quickened their pace. Moments later, they reached

the end of the tunnel and caught their breath with amazement.

Stretching out before them was a huge sectioned-off portion of a fuel cell, flooded with light from a plasma arc artificial sun. The entire interior was covered with lush greenery.
Thick forests and green meadows were planted on the curving inner surface. It was a smaller version of the
Agamemnon, complete with a miniature sea, a narrow band
of blue that curved upward along both sides, like a river encircling the chamber. Clouds floated overhead, and birds
chirped in the trees. The air was fresh and pure, sweet with
the smell of growing things, and small forest animals scur-
ried through the underbrush.

"I don't believe it," Karen said softly, with awe. "It's impossible. How could one person have done all this?"

"One person didn't," said Sharonsky. "Penelope Seldon
merely started the ball rolling. She designed a program and a
new AI, provided the raw materials and had drones constructed, then simply threw the switch, to put it prosaically.
The work has been going on ever since. This must have
taken at least a hundred years. A complete, self-sustaining
ecosystem, independent of the rest of the ship. Inside a fuel
tank." He shook his head in amazement. "It's an absolutely
staggering achievement, and she never lived to see it."

There was a rustling in the bushes before them, and two
dwarves stepped into view. They were both shaggy-haired
and bearded, and came up to just above Karen's kneecaps.
They wore bright green tunics and trousers, red caps, and
tiny red shoes with curled-up toes. They just stood there for a
moment, then slowly approached Karen.

"Careful, Chief . . ." one of her officers said.

Karen already had her stunner out. "Stop right there," she
said. "Where's my daughter? Take me to her, now!"

They nodded and beckoned to her.

"All right, go ahead," said Karen, cautiously. "But slowly,
and don't make any abrupt moves."

They turned and led her through the underbrush as the others followed. They were on a small dirt path leading through
the wood. The dwarves said nothing, leading her on. Before
long, they came out of the wood and into a large clearing.

Karen stopped in her tracks with a gasp. Before her stood a miniature stone castle, slightly larger than the size of an average residence aboard the ship. It had small, crenellated towers, a surrounding wall, and arched, studded, wooden doors. In every detail, save that it had no moat or drawbridge, it was a miniature replica of a medieval keep.

"Will you look at that?" someone behind her said.

The dwarves moved on and she followed them. As they approached the castle wall, the doors swung open to admit them, and a tall figure dressed all in gray stepped through. He was young, and strikingly good-looking, with glossy, black hair hanging down below his shoulders, delicately arched eyebrows, a narrow, sharp-featured face, and pointed ears.

"Allow me to bid you welcome," he said, with a bow.

"Grailing Windwalker?" Karen said.

He smiled. "And you are Chief Kruickshank, of course. Jenny's mother."

"Where is my daughter?" Karen demanded. "Where are the other children? If you've done anything to them —"

"The children are well, I assure you," said the elf. "All of them. Please, come with me."

He beckoned them through the doors, then turned to lead the way, with the dwarves trailing behind him. Karen followed them into the castle courtyard, which was planted with fragrant flower beds and shrubs. At the far end of the courtyard stood the keep, with a short flight of stone steps leading up to double wooden doors like the ones in the wall. In the center of the courtyard, on a pedestal, stood a statue of an old woman dressed in robes. Her hair was long, and her face was lined with age, but her features had a proud cast to them, with high cheekbones, a blade-straight nose, a determined looking mouth, and a slightly upraised chin. She stood erect, gazing off into the distance.

"Penelope Seldon," Karen said.

"Our Great Mother," said the elf. The dwarves moved over to stand on either side of Grailing. "All that remains of her is here."

"Seldon's AI," said Paul, softly.

"Yes, Mr. Sharonsky," said the elf. "You are correct."

"I want to see my daughter," Karen said, firmly. "Now."

Suddenly, the statue's head turned to look at her. "Patience, Chief Kruickshank," it said. "The quest is now complete, and the children are all safe, as everyone watching aboard the ship will shortly see. The first of them should be arriving momentarily."

As the statue spoke, the doors of the keep swung open and Ulysses stepped out, gazing all around him with wonder.

"Ulysses!" Karen cried, running toward him. He looked at her with surprise, then grinned. "Ulysses, where's Jenny?"

"I think she'll be right out," he said.

"Mom!" Jenny came running out of the keep and into Karen's arms. Behind her came Riley and Cat, holding hands, and then the others, all of them staring with wonder at their surroundings.

"Congratulations, Ulysses," said the statue. "You solved the riddle of the quest. I knew you would."

"What happened to the others, the ones who died?" asked Ulysses, uncertainly.

"They only appeared to die," said the statue. "They did not suffer the trauma of the experience; they were only taken out of the game. I have already sent for them. They should be here at any moment."

No sooner had the statue spoken than Robert came riding through the gates on a unicorn. Behind him came Tara and Steven, from Cat's team, accompanied by a group of dwarves.

"There's just one thing I still don't understand," Ulysses said, staring up at the statue. "Why us? Why were we chosen for the quest?"

"Because you were born for this purpose," said the statue. "My task was the creation of all you see around you, while the quest program slept within the network databanks. When the initial stages of the crisis I predicted came to pass, the program was activated, and you were the first result. Twelve children were selected from the Reproductive Centers, according to criteria applied to the profiles of their parents, and some of my own genetic material was introduced during the fertilization process."

"You mean . . . we're all brothers and sisters?" asked Ulysses, glancing at Jenny with dismay.

"No," said the statue. "You all had different parents, as is obvious by your appearance. You are not clones. But a small part of my genetic makeup is in every one of you. That is why you were all a bit different from the others of your generation, brighter, more creative, more inquisitive and more independent. It was necessary to revitalize the colony by bringing back certain traits which had become atrophied with disuse over the generations. Even in my own time, I saw people beginning to lose touch with their imaginative faculties, becoming passive and complacent in an atmosphere of noncompetitive social equality. You were all born with a greater degree of independence, aggressiveness, and creativity, so that you could reawaken those traits in others.

"Of course, this entailed certain risks, and there were ethical considerations involved, questions over which I had agonized for a long time. You may ask yourselves, what right did I have to do this? I asked myself that question repeatedly, and the only answer I could find was that I had no right, but I also had no choice. What I was doing would interfere in the birthing process, and yet, technically speaking, we as a society had already made that choice. Our reproduction was no longer natural. The Reproductive labs controlled virtually all aspects of the process, and automatically corrected for any genetic abnormalities. However, they had not been designed to correct for defects which, over a long period of time, came about as a result of environmental factors. We had tried to make our society so perfect that a sort of reverse Darwinism had come into play. There could be no survival of the fittest if no one was truly fit. Humanity could not continue to evolve if we had produced an environment that was only conducive to stagnation.

"A society committed to balanced political correctness and social productivity does not produce creative individuals, who are by nature incorrect, unbalanced, and irresponsible. In designing a program to select for those traits and inculcate a greater degree of aggressiveness, independence, and creative thinking among members of a future generation, the risk was that I would be midwifing the birth of misfits who would be misunderstood and possibly rejected and abused by the very society which so desperately needed them. And there were no guarantees. Even with all our scientific knowledge and technical capabilities, we cannot make our children be what we want them to be, especially if they possess a greater degree of intelligence and independence. The most that I could do was provide the optimum genetic matrix and add stimulation at the proper time. Ultimately, it would be up to the children to rise to the challenge and ensure the future. It always is."

"You keep referring to yourself as if you were Penelope Seldon," Karen said, frowning. "But you're not. You're an AI that she created."

"A part of me is also Penelope Seldon," said the statue. "Or what is left of her. Before she died, she used direct interface between us to create part of my programming. Penelope Seldon lives on, through me and through the quest program that is now part of the network."

"So you've taken over the ship for our own good, is that it?" Karen asked, tensely.

"No, not at all. The quest program, having served its purpose, will execute a subroutine for self-deletion within 24 hours. And since I have no link to the network, my control begins and ends within this chamber. The AI Network has controlled the ship from the beginning, and essential functions were never interfered with. Humans were always nonessential personnel, at least so far as the functions of the ship were concerned. The ship was designed to free the colony from that burden, but with all challenge removed, with creativity and competition stifled, and with natural aggressive instincts suppressed, the colony began to stagnate.

"People need challenge to thrive. They need the revitalizing element of risk in their lives. They need to compete and fantasize. A thriving society needs individuals who are creative and disruptive, and in order to be something more than mere existence, life cannot be fair. The AIs have no interest in controlling human destiny. Their function is to maintain the ship. You must maintain yourselves, and you were not doing it."

"What about the creatures?" Karen asked.

"They all have a programmed life span of one generation, 150 years, and they cannot reproduce themselves. What you choose to do about them is entirely up to you. If the Assembly decides they need to be recycled, then they shall not resist. If you decide to have them live among you, and take part in your society, they will cooperate with whatever plan you may devise. But if I might make a suggestion, I would recommend you leave them here, and treat this section of the ship as an environment for stimulating, interactive play. You are very much in need of it. You need to learn how to use your imaginations once again. There are any number of quests I could devise for live participation. And if, after a time, you decide it would be beneficial to have them continue as part of the ship, then I possess the necessary data to enable you to reproduce them as you see fit. Whichever way you choose, the decision will be yours. But take some time and think about it. You still have a long voyage ahead of you. It need not be a boring one."

EPILOGUE

"Are we late?" Riley asked, as he came in with Cat.

"No, Riley, you're just in time," said Sonja, with a smile. "We're just waiting for Karen. She called a little while ago and said she was on her way."

Jenny and Ulysses got up from the couch to greet their friends with hugs. "So," Cat said to them, "have you two got any news for us?"

"I told you it wasn't going to be a surprise," said Jenny.

"We formally requested our Choice this morning," Ulysses said.

"Congratulations," said Riley, clapping him on the shoulder. "This calls for a celebration."

"Why do you think you're here?" Ulysses said.

"What about you two?" Jenny asked, raising her eyebrows.

"We're not going to rush into anything," said Riley. "I think we should take our time."

"Excuse me?" Cat said, glancing at him with surprise.

"Where is the real Riley Etheridge and what have you done with him?"

"Honey, are you coming down to dinner?" Sonja called.

"I'll be right there," Peter replied, in a strained voice. A moment later, he came waddling down the stairs, holding onto the railing for support and leaning back slightly to compensate for the weight of his big belly.

"Here, let me give you a hand," said Sonja.

"It's all right, I can make it," he said as he reached the bottom of the stairs. He exhaled heavily. "Boy, my back is killing me."

"Hi, Mom," said Riley, putting a hand against Peter's stomach. "Is she kicking yet?"

"Yet?" said Peter, with a grimace. "She hasn't stopped."

"Hey! I just felt one!" Riley said.

"You ought to try it from this end," Peter said, wearily.

"Let me feel!" Cat said.

"Why don't I just set up a chair outside and let a line form?" Peter asked, sarcastically.

"Oooh, that was a strong one!" Cat said. "Have you decided on a name yet?"

"Penelope," said Sonja.

"That's appropriate," said Riley, with a smile.

"When Ulysses and I have a child, I'm going to carry it myself," said Jenny.

"You'll be sorry," Peter said.

"Oh, come on," said Jenny. "Don't tell me you're not loving every minute of it."

"Oh, sure, it's great," said Peter. "Throwing up every morning during the first trimester, having your back hurt constantly; being exhausted all the time and barely able to walk; feeling like you have to urinate 24 hours a day from the constant pressure on your bladder; mood swings; swollen ankles. . . . It's just been eight months of pure delight."

"Stop complaining," Sonja said. "You didn't have to do this. The Reproductive Centers went back on-line as soon as the quest was over. You're the one who insisted on going through with it."

"I must have been out of my mind. I should have listened when Dr. Burroughs tried to talk me out of having a birth canal installed. As soon as this kid's ready, we're doing a C-section and she's coming out of there."

Karen arrived and after she said hello to everyone and felt Peter's stomach, they all sat down to dinner.

"So, how was your vacation, Mom?" asked Jenny.

"You know, I have to admit it, it was a lot of fun," she said. "My team went up against Jorgensen and his bunch from Ecology Support and we beat them by thirty points. He said it wasn't fair because we were all Security and in better shape and had more training, but he knows the Quest Chamber like the back of his hand. He's practically been living in there. It didn't do him any good, though. The elves had him so confused, he still got lost. He wants a rematch."

"And are you going to give it to him?" asked Ulysses.

"I'll think about it," Karen replied, with a grin. "Anyway, tonight isn't about me, it's about you two. I brought some wine made from Second Generation grapes. I've been saving it for a special occasion, and this is it. I want to propose a toast."

"Oh, no . . ." said Peter.

"Well, all right, Peter, since you're the one who's pregnant, you propose the toast," said Karen.

"I meant, oh, no, it's time!"

"Time for what?" asked Sonja.

"What do you think?"

"You mean . . ."

"I mean get me to the hospital, right now!"

"Now?" said Sonja, wide-eyed.

"Yes! Now!"

"My cruiser's right outside," said Karen, jumping up out of her chair.

"Mac, call Dr. Burroughs!" said Sonja. "The baby's on the way!"

"I'm calling right now," said Mac.

"Ohhhhh . . ." said Peter, as they helped him up out of his chair.

"Ulysses, Jenny . . . I'm sorry . . ."

"Don't worry about it, Mom," Ulysses said. "Go. We'll meet you there."

"Sit tight, I'll come right back for you," said Karen, as she helped Sonja get Peter outside to the Security cruiser.

"I guess we'll have to postpone this," Riley said.

"Who cares?" said Jenny. "Isn't this exciting?"

"I'm not sure my dad feels that way about it," said Ulysses, with a grin. "Anyway, we've still got plenty of time for that toast before my little sister's born." He poured the wine and picked up his glass. "To us," he said, looking at Jenny. And then, including Cat and Riley, he added, "To all of us."

"To fantasies that come true," Jenny said.

"I'll drink to that," said Mac.

They laughed and raised their glasses.

****

ABOUT THE AUTHOR

SIMON HAWKE became a full-time writer in 1978 and has almost sixty novels to his credit. He received a BA in Communications from Hofstra University and an MA in English and History from Western New Mexico University. He teaches science fiction and fantasy writing through Prima College in Tucson, Arizona.

Hawke lives alone in a secluded Santa Fe-style home in the Sonoran desert about thirty-five miles west of Tucson, near Kitt Peak and the Tohono O'Oodham Indian Reservation. He is a motorcyclist, and his other interests include history, metaphysics, gardening, and collecting fantasy art.